The Purloined Encryption Caper

by
Rose Ameser Bannigan

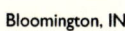 

Bloomington, IN   Milton Keynes, UK

AuthorHouse™
1663 Liberty Drive, Suite 200
Bloomington, IN 47403
www.authorhouse.com
Phone: 1-800-839-8640

AuthorHouse™ UK Ltd.
500 Avebury Boulevard
Central Milton Keynes, MK9 2BE
www.authorhouse.co.uk
Phone: 08001974150

© *2006 Rose Ameser Bannigan. All rights reserved.*

No part of this book may be reproduced, stored in a retrieval system, or transmitted by any means without the written permission of the author.

First published by AuthorHouse 6/14/2006

ISBN: 1-4259-2769-6 (sc)

Library of Congress Control Number: 2006902876

Printed in the United States of America
Bloomington, Indiana

This book is printed on acid-free paper.

Also by ROSE AMESER BANNIGAN

THE SNOWSTORM MURDERS
RIDDLE OF THE FIVE BUDDHAS

DEDICATIONS

With love to my husband John for his
constant encouragement and to my good friends
Lee Miller and Melanie Brown who
provided valuable critiques
of my manuscripts.

PROLOGUE

Pierre steered the small awninged boat towards the Lake Como shore, stopping at a small dock at the foot of a trail leading to a centuries-old monastery half-hidden high among the olive trees. There, a handsome Italian man climbed aboard and greeted his three friends.

"We are meeting Hans at the far end of the lake," Pierre said, after embracing the new arrival. "He's bringing lunch."

When the boat reached the picturesque village nestled at the foot of the Italian Alps, Hans climbed aboard. Pierre quickly headed toward the center of the lake. The blue water, together with the snow-dusted mountains in the distance accenting the multi-hued trees, was a perfect setting for their rendezvous..

Pierre looked at the assembled former NATO intelligence officers whom he first met in Brussels. At the end of their tour there, they all were assigned by their countries to the office handling industrial espionage. Subsequently, they agreed to join Pierre in his secret scheme to sell the most valuable technologies they could steal to the highest bidder on the world market. They all had excellent contacts in countries willing to pay a handsome sum for leading edge computer technologies, countries mainly in the Middle East and considered rogue nations by the American government and through them to China and North Korea.

"I am pleased we could meet today. Soon we will be deeply involved in our new jobs and I did not want to phone you or use electronic communications to finalize our plans. It would be too risky with the high tech satellite listening devices the Americans have. Our discussions are secure here. No one will question tourists, obviously enjoying a lovely autumn day on this beautiful lake with good food and drink." Pierre looked with pleasure as Carlo and Hans carefully assembled the lunch spread on the boat's small table.

Pierre worried about the lax attention of the Brit, who seemed consumed with his drink. "Hans, the next time, please bring beer, too. Not all of us favor wine," the Brit commented in his clipped accent, his ascot slightly askew.

"Also, the cheese should be French, not German," the Belgian remarked pompously. "German brie is not the same." Hans looked at them with disdain since they had contributed nothing to the lunch.

"It is good that you all have been accepted for participation in the senior fellowship program at the U.S. State Department in Washington next summer. I

will be attached as second secretary to my Embassy there. This will give me diplomatic status and immunity, if necessary. So, when you arrive in Washington, please contact me." Pierre looked at the group, hoping they were paying attention.

"Until then, renew your contacts in what the U.S. terms 'rogue nations', especially those with money to pay for highly desirable goods. And determine the priority they place on specific technologies, software or information. We will then need to identify the American companies or government organizations where these can be obtained." Pierre smiled as he discussed his plan. *"And, most importantly, note the dollar value they place on them."* He paused. *"Remember, those willing to pay the most will be the ultimate recipient."*

Pierre was glad everyone agreed to designate a woman as an alternate in the event a proxy was needed. "I assume," Pierre said, *"that you will choose someone with whom you've had an affair or are currently having an affair."* Pierre definitely had chosen carefully and they all nodded.

After Pierre had given the group sufficient information and instructions, he restarted the engine, retraced the stops and headed back toward Bellagio. The last three men returned the boat, paid the rental in cash, and headed for their cars parked under the trees along the quay. Soon, they were on their way down the narrow mountain road back to Milan to take their flights home.

CHAPTER 1

April in Paris is famous for lovers. As Pierre entered his apartment in Vincennes, he was glad he was going to spend the night with Miriam Gauthier, an old friend and a sometime lover. Like many French women, she was expert at the role of love-making and intrigue. While the main purpose of their meeting was business, some time would be spent in amorous play. He and Miriam had worked together on several projects, originally in French intelligence, but later in lucrative activities falsifying documents to transship stolen U.S. technologies to Middle Eastern countries. They understood each other and had no qualms about devotion to any specific lover or even to one's country.

Soon, a knock on his door announced Miriam. He looked at her with a renewed awareness of how sensual she was. "Mon amie, it is wonderful to see you. Shall we have a drink here and then stroll to the local restaurant?" he asked after a warm kiss.

Miriam agreed with a smile. As she settled on his divan, she stretched her long legs like a cat, crossed them, and tugged down her short leather skirt so it would accent her slim hips. Her feline movements were not lost on Pierre. As they sipped Pernod a l'eau, they discussed Gallic politics, a natural topic for two people involved in French business and government intrigue.

En route to the restaurant, Pierre asked Miriam if she would join him on a project that could bring in a great deal of money. "C'est un cercle des amis, dans la guerre economique," Pierre told her. "We plan to identify and then borrow, so to speak, certain technologies to sell to the highest bidder, friend or foe." Pierre did not identify his friends, but merely said they were trusted NATO colleagues whose interests were the same -- to get rich.

Miriam listened intently. "And what is my role, cheri?" she inquired.

"My dear Miriam. You know well the art of seduction and getting men to tell you their secrets, and, shall we say, you have no scruples about compromising married men and then reminding them of their indiscretions. American men particularly talk big, yet a word from their wives makes them shiver. Do you know they take out garbage at home, even if they're highly-placed executives? Incroyable!" His shoulders and eyebrows did the Gallic shrug simultaneously. "You can easily put them in a compromising position by plying your expert skills for the knowledge we seek. Then, they

will have to do as we ask." He paused as he lit his Gauloise cigarette.

"Also, you are knowledgeable about technical meetings held in Europe and the U.S. where you can meet these naive Americans." He waited to see her reaction before he continued. She merely gave him a very sensual smile. *"You and Francois are always looking to purchase technologies for legitimate sales to other French or European companies. You are a natural person for American businessmen to talk with regarding their sales to European businesses. I can alert you about American companies we want to penetrate."* He paused again, letting her conjure up some attractive scenarios.

"As you know, the hottest software being sought internationally, including by La Belle France, is secure or unbreakable encryption and biometrics currently being developed in the U.S. Since La Grande Guerre, the United States has been and still is number one in encryption technology and biometrics, far ahead of other countries. But their government thus far has maintained tight control of the export and use of the best software."

"Is this job dangerous, mon ami? I would hate to waste my charms in an American Bastille. I understand the inmates there are not kind to their women." Miriam raised her eyebrows, wondering whether Pierre would come to her rescue if she needed help. She doubted it.

"Non," he assured her. *"Their Congress has passed legislation making industrial espionage illegal, but such laws are rarely enforced by the FBI, mainly because of their incompetence and current focus on*

terrorism. Also, they have many domestic crimes to pursue which their bureaucratic bosses consider their main purpose. American justice rolls very, very slowly. If we are suspected, we will quickly leave the country and use our substantial Swiss bank accounts to relocate on the other side of the world." He grinned and sipped his Pernod.

Miriam looked at Pierre, not knowing whether to believe him. "Is that all?"

"Other things, from time to time," he continued. "First, I would like you to go to the States, to a place called Berkeley Springs in West Virginia, and buy or lease a cabin I have selected as a safe house. It is about a two-hour drive from Washington. Here is the information." He gave her a map and a brochure from one of the local real estate firms describing the property. "When you finalize the negotiations, telephone or e-mail me at my home, and I will wire you the necessary funds. I would like you to do this as soon as possible. I will be assigned to our Embassy in Washington, beginning in July and would like to have the cabin available as soon as I arrive."

"I can leave within two weeks," she said, pocketing her advance payment, "and will contact you as soon as the cabin is registered in my name. I assume this is what you want."

"Indeed," he confirmed. "It may cause some unpleasantness for the French Embassy if it is found to be connected to me. I will arrange for airline tickets to be delivered to you within the coming week."

The Purloined Encryption Caper

After dinner, Miriam returned with Pierre to his apartment where they assumed their role as occasional but intense lovers.

Shortly before Bastille Day, Miriam was sharing another evening with Pierre, this time at her apartment in the semi-fashionable Ile de la Cite area. "Voila. Here are the keys to the cabin. Five sets, plus one for me to keep. It's furnished, I hope, to your satisfaction, with enough overnight sleeping accommodations for five, without women of course." She smiled momentarily with a raised eyebrow giving him a saturnine look. "I have drawn a map that provides three different routes from Washington on how to reach the cabin. I already stocked some tins of food and various beverages, but you will have to buy any perishables since I didn't know how soon you plan to use the cabin."

"Tres bien," Pierre acknowledged. "I leave for the States in two days for up to a year's assignment, depending on the patience of my agency and, of course, the French Embassy in Washington. They do tire easily of having extra members of les services speciale around. And, most importantly, depending upon our success in obtaining the technologies we seek, I shall e-mail you when any needs arise. I have set up a bank account in both our names in Geneva, so we'll have easy access to funds in the event of an emergency." Pierre shifted in his chair and continued as he sipped another Pernod.

"I'm not sure if the Embassy will provide housing or whether I will have to locate my own apartment.

You will always be welcome as an overnight guest. As a matter of fact, it would be a pleasure."

Pierre then took her by the hand into her bedroom. He thought it might be a long time before he would taste her pleasures and he wanted to make the most of their last night together in Paris.

As they lay side by side, Miriam turned to Pierre. "Be careful, my good friend. I've heard that an official American is here, asking about foreigners trying to penetrate American companies, an American working for a powerful U.S. senator."

"Don't worry, my dear," he assured her. "If we find anyone who is being especially inquisitive, I am sure you can arrange to take care of him or her in the usual manner."

Miriam smiled. "My Union Corse friends are always willing to do a public service--for a price, of course."

CHAPTER 2

As Rachel Brown strolled the warm Outer Banks beach in North Carolina, she couldn't believe that it had been five months since she had encountered her childhood friend, Steve Holliday, here. It had drastically changed her life. She had been desperately unhappy then, looking for a new beginning after several disastrous love affairs, and Steve had miraculously helped her. She shook her head as she thought about the e-mail she had received from him shortly after that chance meeting: "Come to Washington. Found the perfect job for you working in a PR and lobbying firm. Jack Warden's company represents small electronics companies and he's looking for someone with your background to assist him with research and mingling. Might not make you a millionaire but it should be interesting." Rachel had immediately phoned Steve and after a few minutes conversation decided this was the change she needed.

"Steve, you'll never know how you saved my sanity," Rachel said after she settled in suburban Virginia, a short commute from her K Street Office, and had become a vital part of the Warden Associates office. "I love my job and Jack's really given me my head. And I appreciate your showing me around the Hill and introducing me to all your fellow Hill staffers, especially your roommate. Tom's been like a brother and has filled your shoes when I've needed advice and TLC, especially since you spend so much time sleuthing around Europe."

"I'm glad to help out an Outer Banks pal, but I'm afraid you're going to have to lean on old Tom for the time being. I'm off to Europe again, checking out rumors about industrial espionage." Then Steve paused. "Remember the report I was writing last winter at the Beach? Well, there are a few more details I have to get before I submit the gory story to my senator's committee. Then, I hope to hang around Washington, maybe even spend a month or so recovering on our favorite sun-drenched sands."

Rachel had remembered how nervous Steve seemed, almost remote. As she now passed in front of Steve's beach house, she experienced a slight chill, as if for some reason the house transmitted a warning or alarm for Steve's safety. She shook her head as if to drive such thoughts from her mind. "He's a big boy and can take care of himself," she said aloud, causing nearby sun bathers to look up at her.

The Purloined Encryption Caper

Rachel had no sooner returned to her Virginia apartment that weekend when the phone rang.

"I've been trying to reach you," the familiar voice of Tom Fulton rang out. "Steve told me that you should socialize again and forget your past, whatever that is." Rachel remained silent realizing she hadn't confided much in Tom. "How about going to a party with me next Saturday night? Joe Coswell, majority director of the House Science and Technology Committee, invited me to a bash at his place and said I could bring a date."

"Would love to," Rachel found herself saying. "What will the dress be?"

"Elegantly casual is what his wife usually says. It means no sneakers or jeans but a dress or pantsuit. I'll pick you up Saturday night, about six."

Rachel looked forward to this party. Most of Rachel's evenings out, other than with Steve or a friendly dinner with Tom after attending a committee meeting, were as a dinner companion with visiting clients. Almost all were happily married, contrary to the Washington norm, and they talked lovingly about their families and wives.

That week Jack and Rachel had been reviewing their client list. "Rachel, I think you've met everybody with the exception of Jason Conrad, President of Techno Electronics and Systems in Palo Alto, California. He's an especially close friend of mine. He's a busy guy and rarely spends much time here. So in the past, we've normally met for dinner or we get together in New York. He's the guy who works closely with Bill Worth." Bill Worth, President of Electro-Systems in

California, and Jason had started their companies at about the same time. Rachel had had dinner several times with Bill when he was in town.

"Jason's a bright guy. His company is on the leading edge of developing new information software, especially involving advanced encryption. Now, he's also deeply involved in biometrics and other interesting things. You'll like him," Jack commented with a twinkle in his eyes. "So, the next time he comes to Washington, I'll make sure you meet him. I want you to know all our clients since I need you to take charge of the office when I'm away."

Meanwhile in California, Bill Worth had telephoned Jason and asked him to meet at their favorite watering hole for a drink after work.

"You know, Jason," Bill started, "I've heard rumors you're developing new encryption software and other technologies that go well beyond the things we've discussed." Jason looked surprised. "I don't know the details or where the information originally came from, but I think you should be aware that there's a leak somewhere about your activities. You told me earlier that you had filed some new patent applications." Jason nodded, wondering how this info had leaked.

Bill then continued. "The next time you go to Washington, you may want to ask Jack's office to see if any of his other clients are experiencing similar problems. Could be time we talked with government brass concerned with industrial espionage and patent protection."

The Purloined Encryption Caper

"Not a bad idea," Jason said, mentally planning an early visit to the nation's capital.

"I've got to go," Bill said after he finished his drink. "I want to spend time with my kids. If you don't have plans, why don't you come home with me for potluck? I know Kim would be delighted to see you. That is, unless you have a date with Claire."

"No date and dinner with you and Kim sounds great," Jason said, always enjoying time he had spent at Bill's house. It was the kind of homey married atmosphere he himself wanted. Bill had been lucky to find a girl who still had traditional values about marriage and home life.

"And when you visit Jack's office, please give my regards to Rachel Brown. I don't know if you've met her yet, but she's really a great find. I should warn you though, she's the kind of girl a man marries." Bill had taken an exceptionally keen interest in Rachel. She had been recommended to Jack by Steve Holliday, a friend of Bill's from his college days, although Bill never mentioned his relationship with Steve to Jack.

"Will do," Jason said after admitting that he hadn't yet met her. "Now you've really piqued my interest."

The following Thursday, Rachel was called into Jack's office. "I'd like you to meet Jason Conrad." When she saw him, her heart momentarily stopped. She was instantly attracted to him and hoped the rising warmth in her cheeks wasn't evident.

"This is Rachel Brown, Jason. She's the one responsible for putting out the weekly newsletter and gathering much of the info we send you."

"Very nice meeting you, Miss Brown. Your newsletter is extremely useful and well written," he said as he extended his hand.

It was apparent to Jack that Jason readily approved of Rachel. Her shoulder-length dark brown wavy hair, natural fair skin and deep blue eyes told Jason she was probably of Irish descent. She was of medium height with a trim figure.

"Nice meeting you, too." She took his hand, which Jason seemed to hold longer than necessary. She gently withdrew it, acknowledging a strong, warm sensation. Thinking of nothing else to say, she thanked him for his kind words and said, "Please call me Rachel."

Jack broke the spell. "We're on our way to lunch, Rachel. Why don't you join us? Jason needs our help in getting information on data leaks, possibly to foreign companies. The CEO's of other California companies have mentioned similar concerns to him. It'd be useful for you to get details directly from him. That is, unless you have a more important date."

"I have plans, but nothing so important that can't be changed." Rachel felt uncomfortable with Jason. He seemed to be watching her every move. "I'll get my purse and meet you by the elevator."

She was glad to be away from Jason and, once in her office, noticed that her hands were trembling. The chemistry between them amazed her and, for some reason, Jason frightened her. He was handsome in a rugged, masculine way which appealed to her. She had never been so physically attracted to any man and even took time to apply fresh makeup, something she rarely did during office hours.

The Purloined Encryption Caper

The maitre d' at Luigi's seated Rachel and Jason took a seat across the table from her. She could feel his eyes on her and every time she looked at him, he smiled.

After they finished lunch, Jason looked around to make sure no one could overhear and leaned closer.

"Jack, you know my company's developed several new computer-oriented technologies. We've applied for patents which we hope to get within the coming year. At the same time, we're working on extraordinarily secure encryption software and developing biometrics that will be invaluable for our government as well as companies concerned with privacy. Some data which has been held very close in our company, limited to only a half dozen people at most, is suddenly being whispered about in high-tech business circles. I think companies such as mine are being targeted by foreign agents. If true, this is very worrisome." Jason stopped for a minute to let Jack absorb the information.

"Several months ago," he explained, "to avoid possible competitor cyber sleuthing, I installed a system where each of my technical staff has two computers, a stand-alone computer for R&D work, and another computer attached to the Internet or for networking purposes with colleagues. The stand-alone computers have no hard drives and only use floppy disks with an identifying chip in them. These chips work like the plastic security attachment on clothes at department stores and cause an alarm to ring if they are taken off the premises. It's a rather expensive security device, but I felt it was worth it. It's almost impossible for any technical staff member to duplicate these diskettes and sell them to competitors or for techno-hackers to break into these stand-alone systems." Jason took another sip of coffee.

"I had drinks with Bill Worth last week," he continued. "He was told details about software my company still has on the drawing board and he told me about leakage of his company secrets. Are other companies having similar problems? Perhaps you could put me in touch with someone at the FBI or Commerce or other offices concerned with these problems." Both Jack and Rachel listened intently.

"Also, I'm planning to expand sales of our present technologies in Europe and possibly Asia. Our company needs more income and our older technologies still under patent protection are very salable. I've already had several inquiries from French and German companies, but I need to know of export limitations imposed by the Administration and how Congress and the Administration feel about high-tech companies negotiating directly with foreign entities without prior clearance from the Defense, Commerce or State Departments, especially with all the hubbub of the coming millennium. And then 2000 is an election year and we'll have a change in leadership." As Jason was talking, Rachel had taken out a small notebook and began making notes. Jason continued.

"I've heard there's a wide range of conflicting opinions among various government departments and Congress, especially with all the corporate scandals that took place during the past few years with the advent of the millennium. And now, since 2000 is an election year, problems are bound to increase and bring more

The Purloined Encryption Caper

snooping. Is there any possibility that you can get this info for me quickly? I plan to go to Europe within the month, so anything you can find out would be critical to my visit. Also, any suggestions of possible buyers. I've a list of those who've already expressed interest and identified other potentials, but any help would be appreciated."

Jack frowned. "I'm going on vacation for a week starting tomorrow, Jason, and my plans are hard to change now. But Rachel could get some preliminary clues on the situation and could find out who in the government is focusing on this problem. Could be the CIA, Defense or Commerce or possibly the FBI. How about it, Rachel?"

She nodded her head. Jack then went on.

"And if you need any contacts abroad, you're also in luck. Rachel lived in both Europe and Asia when she was with the State Department, dealing with U.S. and foreign companies and might be able to give you some pointers or leads. At least she could tell you about the best restaurants," he said with a smile.

"Yes, I think I can," Rachel commented. "Perhaps when we go back to the office, Mr. Conrad could give me more specific details. There's a reception in Congressman Smith's office this afternoon and I could begin to ask around. Also, if Tom is there, I'm sure he would be happy to help me." Rachel had assumed her most professional tone in talking with Jason.

Jason looked at Rachel and for some reason resented Tom, without knowing anything about their relationship, but becoming aware of his strong physical attraction to her. "I'll be happy to give you more information. I'm sure you can be a big help. Maybe we can spend some more time together," his eyes questioned mischievously as he looked at her. "Perhaps I could go with you to the reception, or don't they let you take *a date*? And, by the way, call me Jason."

His emphasis on the word *date* wasn't lost on her. "You'd be more than welcome, although the receptions are usually very boring. They're normally large affairs with no specific guest list, so no one checks off who is or isn't invited, as long as you can clear security. It's scheduled to start this afternoon at five-thirty and normally ends about seven."

"It's a date," Jason said to her. "I have a question, though." He paused "If it's so boring, why do you go?"

"Part of the job. That's where I pick up miscellaneous information and meet individuals who are useful in my work." As he looked at her, he wondered what it would be like to take her in his arms and kiss her. It was what he wanted to do.

The reception was the usual crush of people: lobbyists, staffers, friends and even a few congressional representatives. There was the usual drinking, nibbling and politicking as well as individuals just watching each other, trying to figure out who was who. Rachel enjoyed these, not because they were necessarily amusing, but she did like watching the body language between people, especially between the young women and any prospective suitors.

Many of the Hill "girls", as Tom and Steve called them, were really looking for husbands, preferably nice young congressmen with a good future. But the women also seemed satisfied to latch on to a prosperous lobbyist or constituent who could show them a good time or be useful. Whether the men were married or not didn't seem to matter. These women would search out Hill parties and, if they weren't too particular or bothered by political persuasion, they could find a party almost every night.

When Jason entered the reception area, it was only natural that the young women would make a play for him. He was a new face, good looking, very masculine and tall compared to most of the male staffers. It seemed to Rachel that many men on the Hill were rather short. She wondered if they had Napoleonic complexes.

Rachel wandered away to check out the players but, out of the corner of her eye, surreptitiously watched Jason's interaction with the women, first flirting and then trying to fend them off. Maybe later she should just drift away and leave him alone so he could ask one of the women out for dinner.

Suddenly, she became aware of someone nearby speaking with a French accent. His face was familiar, but she couldn't remember whether she had met him before. She looked around and noticed that there were several other foreign-looking men nearby.

She soon spied Tom and, when they were alone, asked him who they were.

"I don't know." he said. "I think they're visiting officials attached to the various European embassies in Washington. You know that we maintain close ties with friendly embassies, brief their visiting dignitaries about our activities and on how we operate. Maybe there was a briefing today and someone invited them along."

When Tom identified the Frenchman as Pierre Ledent, Rachel recognized the name as someone on a "black list" when she lived in Germany, but couldn't recall the details. As soon as she had time, she would rummage through her past papers and see if she could find any information that would clear up the mystery. Tom promised to give her a complete list of the other foreigners.

"By the way, Steve was supposed to return from Europe yesterday, but hasn't shown up yet. Have you heard from him?" Tom asked.

"No. I haven't seen him for several weeks so assumed he was still sleuthing in Europe. I hope nothing has happened to him." Rachel couldn't imagine that Steve would have encountered any difficulty. He was resourceful and always seemed to extricate himself from any encounter.

As seven o'clock approached, she returned to Jason's side. "I'm about to leave, but please feel free to stay," she said, looking at the pretty, leggy blonde who managed to corner him most of the evening.

"No, I've got to go, too. Goodnight, Myra, it's been very nice talking with you" he said to the blonde. "Thanks for the conversation."

She gave Rachel a very dirty look. I hope she doesn't work for an influential senator or congressional representative, Rachel thought, or else I'll be dead meat in that office. Rachel then gave Tom a short embrace and said, "See you Saturday night. When Steve returns, have him call me."

The Purloined Encryption Caper

When they got outside, Jason said, "Whew! No wonder Jack didn't like going to these things and why his wife hated for him to go. Those women are so forward. Thanks for rescuing me."

"I didn't think I was rescuing you. I almost left without saying goodbye. I can't believe you didn't like being the new man in the room, with a dozen young hot chickees chasing after you," Rachel teased.

"No," he laughed, "I didn't. They're really not my type. I much prefer less aggressive women with more class, like you." She smiled and started walking toward the Metro.

Jason had been unhappy when she introduced him to Tom as a 'client', thus establishing their relationship as a professional one. This annoyed him, even though it was true.

"If you have no other plans, how about dinner? I heard there's a very good French restaurant nearby. Apparently, they have a room two well-known senators made famous by their amorous antics. Myra called it a 'sandwich shop'. Do you know what she meant?"

Rachel hesitated before accepting his dinner invitation. "You're very good at getting gossip. I've heard about the place. I can only imagine what happened." Actually, someone had walked into a private dining room where two senators from proper New England states had been dining and, as rumors go, saw one senator on the floor and the other on top with a waitress as the filling of the sandwich. Rachel had no intention of sharing these details with Jason.

After they were seated, Rachel ordered a scotch and water, Jason a gin and tonic. "Is this your first visit to Washington this year?" Rachel asked.

"I've been here earlier but I usually never have time to get to know the town. I'll try to change that, now that I've met Jack's able staff." His eyes were smiling at her.

Rachel felt her cheeks redden. She avoided looking at him. "I'll have the sole Veronique," she said to the waiter who suddenly appeared, "and a small house salad."

"The same for me," Jason echoed, "as well as s glass of Chardonnay for both."

"How long have you been with Jack?" he asked. "I believe he mentioned earlier this year that he was looking for someone to help him."

"I started shortly before Easter. Have you been a client of Jack's for long?" Rachel asked. She knew the details of Jason's company, but again wanted to direct the conversation away from herself.

"Jack and I go back a ways. He represented my company while he was with his previous firm. Did you know Jack before you started working for him?" Jason again was trying to find out more about her.

"No. He's a friend of an old friend who recommended me." she replied.

Over coffee Jason provided more details of his concerns.

"Today, it's imperative that we protect sensitive information, not only within the States but internationally as well. Until about forty years ago, most cryptography and encryption were used

The Purloined Encryption Caper

mainly for national security or military purposes. Governments needed encrypted communications to ensure information they wished to transmit was secure. However, with the huge increase in the use of information systems in banking and commerce and confidential data, it's become critical that these systems are also totally secure. My company and Bill Worth's have been the primary developers of new encryption software for protecting data traffic." He paused to see if she was following his narrative. "Also, biometrics systems are imperative these days in order to ensure individuals are who they say they are, and to protect unwelcome illegals from entering our country, as well as ensuring security at installations, both official and private." He paused again.

"One of the current problems is that our government prohibits American companies from selling many technologies beyond a certain level of complexity overseas, because of potential use by money launderers and terrorists. The government wants a 'back door' control in order to circumvent the system's security if necessary. It usually requires an escrowed encryption system that gives access to the data through a key held by a trusted third party. The American public generally doesn't want government to have access," he explained as he lowered his voice.

"We're developing a stand-alone cryptographic add-on product that's designed to provide encryption capabilities for hardware which would permit the individual to protect any information system, yet meet the standards required by government. We're calling it the 'flipper chip'. It lets you disengage or flip off the key system which cuts out a 'back door' recovery capability and establishes a sure proof firewall against hackers. You can also flip on extra security, as well as other very useful features." Jason was very serious in discussing his business concerns. "And another promising software program where no key exists. It will be totally uncrackable." He paused, letting her absorb the import of his statements.

"That's amazing," she exclaimed, trying to keep her voice low.

"I'm sure you understand how confidential this information is and why others, especially foreign governments or terrorist groups, are intensely interested in getting details. They could duplicate our 'flipper chip', insert it in their current operating system and thus have a system that would prohibit other governments from gaining access to it and would prevent anyone from gaining access to encrypted data." Jason didn't want to give too many more details.

"I understand," Rachel said. "Tomorrow, I'll start tracking down leads I got from Tom and others tonight on problems of industrial espionage and about restrictions in doing business in Europe and Asia. I can almost guarantee that the government wouldn't let you sell the 'flipper chip' abroad unless it had some way of circumventing the security system. And your uncrackable system would be totally out of the question."

She then thought about her coming day. "With Jack on vacation and a newsletter to get out tomorrow, it's going to be hectic. I'll fax or fedex what information I

The Purloined Encryption Caper

get to your office so you have it on your desk Monday morning," she assured him.

"Don't bother to send it unless you don't see me tomorrow. I plan to be in your office tomorrow afternoon. I have several morning meetings and a luncheon engagement, but should be free afterwards. Perhaps if you're available, we could talk more then."

Jason then asked about Tom. "Is he a serious friend?"

"No. Just a good friend and the roommate of an old childhood friend, who's also a friend of Jack's. He's been very kind and helpful to me since I've been in Washington and I rely heavily on him for getting information and contacts."

As they were leaving the restaurant, Jason asked Rachel where she lived so he could escort her home. "In Arlington, Virginia. Close to the Ballston Metro station. I can walk to the Metro and be home in fifteen minutes. So you don't need to worry about me getting home."

"Nonsense. Chivalry is not dead," he commented. "I'm an old-fashioned Westerner. I wouldn't let you go home alone in this city. I understand it's not very safe. I'll go with you and then take the Metro back to my hotel." Jason was anxious to see where her apartment was for future reference and, if he were lucky, to have her invite him in for coffee or a nightcap. Primarily, he wanted to see whether there was any evidence of a live-in male friend.

"That isn't necessary. I do this all the time," she protested.

"Not when you've had dinner with me. I'd feel responsible if anything happened to you. Which line do you take?"

"The Orange Line," she said. "It takes me within a few blocks of my apartment."

When they emerged from the Ballston Station, Jason noticed a Hilton Hotel, which he would have to keep in mind for future visits, in the event his current instincts about Rachel were correct. It would certainly be more convenient than staying in the District, especially with the Metro so near. As a matter of fact, he realized it would be extremely convenient because many of his meetings were in Arlington, Crystal City or the Pentagon where the Metro had stations and many consulting firms and defense contractors had offices.

"Here we are," Rachel said as they stood at the door of a newly-built apartment building. "Thanks a lot for dinner and your chivalry in seeing me home." She extended her hand to shake his goodnight.

"You're welcome." He had thought about inviting himself in for a nightcap, but instead said, "Let me at least see you to the door of your apartment. Then I'd know that you were indeed safe." He followed her to the elevator, getting off on the fourth floor, and walked her to her apartment.

"Good night. I enjoyed our dinner." He started to put his arms around her, but feeling her body stiffen, kissed her on the forehead and left. Jason knew, though, that he had to see her again.

The reception on the Hill was the first one that Pierre and his partners had been invited to attend

The Purloined Encryption Caper

since arriving in Washington. The previous week, the group had a quick familiarization meeting in his Berkeley Springs safe house to ensure that everything was in order and to determine the travel time via each route. At that time, Pierre had given the other members of his group an overview of the group's needs and the importance of penetrating key government bureaucracies and leading contracting companies where possible.

"But," he stressed, "the first attempt in gaining data should be from the open press or through requests to the appropriate government office. You will be amazed how loose the American government and its press is with information. In our countries, as you are well aware, it is much different. Also," Pierre continued, "we should try to establish contacts at the various government departments and agencies. High on the list are the FBI, CIA, Commerce, Pentagon, and State Department. Of course, the key targets are the White House and Congress. That's where most policy and regulations are proposed and passed. At our next meeting, we should be prepared to list all of our identified sources so we don't duplicate our efforts." The other four agreed.

Today, the members of the State Department program had their first briefing by staff members of both houses of Congress. Pamphlets describing the structure, activities and purposes of both the House and Senate were distributed to the attendees. They were delighted when the congressional staff person in charge of the briefing suggested they come along to a reception.

"It might be dull," the staffer said, "but you can see how we spend some of our unofficial time and you'll get to see the lobbyists we talked about in action." They readily accepted.

Pierre was not married any more since his wife left him several years ago, and he observed with delight the large number of very attractive young female Hill staffers. He had accumulated a lot of business cards and would check out the importance of each. Sexual attraction is one thing, he thought, but more important is the position and clout the woman has and the less attractive the woman is, he had learned, the more she might be willing to be compromised.

He also noticed a number of pretty women representing lobbying firms or trade and business associations. The key ones were those who could give him the names of firms on the cutting edge of technology development. As he was leaving, someone told him that one of those women, Rachel Brown, had brought the president of a Silicon Valley high-tech company. He would make it a point to become acquainted with her. She might indeed be very useful.

He also learned that day that a Senate Intelligence Committee staff member had questioned the membership of the State Department program. His contact at State told him that Steve Holliday, a senior Hill investigative staffer, could possibly make trouble for them. Pierre would have to stay alert to this problem and possibly ask Miriam to have one of their "friends" in Europe "take care of Steve", one way or another. Pierre couldn't afford to have anything interfere with his plans.

CHAPTER 3

The next day, Rachel telephoned her contacts to track down information for Jason. "There's too much to fax so I'll have to mail it to you," the staffer said. Since she needed it immediately, Rachel asked if she could have a messenger pick it up.

"Sure. It'll show you the rules we're operating under as well as what we'll be facing in the coming months, especially on cyber hacking," the helpful Hill staffer said.

By the end of the day, Rachel had amassed a sizable amount of information on problems facing U.S. high-tech firms in maintaining control over their patents and software, and the type of software and hardware that foreign agents were seeking. Advanced encryption systems and the development of biometrics were on the top on that list.

After she and Cindy finished e-mailing their newsletter, Rachel asked Cindy to photocopy the information she had gathered and federal express a package to Jason in California.

Rose Ameser Bannigan

"Why?" asked Cindy. "Jason's sitting in Jack's office, making some phone calls. I can just hand it to him."

"Oh," she exclaimed, trying to hide her surprise. "Then also give him a copy of the newsletter." Rachel had forgotten that Jason planned to be in the office that afternoon.

Rachel went back to her desk to review the day's e-mail, snail mail and faxes, and answer any urgent phone calls. She was in the process of listing priority matters for the following Monday when there was a knock on her door.

"May I come in?" Jason asked, as he smilingly entered. "I scanned the information you gave me and would like to talk about it. I'm meeting an old friend for drinks now but that shouldn't take long. How about dinner later? I could come by about seven, unless you already have a dinner date."

Against her better judgment, she said, "No, I'm free. Seven o'clock would be fine. Just ask the woman at the desk in the lobby to call me and I'll come down, so you don't have to bother coming up to my apartment."

Jason smiled. "No bother at all. Perhaps you'll even offer me a drink before dinner."

Jason had given the bulky material only a cursory glance, but knew that if he didn't indicate the evening was business, she would have turned him down. He wanted to see her apartment--how a woman lived told a lot about her.

Promptly at seven, Jason knocked on her door. Somehow he managed to escape the watchful eye of the desk clerk. And he liked her apartment. It was warm and comfortable and decorated with various pieces of art and memorabilia she had collected in her travels, as well as older pieces obviously inherited from her family or bought at antique sales. It had character. He hated apartments that looked like a page out of *Better Homes and Gardens.*

"What will you have?" Rachel asked as she walked toward her bar. It was already set up with decanters of scotch, bourbon, gin and vodka, and had a pitcher of water, and bottles of mix handy. The bar was a piece of furniture she loved. It had been her father's and she maintained the exotic contents much as he had.

"Here, let me fix the drinks," he said, as he moved behind the bar. "I'm a good bartender. Do you want a scotch and water or something more exotic?"

"I usually stick to scotch and water." Sometimes Rachel would have a vodka martini, but scotch was usually safer. Two martinis would make her light-headed and tonight she wanted to keep up all her defenses. She would need to, again realizing how physically attracted she was to him

He sipped a gin and tonic while she nursed her scotch. "I must confess," he said. "I haven't yet had a chance to thoroughly review the material but I will on the plane tomorrow. If I have any questions, I'll call you early next week." He paused.

"Where do you want to eat?" he then asked. "I noticed an intriguing place close by. I think it's called Jacques Cafe. Have you ever eaten there?"

"No. I've noticed that it's usually crowded on the weekends, so we may need reservations. Do you want me to call?"

"I took the liberty of making reservations as I walked by on my way from the Metro. We can casually stroll over now if you want and you can show me a little more of your neighborhood."

The maitre d' at Jacques seated them side by side at a cozy corner table which was so small that their thighs touched. Rachel felt a warm sensation as a result of his closeness. Jason ordered a scotch and water for her and a gin martini on the rocks for himself. After he ordered dinner and wine, a small band started playing.

"Let's dance. The music is slow, just my speed," Jason said and led her to the dance floor. It was a tiny area and Rachel and Jason had to dance very close so they wouldn't bump into other couples. He pressed his body very close to hers and, as he held her, she felt her heart race.

Fortunately, the music suddenly changed to rock. "I'm not really up to this," Rachel said, grateful that she had an excuse to sit down.

During dinner, Rachel and Jason talked about the current political situation in Washington and the attitude toward small business.

"Jason, I've been told that many U.S. government officials feel that any technology, regardless of its sensitivity and potential use for military purposes, should be shared. In their outlook of global equality, we, the United States, should not refuse to share data with a country, even if it is still dominated by socialist or communist thought." She hesitated before continuing.

"I understand the only exception is software which the U.S. government feels should be kept for itself or perhaps shared with a few close allies. If this is true,

The Purloined Encryption Caper

it seems unfair to the business community. Many of these countries merely duplicate the hardware or software and sell it for a far cheaper price, thus cutting U.S. business out of possible lucrative markets." She paused as she saw his eyes concentrating on hers. Somehow, Rachel had the impression that Jason wasn't interested in talking business.

After dinner, when the music again became slow and dreamy, they danced for another few numbers. Being in his arms, held so close that she could feel his every move, excited Rachel. She found herself trembling and tried several times to put some distance between them. When the band paused between songs, she tried to return to their table. But each time he just held her closer not letting her move, and then continued dancing when the music started again.

When they returned to the table, Jason questioned, "Do you always set up barriers with someone who may only want to hold you?" He watched her reaction to his candor.

"It's a natural female reaction to keep one's defenses up," she said with a touch of sarcasm. Rachel knew that if she didn't fight him, she was liable to find herself in a compromised position. She knew the decision would be hers and serious emotional involvement was not something she wanted at this point in her life.

They strolled back to her apartment building, hand in hand. When they arrived, Rachel turned and said, "Thanks very much, Jason, for a lovely evening. Please call me next week if you have any questions or need further information. I'll be in the office most of the time with Jack away."

"I'll walk you to your apartment. I left my briefcase there." Rachel was about to volunteer to bring it down to him, but she felt it would make her look ridiculous.

"You'd better be careful about where you leave your briefcase when you visit Europe," she admonished. "The French have taken to photographing documents in businessmen's briefcases left in hotel rooms during dinner or sightseeing." He assured her he would follow her advice and steered her towards her apartment door. She could hardly avoid inviting him for coffee or a nightcap.

Once inside her apartment, he said, "I noticed a good cognac that would be welcome for my voyage home. I'll get it though. What about you?" For some reason, it was important for him to establish that it was a man's job to fix drinks.

"I'll just have a glass of Perrier with lime. I've had more to drink this evening than I usually do." She watched him behind the bar, remembering her father's bartending skills.

When he brought the drinks, he put them down on the coffee table, took her in his arms and kissed her. She seemed startled at first but responded naturally. Jason felt his passion rise, as if he were on fire. Then she tried to gently extricate herself.

"Don't," he said. "I've wanted to do this since the moment you walked into Jack's office." He then paused, before continuing. "I know the feelings are mutual or your heart wouldn't be pounding like mine."

"Jason," she replied, trying to get her breath, "we've just met and don't really know each other. Also, I don't want to get involved with anyone at the office." Rachel remembered her father saying that if you date someone at the office and the relationship sours, you have to face the breakup every day.

Jason pulled back and took a sip of his cognac. "We're hardly in the same office. As a matter of fact, I'm fully aware that we're several thousand miles apart. And there's no better way to get to know each other, and I do want to get to know you better."

After he finished his drink, Rachel suggested he leave. "You have a plane to catch early in the morning and tomorrow's my day for taking care of personal chores." She wanted to have plenty of time to get ready for the party she was going to the next night with Tom.

He left, begrudgingly, but not without kissing her goodnight. It was a very long and passionate kiss. He desperately wanted to make love to her, but decided he wouldn't press his case tonight.

On the plane back to California, Jason thought about the events of the last two days and somehow knew they were a turning point in his life. The fact that foreign companies and their governments were making a concerted effort to steal industrial secrets was confirmed. Also, after reading the vast amount of material Rachel gave him, it was apparent that the U.S. government intelligence agencies had put most of the onus on private companies to protect themselves. He was sorry he couldn't reach Steve Holliday, Bill Worth's friend and guide to the government maze. Bill spoke so highly of Steve and was sure he could give him good advice.

This meant that early next week, he would have to establish a more stringent visitor policy and isolate his technical teams. His staff was always very friendly and open and wasn't as compartmentalized as many of the other high-tech companies. Their staff meetings were free-for-alls with individuals spouting different ideas. Jason felt this was one of the strengths of his company and the reason his scientific and technical staff came up with so many new ideas. They had rebelled against using two separate computers at first, but later got used to it. But it had taken a while.

Also, it meant that he would acknowledge the advisability of going along with the new wave of restrictions being discussed at various association meetings on the Peninsula and Silicon Valley in California. Both he and his staff would have to be more circumspect in discussing their research and product development at national meetings and on sales trips, both in the States and abroad. He was scheduled to take a sales trip to Europe the end of the month and would have to be especially careful.

He thought a lot about Rachel. He had never before had such a strong physical attraction to or desire for a woman and wondered why she had this effect on him. She was pretty and had a pleasing figure, but no prettier than Claire, his current girlfriend, or other women he had dated. But there was something about her that managed to get under his skin. He wanted her almost from the moment they had met. Now, he was mentally planning how quickly he could return to Washington and continue their relationship.

The Purloined Encryption Caper

Maybe he could talk Jack into visiting clients in California and bringing Rachel with him. Jason would love to show her around the Bay area and have her see him in his own domain. Perhaps he would have more influence over her on his turf.

He also thought about his earlier discussions over drinks with Frank Avery, a former Stanford classmate. Frank had it all, they used to say. He came from a wealthy Chicago family, always drove flashy sports cars, flew private planes and, in addition, was very bright. The women at Stanford were mesmerized by him, and would break any date if Frank asked them out.

In spite of it all, he was a nice guy, a talented writer and journalist with a good sense of humor. Jason liked him very much and regretted that distance kept them apart for so many years. Frank lived in New York and Chicago and traveled to Europe frequently, while Jason lived a fairly provincial life in California.

Over drinks, Jason had been thinking of Rachel and asked Frank if he believed in love at first sight. Frank had been so level-headed about romance. Every woman Frank dated in school and afterwards had to meet certain qualifications to insure that she would fit in with his social standing and be acceptable to his parents, especially his mother. He never wanted to risk falling in love with a woman who didn't measure up, and Frank had found such a woman in Betty. They married shortly after graduating from college. His family had been ecstatic about the union since the families got along well together and belonged to the same social group. His mother heartily approved of

Frank's choice and looked forward to grandchildren to keep the family line going.

"Why do you ask, Jason?" Frank questioned after a long hesitation.

"Because I think I've fallen in love with a woman I just met, had dinner with only twice, and haven't yet made love to," Jason responded. "When I'm near her, I feel like a boy of sixteen again. I've never felt this way before, and I've gone out with a hell of a lot of sexy women. I know very little about her or whether she's going with anyone, but I know she's not married."

Frank looked at Jason and again hesitated before he spoke. "I would never have thought so in college, but I do now. I didn't tell you that Betty and I have been separated for the past five years. We've kept the matter secret because of mother. However, shortly before we separated, during a trip to Europe to cover a story, I was invited to a party given by the American Consul General in Frankfurt and a Stanford alumnus. He said that most of the Americans living in Frankfurt would be coming so it might be useful in making contacts with the business community, both American and German." Frank seemed lost in thought.

"Having nothing else to do, I accepted," he continued. "At one point during the evening, I looked over the crowd and saw a young woman, not extraordinarily beautiful, but when I looked at her, my heart did flip flops. I stared at her and finally, she turned, looked at me and smiled. Not a come-on smile, just a friendly one." It seemed to Jason that Frank's mind was a million miles away in his reverie.

"Before I could move through the crowd to her, she left with her date. Fortunately, the host came up at that moment and was able to tell me who she was and how I could get in touch with her. I think I fell in love the moment I saw her. This had never happened to me before. You know me. I was always thorough in vetting any woman before I let myself have any feelings," he explained with a somewhat apologetic smile.

"The next day, I telephoned and asked her to accompany me to a party that evening. Initially, I was afraid she wouldn't remember me, but she did, and accepted. I didn't tell her that the party would be only the two of us. I was afraid she would turn me down. As it turned out, she was attracted to me as well, perhaps not to the extent that I was. After two months of dating, we became lovers. I'd never been so happy in my life. I lived for the moments we could be together. We met in London, Paris, Vienna, or wherever my work took me. It also happened that her work with the State Department coincided with the stories I was covering. This made our relationship that much more interesting and exciting, and, I may add, useful." He paused to see Jason's reactions. Noting an interest, he continued.

"Betty and I separated shortly after I met Monk. That was what I called her. I asked Betty for a divorce. I told her I'd met someone that I had fallen hopelessly in love with and wanted to marry. Betty asked if I had mentioned it to mother. I said no, that I thought this was between the two of us. It turned out that mother told Betty she would write me out of her will and void my inheritance if I ever divorced Betty." Frank paused. "I was very unhappy, but also realized that my inheritance and having money meant a great deal to me. Yet, I couldn't let Monk go, so I continued seeing her." He knew Jason was not sympathizing, but went on anyway.

"Several months after we started dating and before she let me make love to her, Monk asked me if I was married. I told her that the answer to that was so obvious, I wasn't going to honor it with a response. I didn't want to lie, but I knew that if I told her the truth, she would stop seeing me." Again, he paused, lost in thought.

"Several weeks before her assignment in Europe was over, she asked me what our future together would be. She was being reassigned to Washington, but if we were going to get married, she thought she should resign now because I lived in New York. She didn't want her office to block a position in Washington and have to turn it down at the last minute. It was at that moment I realized how deceitful I had been, and how trusting she was. We had just returned from a farewell party where we had had several drinks, perhaps one too many. I hesitated in responding and it was at that moment she looked at me and said, 'you're married, aren't you?'"

"While I could pretend and give a confusing answer earlier, I was unable to lie to her face that night. She gave me the most devastating look I ever thought possible. She went to her bedroom, came out with a suitcase, handed it to me, and told me to get out. She never wanted to see or hear from me again. I couldn't believe she meant it after so many months together, so

I told her I would telephone the next day. No, she said. Not tomorrow or ever. And she meant it. She wouldn't accept my calls and even refused to accept a bouquet of flowers I sent." He waited for Jason's reaction, but seeing none, continued.

"When I got back to my hotel and opened the suitcase, I saw that she packed all the jewelry and gifts that I had given her. Inside was a card that said, 'Give them to your wife--she deserves them.'"

"Whatever happened to her? Did you ever see her again?" Jason asked, intrigued by Frank's confession.

"No," he admitted. "When I returned to Europe two weeks later, she had already left." He paused. "Poor kid. About a week after my confession, her office told me she had received a message from home. Her parents were killed in a freak car accident by a drunk driver. I really felt like a dog, or as much like a dog as I could. I had just sent her a letter explaining why I couldn't get a divorce. I had become too accustomed to having a lot of money and couldn't conceive of life without it. In other words, I was willing to lose her as long as I could keep my money." His face reddened a bit as he realized how this sounded.

"While I was making a good salary as a journalist, knowing that I had money to fall back on gave me courage to pick and choose my assignments, as well as drive sports cars and fly airplanes. I asked her to understand my situation and continue seeing me and not to throw me out of her life. I see now how selfish and deceitful I was. In my letter, I also told her that I'd see that she would never belong to anyone else, that she belonged to me. You see, I had been her first and only lover." Frank paused. "I guess I thought that if she were willing to continue our relationship as before, my mother would eventually accept my decision to divorce Betty. I wanted time to get up enough courage to talk to mother again. But I never did." Frank was quiet for a few moments as he thought about that stressful period of his life.

"You know, Jason, hardly a day goes by when I don't think of her. I hear a song that we once said was ours, and I go numb. I tried to locate her in Washington, but she must have had an unlisted number. I made excuses to my newspaper to visit Washington to look for her. I even tried to get a friend, a police officer in Washington, to see if he could use his office to check her number or location. He refused. He had too much respect for a woman's privacy. If she wanted me to locate her, he said, she'd give me her number. I guess he had more integrity than I did."

Frank looked at Jason. "My advice, good friend, is not to let this girl go, especially since she's not married. Strong feelings like that are hard to come by."

Frank glanced at his watch. "It's after six. I have to catch the seven-thirty flight to Chicago. Mother's been ill and I promised that I'd spend a few days with her. I really don't know if she's really ill or whether it's a ruse to get me there. She's still hopeful that Betty and I will get back together. As you can imagine, my relationship with Betty is nonexistent."

They left the bar, shook hands, and went their separate ways. Jason had always envied Frank, but obviously Frank was a very unhappy man. In a strange way, Jason was glad. He and Frank had been

The Purloined Encryption Caper

competitors, and Frank had always been so smug about his ability to buy anything he wanted. He finally found something money couldn't buy: love and honor.

Jason thought about his own personal life. He was in his mid-thirties, fairly successful in business and more or less happy with his current situation. However, after meeting Rachel, he wondered if he wasn't missing the excitement of a woman's love, a happy marriage and family. Was Rachel a traditional woman, someone who would be content to share his life and have his children?

His thoughts went back to Terry, a girl he had been engaged to shortly after he started his company. She was also a Stanford graduate, although a few years younger. They planned on getting married as soon as Jason was on his feet financially. Terry moved in with him and was there waiting when he returned late at night or from business trips. She accepted the fact that at this point their time together was limited, because getting his business started was his first priority and required so much of his time.

He remembered the day his mother came to his office, something she rarely did. "Jason, if you're really serious about Terry, I suggest you start spending some time with her. It's not fair to leave her alone so much, regardless of how busy you are," she admonished

Jason headed for home early that day, made reservations at a French restaurant in the city and planned to take her dancing afterwards. He even stopped and bought a bouquet of flowers. However, when he got home, he found Terry in bed with another man. Apparently she didn't mind Jason's being away so much. She had taken a lover.

"I was going to tell you about him as soon as he gets a job and is able to support me," was Terry's response. "But now, he has time to be with me, something you don't have." Jason kicked the man out of his apartment and told Terry to pack her clothes and get out as well.

What puzzled Jason was how a woman could profess love, as Terry did to Jason, sleep with him and yet have an affair and plan to abandon him for someone else. Jason was devastated but soon realized that a damaged ego was causing more pain than losing Terry. It was then Jason decided he wouldn't become seriously involved with another woman until his company was on firm footing and he had enough time for his business, a wife and, hopefully, children as well, but he would have to have complete trust in the woman he married.

Jason suddenly remembered his dinner date that evening with Claire. There was a telephone on the plane and he considered canceling their date. He didn't really want to see her, but realized that it wouldn't be fair to her. Perhaps being with Claire and resuming his normal life in California would take his mind off Rachel.

He was very, very wrong. That evening he took Claire to one of their usual hangouts in Palo Alto.

"Did something happen in Washington that I should know about?" Claire could sense that Jason had seemed preoccupied.

"No, it's just business. It was a tiring few days. Perhaps we should go. Do you mind if I don't stay over and go home tonight?"

The Purloined Encryption Caper

"No," she said, "whatever you like."

If Jason had been honest with Claire, he would have mentioned Rachel and her spell over him which even he couldn't explain. Recently, he had thought of asking Claire to marry him, but somehow just couldn't do it. They were good friends and they spent nights together, but there was no magic. He wanted more out of marriage. Jason knew she dated other men and probably slept with them as well, but she was convenient for him. She was very good for his business entertainment or as his partner for evenings out with business friends.

In only two days, Rachel changed all that for him. He had stronger sexual feelings for her than he ever had for Claire, but he didn't know what would happen with Rachel and didn't want to break off his relationship with Claire yet. Claire was a lawyer, fit in with his crowd, very self-sufficient and a damned pretty woman. Also, sex with her was very comfortable, and sex was very important to Jason.

CHAPTER 4

That night after Jason left, Rachel sat down and poured herself another scotch and thought about the past few days. She had only known Jason Conrad for two days, but he already had a strange hold on her. His kiss made her heart pound and she felt all the sensations and sexual urges that she had always read about but never before experienced. She knew little about him, whether he was married, engaged or had a steady woman friend in California. She had just begun to get back her emotional balance and didn't want anything to happen that could upset her. Not that she was normally neurotic, but during the past four years, she had lost everyone she loved or cared for

Jason had confided to her what he hoped to accomplish in the future with expanded sales to Europe and Asia. Her past job under State Department cover but working on a project for the Department of Commerce and the CIA was to help keep new technologies from reaching foreign entities. Since FBI "bag operations", under cover illegal break-ins or burglaries, to get information had recently been blown, new methods for gaining information had been explored.

Now, her job was to get key information that would permit U.S. industry to sell its technologies abroad, some that perhaps she felt shouldn't be sold. How different was her current attitude. How quickly Jason and Jack were able to change her moral and intellectual attitude. The major concern of U.S. industry was to prevent their technologies from being stolen ensuring a loss of profits, not necessarily to reserve them for U.S. national security purposes.

Tom picked her up that evening at six. "You look very sharp," he said. Rachel wore a plain steel blue silk sheath dress with pearls that would fit almost any dress code. And, it was pleasantly flattering.

It was a forty-five minute drive to the ultra-fashionable suburb of Potomac, Maryland, where the party was. Tom briefed her on the possible guest list and also gave her a list of the foreign visitors who had attended the Hill reception.

"I thought this might be useful. Several of these individuals may be here tonight. I know the Frenchman, Pierre Ledent, has been invited. He works for the French foreign ministry and is temporarily assigned to the Embassy here. But, I heard confidentially that he's really an electrical engineer, so I doubt that he's a career member of their diplomatic corps. My hunch is that he's a member of the DGSE, the French Intelligence,

The Purloined Encryption Caper

but I'll let you reach your own conclusions after you meet him."

She would make a special effort to observe Pierre tonight, perhaps even try to talk with him. It would be interesting to see who he came with. Maybe she could uncover his main purpose in his current assignment.

Rachel enjoyed the party immensely. Toward the end of the evening, Pierre approached her. "Hello, I'm Pierre Ledent. I understand, Miss Brown, that you are one of those established Washington institutions, a lobbyist. It must be fascinating." He exuded Gallic charm.

"I wish I were," Rachel replied. "My boss is. I'm only his research assistant and not yet very versed in the ways of Washington. Are you visiting Washington or assigned here?"

"I am attached to the French Embassy for the coming year to learn how your country works, especially how the American business community interacts with your government and academic community. We Europeans feel that your country has been very successful in integrating all parts of its productive society. Tell me, Miss Brown, who does your boss lobby for, or is that a business secret? And what kind of research do you do?"

"Our clients are mostly small companies in information technology and electronics," Rachel explained. "We have an overly active Congress which feels it must pass laws to justify its existence, many of which can inhibit business and limit their ability to sell their products abroad. It's our job to keep our clients informed of the current thinking in Congress and in the Administration, especially in advance of the passage of laws."

He reacted with some enthusiasm. "It sounds fascinating and an excellent service to your private sector. I can understand why firms feel having lobbyists in Washington look out for their interests is so important. This is a most complicated system. I hope you'll have dinner with me some evening, Miss Brown, or may I call you Rachel? Do you have a business card?"

"Yes, I do, and by all means call me Rachel." She gave him her card and took one of his. He was listed as a Second Secretary, French Embassy, with another address listed in French on the back that showed him as an industrial consultant to their Ministry of Foreign Affairs. Later, she saw him talking with several of the Commerce Department staff as well as a man someone had identified as a personal assistant to the President. She would have to get their names from Tom.

Rachel also met several political appointees assigned to the Commerce and State Departments. Everyone she met always asked who she was and tried to determine how important she was. When she told them about her research job, it seemed they quickly lost interest. This was one thing she learned very quickly in Washington. The first question anyone asked at a party or a reception was "...and what do you do?" Perhaps Jack could give her a better title which would suggest more clout. It didn't seem to matter much on Capitol Hill since your clout came with the companies you represented. But when you got beyond that world it seemed to make a big difference.

The Purloined Encryption Caper

She assumed the men she met were single, since they hadn't come with wives or girlfriends, or else gay. She made special note of the "single" men on the back of their cards. They would be good prospects to invite to a party, even though none had particularly appealed to her.

On the drive home, it was fun gossiping with Tom about who was there and what they said.

"Watch out for Pierre," Tom cautioned. "Joe told me to tell you he eats little girls for lunch. And I hear that he's very interested in getting access to high-tech companies. He seems to be very cagey, and I certainly wouldn't trust him."

"Thanks for the warning, but I realized he was very slick. He asked me to have dinner with him, but I have no intention of doing so alone. Anyway, I think he's more interested in meeting Jack than wining and dining me. Jack's away now, so I'll have to forewarn him before lucky Pierre strikes. Perhaps some night next week, I can fix dinner for you and we can talk about the people I met tonight. There are a number I'd like to keep up with and I feel I should get to know a little more about them before I follow up or before anyone calls me. I seem to have handed out a lot of cards tonight."

"It's a date," Tom said. They settled on Tuesday evening.

"By the way, Rachel," Tom asked as they got out of his car, "have you heard from Steve? He was supposed to be back from Europe by now."

"No, I haven't. Maybe he decided to take a short vacation," she replied. "Can you phone him in Paris and see if he's still there?" Tom thought he would try the next day, unless he had word waiting for him.

The next day was Sunday and a beautiful warm autumn day. Rachel decided to take a drive in the countryside. She remembered a wonderful little town in West Virginia-- Berkeley Springs--she and her mother had visited before Rachel left for Germany. Her father had been away on a consultancy and her mother was staying with her in Washington.

Berkeley Springs was originally called "Bath" after the town in England, since George Washington and his colonial cronies established the town around the warm springs located there. A state Park in the middle of the city is famous for its bathhouse and spa treatments where she and her mother had enjoyed a massage and mineral bath. Then they had a wonderful time poking around the Old Factory Antique Mall that sold antiques or near antiques. Her mother had bought her several pieces of old jewelry which Rachel still treasured.

The drive through the Virginia countryside to West Virginia was a picture waiting to be painted by a master. Autumn was just starting to show its multi-hued colors and the trees were beginning to display their brilliant red and gold foliage. She drove slowly to enjoy the scenery and when she entered the center of Berkeley Springs, she realized it had changed very little. The Country Inn looked the same, with its manicured gardens and large baskets of flowers hanging around the entrance on the large porch. A few more shops and boutiques had opened in the town but the rustic charm still prevailed.

The Purloined Encryption Caper

She followed the signs directing her to the Old Factory Antique Mall where she hoped to find a few items for her apartment. She desperately needed attractive and unusual flower vases. She left all of hers in storage and missed not having fresh flowers in her living room and bedroom. Flowers made an apartment look alive and, according to her mother, no dining room table looked complete without a bowl of fresh flowers.

She found four wonderful old vases, in different sizes and colors. As she was getting ready to pay for them, she looked up and saw Mary Howard, whose husband, Philip, had been her boss in Hong Kong.

"Mary! What are you doing here? I thought you were still in Hong Kong." The two women embraced.

"I should be asking you that question, Rachel. Are you passing through or are you and Jeff living near here?"

Rachel hesitated. "I'm working in Washington now. Are you on home leave?"

"No, we're living in the area as well, in Falls Church. Philip was promoted to head the project you worked for and so about six months ago we were transferred back to the States. He'll be so glad to know you're here. How's Jeff?" Mary realized that this might not have been the best question to ask since Rachel hadn't mentioned him or responded to her questioning earlier.

"Jeff was killed in a plane crash on his way home, right before we were to be married and after I had resigned from the Agency." Visibly shocked, Mary began to say how sorry she was, but Rachel stopped her and said, "Don't feel badly. It's not so painful any more."

"Rachel, we have a cabin in the mountains nearby. If you don't have any more shopping to do or any other pressing plans, please come back with me. I know that Phil will be glad to see you. He'll also want to know why you didn't get in touch with us after Jeff died. After you left, we wrote you at the last address you gave us, but our letter was returned."

Mary had remembered Rachel when she first arrived in Hong Kong. The bright young lady had just lost her parents and was also suffering from a broken love affair. While Rachel never actually told them about her affair, Mary's instincts could tell. It also explained why Rachel hadn't been interested in meeting young men, and always declined dates. Mary considered Rachel too young to have had so much sadness in such a short time.

Rachel followed Mary up a winding road for about a mile from the main road to a mountain development area called Whispering Pines. The view was spectacular, with hazy mountain ranges rising in the distance. The smell of pine and the blanket of falling multi-hued leaves enchanted Rachel. Mary turned into a driveway and stopped at a lovely cedar-sided cabin. It was hidden from the road and made Rachel think what a good safehouse it would make.

"Mary, is that you?" Philip called, as Mary and Rachel entered the cabin..

"Yes, Phil. But come see who I found rummaging in our quaint antique shops."

"My God, Rachel," the startled husband exclaimed as he embraced her. "What are you doing here?"

The Purloined Encryption Caper

    Mary got a pitcher of iced tea and poured a glass for everyone. Rachel told them about Jeff's death, her long seclusion on the Outer Banks and about her new job.

    Phil then asked" "Why didn't you call us when you got back to Washington? We would have been glad to help you get settled or find a new job."

    "Phil, I didn't know you were here and I was in a blue funk. I wanted to do nothing but hide. I was too proud to contact the Agency and ask for a job. I was so shaken when Jeff was killed. I had no one and felt totally alone. Jeff's family treated me like an intruder who had no business trying to 'snare' their son and press him into marriage." Rachel took a long gulp of her drink. "You see, Jeff never told his parents about me. His mother already had selected someone for him--the perfect wife who would fit into their social circle and ensure that he became an admiral or some such senior officer." She paused a moment before continuing.

    "At the base memorial service for Jeff, I was relegated to the back row and his mother kept introducing a young woman she had in tow as Jeff's fiancée. I think Jeff had dated her before he went to Asia. His mother was horrid and embarrassed Jeff's friends. They all were going to attend our wedding reception and so knew the truth. I didn't say anything to anyone and left before the end of the service." She paused, reliving the humiliation she had felt.

    "I was so devastated that for three days I hid in my hotel room in San Francisco trying to figure out what to do. I had no family, no job and had just lost the man I was to marry. I was feeling sorry for myself and wallowing in self-pity. It was at this point, I had to go somewhere that had familiar memories that was part of my past." Rachel paused, trying to keep her emotions under control.

"My parents owned a cottage on the Outer Banks in North Carolina near Kitty Hawk. We used to spend all our summers there when I was growing up. I telephoned the real estate agent and asked if the house was rented. It was available so I asked him to take it off the market, that I wanted to spend some time there." Rachel had the beginning of tears well up in her eyes.

"I flew to Norfolk, bought a car and drove down to North Carolina. When I walked into the cottage, I sat down and sobbed. All the pent-up emotion seemed to come out. I couldn't understand why all these bad things were happening to me. I walked the beach every day, trying to make up my mind what I should do. I was lucky that I didn't have to worry about money. Since my family had managed their money well, no mortgages were left on either the Pennsylvania house or the beach cottage. And, at my father's advice, I had invested most of my salary while I was in Germany and Hong Kong." Rachel paused as she painfully reviewed that trying time.

"I didn't want to see or talk to anyone. Fortunately, the tourist season was over and I almost had the beach to myself. I read a great deal, more novels than I'd ever read before and bought the *Washington Post* and *Washington Times* every day to try to reacquaint myself with the U.S. since I'd been overseas for over four years." She sipped the iced tea before continuing.

The Purloined Encryption Caper

"I scanned the employment ads to see what jobs were available. I even thought about going back to school to get my graduate degree, something my father always wanted me to do." She paused and looked up at the Howards, who were visibly empathizing with her.

"After about six months, I knew I had to pull myself together and stop feeling sorry for myself. I updated my biodata and began to respond to some of the want ads listed in the Washington papers. But then I got lucky. Steve Holliday, a guy I had known since I was a kid whose folks had a beach cottage near ours, was vacationing from his Washington job on Capitol Hill. After hearing my tale of woe, he recommended me to a friend who runs a PR and lobbying firm in D.C." She thought a moment before making the next statement. "I didn't want to go back to government. I needed to make a success of myself, yet not get locked into a job that I couldn't leave if I wanted to." The Howards sat motionless, fascinated by Rachel's story.

"I came to Washington and was interviewed by Steve's friend, Jack Warden, who runs Jack Warden Associates. Remember when we used to bad mouth lobbyists? Jack needed someone to do research on legislation that affected the high-tech industry or could restrict their foreign sales. It's very much in line with what we did in Asia, gather information, except it's for the private sector, not the government. It was a good move and Jack's really a good guy. I found an apartment in Arlington, Virginia, near the Ballston Metro. I'm now a settled Washington suburbanite, working hard to develop a career." She looked at Phil and Mary and smiled.

"But enough about me. How's the project going? Are you located in the big Langley fortress or are you at Commerce now?"

"Well, I'm still with the company, but they stopped the project. I have two offices, the main one in Langley, with an auxiliary one in Rosslyn, but we are mostly involved in Mickey Mouse kind of work. The Agency isn't what it used to be. I keep wondering who we're working for, the U.S. or the opposition. While I'm glad our country is concerned about refugees and political correctness, there are so many more important things for the Agency to do. Other government organizations or private voluntary groups using government money are far better suited to do social or community work." Phil smirked as he regaled Rachel with his situation and the Washington squirrel cage atmosphere.

"Who's keeping track of the abuses of U.S. export control laws by high-tech companies or protecting companies from foreign industrial spies?" Rachel inquired.

"No one that I know of at CIA. Not seriously," Phil replied, shrugging his shoulders. "Maybe a low-level political operative, a GS-7, or a private sitting in an office in a Treasury supply closet. This isn't of concern anymore at the top. I've really been worried. There is great unhappiness among the career CIA staff and there are all sorts of rumors going around about congressional people trying to shut down the whole CIA or at the very least emasculate it. A lot of the old timers at the Agency have left or are planning to resign. We're hopeful that a new Administration will change this but we need change at the top of the Agency first."

The Purloined Encryption Caper

He paused to see her reactions. Apparently satisfied with her nod, he proceeded.

"We're trying to fight back in our own little way. There is an informal group of the old hands that get together. Unofficially, we keep each other informed of what we consider gross misuse or lack of interest by the intelligence organizations. We even have a few FBI guys who have joined us, as well as some of the people from the defense intelligence groups. They're unhappy as well. When things get too bad or out of hand and we feel that we're being asked to do things that may be against the best interests of the country, we quietly and informally let some of the sympathetic Hill staffers know. They can then begin to send inquiries to the Pentagon or the CIA and build some pressure or reaction." Phil stopped talking and relit his pipe.

"Enough about the company. Mary and I come up here to forget about all the Washington nonsense. Let's get a real drink now and take a walk. I think you'll like it, Rachel. We have about ten acres of woods and about a half-mile to our nearest neighbor. You'll stay for dinner, I hope."

Their stroll through the woods behind the Howards' house was invigorating and required a lot of physical exercise, since the walk was up and down a forested hillside, strewn with a wide variety of stones. But it was beautiful, especially at this time of year. The oaks, elms and maples all had formed a tent of brightly colored leaves, occasionally falling, that made the ground a mirror of the canopy. There were traces of animals as well. Rachel wished she had brought her camera as a small herd of browsing deer scampered away when they saw humans approach.

Rachel was delighted to stay and talk about their old days in Asia. After dinner, Rachel thanked them for the day. "I've got to go now. This coming week's going to be a hectic one, especially since my boss is on vacation."

Phil and Mary said they were staying over and not going back to Washington until Monday night.

"Phil, can we get together one day this week for lunch?" Rachel asked as they were walking to her car after dinner. "I need your good advice on problems several of our clients have encountered regarding foreign industrial espionage. Also, since our Patent Office now contracts its work to private firms and releases proprietary information before the patent is final, the leakage and plagiarism are rampant. I've hit a brick wall in getting information from government offices other than the usual pap that's available to the general public. How about Wednesday or Thursday? If you can get away, come over to my office and I'll show you my new digs."

"Thursday will be better since I'll be in Rosslyn that day. I'd invite you over to my office, but you know how difficult it is to meet visitors on our home turf."

On her drive home, Rachel thought about her good luck in running into Mary and Phil. She was very fond of them and they had helped her through some bad days in Hong Kong, especially when she first arrived. Phil would be a good sounding board, too, regarding her current concerns.

The Purloined Encryption Caper

That afternoon when Rachel was following Mary to her mountain house, Pierre Ledent was just leaving the 7-Eleven Store in Berkeley Springs on his way to his cabin. He recognized Rachel Brown following another woman in a car, driving up the road where his cabin was located. He had to see where Rachel was going. He hurriedly got into his rental car and discreetly followed her. Fortunately, another car was between them so Rachel couldn't identify him in her rear view mirror.

After about a half mile when Rachel and Mary turned off into a vacation home development, he waited ten minutes, and then drove around the development until he spotted the cabin where Rachel's and her friend's cars were parked.

He noted the lot number and had every intention of identifying the owners or renters, whoever they were. This was a very unfortunate twist of fate. Pierre considered his West Virginia hideout in the Blue Ridge Mountains safe but now realized it could be compromised. He would also have to do a little more checking on Rachel Brown. Was she really just a junior worker in a lobbying firm or a clever agent keeping tabs on suspicious foreigners?

He thought about the party the previous evening and was grateful to his friends for asking Joe, the head staffer in the science and technology committee on the Hill, to invite the small visiting group of participants in the Department of State's program to the party. It had enabled him to meet a large number of people who could be extremely useful and he hoped that his fellow conspirators were taking full advantage of the situation.

He planned on holding a meeting of his group in Berkeley Springs soon so they could plot their strategy. Prior to that, however, he would have to get certain questions answered, some involving Rachel Brown. He would also arrange for someone to start a watch on her.

It was almost ten-thirty that evening when Rachel returned to her apartment. Her phone was ringing but stopped just as she reached it. A half-hour later when she was about to turn out her light, it rang again.

"Hello," Rachel said.

"Where have you been? I've been trying to reach you all day." the voice questioned, almost angrily. It took her a few seconds to realize it was Jason.

"It was such a beautiful autumn day, Jason, I went for a drive in the country," she replied enthusiastically. "The leaves are turning color and it was breathtakingly beautiful."

"All by yourself? Where did you go?" he asked.

Rachel was slightly taken aback by his attitude. "Yes, all by myself. There's this wonderful little town in West Virginia, about a two-hour drive from here, where they have a lot of old antique stores. I wanted to poke around and see if there were any bargains or items I couldn't live without. I found some lovely vases for my apartment." She paused. "Is there something you want, or any questions about the information I gave you?" Rachel asked, suddenly aware of her informal and personal manner with him.

The Purloined Encryption Caper

"No. I wanted you to know how much I enjoyed Friday evening. I already am looking forward to my next visit to Washington," he continued in a gentler tone.

"I enjoyed it, too." She paused.

"I want you to save Thursday and Friday evenings for me next week for dinner. I'll be arriving on Thursday afternoon, and I'd like to get on your calendar before you make other plans. And I won't take no for an answer. I need something to look forward to." He paused, waiting for a comment. But none came. "I read all the material you gave me and realize how much I have to do before my company's Scientific Advisory Committee meets this coming weekend."

"Is this meeting an important one for you?" Rachel asked.

"Very. I think it'll be a turning point for our company. Possible industrial espionage against our firm is going to come as a shock to a lot of the technical and scientific staff as well as the Committee. The new security systems which I've been working on and plan to discuss at the meeting won't be welcomed by them. They're free spirits and used to free movement." He paused before he continued in a more personal tone.

"I wish you could be here with me." He wanted to say "not only would your presence be a great comfort," but instead said "you could help me with my presentation. After all, much of what I have to say is taken from the material you gave me, as well as your interpretation of comments from your visits on Capitol Hill." He again waited for any reaction she might have before he proceeded. She made none.

He continued to keep her interest. "You know we've applied for patents for some new advanced encryption software, and have plans for others currently on the drawing board. If they turn out as well as we think, it could be a big boon for our little company. I think we have a beat on most of our competitors, both domestic and foreign. Also, I think we have the leading edge in biometrics which is now desperately needed in view of the tightening of security." Jason was hoping to have their products available within the next six months. He continued. "One of the topics on the agenda for discussion is whether we should go public with the company. None of the investors want to deal with SEC lawyers and stockholders. Nor do I. But we'll need a lot of cash to go into full-scale production to establish a large niche in both markets."

Rachel followed up. "I think I might have some more detailed information for you by the time of your meeting. Is your cell phone or telephone at the office secure, or is there a number where I can reach you that is secure? I have a feeling about something, linkages, and people I've met, but I don't want to e-mail info or put anything on paper yet, and I wouldn't want to have anyone listen in." She paused before continuing. "I'd advise you not to admit any foreign visitors or other suspicious looking people into your offices until you have your security system up-dated and vetted them. Have I frightened you enough?" Rachel had a theory about how information was getting out, especially after meeting all the individuals at the Saturday night party, but wanted to test her theory on Phil on Thursday.

"Why not call me here at home?" He gave her his home number and realized there was a long period of silence before she spoke.

"And if a woman answers, should I hang up?" Rachel asked hesitatingly.

"No one else will answer but me. No wife, no live-in lover and I don't live with my parents." Jason hadn't realized that Rachel might have thought he was married. "Is that why you gave me such a hard time when I tried to kiss you? You thought I might be married?"

"It's been known to happen. Married men do pursue women after taking off their wedding rings. Look at the Hill scene." She paused for his response.

"Rachel, that's not my style. I'm usually very honest in my private relationships. Remember that in the future. I should have told you I wasn't married. Maybe then you would have let me make love to you."

Rachel didn't answer, so he continued. "I'll call you again in the next few days. Good night, dear one."

After he hung up, Jason knew he would try to make love to Rachel the next time they were together. He wanted her too much. Just talking to her this evening aroused him sexually and his dreams didn't help.

CHAPTER 5

As she entered her apartment building Tuesday after work, the desk clerk stopped her. "I have some flowers for you, Miss Brown."

The enclosed note read, "For your new vase. Love, Jason." She couldn't remember the last time a man had sent her long-stem red roses. Jeff had never sent flowers since there were just too many inexpensive flowers available in Asia. Instead, he had given her lovely pieces of jewelry, including a long strand of pink pearls which she treasured.

This evening she decided to share with Tom her theory of how information on new technologies being developed by U.S. companies might be compromised and data given to unauthorized individuals. She had listed government officials who might receive highly technical info on new or proposed high-tech software or hardware from U.S. companies and could then pass it on to other government officials. They could then leak the info to foreign parties or competitors for payoffs, for their own benefit or for spite.

She then added names of individuals she knew who were assigned to each office and began cross-referencing them to see how the information flow could work. What had emerged was a frightening pattern. Someone at the Patent Office or one of their newly-authorized private contractors could pass confidential information on newly-filed patent applications to individuals at Commerce, the White House or the State Department. From there, the information could flow covertly outside the government to foreign entities, such as Pierre, or rival companies. Limited Patent Office information was in the public domain, but Rachel was certain that the information leaked far exceeded the authorized amount. This enabled unauthorized individuals to pinpoint the companies foreigners may want to penetrate and learn exact details on technologies being developed.

This was why Pierre was interested in getting to know her--to identify the companies her office represented. He had already telephoned her twice and it was only Tuesday.

"Tell him I'm busy," Rachel instructed Cindy, her office colleague. "Say I'm in conference or out of the office." Rachel didn't want to meet with him until she had an opportunity to talk with Jack and to get advice from Phil.

Dinner was ready when Tom arrived. She first fixed a scotch and water for each. "I really need this," Tom said. "It's been a very hectic day. I suppose all days will be like this until the pooh-bahs leave for the Thanksgiving and Christmas holidays. But let's get to the reason you invited me." He took a long sip of his drink "Last night I made a list of the individuals you were interested in from the party Saturday night. As you can see, the most important ones are political appointees and they are everywhere." Tom passed her copies of the information he had collected for her.

"But before we start, let's be honest with each other. I know you didn't work for the State Department when you were overseas. Steve hinted that you really worked for the CIA, so I took the liberty of checking you out. Don't be upset. But if I'm going to go out of my way to help you, I had to make sure I wasn't giving assistance to the enemy." He paused to watch her reaction. He noticed that she looked startled by his statement. "I consider you a good friend, Rachel, but I don't want to play games." He smiled.

"Also, I don't want you or me to get into any trouble," he continued. "People like Pierre play for high stakes. So do certain government officials and company officials as well. Not necessarily the top echelon, but many of the second- or third-level employees may not have many scruples in undercutting the company they work for, especially if it helps them either in their career, with a competitor, or for money. Since coming to Washington, I've been amazed at what people will do for money. And it doesn't have to be much. Some sell their souls for a few thousand dollars or a willing woman. My folks used to drill into me the importance of integrity. In Washington, integrity is almost a dirty word."

Rachel was taken aback by Tom's statement and wondered whether Jack was suspicious of her past as well, or even Jason.

"I thought you were being so helpful because you liked me and thought I was a nice person," Rachel chided. "By the way, have you had any word from Steve?"

"No. I telephoned the Embassy in Paris. The Economic Officer told me he had left for Marseilles last Thursday evening, but they haven't had any word since. They assume he's either following up on leads or went to the French Riviera for a few days vacation. You know how secretive Steve can be at times. I guess we'll just have to wait until he pops up somewhere or we get a phone call. And yes, I do think you are a nice person," he added smilingly.

"It's true," Rachel explained. "I did work on a joint project between the CIA and Commerce. We operated out of the commercial or economic section of the Embassy, but our instructions came from the CIA. Most of our reporting went back to CIA headquarters, although sterilized copies of our reports were circulated to the Consulate and Embassy country staffs." She looked up and smiled. "I guess I have no secrets from you now, Tom."

"Have you told Jack about your past?" Tom asked.

"No. Jack doesn't know unless Steve told him, which I doubt. I told Jack that I worked in the economic section at State and was in the Foreign Service, which was technically true. He seemed impressed that I could operate and get information on local industries overseas. The fact that I dealt with U.S. business officials also seemed to impress him. He also liked the idea that I was fluent in both German and French, had a

The Purloined Encryption Caper

good grasp of Spanish, and studied Chinese, although I don't claim fluency in that language," she smiled

"And Jason?" Tom queried.

"No," Rachel replied. "Why do you ask about him?"

"Rachel, it's obvious, at least to me, that you were both rather taken with each other even though you may not want to admit it," he said with a smile.

The evening proved very fruitful and Rachel was glad that Tom knew about her past. She even told him about her parents' accident and about Jeff. Apparently, Steve hadn't confided this info to Tom. He had wondered why she hadn't continued working for the CIA or hadn't applied for a job at Commerce..

She checked her theory with him. "I'll keep my eyes and ears open and see if I can find any other possible linkages, or get evidence that this is actually happening." He then looked at her sternly.

"Be careful, Rachel." he warned. "I don't want you to get hurt. If you run into any problems, don't hesitate to call. I have a number of contacts that could prove useful if we need to use them. Also, be careful with your clients."

"Tom, do you think Joe Coswell could be in on a plot of this type or could be on the take from either foreigners or private business?" Rachel asked.

"I can't imagine." Tom was stunned by her question. "The committee chairman is a very honest guy who wouldn't put up with any nonsense. Even the hint of corruption of a staffer would send the chairman into a rage. He wouldn't hesitate to fire that person on the spot. Joe's a good director and a good friend."

Tom made a mental note to himself that it might behoove him to keep his eyes open and be careful what he told Joe. There was no use in taking chances. On the drive back to his apartment, he thought about Rachel's theory. By giving her the list of the people at the party, he knew that Rachel would put names to offices and make special note of the people she dealt with at those offices in the future

As soon as Rachel was alone, she tried to phone Jason at his house to thank him for the flowers, but there was no answer. All she could do was leave a message on his answering machine. She wondered where he was and with whom. She didn't want to call him on his cell phone. It might be embarrassing if he were on a date.

Earlier that day, Pierre had driven to the county courthouse in Martinsburg, West Virginia, to check on the cabin in the Whispering Pines development. Philip Howard, the name registered in the books as the owner, rang a bell with Pierre, and he suddenly remembered why. Howard had once been head of a project within the CIA, now defunct, which traced the export of U.S. technologies. What was he doing now, Pierre wondered.

He learned that Rachel had also worked for the CIA. His source at the FBI had confided this tid-bit to him but said Rachel had resigned over a year ago to get married. Did her marriage go wrong, or was she still married? She didn't wear a wedding band. Also, he learned that Steve Holliday had arranged for her job with Jack Warden. Perhaps she had been rehired by the CIA and then put under non-official cover. Was Jack Warden's company a CIA front? The plot thickens, he mused.

That evening while Tom and Rachel were having dinner and discussing her theory, Pierre was on the phone to a "contact" at the CIA. "Hello, my friend," Pierre started. "I am interested in finding out about certain people. One is Philip Howard and the other is Rachel Brown. It would be of great importance to find out what Mr. Howard does now and if Ms. Brown is still a colleague. I will telephone you Thursday evening at the same time."

At lunch on Thursday, Rachel outlined to Phil the problems of several of their clients and her theory about leaks in the government. "What do you think?" she asked.

"Good possibility," Phil said. "I don't know how much of it is illegal, but you know, Rachel, we have the 1960's boomer crowd in charge of the many government departments. They feel that if a technology is good for America, it will be good for other countries, too, and should be shared, for a price of course, such as an impressive contribution to appropriate reelection campaigns. They believe the technology should be given to everyone, especially if *they*, our erstwhile government elite, can decide who everyone is. Giving this information away and the leakage of technical information abroad, especially to enemy countries, is increasingly dangerous," he added.

"But in our country, they want to make us have chips inserted in our computers to permit the FBI or police to eavesdrop or tap into our information systems on the premise of national security or other such reason. And through ECHELON, they can monitor our every word uttered over a phone line. I think it's one step away from a police state." Phil seemed very introspective as he thought out loud.

"You mentioned the two foreign individuals you talked with last Saturday evening, Pierre Ledent from the French Intelligence Office, and Hans Schmidt from German Intelligence. Have they contacted you yet? Also, did you talk with any of the other foreign individuals on this list or give them your card?" Phil asked Rachel.

"Pierre has already telephoned twice, but I put off talking with him. I also had a note from Dr. Schmidt. Being German and formal, he said he enjoyed meeting me and would have his secretary call my secretary for an appointment or lunch, whichever I preferred. I didn't tell him that I had lived in Germany and was fluent in German, but I'm sure he knows it by now. They probably both have checked me out with their intelligence agencies." Rachel shook her head in disbelief as she told Phil this.

"Rachel, I'll ask around. Our informal group is meeting tomorrow for drinks. If I get any information, I'll call you. But I would say offhand that I think your supposition is correct. By the way, does Jack Warden know about your background?"

"No. I indicated that I had been in the Foreign Service and told him the cover story provided by the Agency when I left to marry Jeff."

The Purloined Encryption Caper

"Be careful, Rachel. I'll get back to you. Give us a call and come to dinner some night soon, unless your evenings are fully booked."

"That's one thing I'm not, Phil. There's a nice guy on the S&T committee who's been very helpful in taking me around on the Hill. His name is Tom Fulton, but it's a very platonic relationship. He told me he had checked me out before he offered his help, so he knows my background. And his roommate, Steve Holliday, whom I've known for years. But he travels overseas a lot. He works for the Senate Intelligence Committee as an investigator. It's hard to make close gal pals in a short time. They're either living with someone or too competitive."

"Watch out for those platonic types, Rachel. They can sneak up on you. Remember Jeff?" Phil winked at Rachel. "I think I'll see what information I can get on Tom. I've met Steve. I hear he's really been making waves on the Hill as well as with our supposedly NATO allies. I'll have Mary call you soon."

It was good seeing Phil and being able to talk with him. She felt more secure having friends like Phil and Mary in the area. She was anxious to start entertaining again and was mentally planning a dinner party. Maybe when Jack returned, she could invite Jack, his wife Jean, Mary and Phil over for dinner. She knew they would get along. Maybe she would ask Tom or Steve, or perhaps even Jason, if he was in town.

That night Rachel called Jason in California at his home number. She waited until about eleven to be sure he was there. He answered on the first ring. She explained her theory and asked him to go back and review all the information he had outlined in his patent applications to see if any comments could be traced to these descriptions.

"If so, make a list of all of your employees who have had access to the patent information as well as those who already left or might be vulnerable." She didn't mention Phil by name, but said she was trying to get more information from confidential sources.

"Does this involve Tom?" he questioned. He was beginning to resent Rachel's seeing Tom so much and her reliance on him. Also, Rachel was beginning to sound like an intelligence agent.

"No, it's not Tom," she responded guardedly. "But good luck with your meetings."

That same evening Pierre telephoned his CIA contact. "What did you find out?"

"According to the files, the technology project that Howard once ran has been shelved. He's been reassigned to a middle level bureaucratic job in the current reorganization. Rachel Brown officially resigned over a year ago to marry a Navy pilot she met in Asia," the contact confirmed. "In Hong Kong, Brown worked for Howard which explains their close relationship. There's no evidence in the file whether Brown ever got married or what has happened to her fiancé or husband. But, I can definitely confirm that she doesn't work for the CIA now." The contact paused.

"You may want to get to know her better," his CIA contact advised. "In her current position, she should have access to the CEO's of small technology firms that could be of interest. Remember, too, she got her

current job through Steve Holliday. I will also identify an appropriate CIA secretary here ideally placed for one of your group to get to know."

Even though Jack had been available by phone during his vacation, it was good to have him back in the office again. His vacation at Rachel's beach house had been ideal because Jack's sister and her family vacationed with them.

"You're lucky to have that place, Rachel. You must have loved it while you were growing up. My nephew and niece didn't want to leave. How did things go while I was away?"

Rachel wanted to discuss pending matters with Jack but decided to wait until he went through his in-box. "When you're finished seeing what's on your desk, let me know and I'll fill you in."

"Why not lunch?" Jack asked. "I haven't given Luigi's any business for awhile."

"You're on. I'll even join you in a glass of wine today," she replied.

During lunch, Rachel briefed Jack on her theory, her conversations with Tom and Jason and told Jack that Jason would be in town toward the end of the week.

"It seems Jason has recently become enchanted with our city," he chided. "He never liked to spend much time here before."

She also mentioned that she ran into her old boss and his wife from her Hong Kong days on a visit to Berkeley Springs and some night soon wanted to have Jack and Jean over for dinner to meet them.

"Great. I'd like that and so would Jean."

When they returned to the office, Jack phoned Jason. "Anything I can do so you don't have to make the trip East? I know this is a busy time for you."

"Thanks, Jack, but I don't need you to act on my behalf this time. I have several social engagements I want to keep and I think you know with whom."

When Rachel came home Tuesday, her phone was ringing. It was Jason. "I have to be in New York Thursday, so wondered if you were free Wednesday night as well? If so, I'll arrange to arrive on Wednesday and then take the shuttle up and back to New York on Thursday." Rachel agreed, suddenly realizing how anxious she was to see him again.

Wednesday, when Rachel arrived home from the office, a box of roses was waiting for her. The enclosed note said: "I'll be over at seven. We'll go to a small ethnic restaurant near your place. Love, Jason".

At precisely seven, there was a knock on her door. When she opened it, Jason was standing there, dressed casually in a tweed jacket and an open collared shirt. He looked strange since she had never seen him before in anything but a suit and tie. The tweeds suited him, she thought.

"Hi. It's good to see you," she said.

Jason put his arm around her and kissed her gently on the lips and then the forehead.

"You don't know how good it is to see you. What will you have?" Jason asked, as he headed toward the bar. "The same?" Rachel nodded. He mixed their drinks as he chatted about how helpful her info had been.

The Purloined Encryption Caper

Jason sat on the sofa next to her. "Everybody's very unhappy about the new security system and being told that they had to be more concerned with espionage and hackers. It's been hectic and I've been working every evening until midnight. That's why I need these evenings with you, to help me relax," he said as he took her hand. "Tomorrow, I have to brief two of my Advisory Committee members in New York who couldn't make it to the California meetings."

While they were finishing their drink, the telephone rang. Rachel excused herself and answered the phone in her bedroom. It was Mary Howard inviting her to spend the weekend with them in Berkeley Springs.

"We're going up early Saturday morning. Why don't you drive up and join us for lunch that day and stay through lunch or dinner on Sunday? You can bring someone if you like," Mary said.

"If I can find an interested party, I will. But at this point it seems rather doubtful." Rachel thought about asking Jason, but quickly dispelled the idea. He already told her that he had airline reservations back to San Francisco on Saturday morning.

Rachel returned to the living room and found Jason, sitting on the sofa but sound asleep. She got an Afghan to throw over him, and as she did, he awoke.

"Sorry, Rachel, I guess the stress and work of the past two weeks is catching up with me," he said as he yawned. "This is not how I planned our first evening together."

"No reason to apologize, but I have a proposition. Why don't I fix a cheese omelet, toast and salad, and then you can go home early for a good night's rest. I'll even drive you back to your hotel."

"An omelet does sound perfect, however, why don't I just stay here with you tonight?" Rachel gave him a very stern look.

"Okay," he said, smiling. "But I'll take a rain check on the overnight stay. I'm at the Hilton here in Ballston, so if you'd like to walk me home after you feed me, you can stay with me," he teased, but only half-jokingly.

The meal was good but his drowsiness was evident and he realized he'd better get some real sleep. At the door, he gave her a tender goodnight kiss and told her that she was lucky he was so tired, otherwise he would have insisted on more than a kiss. Rachel, teased him by returning his kiss, as passionate as his.

"You are a wench," he said. "I should insist on staying, but I want our first night together to be the best." He kissed her again and then left.

"How did your meetings go?" Rachel asked Jason the following evening.

"It was actually easier talking to the committee members one on one rather than as a group. Being Easterners, they are much more aware of the realities of doing business these days. And how was your day? Did you miss me after I left last evening?" he asked, as he handed her a drink.

"It seems every day is a busy one when Congress is in session." Rachel replied, almost coquettishly.

Dinner was at Jacques. The small combo played again and they danced to every slow song. They left fairly early, however, and returned to Rachel's apartment.

"Nightcap?" Jason asked.

"I think I'll settle for some Perrier and lime since tomorrow's a school day."

He handed her the drink and then took her in his arms. She put her drink down, afraid she would spill it. She was shaking.

"Rachel, I want to stay tonight and make love to you," he whispered, and then kissed her, first gently and then passionately. Her response was as passionate as his. He pressed his body close to hers, and they could feel the throbbing of their bodies and the wild beating of their hearts. He kissed her face and neck and started to unbutton her blouse.

Jason whispered to her. "I want you so much," and kissed her passionately again, beginning to caress her body. Rachel tried half-heartedly to deter him and ask him to leave, but she couldn't get the words out.

"Rachel, don't fight me."

"Jason, why don't we wait," she said breathlessly.

She tried to break away, but Jason held her and wouldn't take no for an answer, especially since Rachel's objections seemed to diminish. Rachel knew she was falling for him and wasn't sure whether giving in would actually enhance or end their relationship. She finally succumbed, realizing this evening he was determined to make love to her. Also, in her heart, she wanted him to.

He led her into the bedroom, undressed her and then himself. He caressed her body, kissed her neck and breasts, and finally brought their bodies together.

Rachel felt as if she were on fire. Their lovemaking was intense and Rachel knew that if she didn't hold back, this kind of passion could easily destroy her.

"I want all of you, Rachel, darling." But she was afraid of getting hurt again and couldn't fully commit herself to him.

Afterward, Rachel said, "Jason, we can't let this happen again, at least not for a while." But she was not sure he even heard her. He was already fast asleep.

Rachel slept in Jason's arms that evening. Sometime in the middle of the night, Jason softly caressed her, kissed her awake, and made love to her again.

"Jason, we've got to cool our feelings. We don't really know each other."

He knew she was saying things that her body didn't feel. He would have to convince her that it was inevitable and right. Also, he wanted to tell her he loved her, but was afraid that she wouldn't believe him.

When Rachel's alarm sounded that morning, Jason had already left for his seven-thirty breakfast meeting. Although last night she had wanted him to make love to her, she was disappointed in herself for having succumbed so easily and quickly and to her own passion as well.

Rachel dressed especially nice for the office that day but Jason never made it in. He had meetings with patent attorneys in Crystal City in the morning, and then Jack met him and other business contacts at a restaurant near the Pentagon for lunch.

"Jason told me he'll pick you up at your apartment at six-thirty," Jack told Rachel when he returned to the office. What Jack didn't tell Rachel was that he had an

The Purloined Encryption Caper

extra pair of tickets for the new musical opening that evening at the Kennedy Center which he knew Rachel wanted to see. Jack offered the tickets to Jason, who accepted them with one caveat: Jack and his wife would join him and Rachel for an early dinner before the theater.

When Jason arrived at Rachel's apartment, he noticed two rather foreign-looking individuals standing in front of the building but forgot about it when Rachel opened her apartment door. It always intrigued Jason that while Rachel looked so efficient and business-like during the day, in the evening she looked like a different person in her feminine yet elegant dress. He gave her a quick kiss and asked if she was ready.

"Jack and I have arranged a special evening together," he said. "We'll meet him and Jean in Foggy Bottom for dinner and then walk to the Kennedy Center. I understand there's a new musical you want to see."

"How marvelous," Rachel exclaimed. She was thrilled. She really liked Jack's wife a lot and was pleased that the four of them would be together. She was aware, however, that when Jean saw her and Jason together, Jean would realize the strong feelings and familiarity between them.

Rachel had to admit that much against her better judgment, she was more than enamored with Jason. He was good company and now also knew how exciting it was to have him make love to her.

In the taxi en route to the Kennedy Center, Jason put his arm around her. "Darling, I can't tell you how wonderful last night was. I dreamed often of making love to you. Also, it answered one question I had the moment I first met you."

Rachel looked at him questioningly. "What's that?"

"How you'd look in the morning after a night of making love," he said, as he kissed her hand.

The taxi driver was listening and smiled. Rachel could see his reaction in the rear view mirror and was embarrassed.

"Perhaps tonight I can show you again how much I care for you," Jason continued as he brought her close to him. "But tonight, I want all of your passion."

"Jason, we can't continue this way. We don't know each other well enough," she whispered to him, making sure the driver couldn't overhear her.

Jason only squeezed her knee. He already had made mental plans for later on after the theater.

Rachel was in a dilemma. She never took sex as a casual encounter but was afraid that Jason might. She didn't want to get hurt again and Jason definitely could be a heart breaker who might use women and then throw them away. She didn't want to end up on his body pile.

They arrived at the restaurant exactly at seven, but Jack and Jean were already waiting. The restaurant was crowded with the pre-Kennedy Center diners, and Jason was glad that Jack had Cindy make reservations. The dinner was enjoyable, even if it was a bit hurried.

The show was excellent and lived up to its rave reviews. Jason enjoyed seeing Rachel laugh and have a good time. Also, he realized how right it was being with Rachel, that they already seemed to belong together.

The Purloined Encryption Caper

Jack and Jean drove Rachel and Jason back to her apartment. "How about coffee or a nightcap?" Rachel offered.

Jack parked the car and they all headed for her building. Jason suddenly remembered the strange looking individuals who had been outside the building earlier and looked around. They were no longer there or else were out of sight.

"You know, Rachel, when I arrived earlier, there were a couple of strange-looking men lurking around the entrance. Have you noticed them?" Jason questioned.

"Yes. The other day I asked the desk clerk if they were tenants. She said no. I've actually seen them off and on for the past week Maybe we have mafia living here and someone will be plunked off one of these days."

Jack and Jason looked at each other. Could they be after Rachel and, if so, why? Who else lived in the building? Just that day, they had been briefed by several officials of the Defense Intelligence Agency who said a European businessman had recently been kidnapped. In conjunction with a U.S. counterpart, his firm was developing software dealing with artificial intelligence. He was drugged, kept for thirty-six hours and then released. The man didn't know whether his kidnappers had actually gotten him to talk, because they had given him a shot of a new truth serum the Czechs had developed. The DIA agents were now debriefing the individual to get as much information as they could.

"You'd better be careful and not go out at night alone. They may even be rapists," Jack warned.

Rachel thought differently, however. When she first noticed them, she mentioned it to Phil. He had one of his men secretly take pictures of them and was now checking them out. Rachel hoped to get word from Phil this weekend.

"Don't worry about me. I have a black belt in karate," she joked. Jason looked at her as if she just might.

And he was right. Perhaps not a black belt, but in Hong Kong, she had taken lessons in basic self-defense. She even managed to take on a most aggressive Australian at one of the local pubs who tried to make a pass at her. Although he was taller than her five foot five and weighed twice as much, she grabbed his arm and flipped him onto his back. He was so dumbfounded that the Aussie got up, looked at her, and walked away shaking his head. Rachel gained new respect in the international community after that. It kept all the hot-blooded guys at bay.

While Jason was getting drinks, the telephone rang. It was Mary Philips asking if Rachel was bringing anyone. "No, I'll be alone," Rachel responded.

Jason served Jack and himself each a cognac and gave Jean a Grand Marnier. Rachel decided she had better stick to Perrier water. "I have a long drive early tomorrow morning to West Virginia so I'd better skip any more alcohol for tonight."

"How long a drive is it? Will you drive up and back in one day?" Jason asked, slightly irked.

"No, I'll be staying overnight," she responded, not giving any further details.

The Purloined Encryption Caper

Her attitude of apparent nonchalance irritated Jason and he had to control himself from making some sarcastic comment. He didn't want to admit it was pure jealousy. Their passion had been so intense the night before, he felt certain she would ask him to stay over, possibly for the whole weekend. He suddenly became angry with her. The previous evening, he assumed, had obviously meant nothing to her.

Jason left with the Wardens, gave Rachel a perfunctory good night kiss, and went for a long walk. He realized he had already fallen in love with her. Why didn't she want to admit to her feelings? Was she involved with someone else and only saw him because he was a client? And who telephoned her this late at night? He automatically assumed it must be the man she planned to meet in Berkeley Springs. He became enraged. The little green monster had come to life and the temper he had usually managed to control suddenly returned.

Against his better judgment, he returned to her apartment building, determined to talk with her, when a taxi pulled up and a young man in his early thirties got out. In Jason's mind, it all came together. This must be the person who had telephoned Rachel earlier, the man in the photo he had seen in Rachel's computer room, the one which was signed, "My love forever, Jeff." Jason wheeled around and walked quickly back to his hotel, furious with himself. "So much for Rachel Brown," he said out loud. "What a fool I've been."

When he got back to his hotel, he called United Airlines and arranged to get an early morning flight. Originally he had arranged for the afternoon flight since he planned to spend the night with Rachel and have a leisurely morning together over breakfast at one of the charming little places around his hotel. Or possibly change his plans and not return to the Coast until Sunday.

Rachel was curious about the change in Jason's attitude. Suddenly, he had been cool toward her and barely kissed her goodnight. She planned to talk with him and put their relationship on a more even keel, even though she knew it would be difficult. Maybe Jason didn't want Jack and Jean to know there were such strong feelings between them. He didn't even say anything to Rachel about future visits. She was sure Jason wouldn't end the evening this way, that he would phone from the hotel and return. After waiting for half an hour, she tried to phone him. His line was busy.

The next morning before she left for West Virginia, Rachel phoned Jason at his hotel, on the pretext of thanking him for the previous evening. "He checked out early this morning," the hotel operator said. This really perplexed Rachel because his original plan was to catch an afternoon flight.

Rachel continued to ponder Jason's behavior on her drive up to West Virginia and decided to phone him during the coming week, if he didn't call her. Why did it matter so much, she wondered? But she knew why. She was falling in love with him. Why had she given in to his advances and slept with him? Otherwise, she might not have become so emotionally involved.

It was almost noon when Rachel turned into the Whispering Pines enclave. Phil and Mary were sitting in their large screened-in porch waiting for her.

"Hi, welcome to West by God Virginia," they said, as each embraced her. "I see you've come alone," Mary said disappointedly. "Here, let me show you to your room."

After lunch, Phil and Mary suggested they go for a walk in the woods. When they were finished with small talk, Phil told Rachel that the Agency had identified the thugs who had been hanging around her apartment. "Apparently, they've been involved in doing dirty jobs for French intelligence. Just to make sure that you'll be okay, I contacted a friend at the FBI, Mark Strait, who said he'd assign someone to keep an eye on your building to see what the thugs are up to." Rachel looked surprised.

"Do you know of any information or have access to info that would be of interest to the French? Of special concern are encryption systems." Phil waited for a reply from Rachel.

Her heart sank. She hesitated before answering. "Yes. You know most of our clients are small companies with very bright people doing a lot of creative work. Of particular importance may be Jason Conrad's company, which is working on several novel encryption systems. Plus other capabilities in biometrics which Jason hasn't fully explained to me." Rachel thought a few minutes before betraying too much of Jason's trust. She decided to continue.

"They're developing something called a "flipper chip", which can be added to any system to bypass the current U.S. requirement of having a third party hold a key which enables our law enforcement to eavesdrop." Rachel shifted uncomfortably in her chair. "Also, I overheard him telling Jack about a system they plan to patent that is totally unbreakable--one no one could possibly hack into it." Rachel shrugged her shoulders. She noted Phil's increasing interest in her comments.

"Most of the companies we represent have Defense contracts," she explained. "We're not privy to many of the details of this research. We know more about the work they're doing with R&D funds from their own backers, company profits or from larger corporations that subcontract for their expertise." She paused, almost in deep thought. "I can't imagine what they'd hope to get from me though. Those details aren't given to us. What information we do have on their upcoming plans is locked up in our office and the key material is in notebooks that never leave the office." Rachel smiled nervously as she looked at Phil. He was listening intently.

Rachel told them that just last night Jason mentioned that he saw the strange looking guys hanging around the apartment building when he came to call on her. "And Jason's the CEO of that company involved with encryption?" Phil asked.

She smiled and said yes, he is one of Jack's clients, but someone she had been out with on several occasions.

"Perhaps the next time he comes to town, we can all get together for dinner. I'd like to meet this guy and give you my approval or disapproval, now that I'm your surrogate big brother. I'd also like to make sure he's an honest type who wouldn't sell technologies for a fast buck and go around U.S. laws, or make it impossible for our government to track the transfer of drug money to the Cayman Islands or spot potential terrorists."

Rachel smiled. It was just like Phil to joke about the matter. What he really wanted was to find out more about Jason and his company.

"Come to think of it, Phil, I never saw these guys before Jason's visits. I don't know when he's coming next, but I'll probably be talking with him this week and will find out. You know, I almost asked him to come up with me this weekend, but he had a flight scheduled back to California today."

"I'm going to ask you a question, Rachel, which you can refuse to answer. But, if you do, I'll know the answer anyway. Are you having an affair with him?" Phil looked Rachel straight in the eye.

Rachel hesitated before giving her answer. "Not really an affair but I have had dinner with him several times. He's stayed over once, and that was the night before last." Rachel had thought about not telling Phil the truth, but was afraid that one of the FBI agents would report differently. "But Jason said he left by the garage so he wouldn't compromise me at the apartment."

Rachel and Mary poked along the small streets in Berkeley Springs the next day and Rachel found a small trinket that amused her, a whimsical brass camel. She thought of Jason when she bought it and planned to give it to him the next time he came. If she didn't hear from him within the next few days, she would mail it to him.

Phil met them for lunch at a small local restaurant that was one of Phil's favorites, formerly called the Appalachian Springs. "Phil likes the Country Inn for dinner, but feels it's too touristy for lunch. Perhaps if and when you bring Jason up, we can have dinner there on a Saturday night. They even have dancing sometimes." Rachel secretly wondered how Jason would like this little town. He was such a California man and used to big city living.

When Rachel returned that Sunday evening and parked her car in the apartment garage, she looked to see if there were any people loitering around, but saw no one. She hoped she wasn't getting paranoid, but kept handy the pepper spray Phil gave her that would stop anyone who came within three feet of her.

She half expected the telephone to ring and stayed up until midnight in case it did, but Jason didn't phone. She finally turned off the light, put down her book and went to sleep.

Rachel and the Howards weren't the only Blue Ridge visitors from Washington that weekend. On Thursday evening, after he talked with his CIA contact, Pierre telephoned his four partners and asked them to meet him at the cabin to discuss their progress in making contacts. Pierre had found out how essential it was to know people in key positions in the targeted departments or agencies. His CIA contact, courtesy of Miriam, had been critical in identifying Phil Howard and getting information on Rachel. He now knew that she was more or less clean but had access to the CIA through Phil. But more critical was the fact that she had male visitors who were prime targets for their group. Pierre had identified at least one thus far, Jason Conrad.

The Purloined Encryption Caper

At Joe Coswell's party, the group had struck gold. There were staffers from all the offices of interest to them. Pierre wanted to know what follow-up his compatriots had done and how soon they could begin to profit from their plans.

Clive Fyffe, his British co-conspirator, who Pierre knew was bi-sexual, said he had already been invited to a party that evening by the two staffers from the Patent Office and the Department of Commerce. At least he thought they were homosexual or, like Clive, bi-sexual. He could tell by the vibes that seemed to exist between them. If Clive could get them compromised, he would be able to get confidential information on technologies currently being developed and could identify the companies. He told Pierre he had ways of insuring they would provide the info he wanted.

Hans Schmidt, his German co-conspirator, was working on someone in the FBI. This FBI staffer was planning a vacation in Germany, and Hans had offered to help him with his itinerary, recommend places to stay and people to call. If possible, he would arrange to get the FBI person compromised during his Germany visit.

Carlo Vecchio, the Italian member of their group, said he had managed to meet the young secretary at the CIA whom Pierre had identified as a target and had arranged a dinner date with her the next evening. She confirmed that she worked for a high-level official involved in counteracting industrial espionage against U.S. firms. She didn't identify her boss, but Carlo hoped to get more information over dinner.

"Is she pretty?" Pierre asked, since he had a roving

eye for good-looking women.

"Not very," Carlo answered, "and her figure isn't that great. But she might be good in bed. I think she's lonely and hungry." Those were the easiest kind to use.

"I've discovered that Berkeley Springs may not be the best place for our safe house. It's a very popular weekend and vacation retreat for the Washington residents. One, in particular, may give us problems. Philip Howard from the CIA owns a cabin in the Whispering Pines development, about a mile and a half up the mountain. So, from now on, we should not use the route via Berkeley Springs," Pierre warned them.

"And we have to be much more careful. Although it might be more inconvenient and time consuming, I suggest we schedule our arrivals at the cabin at different times, allowing ten minutes or more between arrivals. This will make it more difficult for anyone to tie us together. Also, we will assign one person to arrive first. The other four will then telephone that person at the cabin when he is within fifteen to twenty minutes away, to ensure there are no problems. I don't think anyone knows about this place, but precautions are de rigueur by necessity." The other four agreed. Pierre then continued.

"Also, we must identify a place where we can install some high-powered computers as well as find hackers to work for us, those not working for reputable companies. Government techies would be best since it would not be in their interest to tell anybody about our operation. You, Julian, know more about computer systems and technologies than the rest of us. We will

The Purloined Encryption Caper

leave this to you, but of course, we will help in the identification of the hackers." Pierre was addressing Julian Vanderhaag from the NATO headquarters in his native Belgium.

They also listed their markets for new technologies so they wouldn't cross wires. Giving information to their own governments had long ago been forgotten, other than any medical info which wouldn't bring in any sizable amounts of money from the other nations. Of paramount importance was obtaining the latest encryption software, such as those being developed by Jason Conrad and Bill Worth's companies.

Carlo, the Italian, had good contacts in Libya and he knew President Gaddaffi would pay handsomely for any of these new products. Pierre had served previously in Iraq and Afghanistan and had already been contacted by Saddam Hussein's government who knew of Pierre's intentions in the States. He also had contacts in the al-Queda network.

Hans had served in Syria and Iran and had promised the key mullahs there that he would give them first options on any technology he could acquire. He already heard that the "flipper chip" would be most desirable. As in Afghanistan, it would permit funds to be transferred easily, especially drug money. The mullahs in Iran and Syria were also looking for a secure way to transfer money to the States to fund terrorism. Clive who had once served in Israel had identified several potential buyers in Tel Aviv. Also, through these contacts they were sure both China and North Korea would be willing and profitable customers.

Clive was the wild card. He had been deeply

involved in identifying terrorist groups for NATO, and, unbeknownst to his government or NATO, felt that the terrorists had every reason to attack the developed countries. They had been neglected in his estimation and their causes were not being given the serious attention they should have in the past. He did not want to identify terrorists as his customers since others of this group might suddenly develop a conscience, especially if the terrorists started killing their countrymen.

"I thought we should have a name for our activity. How about Lovenest? No one would think that was necessarily bad and if anyone associated our operation with this hideout, it could easily be explained." The other four agreed and soon left, everyone except Pierre.

The name for the activity, Lovenest, was in Pierre's mind since he was awaiting the arrival of Miriam Gauthier who would spend the next two days with him. He was anxious for her arrival. Pierre was a very sexual man who needed women. He couldn't understand men like Clive who could content themselves equally with men. And Pierre had not yet been successful in finding someone he could enjoy himself with on a continuing basis, without getting entangled in an affair. He was searching for a woman bored with her husband, who was looking for a lover and wouldn't talk.

He wanted to take Miriam to the Country Inn for dinner, but decided against it. The Inn was too close to the cabin and if anyone should see them, it might raise suspicions. He decided a drive to the Bavarian Inn in Shepherdstown would be more discreet and, hopefully, more Continental in cuisine. Perhaps if the Inn had accommodations available, they could spend the night there rather than return to the cabin.

As Miriam dressed for dinner, she went over to Pierre and kissed him. She missed him in Paris. "And how are things going, mon ami?" she asked, smoothing her skin tight woolen dress over her voluptuous body.

"Tres bien. It does take time to get to know one's way around, but I think we've made remarkable progress in only a few months." He then told her of the parties and contacts operation Lovenest was working on. She was highly amused and gave her throaty laugh when he had told her about their cavorting.

"And you? How was the information technology meeting you attended in New York? Did you make any useful contacts?" Pierre questioned.

"Yes, I think so. I met an interesting man from a company in California called Techno-Electronics and Systems, which is doing very state-of-the-art research on encryption and biometrics. His name is Sam Penderton. Have you ever heard of it, or him?" Miriam asked.

Pierre was jolted with the knowledge. It was Jason Conrad's firm. He had Rachel Brown's apartment building watched occasionally and was surprised to see that Jason was a visitor when he was in town. He found that Jason also was a Warden client, but his relationship with Rachel didn't seem to be only business. He would have to keep closer track of her in the future.

"And is Sam Penderton a good lover?" Pierre asked, admiring her figure. He was not jealous of Miriam's other escapades, but was always curious

about other men's abilities.

"Not as good as you, my dear," she reassured him, "but he may be useful to us if his company has value. He didn't wear a wedding band, but I know he's married. I noticed that the third finger on the left hand had marks of a ring that had been removed."

Pierre then told her about Jason Conrad and Rachel Brown. Perhaps Sam Penderton's wife didn't know about his extra marital activities at technical meetings. Pierre and Miriam stored this bit of knowledge in their memory bank as they left for Shepherdstown.

During their drive over, Miriam looked at Pierre. "You know that matter you asked me to take care of? Steve Holliday? Don't worry about it any more. Just act surprised when you read about his unfortunate accident in the Washington Post. I understand that he wasn't a very good swimmer."

CHAPTER 6

Sleep did not come easily for Jason after his evening with Rachel and he tossed and turned until his wake-up call at five a.m.. Now, he was sorry he had been so impetuous and changed his flight. Perhaps he should have called Rachel and asked her to have an early breakfast with him.

The flight to San Francisco was frustrating. Tired after getting up so early and still wondering why Rachel was adamant in having them leave, he was angry because she did not ask him to stay.

Although his flight arrived in San Francisco at midday, he couldn't bring himself to do any work. He tried to read but Rachel and his irritation with her continually clouded his mind. He considered calling Claire or one of his other female friends but his heart really wasn't in it. Sunday afternoon he phoned his mother to see if she would invite him over for dinner. Being with his family always cheered him.

"Jason, are you okay?" his mother asked. "You seem so distant and preoccupied. Is there something you want to talk about?"

"No. I guess I've been awfully busy and haven't been sleeping well. Don't worry so much about me," he responded testily. His mother knew better. Something was bothering Jason. He never was like this unless he was upset.

Recently, Jason had begun to think more and more about getting married and starting his own family. He had enough of the happy bachelor's life. The reason he was so angry with Rachel was that he had begun to think of her as a future wife.

When he returned from his folks' home Sunday evening, he had to fight to keep from calling Rachel. He longed to talk with her, hold her and make love to her. His body ached, an ache he knew could not be soothed by another woman. The next month would be the real test, since he didn't plan to return to Washington soon and hence wouldn't see her. He was going on a business trip to France and Germany and would be busy making appointments for his visit and preparing necessary sales materials. Also, he had to identify several reputable law firms in Europe who could handle licensing and trade contracts with foreign buyers or licensees, in the event he was successful.

It was during one of his staff meetings the following Wednesday when Jason's secretary, May, interrupted and told Jason that Jack Warden's office was on the line. "Tell them I'll call back after the meeting," he told her.

The Purloined Encryption Caper

"Okay," May said. She did not mention that it was Rachel on the phone.

When Jason called the Warden office, Jack answered. "Hi, Jason, what's up?"

"I'm returning your call. I was in a staff meeting when you called earlier," Jason replied.

"I guess Rachel was the one who called you but she's not here now. She's attending a reception on the Hill. I told her about your upcoming visit to Europe and she offered her help. Also, she said the next time I talked with you to thank you again for last Friday night."

"I think I have everything under control," Jason said coolly, ignoring Jack's reference to Rachel. "I'll e-mail you a list of my appointments in the event you and Rachel have any comments or suggestions."

"Fine," Jack said, noting the continued coolness in Jason's voice.

However, Jason couldn't keep himself from asking. "How was Rachel's weekend in Berkeley Springs? It must've been important, since she was looking forward to it so much."

"She said she had a wonderful time. I think her friends there are rather special to her."

Jason sounded so angry and upset Jack decided to change the subject. "I'll look forward to receiving the list and either Rachel or I will fax or e-mail you any comments or suggestions before you leave. What are your travel plans?"

"I'm taking the polar route to Paris, leaving here next Saturday. I'm sorry I don't have time to stop over in Washington, either going or on my way back."

As a matter of fact, Jason would again relegate any future visits to Washington to his associates. Then it would be the holiday season. Thanksgiving and Christmas had always been very special to him and his family, and over the holidays he usually moved back into his old room at his folks' house.

The next day Jack told Rachel about his conversation with Jason. "I'll be happy to help any way I can," she said. "I hope you remembered to thank him for last Friday evening?"

"Yes, I did." Still Jack wondered what had happened. They had been getting along so well during dinner and the theater. Jack decided not to say anything to Rachel, but wait until either she or Jason mentioned it to him.

Jason was still angry and had spent the past five days thinking the worst of Rachel, even comparing her to Terry. But perhaps he should have asked May who was on the line and talked with her when she called. It might have cleared up his suspicions but he doubted it. He was angrier now that they had made love. His body ached for her and now he had no desire to be with any other woman.

Over the weekend, Rachel packed up the whimsical camel she had bought and mailed it to Jason with a note of thanks, saying she looked forward to his next visit. She thought that perhaps then she would have him and the Wardens over to the apartment for dinner and also invite the Howards.

When Jack received Jason's list of appointments, he asked Rachel to look it over. One or two names were familiar to her and possibly on the watch list the CIA had when she was working in Europe, but she couldn't remember anything specific about them. She decided to call Phil and arrange to meet him in Rosslyn for lunch. She faxed a copy to him so he could check out the names and companies before they met.

"I've checked off the ones who are not very reliable," Phil explained when they met. "My sources say they don't honor agreements and have transshipped a lot of technologies they had under license agreements to Iran and other rogue countries in the Middle East not eligible to receive them. Also, they have access to top-notch technical experts who sometimes ignore patent agreements, duplicate or back-engineer the software or hardware, and, regardless of how many safeguards and codes the U.S. companies have installed, they reproduce the technology under a different name. To make matters worse, some of their best engineers or companies which duplicate the technology are located in the States. These companies and a few of their engineers ignore patents and intellectual property rights, regardless of how many laws are on the books."

Rachel asked if she could tell Jack or Jason the source of her information.

"Tell them both that you have 'confidential sources' without any explanation." Phil then hesitated and looked at Rachel. "Do you think they'll buy it? I don't want to tip our hand at the moment. Our group is making headway and Congress has almost convinced those in charge to reinstate our old project. I guess there has been quite a lot of unhappiness among the CEO's of several the high-tech companies."

"Okay. I'll ask Jack to give the information to Jason in a straight forward manner and tell him if he has any questions, he can call us. I don't want to make too much of my source in written documents," she assured him.

When Rachel returned to her office, she drafted a report for Jack's signature. She didn't tell Jack who the comments were from since he automatically would assume the information she got was from staffers on the Hill or at Commerce or Treasury since Rachel had made a lot of contacts and was now part of a group that met occasionally in the evening for drinks.

"Are you sure you want me to fax this to Jason? Don't you want to telephone the information to him?" Jack asked.

"No. Tell him to call me if he has any questions," Rachel responded in a very business-like manner. She was miffed that Jason had refused to accept her telephone call and when she phoned him later at home, his answering machine came on. She started to leave a message but instead hung up. "No more," she said to herself, "will I permit a man to get under my skin."

But her main concern at the moment was the strange men standing outside the entrance to her apartment building. She found herself looking over her shoulder when she walked around the Ballston area now and recently hated to go out at night alone.

That weekend while Jason was winging his way to Europe, Rachel decided to go shopping in the Ballston Mall. She found several dresses she liked, suitable for both the office and evening dinner parties. After buying shoes and matching accessories, she took the

The Purloined Encryption Caper

escalator to the eatery area in the basement and ordered a coffee latte from the coffee bar.

"May I join you?" a voice asked. She looked up and saw Pierre Ledent. She had forgotten all about him and never did return his calls. As a matter of fact, she forgot to even mention him to Jack.

"Yes, please do," she said. He had a cup of French cafe filtre in his hand.

"Do you shop here often?" Pierre asked, knowing exactly where she lived since he had assigned two of his men to report on her movements and any visitors. Thus far, the only visitors other than her boss and his wife and Tom and earlier Steve, had been Jason. Initially, Pierre thought Jason's visits might be business, but when he heard of their repeated dates, walking hand in hand, he thought otherwise. Was Jason married? He would have to find out.

"Yes. I don't live far away and it's convenient. How about you?" Rachel didn't believe for a minute that his being here was accidental. He ignored her question.

"Are you free for dinner this evening? I hear there is a very quaint French restaurant nearby. It would be my great pleasure to have you as a dinner partner." It was apparent that one of his men had followed her and Jason to Jacques Cafe.

"No. I'm sorry I'm not. I have plans for this evening and tomorrow. It's a busy weekend." She hoped this brush off would preclude his pressing for another day.

"Perhaps another time, then," he said. "You're not only an attractive and bright young woman, but a very busy one as well, Rachel Brown," he said mockingly.

He finished his coffee, got up, bowed his head slightly and walked away.

Pierre was in the Ballston area today to meet one of the men watching Rachel's building. Pierre felt like a cup of French coffee and was surprised when he saw Rachel. What had totally confused him was that his man said that either he was being watched by someone or someone else was watching Rachel's building. He didn't know by whom, but certainly it was no one from her office.

There was more to Rachel Brown than she let on, he thought. He would ask French intelligence to see if they had any background information on her, possibly through their contact at the CIA's Paris station. He wanted to find out exactly what she did when she was working in Europe, and whether she had access to anyone who could identify him as a French intelligence official. He also wanted to know if Rachel had heard about Steve's death. So far, there was nothing in the Washington papers.

Pierre decided it would soon be necessary to arrange an extended day's meeting at the West Virginia cabin so he could ask the others to find out anything about Rachel and Phil Howard from their contact at each of their country's CIA station. The CIA was getting to be a very leaky organization and many of their staff, especially the newcomers, were careless giving out information from individuals' files and sharing it with miscellaneous countries, especially members of NATO and some UN countries.

The Purloined Encryption Caper

Shortly after Pierre left, Rachel picked up her packages and returned to her apartment. She decided not to go out for the rest of the weekend and, if she had to, would drive. All of a sudden she was beginning to feel like a prisoner and wonder whether all this interest had anything to do with her current or her past job, or whether it had everything to do with Jason Conrad. If it were the latter, she would probably be left alone soon since it was obvious that he considered their relationship only a fleeting episode in his life. Earlier, she had vowed not to get emotionally involved with another man but Jason managed to shatter her resolve and she was angry at herself for this weakness. .

In Paris as Jason walked through the Tuileries the next day, he thought about Rachel. He realized that he had fallen in love with her, but might there be someone else in her life, the man in the picture, for example, and that she only considered her evenings with Jason an extension of her office commitments. He knew that she seemed frightened of him yet she responded to his kisses and lovemaking with an intense passion he never would have imagined. She told him that night she wanted him to make love to her, but later said she didn't want to get emotionally involved. Jason couldn't understand her at all, unless, of course, there was already someone else she was committed to.

He had to put her out of his mind. He couldn't afford to be distracted from business. His company needed his full attention as it was entering a new phase. His staff were developing new technologies which could transform his small company into a major player in the encryption field. If he were successful with sales in Europe and managed to break into the international markets in a big way, travel for him would be limited. One of his staff would be assigned those duties.

The week went quickly for Jason. He was grateful that Jack's company had given him such good advice and was especially grateful for forewarning him about several of the people on his schedule. Had he not had that information, he might have made some very bad decisions. They were interested in his company's software still in the final design stage. He couldn't figure out how they knew anything about it except through insider information. He was also appreciative of the warning Rachel had given him about not leaving his briefcase unattended in his hotel room when he went out. She explained that the French intelligence operatives made it a habit to enter a visiting business or government executive's hotel room in their absence, photograph all documents in their suitcase or briefcase and use the information for their own purposes, economic or political. She suggested he keep key documents in the hotel safe when he didn't need them or take them with him and he dutifully followed her advice.

When he got back to California, he would again have to follow Rachel's advice. He would reread the patent applications to see if he could figure out where the leaks might be and see if the applications included some of the data these individuals mentioned. Jack or Rachel could help, if he asked them, but Rachel told Jack she had to use a lot of her "chips" to identify the bad guys on the list. What did that mean? What chips and with whom?

It was curious that one of the men that Rachel warned him about in Paris was suddenly called away. The French official's deputy, a sensual and well-shaped French woman named Miriam Gauthier, met with him instead. Their meeting turned into a very long evening of drinks and dinner and an invitation back to her apartment for a nightcap, and whatever else Jason might want. Jason had to use all of his strength not to succumb to her very experienced advances especially since he had had a lot to drink.

During the evening, she mentioned that she had recently met one of his associates, Sam Penderton, at a scientific meeting. Jason had the feeling that she probably managed to get more information from Sam than Jason thought was good for his company. Also, it seemed that their encounter had been more than mere conversation and she obviously had been successful in her seduction of Sam. Jason would have to check with him as soon as he got back to the office. However, he was afraid Sam might not level with him--Sam was a married man.

Jason almost went to bed with Miriam, but had a sixth sense not to. If Rachel found out, it would kill any possible future relationship between them, as dim as that seemed at the moment. And he didn't want to end up like Sam, even if he could justify to himself that he had spent the night with Miriam only to find out what Sam may have told her.

He accepted another dinner invitation from Miriam later in the week, but again, he managed to leave before he succumbed to her advances. As he left, she said, "Perhaps I'll see you in California. Sam asked me to visit him sometime and I am thinking of going next January, perhaps. California should be warm, and Paris will be very cold." Jason agreed and left for his hotel a bit hurriedly.

"Not as cold as the reception you'll get from Sam's wife," Jason thought to himself.

Jason sent a postcard to Rachel from Frankfurt. It merely read: "Your former city says hello. I want to thank you for the advice--it was very useful. Also, for the whimsical brass camel you bought me in Berkeley Springs. Who knows what secrets his caravan carries, ones that only you know. Always, Jason."

Jason stuck to his schedule and flew back to San Francisco over the Pole. He was exhausted when he arrived in San Francisco. On Sunday, he called his secretary.

"Hi, May. I made it back on schedule. Would you please arrange a meeting with the senior staff at two tomorrow and ask Sam Penderton if he can meet with me immediately following the meeting? I'll be in sometime in the morning, but frankly, I'm suffering from jet lag, so I'm not quite sure when."

He had thought about calling Rachel, but was afraid that if she weren't home, it would upset him. He had tried to telephone her from Paris late one evening after he returned home from Miriam's apartment, but Rachel hadn't answered. He couldn't sleep much the rest of the night, wondering where she was.

If he could put off calling her for another week, it might mean that his feelings for her weren't as deep as

The Purloined Encryption Caper

he thought and again, it was just his ego.. He invited Claire to join Bill Worth and his wife the following Friday night to try out a new restaurant which had just opened in Palo Alto.

CHAPTER 7

That same week, Rachel realized Jason probably wouldn't phone her. She had hoped that he would call Sunday after he returned from Europe and stayed home all day waiting by the phone. But the call never came.

Early the next week, she got a call from Phil. "Any chance of getting together for lunch tomorrow?"

"Of course," she said. "Shall we meet in Washington or in Rosslyn?"

"Rosslyn," he replied. "Let's make it at the ground floor of my building at noon." Rachel agreed.

After they had ordered, Phil lowered his voice. "I didn't want to tell you on the phone, but the Agency has reinstated our old program, expanded its role, and asked me to head it. The first major effort will be to identify individuals overseas as well as in the States who are trying to infiltrate U.S. companies on the cutting edge of cryptographic technology development and our advances in biometrics. Three of the companies listed as prime targets are your clients. Apparently, they've heard of the new technologies Jason's company is developing. The Brass feels it's imperative that technologies such as these be available only to them so they can control their use. You understand their position on this, don't you?" Rachel nodded. Phil then continued.

"Jason and his company suddenly loom as being important. The situation is a little awkward. Initially, Jason had applied for funding from the Defense Department to develop his system, but his request was turned down, hence a great deal of antagonism on the part of Jason's colleagues and members of his Scientific Advisory Committee." He hesitated, and then continued.

"Also, Rachel, I'd like to take you up on your offer to have a dinner party so Mary and I can meet Jack and his wife. I want to see exactly what kind of guy Jack is and if he would be willing to cooperate with the company in the event the need arose, but I don't want to mention anything to him yet. I assume you understand."

After lunch, Rachel called Jack from Rosslyn to see when he and Jean would be available. Wednesday evening was good for them, however, Rachel told Phil she already had a commitment for dinner but would break it.

"Is it with the staffer from the Hill, Tom Fulton?" Rachel nodded her head. "Invite him. I think he could be useful. As a matter of fact, my FBI contacts tell me that he's one of the Hill staffers that our "Fifth Column" reports to. Sometime soon, I want you to meet an FBI friend of mine, Mark Strait. We CIA spooks can't operate within U.S. boundaries without presidential

The Purloined Encryption Caper

permission. You'll like Mark and he's unattached now." Phil winked as he said this.

Phil knew that Rachel liked Jason even though she wouldn't admit it. Phil had also been told by his colleagues in the Paris station that Jason had spent several late evenings with Miriam, a known French intelligence agent, as well as a lady of loose morals who sometimes sold information to the highest bidder. Miriam and her boss, Francois Dupont, who had the original appointment with Jason, were fellow French agents.

What worried Phil most was that there was a leak somewhere because Francois had found out that Jason had his list of appointments in Paris checked by the CIA. Was the leak at his office, the Paris station or in Rachel's office? Or perhaps in Jason's company? He would ask Rachel who in her office received a copy of Jason's appointment schedule or knew about her vetting the list with him.

That evening there were two postcards waiting for her. The one Jason sent her from Frankfurt and one from Steve. Steve said he decided to check out the Mediterranean and would telephone her as soon as he returned to Washington.

Wednesday evening proved very useful. Phil liked Jack and felt he would be trustworthy. "Jack, I'm going to trust you with information that is fairly confidential, even within the intelligence community. First, when Rachel worked with me in Hong Kong as well as in her assignment in Europe, she was under cover as an foreign service economic officer where she worked on a CIA project administered in conjunction with Commerce.

At that time, the focus was on enforcing control of exported American technologies and intellectual property rights. Many countries, as you know, are not honest in their dealings with American companies. Likewise, some American companies weren't very honest in their dealings either. There were a number of technologies forbidden by U.S. law for sale to terrorist countries, but these countries still obtained what they wanted through intermediary contacts in France or Germany. Those governments weren't necessarily involved in these transfer sales, but we still had to have a government instrumentality assigned to keep track of them." Phil was glad that both Jean and Mary were in the kitchen helping Rachel when he confided in Jack.

"Do you mean that Rachel is working for the CIA now?" Jack asked, a little startled by the news.

"No. She resigned when she left Asia to get married." Jack looked up for more explanation, but Phil decided to continue with his story.

"Now, some in Washington think that these technologies should be shared with communist or formerly communist countries for political purposes or for political contributions and some American companies are just as eager." Phil took time to relight his pipe, watching Jack's reaction to his story.

"Many Western countries, who are supposedly our friends or fellow members of NATO and the United Nations, are rather miffed about our refusal to share our technologies so have stepped up their attempt to acquire them through industrial espionage. They are right to think that the CIA with its focus more on human rights and less on counterintelligence was no

The Purloined Encryption Caper

longer as vigilant about the concerns of American high-tech companies as it should be. However, that's being changed now. There's a lot of pressure being applied on the Hill for something to be done about it."

Jack listened intently to Phil's words. "And how does this involve me? Are you going to ask Rachel to go back to work on your project?"

"No. I'd take her back in a minute, if she wanted to come, but what I'm hoping for is your cooperation. Rachel tells me that several of your clients are concerned about foreigners trying to penetrate their systems to steal technologies and not necessarily technologies already available. They fancy new ones still in the design and development process." Phil stopped to take another puff on his pipe and let Jack absorb his explanation.

"We can be of help," he continued. "Likewise, you can make it easy for me to talk to these CEO's on an informal basis. With you or Rachel as intermediaries, we can pinpoint which company executives we'd like to talk with. We don't worry about the big companies. They have more clout than is necessary." Phil paused making sure Jack was still with him.

"The worry I have is about the small and mid-sized companies. That's where most of the creative work in the information technology field is now being done, either on their own or under subcontract to larger companies or the U.S. government. We know that a few of our European allies, for example, and some renegade members of their intelligence organizations are anxious to steal encryption software. Several of your clients are leading the target pack in this field."

Phil got up and refilled his drink. Both Jack and Tom also got up and joined Phil at the bar.

"How about it, Jack?" Phil asked.

"I can't assure their willingness to cooperate with you, but I'm willing to talk with them. Perhaps it might even be better for Rachel to make the first pitch, especially to one or two specific companies where she has close friendships." Jack was thinking of Bill Worth and Jason.

At this point, the women rejoined the men and the conversation turned to golf, restaurants, and other topics, normally conducive to social chatter. However, Jack was still giving thought to what Phil had said and what he had asked of him. Jack also now understood why Rachel was so good at her job.

When Rachel was reading her *Washington Post* several days later, her eyes immediately went to a story headlined below the fold. "Hill staffer's body found washed up on Riviera beach." She read on and realized that it was Steve. Her hand was trembling as she phoned Tom.

"I heard late last night and almost called you," Tom said, "but since it was after midnight, I thought you'd be asleep and there was nothing we could do. The FBI said his body was found on the beach near Juan les Pins on the French Riviera. Apparently, he had been dead for well over a week. He only had on swimming trunks and there wasn't any identification on his body." Tom hesitated to continue since he could hear Rachel crying.

"Anything else?" Rachel asked through her sobs.

The Purloined Encryption Caper

"When the French police finally determined he was American, they phoned our Embassy in Paris to send someone down. The French police don't think there was any foul play and are listing it as an accident. None of his possessions were found. They don't know why he was found on the French Riviera since he wasn't registered in any of the hotels or wasn't on any airline manifests." Tom could hear Rachel still crying.

"Tom, I know it wasn't an accident," she sobbed. "He was murdered because of what he knew. He mentioned that what he was investigating was dangerous. Did he leave any copies of his reports at the apartment?"

"I'll look, but I don't think so. He was usually so careful. I'll check with his office today."

"I'm going to start asking questions myself, if you don't mind, Tom. I think he was killed to try to stop the report he was writing. Also, I'm going to ask Phil about it. Maybe the CIA knows something that's not in the press." Rachel suddenly remembered Steve's last words to her before he left for Europe. "If anything happens to me, you'll know the bad guys won."

Pierre had watched at a distance as Rachel walked back to her apartment house from Ballston that Saturday afternoon he had coffee with her and was surprised by later reports from his men that Rachel hadn't left her apartment for the rest of the weekend. She either didn't want to have dinner with him, or had left through the garage. He would ask his men in the future to cover the garage exit as well.

He found the thought that she had stayed home all weekend alone hard to believe. He would have enjoyed spending an evening bantering with Rachel and might even be successful in seducing her, something which his men told him they didn't think happened with her other visitors, other than Jason Conrad. Her male friends had left not long after they brought her home.

That Sunday, he contacted the other Lovenest members to see if they were making any progress. Carlo was doing quite well in seducing the young CIA secretary, identified by Pierre's contact as being involved with tracking industrial espionage. She even told him about Phil's checking the names of people Jason Conrad was going to meet in Paris.

Clive and Hans had not made much progress on their assignments, but Clive had been invited to a large party over the Thanksgiving weekend being given by several political appointees. Some were old friends, and some were lovers. Julian had discovered that while there was a federal law dealing with the theft of technology, it was rarely enforced. Also, a large number of States had individual laws on the books. This fact would limit the place they could establish a cyber operation. It might be best just to set it up at the West Virginia cabin.

Pierre told them he was returning to Paris over Thanksgiving because he had no meetings scheduled and would contact them immediately upon his return to Washington. What Pierre had not told them was that he had managed to convince someone in Reston to sell him illegal software which Pierre planned to give to Miriam to peddle. It wouldn't bring in the fortune they longed for, but his contacts in both Iran and Syria were interested in this bit of technology which could secretly

The Purloined Encryption Caper

give them access to a large Internet operation. Also, Miriam had been contacted by other individuals from the Middle East who were interested in miscellaneous technology that could address specific needs, both for their own use and for transshipment to China. She had a detailed list she wanted to discuss with Pierre in person.

While a meeting of the conspirators at the country place might be useful, he warned his partners not to use the cabin over the holiday. "It's the time when people from Washington spend the long Thanksgiving weekend at their cabins. If anyone we know or have met spot you in or near Berkeley Springs, questions might be raised."

Pierre wanted to be out of the country for another reason. He had asked one of his men to bug Rachel's apartment and put a tap on her telephone. He had heard from Carlo that Phil was going to be in Berkeley Springs, and Pierre was certain that Rachel would be there, too. His men would have to make sure she left and watch the garage door since she would undoubtedly drive. He couldn't take any chances. They might just connect him to the disappearance of Steve Holliday, since he had heard that Rachel was beginning to ask a lot of questions of Steve's friends on the Hill.

CHAPTER 8

Rachel's Wednesday night dinner enabled Phil the opportunity to ask the other men to meet for lunch the following week. "You've probably noticed that occasionally," Phil commented to Jack, "there are men standing outside Rachel's apartment house, so we can't use her apartment for meetings. Dinner parties that include wives are one thing, but meetings after work there or for lunch would raise suspicions."

Rachel told Phil earlier that the foreign-looking men were still there but she wasn't sure whether it was someone watching her or someone merely loitering in the busy Ballston area.

It seemed that life had grown less intrusive now that Jason no longer visited her. However, she would gladly put up with any inconvenience to see him again. She seemed to think of him more each day.

Phil was right about the FBI agent, Mark Strait, who Rachel found intriguing. He would never replace Jason in terms of physical attraction, but since Jason was out of the picture, it would be nice to have someone like Mark to fall back on. Mark was stocky and broad-shouldered, an inch or two shorter than Jason, with light brown hair and a pleasant face, almost nondescript who wouldn't stand out in a crowd as Jason did.

Luckily she was busy at the office, doubly so since she was trying to train her office mate, Cindy, to assist her with the newsletter and be more than a receptionist. She told Rachel her new tasks even increased her boyfriend's appreciation of her and he now seemed much more interested in her work. He worked at the Department of Commerce and frequently asked her about their clients.

At the luncheon meeting, Phil asked Jack's permission to use Rachel to review pictures of individuals she might remember seeing before, either in Europe or Asia. Also, with Rachel's language capabilities, she could be invaluable attending meetings abroad that dealt with these topics, if the need arose.

"She looks so young and innocent that no one would suspect that she'd know so much about foreign espionage and encryption. Also, the European men are very sexist," Phil quipped. He remembered the stories Rachel would amuse him and Mary with about her encounters in Europe with men who assumed she was an airhead.

Another area of interest of the CIA and FBI was information they might be able to gather on cyber-hackers who could break into the computer systems at Commerce, CIA, FBI, Pentagon, or even the private companies themselves. Some of Jack's clients told him that several of their youngest and brightest staff had hacked into the computer of the Secretary of Defense, just for a lark. When Jack found out, he asked Rachel to tell Phil.

In her latest newsletter, Rachel asked their clients to let her office know if their companies had any penetration attempts on their networks or systems or had heard of any. Rachel also had started a new column dealing with hacking, both fact and rumor.

On one hand, Jack liked being part of this intrigue, but, on the other, he was reluctant to be identified too closely with the FBI or CIA. He didn't know how it might affect his business.

Several days later, Bill Worth was in Washington and asked Rachel out to dinner. "I've heard from Jason that there's an excellent French restaurant near your place. Jacques, I believe he called it. How about going there?" Rachel felt as if the wind had been knocked out of her.

"That's fine. Since it's not a weekend, we shouldn't have any trouble getting a table," she finally answered.

It was strange having dinner there with someone other than Jason. Apparently, Jason had not told Bill about their relationship.

After they had ordered drinks, Rachel asked casually, "And how is Jason? I haven't talked with him for quite a while. He must be very busy."

"Yes, he is. I understand from Claire that he spends long evenings at the office. Last week, I managed to get him to break away so they could join Kim and me for dinner, the first time for a long time."

"I didn't realize that Jason was married," Rachel said innocently, feeling nauseous.

"No, he isn't yet, but I assume he'll get married soon. He's been dating Claire for a long time now. She plans to come to Washington with him sometime so don't be surprised if she arrives at your office with Jason the next time he's in town."

That evening back in her apartment was the first time that Rachel cried over Jason. "What a fool!" she told herself. "And to think I actually began to believe him when he said all those words of love to me. Tonight's the last time I'll shed a tear over him."

Rachel still felt badly about Steve's death and had contacted Steve's folks to express her regrets. She promised to keep in touch and keep them informed of any news. But she was convinced his death was not accidental and wondered what happened to his papers. The last time she saw him, he told her he almost had completed his investigation of economic espionage by NATO members, France in particular. She was certain that was why he had been murdered. Phil had telephoned the Paris station, but they hadn't had any new information. She even asked Mark about it. A friend of his in another office was checking it out and Mark promised to let Rachel know if he heard anything. Steve's fellow staffers on the Senate intelligence committee only had a preliminary draft of Steve's report, but it didn't provide any clues as to what might have happened. It did suggest that since Nice was becoming France's version of Silicon Valley, our government agencies were going to pay more attention to that region.

Thanksgiving came and went, with Rachel spending the long weekend with the Howards at their mountain cabin. Mark was invited only for Thanksgiving dinner. Phil didn't want to take any chance in having Rachel and Mark spend a whole weekend together with bedrooms across the hall from each other. Phil was aware of Rachel's feelings for Jason and that they had had a disagreement, but Phil didn't want to throw Mark at her. Rachel would be vulnerable since her breakup with Jason and Steve's death and she might just use Mark on the rebound. It wouldn't be fair to Mark, especially since he had just recovered from a painful divorce.

The holiday weekend was a wonderful interlude, and she and the Howards reminisced about the old days in Asia and laughed at some of their funny experiences. Rachel also had a long girl-to-girl talk with Mary, telling her about her past short affair with Jason and her recent dates. Mary was a perfect confidante. She just listened and didn't criticize or give advice.

"Mary, I'm so glad I have you here as a woman friend to talk to." Rachel had often felt lonely not getting to know any women well enough to confide in.

When Rachel returned to her apartment Sunday evening, she knew that someone had been there. She telephoned the desk and asked if anyone had asked for her while she was out of town, or whether there were any messages.

"Welcome back, Ms. Brown. Yes, a gentleman was here, several times. I remember him because he was foreign. I told him you were away and I didn't think you'd be back for several days. Then another gentleman, a private detective I think, asked if you lived here. I told him you did. When he asked for your telephone number, I told him he could call us at the desk and we would connect him or leave a message for you to call him. I hope you don't mind."

"No. Did either of them leave their name or a message?" Rachel questioned.

"No. They said they'd call early this week."

Rachel looked through her desk, her jewelry box and her personal drawers. Nothing was missing. She didn't usually keep any confidential office material at her apartment, but then remembered the files she had set up on their clients. Also, she had reconstructed a lot of the information she had in Europe on people of questionable character. Phil had advised her to get a small safe with a combination lock to keep any sensitive material she kept at her apartment, so she had bought a half-size combination lock safe which she kept in the back of her clothes closet. It was well hidden from view if one just opened the closet door but would bump into it by walking to the very back of the closet. No, Rachel didn't think anyone had disturbed it.

She wondered if they had put a tap on her phone. They had to have some reason for entering her apartment, although she couldn't imagine why. She never made business calls from her home phone other than the past ones to Jason.

As soon as she arrived in the office the next day, she telephoned Phil. "Don't touch anything," he said, "and don't use the phone. Tell Jack. I'll call Mark and ask the FBI for help. Will you be able to let someone in today at noon so they can sweep the place for bugs?"

Rachel said she could.

The Purloined Encryption Caper

When Rachel heard a knock and opened her door at noon, she expected to see Mark. Instead, she looked in the face of Ruth Brennan, a Pennsylvania girl she had known years ago in college. "Ruth, what are you doing here?"

"I thought it'd be fun to get together for old times sake," Ruth exclaimed as she entered, putting a finger over her mouth. They started talking about the old days like long lost sisters.

In the process, Ruth took out some equipment and started panning the room. The machine lit up and Ruth quickly identified several bugs, one in the living room and one in Rachel's bedroom, as well as a tap on her telephone. Rachel wondered how long they had been in place and whether her evening making love with Jason had been recorded.

Ruth didn't disturb the bugs. It would have been too obvious that she was a professional law enforcement official if she had removed them as soon as she walked into the apartment in the event anyone watched her. They made small talk about going to lunch and Ruth's need to find an apartment in town. Rachel led her to a small nearby restaurant where they could talk.

"Don't tell me you're in the FBI," Rachel asked Ruth, looking somewhat skeptical.

"Bingo! Special Agent Ruth Brennan, at your service," she said with a smile on her face. "It was very strange. Mark wanted to send someone who didn't look like an FBI agent. When he mentioned your name, I asked him if you were from Pennsylvania, and, if so, I told him I might have known you in college. He was astounded and said yes, and as a matter of fact, the two of us looked very much alike." Ruth paused. "You could almost pass for sisters, he said. You see, Rachel, I just transferred here from Philadelphia, so I'm new to the area and available to help Mark."

"I thought you were getting married as soon as you graduated? What happened?" Rachel asked. "I lost touch with your whereabouts when I went to Europe."

"My fiancé and I broke up shortly before we were to marry," Ruth explained. "I guess it wasn't meant to be. So I went back to school, studied criminal law and joined the FBI. I had a good background in technology and engineering so I was a natural. I'm looking for an apartment but, at the moment, I'm in a small hotel not too far from FBI Headquarters."

"Why not move in with me until you find one? I've got a spare bedroom, if you don't mind sharing it with my computer. And if this building suits you, I hear they'll have some vacancies in the next few weeks. It's a super location and it would be wonderful to have you live nearby."

Ruth said she would be only too happy to move in the next day. "I'm really tired of the hotel and this location seems ideal."

"Do you think both friends and foes alike are targeting our companies, and that they can steal industrial secrets by stealing documents--contracts, patent applications, proposals--or do you think that there are willing accomplices in government offices, as well as in the companies themselves?"

"All of the above, Rachel," responded Ruth as she moved closer and lowered her voice. "The FBI has set up a special counterintelligence program to investigate

The Purloined Encryption Caper

economic espionage. This is my area of expertise and the reason I was transferred to Washington. The FBI thinks that well over a $100 billion a year is lost by U.S. business through stolen technologies. And we've already identified over 50 countries that now have spies in the States trying, in addition to all the espionage going on abroad. It's not penny-ante business anymore." Ruth shook her head to show her dismay.

"And the foreign countries are playing hardball, working overtime to get as much information as they can. There's little we can do about espionage overseas, except pressure our allies to behave. We know, for example, that until a few years ago that Russia was still using Cuba as a listening post."

"The flip side of this," she continued, "is that we don't want to limit our companies from selling their technologies overseas because this could inhibit development of new ones. Secure encryption systems are imperative in this day and age. So much business is done by smart cards or electronic transfer systems. And even for U.S. firms to use effective encryption technology in their global businesses, they must get permission from appropriate government security offices." Rachel nodded her head knowingly.

"It's crazy. Other countries have developed technologies far better than those the U.S. government permits U.S. firms to sell abroad, and the encryption technologies which we can sell have to have certain specifications to enable us to penetrate the codes. For this reason," Ruth continued, very slowly and quietly. "Mark's very concerned about your safety. He knows you have contacts on the Hill, as well as the FBI and

CIA, and your office has a list of clients the opposition would like to infiltrate, if they haven't done so already. That's what they might have been searching for in your apartment. He'll be delighted to know I'll be staying with you and that I might even move into the building. He didn't realize that when he initially talked to me, we had previously been such good friends." She smiled as she remembered his comments.

The next day Rachel gained a roommate. The first thing Ruth did was change the locks on Rachel's apartment door. If anyone had made a key, it would now be useless. She also brought with her a telephone answering machine so Rachel could screen callers. Ruth removed the bugs and took them to FBI headquarters the next day to see if they could determine their source.

That week, Phil asked Jack to join him for lunch. "I've heard that Congress is scheduling hearings on industrial espionage. Tom, Mark and I feel it would be useful to get input from small innovative companies and warn those companies about foreigners' efforts to penetrate or to steal desired technologies. We also want to know if companies have reliable security systems and, if so, how they're working. Do you think that Jason would agree to meet with us?" Phil questioned.

"I'll call him and see if he plans to come East soon. Otherwise, we may have to fly to California and meet there, possibly inviting officials from other companies." Jack made a notation in his diary to that effect.

"Good. Make sure Rachel participates in the talks," Phil interjected. "In the event there's any follow-up needed, Rachel would be a natural person as the central contact point. She knows everyone involved. It

The Purloined Encryption Caper

isn't appropriate for you, Jack, to play that role, and I'm sure you don't want to get compromised either." Jack concurred.

"As I mentioned before," Phil explained, "it may be necessary in the future for someone to attend meetings abroad for my office. Rachel's not officially connected but knows the scene, has good language skills and previously had a security clearance. She could be approved by the Agency quickly so I can reimburse you for her services if I need to use her too much." He paused.

"I'd like a way to reimburse you for Rachel's time, but I'm not sure how I can do it at the moment." Phil was hesitant to put her on the CIA payroll now because he feared there was a mole or moles at CIA headquarters. He didn't know who they were, but too much information was leaking out. He didn't want to chance tainting Rachel's name.

"Don't worry," Jack replied. "Let's consider it a quid pro quo. You're being very helpful to me and my clients. If her time away becomes excessive, we can figure something out then."

That afternoon Jack telephoned Jason. "I haven't talked to you for a few weeks and wanted to find out how things were going."

" Fine," Jason replied. "We're moving along quite well and have been very busy."

"Are you coming this way soon?" Phil asked casually. "I'd like you to meet with some people here."

"I'm planning another visit to Europe next week to negotiate some contracts and licensing agreements.

I could transit Washington this coming Saturday. I could catch an early flight out of here, arrive at Dulles mid-morning, but would have to be back at Dulles to catch a flight to Paris by late afternoon," Jason replied thoughtfully.

"If it's any easier for you, we could arrange to meet you in California on Friday," Jack offered.

"No. Friday's a busy day. It'll be better for me to meet you in Washington. Any advice you may have could be useful in my negotiations in Europe. It certainly was the last time." Again, Jason promised to e-mail a list of his appointments to Jack, who promised to review his plans, and meet him at the airport the following Saturday to drive him to the meeting.

The Lovenest group was diligently attending all the briefing meetings being set up through their State Department program, but were a little disappointed that most of the meetings were with U.S. government officials, members of the legislative branch, or with staff of the various policy think tanks scattered around the capital city. Pierre, as well as the other foreign attendees in the program, had expressed keen interest in meeting U.S. businessmen. Arrangements had then been made for the visitors to meet with members of the U.S. Chamber of Commerce and various local Rotary clubs. This is not what they had in mind. They were interested in visiting specific, small high-tech businesses where they could identify individuals who could be compromised. However, they did not mention this latter purpose. Apparently, State was hesitant in scheduling visits with private company officials, or

The Purloined Encryption Caper

rather the companies weren't willing to respond to State's request.

Miriam Gauthier had tried to compromise Jason on his last visit to Paris, but didn't succeed. She had told Pierre that she had another meeting with Jason the following week and would try again. If she didn't succeed this time, she would have to depend on her relationship with Sam Penderton, unless Pierre and his group had better success.

"Mon amie," Pierre confessed "thus far we haven't gotten very far with Jason and his company. One of the cyber-hackers recruited by Julian broke into Jason's company's system, but weren't able to obtain any useful information. Apparently, he's taken precautions to prevent hackers penetrating his company's system."

"How about the others?" Miriam asked.

"Not too much success, I'm afraid," Pierre said dejectedly. "I plan to return to Paris over the Christmas holidays and will bring you up to date. You should accept Sam Penderton's invitation to visit California in January and afterwards plan an extended visit to the West Virginia cabin so I can acquaint you with our colleagues." Pierre wanted the others to think that Miriam was as deeply involved in his scheme as he and perhaps even imply that she was the main organizer in the event their scheme was blown. He could then cut and run.

"I've never met any of your group," she said, "so such a meeting will be most useful."

That Saturday, Pierre invited his group to the West Virginia cabin. "Bring any special food or drink you may want," he told them. "I'll have the basic food, but it will be a long day. We should begin shortly after ten-thirty in the morning. The meeting may last until about four or five, but you should be prepared to stay longer. With the Christmas holidays coming, it will be our last meeting this year. We not only must review our progress but also plan our next moves. Christmas season in Washington is when a large number of office parties are held and, I understand, liquor flows and tongues loosen. We should take advantage of these parties to gain as much information as we can or make new friends."

Pierre also thanked them for obtaining data on technologies to add money to their bank account.

CHAPTER 9

"Welcome to Washington," Jack said as he opened his car trunk to stow Jason's luggage. "We have a little over an hour's drive to the meeting place, but I promise I'll have you back here in time to catch your flight to Europe." He then continued.

"The meeting's going to be at the Howard's West Virginia cabin. He's with the government and involved in counteracting industrial espionage by foreign agents. He knows you're a client and wants to talk with you privately about your concerns, as well as get your reaction to proposed strengthening of federal regulations. My role is only to bring you."

During their drive, Jack described the Virginia countryside and the area's role in the American Revolutionary and Civil Wars. When they drove through Winchester, Jack pointed out George Washington's Revolutionary War office and Stonewall Jackson's Civil War headquarters. "George Washington was a surveyor and much of the land around here was initially surveyed by him," he explained.

"Phil and Mary Howard have a cabin in the West Virginia mountains above Berkeley Springs, and the meeting's going to be held there."

At the mention of Berkeley Springs, Jason thought about Rachel. He wondered how she was doing and whether he could telephone her from the Howards on the pretext of saying hello from Berkeley Springs. He still missed her.

When he walked into the cabin and saw Rachel talking to a very elegant looking man smoking a Meerchaum pipe, his heart stopped. She was looking at the man by her side, but suddenly turned and casually said hello to Jason. Jack then took Jason's arm and introduced him to Phil and Mark. "I think you already know Rachel."

They both nodded silently. Rachel left to help Mary bring in coffee and tea, and then joined the others seated around the dining room table.

Phil took charge of the meeting. "As Jack probably told you, Jason, our government is concerned about industrial espionage and the stealing of U.S. technologies by foreign elements. We're losing a lot of money, or I should say business is losing a lot of money and the nation is weakening its security. We need advice and information from small businessmen like you who are the targets of the agents. This is a confidential get-together and we hope you'll treat it as such." Phil looked at him trying to size up this man who evidently was not only bright but had stolen Rachel's heart.

"We know companies like yours are having problems with potential infiltration or are losing secret information. Foreign competitors are especially

The Purloined Encryption Caper

interested in encryption systems and biometrics. Since your company is one of the foremost in these areas, we wanted to get together and exchange information and ideas. Rachel and Jack told me of your continuing concerns." Jason was astounded at how much Phil knew about his problems and his company.

"First," Phil continued, "I should let you know our connections with the government. I'm with the CIA, and Mark is with the FBI. You already know Rachel. What you probably don't know is that she used to work with me in Hong Kong and was with the CIA at that time, as well as during her tour in Europe. She's agreed to help us out as her time permits for the next few months." He paused to let the details sink in as Jason tried to cover his surprise.

"I think, Jason, you'll like what we're doing. We've established a central coordinating agency to strengthen enforcement of industrial espionage laws. The government wants to eliminate unnecessary restrictions and the current registration required for the export of existing technologies as well as some you may have on the drawing board."

Rachel mostly kept her head down pretending to review material in front of her. This was not the case with Jason, however. She could feel his eyes on her and, whenever she looked up, he was staring at her. He never smiled and neither did she.

Jason could hardly keep his mind focused on the discussions after hearing about Rachel's past. Was she still involved with the CIA? Was she merely using him as a pawn? His imagination began to spin, but he kept outwardly calm.

Mark outlined Rachel's theory on the leakage of company secrets and that the FBI and CIA were quietly checking out people who could be involved. Jason recognized this as the information Rachel had confidentially told him earlier.

Mark then continued. "One of our priorities at present is to determine the leaks in the system. We know there are leaks somewhere internally. There are only a few U.S. companies on the cutting edge of encryption. Therefore, we think it'll be easy to trace information and people.

"We know, for example, that a Frenchman, Pierre Ledent, who has been pursuing Rachel, is interested. I understand, Jason, you met him at a reception on Capitol Hill several months ago. Also, the Germans. They are notorious for not sticking to technology agreements. We think the Chinese are trying to obtain advanced encryption capabilities as well as high speed computers, but we still haven't figured out whether they've penetrated our government, companies such as yours, or are working through intermediaries. It's even possible that some U.S. companies ignore our technology export laws to get into that big market. One of the ways used by foreign companies and governments is to buy off disgruntled employees who will gladly share information for money." He paused to let this information sink in.

"As I mentioned before," Mark went on, looking directly at Jason, "we know there is an information leak on your company's R&D activities, as well as on your visits to Europe. It could be from someone in Jack's office, although neither Rachel nor Jack believe that's possible. But we'll have to check that out." Jason looked shocked.

Jason was then told by Mark that Rachel's apartment had been bugged, probably during the Thanksgiving weekend while she was here with the Howards or possibly on an earlier weekend. "I've arranged for a female FBI agent to stay with her. We've also identified the individuals who were surveilling Rachel's apartment building. Thugs like this are frequently hired by French intelligence to do their dirty work.

"In trying to find a suitable agent, I found the perfect individual, a woman who strongly resembles Rachel. It turns out that Ruth Brennan and Rachel were good friends in college, but had lost track of each other over the years. I understand from Phil that Rachel is good at karate and self-defense, but if anyone tries to tangle with Ruth, they won't know what hit them. She's very good at taking care of herself, and others." Mark hesitated, poured himself a glass of water and continued.

"You probably know that Rachel's telephone number has been changed. We asked her to notify only those people she wanted to maintain contact with of her new number." From the surprised look on Jason's face, it was obvious that Rachel hadn't given him her new number.

Jason hadn't liked Mark when he first met him, but he knew it was because Mark acted protective of Rachel. Now, he saw that Mark was the one concerned for Rachel's safety. Jason wondered whether it was for personal or professional reasons.

During lunch, Mark looked up and said, "Mary, I can understand why you and Phil come up here any chance you can. I keep forgetting how serenely spectacular it really is. And it does take you away from everything."

"Mark, you know you're always welcome here. And if you want more privacy, I highly recommend the Country Inn in Berkeley Springs. It's a very romantic place to stay, and on weekends, they usually have a live dance band."

"I'll keep that in mind," Mark replied.

After lunch and before the meeting resumed, Jason left the room to exercise his legs and get a breath of fresh air. On his way out, he ran into Rachel.

"How have you been, Rachel?" he asked, gently taking her arm.

"Fine," she responded, rather coolly, showing no emotion.

"So this is where you spend your weekends in Berkeley Springs," Jason remarked not taking his eyes off Rachel.

"Yes. The Howards are my closest friends, almost like family."

Jason hesitated before remarking. "You never told me." He gently brushed a strand of hair from her face and felt the same thrill as before at being so near.

"You never asked," she replied curtly and headed back to the dining room.

At this point, Phil joined Jason. "Rachel, Mark and I reviewed your upcoming schedule of appointments, Jason. I noticed that you're meeting with a Miriam Gauthier. She's a French intelligence agent, sells any

The Purloined Encryption Caper

technologies or information she gets hold of to the highest bidder. I recommend that you be careful in your dealings with her. I know you saw her the last time you were in Paris and know about your late nights at her apartment." Jason looked at Phil in amazement.

"I'm not trying to tell you how to live your life, but I'd be very careful on that score if I were you. Blackmail or misusing people is a principal feature of her bag of tricks." Phil smiled at him as he again tapped his pipe. "We didn't follow you around, Jason, but we do keep our eyes on certain people in Paris, and you came up in our scope."

Jason looked toward the dining room where Rachel had gone.

"No, Jason, I didn't mention your visits to Rachel, Jack or even to Mark who's deeply involved in this project. I thought it best for your professional and personal relationships not to. But if you continue to see Miriam, I won't be able to conceal it any longer." Phil then led Jason back to join the others. Jason never did get a chance to mention Sam Penderton's past involvement with Miriam.

Shortly thereafter, Jack looked at his watch and stood up. "Jason and I should leave for the airport to avoid traffic problems." Jason was hesitant to go. He wanted to talk further with Rachel.

As he was leaving, Rachel wished him success, said goodbye and started to walk back to the cabin. Before she left, he said, "Maybe we could have dinner the next time I'm in Washington".

"Fine," she responded, thinking what a bastard he is to talk of having dinner when, according to Bill Worth, he is on the verge of getting married.

Mark had given Rachel a ride to the meeting. They were about to turn onto Route 9 from the Howard's development area when Rachel noticed a car with District of Columbia rental car tags and recognized the driver as Hans Schmidt.

Pierre's group had run out of beer and Hans insisted on going back to the 7-Eleven store to replenish their supply. The meeting was lasting much longer than had been anticipated, and he needed his libations to get him through the rest of the afternoon and possibly the evening as well.

"Mark, can you discreetly follow that car? The driver looks like Hans Schmidt, the German I met on the Hill and at various parties. I can't imagine what he's doing up here or why he's driving a rental car, not an Embassy vehicle."

"Of course," he replied and dropped back, but managed to see where the car was going. Hans turned into a driveway to a cabin called Rainbow's End, where two other cars with DC tags were parked. Rachel wrote down the license numbers as they passed by.

Mark continued to drive to the end of the road and noticed another cabin not very far away with a For Rent sign on it, which would give a good view of any activity at the other cabin. He wrote down the name and telephone number of the real estate company. It might be a good place to station some FBI agents if the situation warranted.

The Purloined Encryption Caper

"What do you think this is about, Mark?" Rachel questioned.

"I don't know, but I'm sure as hell going to find out. It looks rather strange, especially since all the cars are from rental companies."

"Maybe they're having a sex orgy with local women," Rachel said humorously.

"Embassy officials usually don't worry about such things, my dear, or have to hide out in the countryside."

On the drive to the airport, Jason thought a great deal about his meeting at the Howard's and about Rachel's past. He knew he was in love with her and realized their long separation hadn't helped him forget her.

"Thanks for everything, Jack," Jason said as they neared Dulles. "I can't tell you how helpful this is for me and my company. I never realized that I would get intelligence briefings from my Washington office as well as good service."

"The thanks really go to Rachel. She's the one who started it by checking your first appointment schedule with Phil. I hadn't even met him at that point. By the way," Jack suddenly said. "I don't know what happened between you and Rachel or what didn't happen, but all I ask is that you don't cause her any grief. I've gotten to know a little about her past from Phil and she's had a lot of sorrow and unhappiness in her short life. I don't want to be responsible for adding to it." Jason wanted to ask Jack what he meant, but by then, they had reached the airport.

When Jason reached his Paris hotel, he rechecked his schedule. It was rather crowded and he wondered if he could manage all the appointments. The first thing he would do Monday would be to cancel his Tuesday evening meeting with Miriam. It would permit him to fly to Frankfurt late Tuesday afternoon after his last meeting. His meeting with her was really to reconfirm some information he had managed to squeeze out of Sam. That now changed with Phil's warning. Phil would hold back on telling Jack or Mark about the late night he spent with Miriam once, but not twice, and Mark would delight in telling Rachel what kind of guy Jason was. Mark seemed to be a straight arrow type.

Tuesday night when Jason reached the Frankfurt hotel, there were several messages for him, two from individuals he was to meet on Friday. Their offices would be closed that day, so the two men wanted to reschedule their meetings for Wednesday or Thursday. After rescheduling his appointments, he called the airline to see if he could get a flight back to the States, via Washington, late Thursday. He thought it might be politic to meet with Jack and possibly Phil, but mainly he wanted to see Rachel again.

No wonder Rachel seemed to lean on Mark so much, Jason said to himself. Mark was there when she needed help. He blamed Terry for his distrust of women, but if he were really honest, he would realize that it was because he had become a selfish man, living alone all of these years, concerned only for his feelings. Could he change, he wondered? He had thought of

The Purloined Encryption Caper

asking Claire to marry him recently but he realized he didn't love Claire. She was only convenient.

Jason wanted to call Rachel at her apartment and ask her to save dinner for him Friday night but remembered that she had a new phone number. Mark said that they asked Rachel to give the new number only to those people she wanted to have it. Jason realized he had not made that list.

Thursday after his last appointment, he telephoned Jack's office. Cindy answered and agreed to make hotel reservations for him at the Hilton Hotel in Ballston for the weekend as well as an eight o'clock dinner reservation for two Friday night at Jacques Cafe.

Rachel was at Cindy's desk when Jason's call came through and overheard the conversation. If Bill Worth was right, Claire was probably meeting him in Washington or had already met him in Europe. Rachel didn't want to be here. To think that he was taking someone else to Jacques really hurt.

Rachel hurried into Jack's office. "Is it okay with you if I leave now for the beach to give me a head start on the traffic?" Rachel already planned to take several days off starting Friday to attend to some business regarding her beach house.

"I've finished everything and am up to date," she explained, "and the House and Senate won't be in session again until after the holidays. The only item pending is my next newsletter which will include a lot of government reports. And this one I'll mail."

"Sure, go ahead," Jack responded as he reached for the telephone. "Just wish we were going with you."

"Why don't you and Jean join me? I'll be all alone." Jack shrugged his shoulders and said he'd talk to Jean. "I doubt it, though. She has a lot of honey-do projects for me."

Jason arrived in Washington late Thursday and checked into his hotel. The next morning, he arrived at Jack's office early, in plenty of time for their ten o'clock meeting. "Boy it's good to be back in the States again," Jason said. "Where's Rachel? Her office is dark."

"She's taking a few days off to spend at her beach house," Jack said casually.

It had never occurred to Jason that Rachel would not be here. She always was. "How far is that from here and when did she leave?"

"About five hours by fast car. She left late yesterday morning so she could enjoy a quiet walk on the beach, shaking visions of company secrets and international intrigue out of her head." Jack tried to be funny, but soon realized that Jason didn't appreciate his humor.

"When's she coming back?" Jason was mentally trying to decide if he would have the patience to wait.

"Monday or Tuesday evening, I believe. Congress isn't in session so things are slow now. It's been a hectic few months for Rachel, so I thought she deserved the break."

"Too bad you'll miss Rachel," Cindy commented as Jack and Jason were leaving the office.

"So am I," Jason replied, seemingly dejected.

"If you had only telephoned a few minutes earlier, you might have caught her before she left. But why don't you fly and drive to the Outer Banks? I can see if

The Purloined Encryption Caper

I can get you a plane ticket to Norfolk and reserve a car for you to drive down to Kitty Hawk? It would get you there by late afternoon. My boyfriend used to fly back and forth to Washington occasionally when we were using Rachel's place and said it was fairly easy."

"Please. I'd appreciate it," Jason said gratefully returning to Cindy's desk. "You don't mind waiting a few minutes, do you, Jack? It will also give me a chance to grab another cup of coffee."

Cindy managed to make the appropriate reservations. "Also, would you please tell Rachel that Mark's been trying to reach her and wants her to call him as soon as she gets back."

Jason said he would. At least Mark isn't with her and doesn't even know that Rachel left town.

Jack and Jason finished their meeting by noon and Jack drove Jason to his hotel to pick up his luggage.

"This is quite a nice hotel," Jack said. "Is it comfortable? "

"Yes, very, and extremely convenient." When Jack gave him a knowing look, Jason continued "Not only because it's near Rachel's apartment, but also located next to the Ballston Metro Station. It's the fastest transportation around Washington and I don't have to be afraid to walk around this area at night. Washington's not only more expensive, but dead at night. The Ballston area really hums, especially with the yuppie set. I especially recommend a nice French restaurant nearby. Perhaps some time you and Jean and Rachel and I can have dinner there together."

Pierre was upset. He had heard from Miriam

that Jason Conrad had canceled his meeting with her. "Did Pierre know why?" she asked. Was there a leak in their group or were the people they had used to get information now using them? The one person who might fit that was the CIA secretary being courted by Carlo.

This was very bad luck considering the good meeting which they'd had the previous Saturday. He'd have to get in touch with Carlo and have him double check with his lady friend. Carlo had been so sure that she was so compromised at this point and dependent upon him as a lover that he could get almost any information he wanted. And she worked for Phil Howard's boss.

Also, Miriam heard from her CIA contacts in Paris that their headquarters were asking all sorts of questions about the death of Steve Holliday. Did Pierre know who in Washington was pressuring the CIA? Was it the representative for whom Steve worked? Or was it a CIA employee?

CHAPTER 10

It took Rachel only five hours to drive to her beach house that Thursday and return to the one place she could hide. She certainly didn't want to be in the office when Jason walked in the next morning with Claire.

Friday, she awakened early and went for a long walk on the beach, thinking about her time here the year before and her chance meeting with Steve. She missed him and still couldn't believe he was dead or that his death was accidental. But apparently that was the verdict of the French police and they now considered the case closed. Phil was trying to exert pressure to reopen the case, but the CIA's Paris station wasn't sure the gendarmes would respond favorably. Rachel planned to visit Steve's cottage while she was here to see if she could find any papers that might provide a clue to his disappearance. His parents had sent her the cottage key and asked her to check its condition, something that Steve normally did for them.

So much had happened since then. She loved her job and her apartment and had met someone she could

Rose Ameser Bannigan

love, and, if she were honest with herself, had already fallen in love with. But somehow it did not all come out as she might have hoped with Jason. She had to admit being badly hurt again and vowed to totally ignore men in the future. She was too unlucky in love.

When she returned from her walk, Rachel telephoned Ben, a handyman her father had used to look after the beach house during the winter months. She was glad he was still available to keep watch over the place and make sure the water pipes didn't freeze. It never got as cold on the Outer Banks as it did in Washington or Pennsylvania. Yet freezing snaps did occur, and woe to the owners who didn't either have the water dripping or turned off completely. Frozen and eventually broken pipes could be the consequence with formidable damage and expense for the owner.

She felt strange entering Steve's empty cottage. It was cold and foreboding. She rummaged around the small room he used as an office, but found nothing, not even a computer. Then she remembered that he always carried his notebook computer with him. She finally located a small printer in a closet which he used to print hard copy. The only clue that emerged was a sheet of paper with two sentences, which must have accidentally got mixed up with the blank paper. It read, "I plan to corroborate evidence during my next visit to France. My informant (see Identity A in appendix B) said it may be necessary for me to visit Nice and Marseilles or possibly Corsica to get the data needed from several Union Corse informants to finalize report." Unfortunately, no copy of appendix B could be found. She neatly folded the page, put it in her

The Purloined Encryption Caper

pocket and returned to her cottage. She was suddenly frightened. It confirmed to her that Steve had indeed been murdered.

She purchased several light novels to read and stocked up on what food she would need for her short stay, mainly salads and fruit. She didn't feel like cooking much for herself. The Market Place, with its Food Lion grocery store, was always close by in the event she craved more solid food, as well as Carawan's Fish Store across the road from the Market Place for her seafood desires. Carawan's had the freshest and best seafood on the Atlantic Coast, her father used to say, and he always insisted that Rachel's mother serve mostly seafood during their stays.

The year before, she had lived on a similar diet and was amazed that she was able to lose more than 10 pounds. Her only compromise on calories was her Scotch and water after a long walk on the beach or as she watched the sunset over the Sound at the little private beach on the opposite side of Southern Shores.

It was Friday afternoon and having taken care of her domestic chores, she decided to take a long walk on the beach to clear her mind. She thought of her involvement with Phil and Jason's concerns for industrial espionage and wondered how it would end. One thing was certain. The excitement it had given her would certainly diminish when it was resolved Maybe Mark would ask her out but she doubted it now that she had become so involved with Jason. She was glad Ruth had entered her life again. It was a strong tie to her college days and happier times.

She would probably leave her job in Jack's office. Too many memories of Jason, and her job would require her to work closely with his company, even though it would probably be with one of his associates. She was ready for a bigger challenge now anyway. As soon as I return to Washington, she mused, I'll begin to look at the employment section of the *Washington Post* and the *New York Times*. Perhaps Tom would be willing to help, or serve as a reference. Sadly, Steve wasn't around anymore. But she didn't want to dwell on that subject.

"Maybe I'll move to New York or Boston, somewhere I won't run into Jason," she thought. A last resort would be to return to the CIA and work for Phil. He told her a job was always waiting for her, either in Washington or overseas.

After crossing the Causeway over Currituck Sound, Jason easily found Rachel's place in Southern Shores. The directions Jack gave were flawless. Jason spotted her car in the driveway of a weathered redwood beach house and parked beside it. No one answered the doorbell so he walked around to the back and sat at a table in a screened-in porch facing the Atlantic Ocean. The beach looked isolated and lonely, so unlike the Pacific Coast beaches. Also, there, hills, and in some cases, mountains plunged down to the beaches. Here, everything was flat, and the engineers had to shore up the dunes to keep the sand from washing away.

He was amazed that the doors to the porch and then into the house were open and thought how wonderful it would be not to worry about locking a door every

The Purloined Encryption Caper

time you left. He sat there for over thirty minutes, fighting the urge to go into the house and fix a drink. It was now nearing six o'clock and daylight was fading fast. He turned and looked across the beach, its golden sand framing the foaming waters. Suddenly, in the distance he saw a solitary figure casually strolling in the direction of the house, watching the last shreds of daylight as a group of pelicans skimmed the water. He knew it was Rachel. Her movements were so familiar.

When Rachel was directly in front of him, she looked out toward the ocean, waiting for the last pelican to fade from view, and said aloud, "goodbye little bird." She then turned and walked up to her house. Suddenly, she noticed a figure standing on the porch steps.

"Jason, what are you doing here?" she asked, obviously startled

"I could say that I was in the neighborhood and stopped by for a drink, but that would be lying. You agreed to have dinner with me, remember? I thought that the Outer Banks was as good a place as any."

When Rachel didn't laugh or respond in a flippant manner which had once been her style, he told her he wanted to talk with her. She finally came onto the porch and into the house and stirred the fire. She said nothing, which made Jason feel slightly uncomfortable.

"Would you like a drink? Is it still gin and tonic, or would you like something else?" Rachel offered.

"No. Gin and tonic will be fine." This time Jason let Rachel make the drinks.

"I thought you were going to be in Europe all week? Didn't things work out?" "I managed to complete my appointments in four days and I figured there was no purpose in staying in Europe when I'd rather be with you." He now hesitated. "Rachel, we need to talk. I know I have a lot of explaining to do and perhaps extend a number of apologies."

"You have nothing to apologize for and explanations aren't necessary. You owe me nothing." Her voice was non-committal and distant.

Rachel handed him his drink and sat down on the sofa in front of the fire clutching her Scotch and water. She had taken off her parka, but the chill from her long walk made her shiver. Jason sat down beside her and took her hand. She was on the verge of pulling it away, but his grasp was so strong it would have been difficult to do without making a scene. She felt that might seem too comedic.

"Jack told me you were here and Cindy with her usual efficiency told me how I could get here with a minimum of time and trouble." Jason then paused. "Did you leave Washington yesterday because you knew I would be there for the weekend?" He hesitated before asking the next question, afraid of the answer. "Didn't you want to see me?"

"I'd already decided to come down here for several days, but I won't lie," she replied curtly. "I heard you ask Cindy to make reservations at the Hilton and at Jacques. But since I hadn't heard from you directly, I decided I'd leave and avoid any embarrassment if we met accidentally." They both were nervous, and their conversation was very strained.

After an uneasy silence, Rachel turned and looked directly at him. "What do you want from me?" she asked in a controlled, almost cold, voice. "I can't figure

The Purloined Encryption Caper

you out. You pursue me, make love to me and then you avoid me. Now you come almost three-hundred miles to talk with me." There was a moment of silence before she continued, her voice quivering slightly.

"If you want to thank me for helping your company, a nice letter of appreciation would suffice. We do service you as a client and it is part of my job. Also, such a letter thanking me for my good work would be useful in my file, especially if I need it for a future job." Rachel was very sincere, and she hoped her voice didn't betray her real feelings.

"I'm not sure exactly where or how to start," he said nervously.

"The truth would be nice and you can start with the evening you left after our evening with Jack and Jean. You were so warm and friendly and then turned sullen without any reason." Rachel was still looking directly at him.

"I suppose it was a fit of jealousy. As you'll recall, after our nightcap, you mentioned that you wanted us to leave since you were going to Berkeley Springs early the next day. Somehow, I wondered why your going to Berkeley Springs was so much more important than spending the night with me, especially since I was going back to California the next day." He paused, and kissed the back of her hand.

"I now see I was wrong in thinking that you were going to meet someone there, and I don't mean Phil and Mary Howard. I knew nothing about them. I assumed you were meeting a male friend, a lover, especially after the late telephone call. Since you always tried to keep me at arms' length, I became jealous and angry.

I knew I was falling in love with you and didn't want to get hurt again. I have been in the past, so I was determined not to call you or see you any more."

Jason stopped and when Rachel made no comment, he went on. "After I met Phil, I realized what an absolute ass I'd been. Also, seeing you there made me realize that I had to talk with you and resume our relationship. I don't think you understand how much you've come to mean to me. I hope you know that I'd never do anything to hurt you." He paused for her reaction.

"No, I really don't. And please, Jason, don't use that hackneyed phrase--*I'd never do anything to hurt you.* All I'm waiting for is the next word, *but...*"

Rachel was angry and rose to refill their drinks. Jason took the glasses from her. "Here, let me do it. I still can manage that, even if I am not doing a very good job of explaining my behavior that night. Perhaps you're even enjoying seeing me squirm." Rachel looked at him coolly and shook her head no.

"Not that I want to change the subject, which I do for the moment. Jack said you might offer me a spare bedroom for the night. If not, I'll have to find a local motel."

"I'll give you the room over in this corner. It has a nice view of the Ocean, and you can hear the sound of the waves crashing on the beach at night."

Jason brought in his luggage and put it in the designated bedroom. What Rachel didn't tell him was that this had been her room before she moved her things to the master bedroom after her folks died.

The Purloined Encryption Caper

"Where should we eat tonight? Do we need reservations?"

Rachel laughed, amazed that he could so completely change the subject. "Not at this time of year. The place is practically dead. We can just drive the By-Pass and find something suitable. Don't dress, or I should say, dress down. This area is very casual. Jeans and sweaters are usually the code."

As they were leaving for dinner and Jason was reaching down to open the car door for her, he took her in his arms and kissed her hair. "God, I've missed you." Then, he kissed her lightly on the lips. Rachel did not pull away, yet didn't respond with the ardor she felt. She couldn't afford to let her guard down again.

As they were driving, Rachel pointed out the local landmarks--the Wright Brothers Memorial as well as the old Coast Guard lifesaving station--and interspersing some of the old tales of the Banks to try and keep her impersonal facade secure.

"Many ships have wrecked off the Coast, the latest ones during World War II, when German submarines prowled within twenty miles of the shore. None of this apparently was reported in the press at the time. The American government didn't want to frighten the public." She thought of the present situation and its implications with apprehension and tried to keep up her chatter about the history of the area.

They finally came to Mako Mike's, an attractive seafood restaurant which was open so Jason pulled in. Restaurants on the Outer Banks opened and closed with great frequency. The busy time is summer when the sleepy villages bustled with people, and convertibles with loud music deafened the nearby passengers and pedestrians.

Rachel ordered another scotch and Jason a gin martini. She told Jason she would have broiled catch of the day and a salad. "That's what you had our first night together. Do you remember? "

Rachel smiled. "How did your meetings go in Europe, Jason? You haven't even mentioned whether the trip was worthwhile." She didn't want to reminisce yet.

"Things went very well. With my European lawyer's help, I managed to negotiate several contracts and licensing agreements, now waiting for my California lawyers' approval. But the most successful part of my trip is being here with you. And that I do mean. Do you want another drink, or are you afraid you'll lose control?"

"I'm rather nervous tonight so another drink would be helpful," she said with a slight smile, realizing she never drank this much normally. He didn't ask her what she meant by that and wasn't quite sure he wanted to know.

After dinner, they drove home, mostly in silence. Jason suggested a walk on the beach before they called it a night.

"What did Jack mean when he said that he didn't want me to hurt you, that you already had enough unhappiness during your short life? Rachel, I know all about your office qualifications, now I even know the truth about your past employment. But I don't know anything about this personal part of you," he said putting his hand over her heart. "If we knew a

The Purloined Encryption Caper

little more about each other and our past, perhaps there wouldn't be so much suspicion on either side. How about some true confessions so we can try to wipe away any pain we've caused each other? Perhaps even start with a clean slate."

She was silent for several moments. "What else did Jack say? I suppose Phil told him about me." The latter she said as a statement more than a question.

"He said that you were very dejected when you arrived in Hong Kong, that your parents had been killed in an auto accident and thought there was more, perhaps a sad love affair. Then later, your fiancé was killed in a plane crash. I think he was trying to warn me not to toy with your affections, or something like that," Jason confessed.

"Jack knows you very well and told me you were good friends. Do you usually toy with the affections of young ladies? If he was so worried about me, why didn't he warn me earlier rather than encourage our relationship?" Rachel was very caustic in her statement, but Jason said nothing.

"You said you weren't married, yet I know you're involved with someone in California. I think her name is Claire. Right?" She stared at Jason, but he made no comment. "I've been told how beautiful she is, that you spend nights together and make a handsome couple. And that you'll probably marry her soon, now that your company is doing so well." She almost sounded like a prosecutor closing her case.

Jason was momentarily at a loss for words. Rachel waited before going on.

"What you do and who you go out or sleep with is your business, Jason, and I have no right in asking. But please spare me your remarks about being in love with me, and how afraid you were that I was toying with you as your excuse to suddenly ditch me with no explanation, especially after making love to me. I may be naive but I'm not stupid. I can be taken in once, but not twice." She stopped abruptly to catch her breath.

"You've every right to be angry with me." He took a deep breath. "Claire is a woman I've known for several years. I did sleep with her at one time, but I haven't touched her, or any other woman I may add, since I met you. Yes, she's attractive, poised and very professional. She's a lawyer, but I am not intimately involved with her anymore. I even told her about you. At one time I did consider marrying her, but after I met you, I knew what it was like to really feel very strongly about someone, feelings I'd never had toward Claire or anyone else." He paused before continuing.

"I've never been married. At the time I was starting up my company, I was engaged to a woman whom I believed would be a good, honest and faithful wife. Did I love her? I was convinced I did at the time." He paused.

"What happened?" Rachel inquired, her interest growing.

Jason then told her about his relationship with Terry and how she had betrayed him. "Afterwards I occupied my time building up my company and shielding myself from getting emotionally involved with any woman, not wanting to develop any close or intimate relationships. I could take them or leave them, which I did. As I said, Claire was convenient, a professional lawyer who served as an efficient hostess when I needed one. Now I realize I never loved her, either." Jason then looked at Rachel.

"Out of curiosity," he asked, "who told you about Claire?" He didn't think that Jack had ever met her.

"I had dinner with Bill Worth when he was in town recently and he told me you all had dinner together the week before. You told him you were anxious to settle down and have a family and you promised to bring Claire to Washington with you on your next visit."

Jason shook his head. "With friends like that, who needs enemies." He paused before continuing. "What about your relationship with Mark? Are you sleeping with him, or are you still in love with the man named Jeff? Or is there anyone else? You mentioned that Tom was just a friend, but friends can turn into lovers. There are so many things in your past and present life that I want to know. I feel so uncertain with you. I can compete with flesh and blood men like Mark, Rachel, but I can't box shadows and ghosts."

Rachel answered slowly. "I find it difficult to answer certain of your questions out of context. They could be considered cruel. First off, though, one answer is easy. I'm not sleeping with Mark. I've never kissed him goodnight or goodbye although I would have during the past few weeks if he'd made a pass. He's like Tom to me--a trusted friend who's been very kind and protective. I've turned to him for help when I needed it and I've definitely needed a friend like him over the past month. I know he likes me and once told me he hoped to put our relationship on a more personal basis after we're no longer working together." She hesitated a moment, watching his unease at the last remark.

"I'll always love Jeff for the type of man he was, a good man with a kind heart who never really asked very much of me. But was I *in love with him,* I don't think so, not now. His kindness really saved me in terms of my regard for men." She stopped and thought about her childhood and previous relationships with men.

"You see, I had led a rather sheltered life when I was growing up. I am an only child born to parents who themselves had been only children. We did everything together, and I suppose people would consider that I had an idyllic childhood. I wasn't a problem child, did well in school and college and graduated with honors from Northwestern University. Since my father was a university professor, he guided my schooling, always taking into consideration what I wanted." Her eyes were beginning to mist. She continued, slowly.

"I was recruited by the CIA just before I graduated from Northwestern. They promised an interesting job that would make use of my knowledge of technology and journalism as well as my languages. My first assignment was in Europe, where my parents had taken me for visits. I always trusted people, believed that friends were honest and would never purposely hurt me. How wrong I was." She took a sip of her coffee and then continued.

"About a year after arriving in Europe, I met a man at a party being given by a Consular official. I didn't actually meet him but felt him staring at me from across the room. I knew he was attracted to me, but

The Purloined Encryption Caper

didn't think about it any more that night. However, he telephoned me the next day for a date and we began seeing each other rather regularly." She watched Jason for his reaction. He showed none, so she went on.

"He was based in New York, but managed to get to Europe quite frequently. Since he seemed so sure of himself and easy around women, I thought he might be married. Also, he never brought up the idea of marriage, something other men I dated did after a number of dates. When I asked him if he was married, he said that the question was so silly, he wasn't going to bother to answer it. The answer was obvious, he insisted. Naturally, I assumed, incorrectly I may add, that he was single." Rachel then proceeded to tell Jason about the ending, when she found out that he was indeed married. "He said he hadn't lied to me or never actually *said* he wasn't married, but was afraid that if he told me the truth, I would stop seeing him. He was right. Also, as a journalist, he used me and my contacts for meeting people, although he insisted that it was secondary."

Listening to her story, Jason realized that Rachel could be the girl his friend Frank had been, and probably still was, in love with. Could the world be this small? He had felt sorry for Frank that evening over cocktails when he talked about the girl he had met in Europe and was still in love with. Now he felt sick at the thought of Rachel and Frank making love, and felt a great deal of jealousy toward Frank.

Just two weeks ago he had received a letter from Frank reporting that his mother had died the weekend Frank and Jason had drinks in Washington, and his estranged wife had asked for a divorce. The money issue was now settled and Frank's inheritance ensured. His wife was making it very easy since she had met someone else several years earlier and they now wanted to get married. Both he and his wife in their own way had deceived his mother, and each other.

"I now plan to see if I can find Monk, the woman I loved in Germany," Frank had written. "I don't think she's in Washington since there's no telephone listing in her name. If I don't have any success on my own, I'll hire a private detective to track her down. She may already be married, or may not want to have anything to do with me, but I must find her. If she's still free, I'll do anything to resurrect our love and marry her and start all over again." Rachel's voice brought him back to reality.

"When I closed the door on him that evening, I felt that someone had thrust a dagger through my heart." Rachel continued. "Also, I was very angry with myself. How could I have been so badly duped? The day after I received his letter explaining why he hadn't told me earlier about being married--he loved me too much and he would have been written out of his mother's will--I got word of my parents' accident." Rachel paused again, her eyes lowered.

"I was numb. I flew home immediately, arranged the funeral, closed the door on the Pennsylvania house and drove here. We were going to come here for a few weeks during my home leave anyway so it was all ready for the family vacation." Rachel was near tears as she thought of the day she opened the door to the beach house and realized she was now all alone.

The Purloined Encryption Caper

"When I was a child and upset, I used to sit in a dark closet and think about life and my problems until I felt I could go back to the world. In other words, join people again. This house became my adult closet. When I came here after my parents' funeral, I walked the beach every day, thinking, and trying to come to terms with my loss and my life." Again Rachel was quiet for awhile, lost in her own thoughts, almost if she had forgotten Jason was with her.

"About a week before I was to report to Washington, I got a telephone call from CIA headquarters. Would I be interested in an assignment to Hong Kong? Yes, I said, but I'd need another two weeks to get my affairs in order.

"Fortunately, my father was a very organized person and by spending only a week with his attorney and his stockbroker, I was able to finalize my financial affairs, and give the attorney authorization to attend to any matters that would come up while I was overseas." Rachel was quiet for a moment, recalling those difficult days.

"I had all of the household effects put in storage and turned our Pennsylvania home over to a real estate broker to manage rentals on my behalf. I then came back here, took the personal effects from our beach home, put some in a lock-up closet and some in a storage warehouse locker nearby. I turned this place over to a beach rental agency, said goodbye and drove to Washington. Within a month, I was in Hong Kong. My boss there was Phil Howard." She paused as mixed memories crowded in. Jason sat listening, not making any comments.

Rose Ameser Bannigan

"My days were spent working and studying Chinese. I was fluent in German and French when I went to Europe, but I couldn't even say hello, goodbye or thank you in Chinese. I didn't want to meet anyone romantically and wasn't interested in making any friendships. I was constantly being introduced to 'eligible young men' but they could tell by my body language, 'don't call her', and they didn't." She looked at Jason to see his reaction as she sipped her drink and resumed her tale while staring into the fire.

"Part of my job involved traveling to other cities in Asia. About nine months after arriving in Hong Kong, I attended a meeting in Jakarta, Indonesia. I studied all about the country before I went and decided that after the meeting, I would visit Borobudur, a beautiful eleventh-century Buddhist temple which had recently been renovated by UNESCO, and then tour the island of Bali. When I was coming down a steep stairway inside the temple, I was holding on to the railing for dear life. Heights sometimes frighten me. Suddenly, I heard someone behind me say, 'let me get in front of you so you can lean on my shoulder. It won't be so bad that way.' I turned around and saw a young American, with a kind smile on his face and took him up on his offer. That was how I met Jeff." She shook the ice in her drink, finished it and continued.

"I had taken the local bus out to the temple so Jeff offered to drive me back to Jogjakarta, the closest city to the temple where I was staying. Also, he said there were several other minor temples that I should see that wouldn't be possible by bus.

The Purloined Encryption Caper

"Coincidentally, it happened that we were staying at the same hotel and were on the same flight the next day to Bali. He already had reserved a rental car there, so we toured Bali together, as friends. He never made a pass, but seemed to understand that a buddy was what I needed at that time. When he dropped me off at the airport for my flight back to Hong Kong, he asked if he could telephone me the next time he passed through Hong Kong. That's how our relationship began. It seemed his flights were constantly routing him through Hong Kong. He was a Navy pilot on special duty so I guess he could pick his route." Jason was listening attentively.

"I was in Bangkok, once, on extended business and he managed to come to see me there. We went to Chiang Mai, a lovely city in northern Thailand for the weekend. At this point, I liked him a lot and felt very relaxed and comfortable with him, and thought he considered me only as a good friend, especially since he had never even tried to kiss me on the lips. That weekend proved differently, and it began our love affair." Rachel moved and put another log on the fire.

"A few months later, he asked me to marry him. He said he'd loved me for a long time, but felt I'd been hurt in the past and he didn't want to rush me. He wanted to get married in Hong Kong, but I thought we should wait until I had completed my assignment and returned to the States. He finally agreed, provided I would meet him in San Francisco upon his return so we could get married immediately. Neither of us wanted a big wedding." Tears came closer to the surface of her blue eyes.

Then Rachel told Jason about Jeff's death, the attitude of his family and her decision to go to the beach house again to think things over. "Jeff was a wonderful and kind person. Any woman would have been a fool not to want him as a husband." The tears were close to flowing and she had to struggle to retain her composure.

"I felt as if my heart had been pounded by a mallet. It hurt whenever I breathed deeply. I finally got courage after many months walking this beach to get back into life and I returned to Washington. That's when I started working for Jack. He was a friend of a childhood friend who used to spend his summers at this beach as well." She paused and looked straight at Jason.

"My emotions were well in check until the day you walked into Jack's office. You knew I was attracted to you, and you seemed to enjoy getting my emotions stirred up. But I couldn't take a chance in caring for someone so much again, especially if he were just playing games with me."

No wonder Rachel felt contempt for him. "Why didn't you tell me this before?" he asked softly.

"Why? I don't go around telling everyone my life story. Also, I didn't want anyone in the office to know about my past. I'm really a very private person. I'm sorry now that Jack knows so much. It was much better before. I don't want his or anyone else's sympathy. I got over self-pity when I left here for DC." Rachel hesitated before continuing.

"That's why I didn't want to succumb to your advances. You were too slick and smooth and, frankly,

The Purloined Encryption Caper

I didn't trust you. It seemed that all you wanted to do was get me in bed. When I fought you, you became upset. I don't sleep around, Jason. Too much of Washington already does that. Unloving sex is not for me, or I should say has never been for me." And the contempt in her tone showed she meant it.

Jason took Rachel in his arms and held her tight. "I'd be lying if I told you I didn't want to make love to you tonight. I've never wanted any woman as much. But, I won't press my advances and, if I get overly romantic and lose control, when you tell me to stop, I will."

They sat together a long time in silence watching the fire. After a while, he started kissing her, first tenderly and then with more passion. At first, she resisted but soon her passion was as intense as his. He unbuttoned her sweater and reached under her T-shirt, and started to caress her breasts. He was glad she wasn't wearing a bra. He kissed her neck and her face, and then again kissed her on the lips, her mouth opening to welcome him. He could feel her breast heave and her passion rise to match his.

In the midst of their embraces and passion, Rachel whispered "Jason, please make love to me."

"I thought you'd never ask." He took her hand and led her to her bedroom.

He undressed her, kissed and caressed her body before lowering her on the bed. When their bodies came together, Jason had never felt such fire in his loins. She also responded to him with more passion than she thought possible. Tonight she didn't attempt to control her emotions. Their love-making was intense and almost brutal. She had never been aroused like this by either Frank or Jeff, and it frightened her. She didn't like to lose control of her feelings, but she couldn't help herself.

At the climax of their passion, Jason murmured, "Rachel, I love you so much."

"Please, Jason, don't ever say anything you don't mean, especially in the midst of making love," she murmured afterwards.

"But I do mean it, Rachel, and you must believe me." He held her in his arms the whole night. He was afraid to let her go.

CHAPTER 11

The smell of freshly brewed coffee and bacon frying awakened Jason. It reminded him of home. He quickly got up, put on his robe and headed toward the bedroom Rachel had assigned him. He stopped where Rachel was and held her for a moment. "Why didn't you waken me, or were you afraid I'd never let you out of bed?"

"You were sleeping so peacefully I didn't want to disturb you. You must've been very tired," she smiled coyly. "While you dress, I'll go get the papers." She breezed out the door.

By the time Rachel returned with the *Washington Times* and *Washington Post*, Jason had showered, shaved, dressed and was sitting at the counter enjoying a cup of coffee and a glass of juice.

"The service in this hotel is excellent," he said smiling.

Rachel suddenly realized she had no idea how he liked his eggs.

"Sunny side up, if you can," he answered, smiling.

Rose Ameser Bannigan

Several minutes later, Rachel joined him at the bar after serving breakfast. "I'll give you the *Post*," she said. "I always enjoy reading the *Times* first."

It was almost as if they were married. He passes the breakfast test, she thought. This had been a private joke at college. Spend at least one full night with someone you might marry to see if you want to have his face across the breakfast table every morning for the rest of your life.

Since the sun was shining and only a slight chill in the air, Rachel said she was going for a walk on the beach. Jason insisted on joining her. Little was said for the first five minutes as they listened to the sand crunch beneath their feet and the waves tumble toward the beach.

"How long are you planning to stay here?" Jason asked.

"Until Tuesday," Rachel replied. "When are you going back to California?"

Jason hadn't thought much about his return flight after last night and was determined to stay with her as long as he could.

"Why don't I turn in my rental car and ride back to Washington with you? There's a place in Nags Head so I won't even have to take it back to the Norfolk airport. I'll call and make reservations for a San Francisco flight for Tuesday evening."

That afternoon Rachel drove him to Nags Head and then to Manteo, the Dare county seat, on Roanoke Island in Albemarle Sound. "This is the site of the Lost Colony," she said, "the first permanent English settlement in North America in 1587. The colony had

The Purloined Encryption Caper

been organized and backed financially by Sir Walter Raleigh although he never visited it. The people disappeared before another ship arrived and the mystery of what happened to Virginia Dare, the first English child born in America, and the rest of the Lost Colony has intrigued America ever since." Although she knew she was sounding like a tour guide, she continued. "Some think the men were killed and the women taken as wives by the local Indians. There is the replica of the Elizabeth, the boat that brought the first settlers to Dare County, moored across the Sound," she said pointing to it.

As they were walking along the Manteo Harbor boardwalk, Jason suddenly stopped. "Rachel, I've had enough history lessons for one day. I want to talk about us. Where do we go from here? We can't just go back to our hometowns and lives as if nothing has happened. Personally, I don't want to and don't think I can."

She was silent for several minutes before answering. "For the time being, why don't we just enjoy the next few days together and make that decision later. Come Tuesday, you may never want to see me again," she joked.

"I doubt that very much," he said shaking his head.

"By the way, don't you have to get in touch with your office or follow up on your meetings in Europe? I have a computer set-up and fax machine here so if you want to tackle any correspondence or fax any information, we can do it from the cottage."

Jason allowed as how he would have to do that, probably the next day so the office would receive it by Monday, or Tuesday at the latest. "We even have Federal Express or UPS services if you need to send a lot of material," Rachel told him.

Bringing business and reality into an otherwise perfect weekend, Jason commented on the newsletter which Rachel wrote and edited. "I didn't realize you had international clients."

Rachel looked at him in surprise. "We don't. The newsletter is only for our clients in the States. Why did you think that we send it overseas?"

"I saw a copy on the desk of one of the men I had an appointment with in Paris. I was going to ask about it, but then it slipped my mind. You mean you don't send copies overseas?" Actually, he had seen a copy in Miriam's apartment on his last trip.

"No," Rachel exclaimed. "You didn't happen to see the last page, did you, or get an e-mail or fax number from where it was sent?" The last page that normally had specific comments for the individual company would vary according to which company was receiving it and might indicate who was sending copies abroad.

"The fax area code was 202. That's why I thought your office had sent it." Jason looked as puzzled as Rachel. With other things on their mind, they let the matter drop.

They both knew the weekend had changed their relationship. They were no longer adversarial lovers, but willing participants. Jason kept telling her how much he loved her and Rachel knew she loved him too, but still couldn't bring herself to admit it to him.

The Purloined Encryption Caper

On their drive back to Southern Shores, Jason had talked generally of marriage. "You know, Rachel, when I marry, I want a wife who'll love me and be willing to stay home and raise a family. I don't want a professional marriage, where spouses meet en route to meetings but a marriage like my parents had when I was growing up. This is what I told Bill Worth and why he interpreted that as my interest in marrying Claire." Knowing now that Rachel was willing to enter into such a marriage before with Jeff, he quietly hoped that she would love him enough to share the same with him.

Jason knew that sometime, and the sooner the better, he would have to confess that he might know her first lover and that he was a close friend. However, he didn't want to ruin a perfect weekend by bringing up Frank's name. Also, he didn't know what Rachel's response would be or her current feelings toward Frank. Now that Frank was free, would Rachel want to start all over again, or even consider sleeping with him as she had in the past? The thought of this was more than Jason could or wanted to handle and the intense jealousy he felt surprised him.

They spent the balance of their time together walking the beach, eating and making love. At one point Rachel said, "I hate to confess this but that Friday night after we went to the theater with Jack and Jean and you left my apartment, I was sure you would return. I changed into a sexy nightgown. After about thirty minutes after you didn't knock or telephone, I called your hotel room. I was going to thank you for the lovely evening and hope you'd ask to return. But your line was busy." Jason shook his head.

"The next morning I telephoned the hotel and found you had already checked out. I couldn't understand it since you told me you had reservations on an afternoon flight. It was then that I knew you'd never call again. And I was right. And when you wouldn't accept my call at the office the following week, I thought you had just used me and threw me on the pile of women who must have felt as I did that night." She looked at him now with a glint in her eye.

"There's something else I should tell you which is rather funny in retrospect. That Wednesday night you fell asleep on the sofa, it was Mary Howard on the phone asking me to spend the weekend with them in Berkeley Springs and to bring someone along. Phil specifically mentioned you since he knew I was getting the information from him for your first visit to Europe. I thought of asking you that night, but you were so tired I decided to wait. Then the next day, you seemed so adamant about returning to San Francisco on Saturday afternoon, I didn't mention it. The telephone call on Friday night that angered you so much was Mary, asking if you could make it. Isn't that ironic? If you had come back that night, I would have tried to talk you into spending the weekend with me at Phil and Mary's."

Jason shook his head. "I also have a confession. After Jack, Jean and I left your apartment, I went for a long walk. As I rounded the corner to return to your apartment, I saw a taxi stop in front of your building and a young man got out and went inside. He looked

The Purloined Encryption Caper

exactly like the man in the picture in your computer room, signed Jeff." He looked at her with a smirk. "I confess that I checked out both of the bedrooms during my second visit to your apartment to see if there were any signs of a live-in companion. I was sure he was the person who had telephoned you when you asked us to leave so you could meet him."

"My, you really don't think very highly of me, Jason, do you? So that's why you asked me about Jeff." Rachel vowed to remove Jeff's picture when she returned.

They both hated to think of Tuesday when they'd have to abandon their idyllic interlude. "When will I see you next?" Jason asked.

"It depends on when you next visit Washington."

"I can't wait that long. As a matter of fact, the end of next week is Christmas. Do you have holiday plans that can't be changed? If not, come to San Francisco and stay through New Year's. Your office will be closed. If you're going to become a part of my life, and I hope you'll think seriously about it, you should at least have the opportunity to meet my family first." Rachel was shocked by his statement and wasn't quite sure whether this was a proposal, but didn't want to ask.

"I have no plans. Jack and his wife are joining his sister and Phil and Mary are going to New York for the holidays so I thought I'd catch up on my reading. Much as I'd love to, I don't think it'll be possible to get a plane reservation to San Francisco at this late date."

"If I can get a reservation for you, will you come?" he asked.

"Yes," she said. She thought afterwards that he might think differently after he returned to his home territory.

"I'll phone mother and tell her that she'll have an extra guest for Christmas dinner. I know she'll love you as much as I do." Jason was delighted at the thought of her visiting him for a change.

"I'm not so sure," she said. "I don't do mothers well. My own was, of course, different."

Sitting on the deck that evening, they were quiet and pensive thinking of Tuesday and the real world away from the Outer Banks. Jason had taken several rolls of film that he planned to have developed in California. This time he would at least have pictures of her near him, even if she were almost three thousand miles away.

On Monday night, Rachel fixed dinner at the cottage. Then they packed for the trip home the next day. Jason made a fire and they sat holding hands in silence for a long time. "Let's go to bed, darling. It may be a long time until we hold each other again and feel our bodies meld together." Rachel turned, kissed him passionately and led him into her bedroom.

Since the meeting at Phil's house in Berkeley Springs, Mark had followed up on their chance sighting of Hans Schmidt. Was this an innocent visit to a friend's cabin or was there something more sinister involved? Rachel had given Mark the names of the individuals at the Hill reception which she got from Tom. Since there was no FBI file on most of them, he had faxed the list to Phil to check the CIA files.

The Purloined Encryption Caper

Phil was concerned that there might be a leak at the CIA causing Miriam to see Jason rather than Francois during Jason's first visit to Paris. He decided to do the research himself or ask only those individuals he personally knew would be "clean". What Phil discovered was that five of the individuals, all Europeans, had served together at NATO headquarters in Brussels and were members of their countries' intelligence organizations. Most had spent time in the Middle East and still maintained contacts there. Doesn't the State Department check out the participants in their programs, he wondered?

Rather than e-mail or fax messages to the CIA station chiefs in the five home countries of the NATO conspirators, Phil decided to call the station chiefs directly on a scrambled, secure line so no one else at the stations would have access to the information. What he found out by the end of the week was that all five NATO officials had pulled strings to be participants in the State Department's program, and their governments acquiesced to their requests readily. Also, their governments asked them to have as their highest priority economic intelligence, specifically getting the latest encryption technology any way possible.

However, through penetration of these intelligence agencies, the CIA officers in Europe also discovered that the individuals were considered by their colleagues to be more unsavory than most, with strong ties to suspect individuals in Middle and Far East countries. If they did manage to obtain economic secrets, their governments would be delighted. If the U.S. found out and objected, their governments would have deniability should it become necessary. Phil passed this information on to Mark and Phil asked his colleagues in Europe to continue searching for more information that might be of interest.

Mark had identified several ex-FBI employees now living in the Berkeley Springs area to undertake miscellaneous activities on his behalf. Those former employees were now considered locals who would not raise eyebrows if they asked questions. His assignments were first, rent the cabin he had identified with Rachel near Rainbow's End and furnish it with sufficient supplies to be comfortable for several people to hole up for an extended period. Next, check the County Courthouse to identify who was registered as the owner of Rainbow's End, see if the owners were renting or occupying the cabin, and how long the ownership has existed. When this was completed, Mark asked his people to call him immediately. He wanted to visit the cabin when it was rented and furnished.

By that Wednesday, Mark got his call and headed up to Berkeley Springs. He found his cabin, aptly named Lookout View, was ideal for his purpose. With high-powered binoculars, one could watch the comings and goings at Rainbow's End, especially since it was winter and the trees were barren. With a telescopic lens camera, they could take pictures of any visitors. Mark now had to stock the cabin, find a young FBI man or couple willing to stay there for the next few months to keep a watch on Rainbow's End and undertake the surveillance. By noting the frequency of meetings and those involved, he should be able to discern a pattern

The Purloined Encryption Caper

of its use and by whom. He had thought of bugging the house but decided against it. They were obviously trained intelligence agents who would check out the place each time before a meeting and there was also the possibility of an FBI mole.

Once Mark knew the use pattern and felt it safe, he would enter Rainbow's End with a colleague and see if there was evidence that could incriminate the owners, especially if there were any firearms or possibly a computer setup. He would ask the FBI or CIA to get State to schedule a full day's activities for the European participants' program in Washington so he could enter their cabin without possible detection and see what was there. He could easily get a search warrant within a matter of hours, if necessary.

He learned that the cabin had been sold to Miriam Gauthier, a French woman, who told the real estate agent she wanted a place to bring her nephews and nieces during their school vacations to acquaint them with nature. The name meant nothing to Mark but he would check with Phil or perhaps have him check with the Paris CIA station.

One interesting bit of news emerged. It appeared that while Mark's people were checking on the ownership of Rainbow's End at the Morgan County courthouse, the clerk asked him why the sudden French interest in this area. A Frenchman had visited the courthouse only about a month ago to check on the ownership of a cabin in the Whispering Pines Development, a cabin owned by Philip and Mary Howard.

The next day Mark telephoned Phil and asked to meet him, either for lunch or dinner, wherever or whenever Phil could get away, at Kazan's, a Turkish restaurant in McLean, not far from CIA Headquarters. Mark explained his recent actions and gave Phil the news about Pierre's knowledge of his West Virginia cabin in Whispering Pines. "What I don't know is whether they've had your place watched or have tried to bug it."

"On the latter," Phil noted, "don't worry. I run a check each time I enter and I also have a scrambler phone, so tapping it wouldn't do them much good. My only concern is whether they have identified our PTConcern group together. And I wonder why they checked. Mary and I have owned the cabin for over five years and we've never had to be concerned about being watched or afraid to use it. Mary has even gone there alone at times. I won't allow that anymore."

"Have you ever heard about a French woman named Miriam Gauthier, or could you ask your station chief to check her out for me? The Rainbow's End cabin was purchased by her according to the records at the Morgan County courthouse." Mark asked.

Phil blanched and began to see a few connections emerge. "Yes, but I doubt she'll be a frequent user. She lives in Paris. She must've bought it for the group. She's also a member of the French intelligence service but working under cover as a French technology company vice president. She is more a lady of fortune than an honorable member of the intelligence community, and, as I understand, is not above offering sexual services for information or position." He paused and smiled at his last statement as he reviewed her file mentally.

The Purloined Encryption Caper

"We've been watching her for several months and she spends a great deal of time trying to seduce U.S. businessmen with invitations to her Paris apartment. A few have stayed over night. I hear from our Paris station that she's a sometimes lover of Pierre's, as well as her boss, Francois Dupont." Phil smiled. "It's just like Pierre to be free of any real estate entanglements so he can cut and run. Or else, maybe our Mademoiselle Miriam is the prime organizer of this enterprise." He'd have to make a special effort to warn Jason personally, not through Rachel or Jack.

"What's new with your surveillance of Rainbow's End? Any visitors recently?" Phil wanted to move the subject away from Miriam.

"Phil, I'm still trying to identify somebody or a couple to stay in our cabin for surveillance. So far, none of the young FBI agents has risen to the bait. My next move is to identify a retired FBI agent who'd like to be back in the business for a while. But, I'm afraid that'll take time. When last I talked to Rachel, she said she would be free during the holidays, so I thought I'd ask her to spend the next few weeks up there with me. I'd ask Ruth to come too, except she'll be moving into her own apartment then." Mark studied Phil to determine his reaction.

"I'm against it," Phil said. "I'd like to keep Rachel out of this part of our project, if you don't mind. The less she knows about this, the better it'll be for her. Let me check to see if any retired colleagues of mine would be interested in having a few months there. Many times new retirees are bored being uninvolved and welcome a change. And they wouldn't be encumbered with children to complicate matters."

The next day Phil identified the perfect couple, Jan and Miles Hanson. Miles was a former operations officer in the CIA station in Brussels but had not served in an overt diplomatic position and, therefore, would be unknown to former NATO officials. They were available immediately and looked forward to an exciting few months. Their children were grown with kids of their own who would undoubtedly visit, which would give the occupancy an air of naturalness.

Over the weekend while Jason and Rachel were enjoying the North Carolina seashore, the setup Mark arranged had paid off. On Saturday, four individuals had been sighted and Miles dutifully took their pictures. He also noted their arrival and departure times and who was with whom at the same time. There was a smaller shed or a garage that had a room on top, apparently used as an extra guest bedroom. During part of the visit, it appeared that two of the men entered that room for about an hour. Miles couldn't see what was going on, since it was late in the afternoon and the lights in the room were very dim. Then on Sunday, four people came again. As usual, he noted the arrival and departure times of the individuals and took as many pictures as he could.

On Monday, Mark met Miles at the Virginia Farms Market outside Winchester and retrieved the schedules as well as the film to be developed and rushed back to the city to identify who was involved with the foreign visitors. He was astounded when he identified a fellow FBI employee assigned to the confidential reports

The Purloined Encryption Caper

office. One of the pictures Miles had managed to take showed the FBI employee going into the garage hand in hand with two other men whom Mark could not identify.

There were others, but except for the two of the "dirty five" foreigners and the FBI staffer, Mark didn't know who they were. He took an oversized blank poster and started his linkages chart. He put the two foreigners in the center with pictures of others in satellite positions around them. He wrote in the name of the FBI employee and over his picture identified him as FBI. Would he encounter others as well? Mark was sick at the thought and knew then that he had to be very careful about telling anyone at FBI headquarters about the project and his chart. Ruth could be trusted, so he would request she be assigned to work with him full time instead of on the current as needed basis. He also would need to check with Rachel or Tom to see if they could identify the other individuals as well as any new faces that might appear.

Mark telephoned Phil and asked him to come to his apartment where he was working. Phil identified one woman who worked in his director's office--a mousy and prudish girl who would never fit the profile of a mole. She had arrived with the Italian, who obviously had managed to seduce her, probably for information. They had spent several hours in the house alone and had emerged, according to the photos, with arms wrapped around each other.

"I'm hoping to have dinner tomorrow night with Rachel and Ruth at Rachel's place," Mark commented, "and plan to take the rest of these pictures with me to see who they can identify. I won't mention the details of the project to Rachel but she already knows about the foreigners' cabin so she'll assume we accidentally came across the visitors and took pictures. As a matter of fact, Ruth is working full time with me on this project so she is clued in," he added, and then continued.

"I'm glad that she's living so close to Rachel. I've a feeling that these guys will play dirty. I'll bet the activities up there at the cabin are for blackmail purposes. Let's keep in touch, Phil, and share information as we receive it. I assume the dirty five will return to their home countries during the Christmas holidays, especially since Washington is so dead. I'll call you if I find out anything startling from Rachel or Ruth about the other individuals."

The two members of Lovenest who had used the cabin that weekend did so not for official purposes but for purely personal sexual encounters. Clive had become quite close to his new found friends and enjoyed their sexual relations a great deal. Being a diplomat overseas in Europe, he had been watched more closely, and being married with his wife in residence with him, he had to be on his best behavior. Now, it was different. He had managed to become a part of a network of homosexuals and bisexuals who seemed to be part of the large number of political appointees in various government departments. He didn't understand how the FBI had granted them security clearances since the FBI had usually been so thorough in the past. However, he guessed that times were now different in Washington and homosexuals enjoyed an elevated status.

But that wasn't Clive's problem. He already had received confidential information from the Patent Office, the Commerce Department and a young aide to the President. He hoped that if his new-found friends and lovers started to cool off, he had enough on them for blackmail purposes that would quickly change their minds. Clive had already set up a video camera system in the room over the garage and the pictures he had were quite revealing. He could visualize them on the front pages of the Post or Times in his mind and loved to speculate on the reactions they would provoke. Both he and Carlo were told by Pierre to stay away from the cabin over the Christmas holidays, but neither was going back to Europe as Pierre was and they both agreed between themselves to be discreet and use the cabin whenever they could. Pierre would never know.

CHAPTER 12

On the return to Washington, Rachel and Jason stopped for a late lunch at Nick's Restaurant on the York River.

"My folks always stopped here on our drive home. My father loved this place. I don't know why except he said they have the best broiled flounder in Virginia, so big that it fell off the plate." Rachel thought about her parents and wondered what they would think of Jason. She was sure her father would approve since Jason and he had the same background and her parents would consider Jason a serious businessman who would financially take good care of their daughter. That had been her father's concern when he had his parental talk with her before she went off to Europe.

"A penny for your thoughts," Jason said.

"I was thinking of the times I used to stop here with my folks."

"Do you think they'd approve of me?" Jason asked, as if reading her mind.

"Is there any reason why they shouldn't?"

"None that I can think of," he responded.. "By the way, in Manteo when I asked about our future relationship, you said to wait until after the weekend. The weekend is over and I still haven't heard your answer."

"Let's see how you feel when you get back to California. After all, we've only been together on my turf," Rachel reminded him.

"I'll accept that answer only if you will come to California for the holidays. If not, you'd better give some thought to our future together so we can talk about it before the holidays. I love you and want you with me. I've already told you that." Jason began eating, thereby ending the topic.

After lunch, as they headed to Washington, Rachel thought about his comments and couldn't figure out whether he was proposing marriage or not. He never asked the question: will you marry me? If he only wanted her to live with him, she knew she couldn't do it, regardless of how strongly she felt.

"You know, Jason, after the meeting at Phil's, Mark and I were returning to Washington when we saw Hans Schmidt in Berkeley Springs. He's the German we met at the Hill reception. I don't think he saw me or if he did, didn't recognize me. Mark followed his car and we watched him turn into a driveway about a mile from Phil's place. There were two other rental cars there similar to the one Hans was driving. We took the license numbers and Mark's checking them out. Something very strange is going on. What I can't understand is why Hans had a rental car and not an Embassy car which would be normal. I've been

The Purloined Encryption Caper

curious and am hoping to get more information when I get back."

"Which reminds me, Cindy asked me to tell you Mark wanted to talk with you. I forgot," Jason said sheepishly.

"I'll call him tomorrow or maybe Ruth will know what he wants," she said with a smile. "I can't understand why you're jealous of Mark."

"I never had a jealous bone in my body until I met you," he said grabbing her hand. "And I never felt so insecure with a woman, either."

As they approached Dulles Airport, Jason looked at Rachel. "I'm going to miss you more than you'll know, but I'll call you tonight from San Francisco." When she stopped to let him unload his luggage, he kissed her lovingly. "Don't forget me and remember, I love you very much."

Rachel knew she would, and suddenly realized she had to go back to her regular life in Washington. She had gotten so used to having Jason next to her.

When she reached her apartment, Ruth had not yet returned home from the office, so Rachel went into her bedroom and began to look through the mail that had accumulated. There didn't seem to be much of importance, only bills, ads and a few invitations to Christmas parties on the Hill or at some government offices. There were a few Christmas cards, but not so many that she would have to feel guilty for not yet having sent any. After the first of the year, I'll mail New Year's greetings with an Open House invitation to introduce Ruth to the people I've met so far, Rachel thought.

She had finished unpacking when the telephone rang. It was Jason.

"I've made reservations for you to fly to San Francisco on Wednesday, December 22. I'll talk to you later, but I just wanted to let you know so you could make plans. I arranged to have the tickets mailed to you, so you should get them within the next few days. I've got to run to catch my plane. Thanks again. It was a wonderful weekend. I love you, Rachel, very much."

"Thanks, Jason. I was going to call for reservations tomorrow, but I appreciate this. I love you, too, and will miss you." This was the first time she had uttered those words to Jason.

"Welcome back," Ruth said as she entered the apartment. "Gee, it's been lonesome without you. Mark asked about you several times and Tom called. I said you'd probably call them tomorrow. Did you have a good time? Don't tell me. I can tell by the happy look on your face."

"Yes, I had a marvelous time." She decided against telling Ruth right away about Jason.

Ruth continued. "I'm going to be your neighbor. An apartment became available four doors down the hall, so I grabbed it. It's exactly like yours. The current resident is moving out shortly before Christmas, so I'll have the holidays to get settled. I've already called the storage company and they'll deliver my effects right after Christmas. Soon, you'll have your place all to yourself again, although I sort of enjoyed being your roommate."

The Purloined Encryption Caper

"I'll miss you, too, but am glad you'll still be close. How about a bite out tonight? We'll celebrate your new digs."

"You're on. I hear there's an awesome Vietnamese Restaurant nearby called Nam Viet. Is that okay? And I'm buying. I have to start doing something to repay you for taking me in and saving me from the dreary hotel existence. "

It was good to get back to the office the next day and finalize the end of year newsletter. This one would be marked "confidential" and mailed to each CEO with requests not to distribute to staff or board members. In some cases, it would include a covering letter with specific information pertinent only to that company. Jack and Rachel had Phil check out their clients to see if any were ignoring existing U.S. laws, or had suspicious dealings either in the U.S. or overseas. All had come out clean. A major part of the newsletter was in the column under Jack's name. Rachel wanted the company executives to take it seriously and Jack could also stress the importance of confidentiality.

In his column, drafted by Rachel, Jack mentioned the increase of industrial espionage and the major suspected culprits, the operational methods, emphasizing the need to tighten their security systems safeguarding their product information. Also attached was a sterilized copy of a report prepared by the FBI's U.S. National Counterintelligence Center outlining the number of cases that had been reported as well as the cost to U.S. industry. Jack felt the companies would take an official government report more seriously.

"Many cases go unreported for fear of complaints by company investors," Jack's column stated. "You'll see in the attached FBI report that 73 percent of the incidents took place in the United States, and the company data had been divulged in the majority of cases by either ex- or current employees. Therefore, it is critically important for companies to establish a system to assure the reliability of each employee." Jack hoped in reading Rachel's draft that he wasn't scaring his clients too much, but he continued his advice. "I would, therefore, like to call to your attention key FBI recommendations for your consideration.

"Also, it might be wise for each CEO to review ex-employees personnel files who were fired, dismissed or resigned, or who may hold a grudge against the company. The same is true of board or advisory committee members."

Jack suggested that special attention be given to visitors or individuals who identify themselves as potential customers. "You should be sure to ask for appropriate identification. Corporate espionage is preventable, but the management of each company has the main responsibility for the security of its products. While the U.S. government can help, the private companies are really our first line of defense."

Rachel faxed copies to both Mark and Phil for review before forwarding it to their clients. She didn't want to say anything she shouldn't. Also, she didn't want to use e-mail since she didn't want to leave a paper trail.

The Purloined Encryption Caper

"Good morning, May," Jason said as he entered his office on Wednesday. "I hope you got all my faxes and FedEx packages to distribute to the staff." He was glad that Rachel insisted he complete his trip report at the beach.

"Yes, and I've scheduled a meeting this afternoon at two. I hope you had a productive time in Washington. I hadn't realized you planned on returning by way of Washington." She was awaiting his explanation. None came.

May had been with Jason since he opened his office. Her husband was Jason's former boss at Hewlett-Packard and had been a mentor of sorts since that time. Currently, he ran his own successful consultancy firm. May initially offered to help Jason as a friend when he desperately needed inexpensive labor, but she stayed on and had become his most trusted ally. Everyone loved her and confided in her. This was most important to Jason who could be quiet and reserved at times with his staff.

"You don't have to be coy, May. I know you're really asking me why I stayed over in Washington and the material was sent from North Carolina." May smiled. "Let's say it was for personal reasons." He smiled but did not elaborate.

May realized she would get no further explanation. "As soon as you're settled, I'll bring you some coffee and review the mail with you. There are several items which need your immediate attention, and some personal invitations to Christmas parties. Also, I need to talk to you about our office party that I've scheduled for December twenty-third. I hope that's okay. Here's a tentative guest list. Also, Claire's law firm is having an office party this afternoon at six. I assume you'll attend."

"No, May. Please send my regrets." He scanned the office guest list, adding names and deleting others. "The list for our party looks fine with the few changes I've made." May noticed that Claire's name had been removed and Rachel Brown's had been added.

"Also, would you take these film rolls to the camera shop and have them developed? See if they can be ready by five this afternoon, if possible. I'll stop and pick them up on my way home. I'd be grateful." Jason then sat down and started going through his in-basket.

At the meeting, he told his staff that the office would close during the holidays as usual, starting December twenty-fourth until January third. Normally, Jason used this period to catch up on work and reading but still came to the office. This time Rachel would be with him.

"I'll be in the Bay Area during the holidays, if you need me," May volunteered.

"Thanks, but I don't plan on coming in this year. I think we all should take a rest." May wasn't fooled by Jason's evasive answers. When Jason hadn't returned as scheduled, May telephoned Cindy to find out where Jason had gone and Cindy was her usual talkative self.

May was actually delighted. She didn't like Claire, who treated any woman without a senior professional status with disdain. What Claire didn't realize was that Jason considered May an indispensable professional in his company, who, in essence, really operated like an administrative vice president.

The Purloined Encryption Caper

That afternoon, May picked up the pictures and left them on Jason's desk. At the end of the day, Jason looked at them and selected a number he wanted to frame. He planned to do some Christmas shopping that evening and, in the process, buy some frames. While it might surprise some of his staff, he wanted to have a picture of Rachel on his desk as well as at his house. They would meet her next week at the office party, so they might as well identify her as Jason's woman from the very start. And Jason didn't want any of his bachelor staff asking Rachel out.

The unpleasant part of the day came after the staff meeting when Jason confronted Sam Penderton again about Miriam.

"Sam, I have to talk to you about something rather personal." Jason was not very good at this type of discussion, especially since he and Sam went back several years.

"As I mentioned after my last trip to Paris, I met a woman by the name of Miriam Gauthier, who told me she knew you--intimately. She tried to put the make on me so I assume she did the same to you. You were rather vague about your relationship the last time we talked. But I need to know, did she succeed?"

Sam got up from his chair, walked to the window and looked out. "I'm afraid she did. It was at a time when my wife and I were having major problems and I was lonesome and needed consoling. Miriam only too gladly provided it," he answered hesitantly.

"Did you give her any details about our new designs or planned technologies?" Jason asked, narrowing his eyes. "Please think hard, Sam. This is very important," Jason added.

"No, none more than I discussed in my paper I presented at the meeting. I'm not that much of a fool. But what's wrong?" Sam was getting apprehensive.

"I was told she works for French intelligence and, much worse, screws her own country by selling technology or competitors' intelligence to the highest bidder, including, as I understand, the Middle Eastern thugs, such as Iran and Iraq."

"Jesus," Sam said. "Let me think back a ways and review my paper. Remember, that was the conference I talked about encryption technology and the importance of companies having the right to sell their products, either in the States or abroad, without government interference."

"Sam, what I'm afraid of, and the FBI is as well, is that she'll try to blackmail you. She knows you're married. If she contacted your wife, how would that affect your marriage?"

"God, it couldn't happen at a worse time. A few months ago when I met Miriam, my wife and I were temporarily separated and at the point of divorce. Now, we're trying to put our marriage back together. This might just kill it. And I found out in all this that I'm still very much in love with my wife." Sam looked shaken with the news.

"Don't worry about it, yet," Jason replied. "Miriam mentioned that she might take you up on your offer for her to visit San Francisco in January, so you have some time yet to think about your time with her. The FBI thinks she'll make a play."

The Purloined Encryption Caper

"I really didn't invite her to visit me here. I said she should visit San Francisco some time since it's such a beautiful city. Thanks, Jason, for warning me." Sam sheepishly looked at Jason. "Will you ask me to leave the firm?"

"No, Sam. I've been in touch with several government officials who've had their eye on her. I'll let you know if we hear anything further. Okay?" He put his arm around Sam's shoulder to reassure him that he wasn't angry. Jason was sorry he had to be so blunt with Sam, especially since he himself had almost succumbed to Miriam's sexual advances.

When Jason arrived home the next day, he found his mother waiting for him. They had planned dinner together that evening. She was early.

"My, she's pretty," Jenny Conrad said looking at the pictures Jason had taken on his long weekend with Rachel. "Someone I should know about? You've never had framed pictures of a woman around your house before. Could she be the person who'll join us for Christmas dinner?"

"So many questions," Jason said as he kissed his mother's cheek. "Yes, she is. Her name is Rachel Brown and she works with Jack Warden in Washington. She'll be in San Francisco during the holidays, staying here with me, if you must know."

"Are you in love with her?" his mother questioned boldly. Jason was a little taken aback by her direct questioning.

He hesitated before answering. "Yes, I am. As a matter of fact, I'm crazy about her. I've never felt so strongly about a woman before. Perhaps I shouldn't have told you, in case things don't work, but at this point, it's hard to hide my feelings." Jason then fixed drinks.

"Jason, will you take some advice from an old woman? Marry her. Jump in with both feet and be grateful that you've found someone you love. I confess I've never seen you in this state before, certainly not when you were involved with Terry. And I've always thought that Claire was really a convenience for you. There didn't seem to be any fire. Don't wait or weigh the consequences. I know you're not the impetuous type, but have you asked her to marry you yet?"

"No. I've told her I loved her and I think she loves me, at least she said so when I left Washington. I thought our spending the holidays here together would give us an opportunity to see each other on my turf, give her some idea of my lifestyle here and let her meet the family. That's why I invited her to San Francisco and why I asked if I could invite her for Christmas dinner."

"Actually, Jason, I think it would be nice to have you both spend Christmas Eve with us as well. I don't think you'd shock anyone if she slept with you in your room. I assume you're sleeping together."

Jason looked at his mother with amazement.

"I hope you're not surprised or shocked by my bluntness. I've been hoping that you'd meet someone you couldn't live without. Remember, I was young once myself and know love and passion." His mother had an understanding look on her face.

"I think Rachel might feel uncomfortable sharing a bed in my parents' house without being married, so

The Purloined Encryption Caper

I think I'll decline, at least for now. She arrives the twenty-second and our office party is the next night. To have her move to your house the next day may be a little much to ask. She's not really an aggressive woman." He paused to let that sink in.

"If all goes according to my plan, I'll ask her to marry me at Christmas and if she accepts, we can get engaged on New Year's Eve. If we keep running from one social function to another, I won't have that opportunity." His mother asked for and was given a photo of him and Rachel together taken in front of her beach house. They looked so happy and very much in love. His mother was anxious to meet Rachel.

"You know, my son, this probably explains why you've been in such a dreadful mood these past weeks. I assume you had the normal difficulties and insecurities that arise in relationships. I'm certainly glad you're cheerier. Your dad and I thought it might be something like this, especially since I've received several phone calls from Claire asking about you. Have you told her yet about Rachel?"

"I mentioned to Claire that I'd met someone new after my first few evenings with Rachel. But I think Claire felt that Rachel was a passing fancy and, as usual, I'd go back to her. If it weren't for this past weekend, Claire just might have been right," he smiled impishly.

"Thank God, Jason, for this past weekend. Claire wouldn't be a good wife for you. She's far too competitive and it would be more like a business arrangement."

CHAPTER 13

With the newsletter and cover letters drafted and mailed, Rachel began to focus on Christmas shopping. She arranged to have fruit baskets sent to their clients and bought perfume and bath powder for Cindy and Susan, Jack's administrative assistant.

For Tom, she had found a perfect sweatshirt at a small Outer Banks store and a nice scarf for Mark. She wasn't sure what to give the Howards or her boss, so she settled for a large basket of exotic foods from the local gourmet shop. Not knowing Jason's family at all, she decided to send a similar basket to his mother with a note thanking her for the Christmas dinner invitation.

For Jason, she had selected a beautiful silk bathrobe that she had monogrammed. She was looking for a nice terry cloth one, too, and wanted to find slippers to match replacing his terry bathrobe which looked a little seedy at the beach house. She found a wonderful original pottery casserole dish with matching platter for Ruth which would double as a Christmas and housewarming present at an unusual shop on the Outer

Banks called *Ocean Annie's*, where she and her mother had bought dozens of unique pottery items over the years.

"I invited Mark for dinner tomorrow night, Rachel, since he's been so good to me. Hope you don't mind." Ruth inquired cautiously.

"Not at all, Ruth. I'll disappear if you want me to," Rachel volunteered.

"It's nothing like that. I'd want you here."

"Then, I'll invite Tom Fulton, too, if he's free, and we'll make it a foursome. I don't think you've met Tom yet. He's really a nice guy and has been a real buddy to me. I know you play bridge and Tom plays bridge. If Mark is also a player, perhaps we could have several rubbers after dinner."

"I don't know, but please ask Tom. I'm always anxious to meet nice guys. Most of the guys I've met at FBI headquarters are married."

Tom accepted. Tom knew how Jason felt about Rachel and how she felt about him and was wondering what the current state of their relationship was. It seemed to flow hot and cold.

One time, she asked Tom out of curiosity if Jason was the reason he had never made a pass at her during their evenings together, or was she losing her sex appeal. Tom hesitated a few minutes before answering, but finally confessed that his initial and only sexual experience had occurred when he was 15 years old. An older man in the neighborhood had seduced him and told him he was now gay and one of them. He was very shaken by the incident. Although Tom was now 30 years old, he had never had another homosexual

The Purloined Encryption Caper

experience and was afraid to have or express any feelings for any woman he met because of his past. He considered himself asexual. He seemed embarrassed, but continued his explanation.

Recently he started seeing a psychiatrist. Was he gay? That was the question he posed to his psychiatrist. The answer to that, the psychiatrist said, was his. No doctor could tell him. "Rachel, you know I'm very fond of you and had I been surer of myself, I would probably have made a pass. But I value your friendship too much to mess it up." She smiled sympathetically and dropped the subject.

The evening with Mark and Tom was a huge success. Conversation was easy, and they had fun playing bridge. Rachel told them that she was going to spend the Christmas holiday in California but didn't identify her reason as Jason.

The foursome planned to get together again for bridge in the new year. Ruth said that by then she would have her own apartment, just a few doors down the hall. Mark was pleased Ruth would be nearby since his men told him that occasionally there still was a strange man casing the apartment building at night.

"Which reminds me," Mark responded. "Remember the cabin in Berkeley Springs where we saw Hans enter? We managed to take pictures of individuals who visited over the weekend and I wondered if either you or Tom can identify anybody for me?" Mark took out the pictures of the unidentified people and spread them on the bridge table.

Rachel recognized several as people she had met at Joe Coswell's party but waited for Tom to speak first.

"I've met all of them," Tom said. "With the exception of Joe, the majority staff director of the House science committee, the rest are all political appointees at Commerce, the Pentagon or the White House. Do you have any of those yellow stickies, Rachel, so I can write down the names and positions for Mark?"

Rachel got a pack and handed it to Tom who filled in the blanks for Mark.

"Here," Tom said, as he handed the photographs back to Mark. "What do you think this means?"

"I don't know," Mark responded, "but I may have to get back to you for more information, if you're going to be in town over the holidays." Tom said he would be and gave Mark his home telephone number.

After the men left, Ruth turned to Rachel. "Since you told me that Tom is only a buddy to you and you seem to be serious about Jason, do you mind if I ask Tom over for dinner when you're in California? I really like him and he offered to help me get settled in my apartment over the holidays."

Rachel said no but felt a bit of a qualm not leveling with Ruth about Tom's past, but she felt it would be better for Tom to tell her directly, if necessary.

Rachel was excited as she boarded the plane for San Francisco. If his mother is anything like Jeff's, I'll take the next plane back to Washington, she thought. Jason is close to his family and I couldn't spend a long holiday with someone hating or snubbing me.

Jason met Rachel's flight at the San Francisco airport. "I've missed you so much," he said as he put

The Purloined Encryption Caper

his arms around her. "I can't believe we'll have more than a week together."

Jason led her to his car and began driving up through the neighboring hills covered with lush almost tropical greenery and pulled into a driveway that led to a lovely redwood house, with a vast expanse of land around it. She wondered whether this was really his house or perhaps his parents' home. When he opened the door, she knew it was his.

"This is lovely Jason. It's so California." The house was a Japanese-style redwood, with guest bedrooms on the lower level, down six steps from the entrance. The main living area took over the second floor, which was about six steps up from the entrance. It consisted of a large living-dining area separated by sliding Japanese-style panels and a deck overlooking the valley, a large kitchen with an eat-in breakfast nook and an office-library where Jason spent his time when he worked at home.

The next floor up was a large bedroom, with two areas, one off each side. They were separate dressing and bathrooms, one for each spouse, Rachel thought. Obviously, the house had been designed by a woman. There was also a large deck off the bedroom, as well as a smaller room behind the bathrooms. Probably for a nursery, Rachel thought or perhaps an office for the lady of the house.

Jason carried her luggage up to the bedroom, and when he returned to the living room fixed each a drink. "Scotch and water, I assume."

She smiled and nodded yes.

"Here's to a wonderful holiday season I never thought possible," he toasted. Then he led Rachel onto the deck and gave her a long deep kiss. He could feel his passion rise and knew he had to quench his desires. They had reservations at eight at a local restaurant. Rachel would be tired since she was operating on East coast time, and he wanted to retire early since he had a busy day ahead of him tomorrow.

Standing on the deck, Rachel wondered why Jason had bought this house. Was it for Terry, or another woman?

"I'm glad you like the house," Jason said, almost reading her mind. "My mother is always looking at places for sale. It's a favorite pastime of hers. When she saw this one, she knew it was ideal for me. I had no wife in mind at the time, but mother hoped it would give me ideas. Also, it was a good buy and she said I was throwing money away paying rent for a new three-bedroom apartment."

Over dinner, Rachel asked him about the information the office had sent and whether he thought it was helpful. She hadn't yet had time to receive any responses from other clients and she was beginning to get nervous. It was the holiday season so probably a number of the people had already gone on vacation or closed their offices for the last ten days of the year before the info package had arrived.

"Yes, of course, it's helpful," he said, "but it may have frightened others who haven't had my privileged status of meeting FBI and CIA officials in Washington." He paused to change the subject.

The Purloined Encryption Caper

"By the way, our office party is tomorrow night so you'll be meeting all of the staff and other friends in the area."

Rachel gave him a quizzical look.

He smiled impishly. "Claire or no other ex-girlfriends are coming, so you don't have to protect your back from knives. It'll only last two or three hours. The staff knows your name as far as our business relations go, but they don't know you're my girl. They may have suspected it, since I have a picture of you and one of us together on my desk." He waited for her approval, which she willingly smiled.

"Mother wants us to join them for Christmas Eve and stay through Christmas Day, but I thought that might make you feel too uncomfortable and declined her offer. I still keep my old room at my folks' house with a double bed and she didn't think we'd shock the rest of the family if we slept there together."

"I see we have a busy social season coming up," Rachel commented. "I'm not sure I brought enough of a wardrobe to suit every occasion." She then continued. "I know you've always spent Christmas Eve at home as a regular family tradition so the decision really is yours. You know what conclusions will be drawn by the rest of your family. If for some reason we break off our affair, you'll be the one in the future who'll have to answer questions. I'll be back in Washington." She watched his reaction with mixed curiosity and apprehension.

Jason was a little taken aback with her phraseology. He didn't think of their relationship as an affair. She was right, of course, but he knew what he wanted in the

Rose Ameser Bannigan

future. He wanted to marry Rachel and had hoped she wanted the same.

When they returned from the restaurant, Jason took Rachel directly to his bedroom. "It's almost one o-clock in the morning your time, and I know you must be tired. I also know that I won't be able to be next to you tonight and not make love to you." This they did with passion that neither he nor Rachel thought possible.

When they awakened the next morning, Jason reached over, drew her to him and gently made love to her again. He had never been so happy. He got dressed for the office and went down to the kitchen. He found Rachel busily making breakfast.

"I hope you don't mind," she said. "I just made myself at home." She had a glass of juice waiting for him and coffee perking with English muffins in the toaster. "Will this be enough to get you through the morning?"

"Yes, it's more than I normally have. Usually, I only have coffee and juice and if I get hungry, I ask May to get some doughnuts. By the way, the party starts at five this afternoon. I'll come by about four-thirty to pick you up. Will you be okay here all day alone?"

"Yes. It'll give me time to unpack and relax. Don't worry. I won't get lonely or bored. I'll be ready." He kissed her goodbye and drove off to work.

Rachel went back upstairs, unpacked and showered, put on a pair of slacks and T-shirt and began to explore Jason's house. She was amazed at how neat and clean it was and then realized this was not Jason's doing. He

The Purloined Encryption Caper

had a cleaning woman who came in once or twice a week, as necessary.

The four guest bedroom suites on the first floor were like hotel rooms, each with a separate bathroom. They were neat and clean but decorated with little or no imagination. She started thinking how she would change them if she lived here. The living area on the middle floor was better but very masculine, very much like Jason. Only Jason's den and the bedroom seemed lived in. When she went into the den, she saw all the framed pictures Jason had of their time on the Outer Banks. She examined them and marveled at what a difference that weekend had made in her life and wondered what was next. She would ask Jason to give her copies for her own apartment when she left.

At this point the telephone rang. She thought it might be Jason and decided to answer it.

"Hello, Rachel?" a woman's voice asked. "This is Jenny Conrad, Jason's mother. I thought it might be nice to get to know each other. So if you're up to it and Jason hasn't already booked you, perhaps we could have lunch together."

"That sounds lovely," Rachel said, not knowing for sure whether it was such a good idea. "But you'll have to give me time to change. I'm in slacks."

"Slacks are fine. That's what I'm wearing. California is rather informal. I'll be by in fifteen minutes."

Rachel didn't know how Jenny could be there so quickly. She was under the impression that Jason's parents lived in Berkeley across the Bay near the University of California campus, a good forty-five minute drive away. She fixed her makeup, combed her hair, grabbed a jacket and was downstairs waiting when Jason's mother arrived.

Jenny embraced her and started to lead her to the car.

"I don't have any keys to the house. Can we leave the door unlocked?" Rachel asked.

"Here I have a key. You should scold Jason for keeping you a prisoner," Jenny said shaking her head while she went back to lock up.

When they were in the car, heading down the hill, Jenny explained. "I had to deliver some presents near here and decided to take the chance that you might be free. I've been looking forward so much to meeting you. And, I want to set the record straight. Jason doesn't know I invited you to lunch, but I thought it might be easier for you not to walk into a house full of strangers on Christmas knowing that everyone will be eyeing you up and down. It wouldn't be with malicious feeling, but you are the first person Jason's asked to our house for Christmas dinner for many years. Naturally everyone will be curious. Also, it's obvious that Jason is crazy about you so you'll be considered a possible new member of the family."

"Mrs. Conrad, I do appreciate your being so open and honest with me and, I agree, it is reassuring. Jason hasn't told me very much about you all except that your family is very close and means a great deal to him. To say I'm not nervous wouldn't be truthful and, like you, I do believe in being honest."

"The first thing you can do is call me Jenny."

Over lunch, Jenny told Rachel about the other members of the family, her husband John, and the other

The Purloined Encryption Caper

two children, Allen and Caroline. Being the only girl and the youngest, Caroline was indeed a little spoiled by the family. None of the children were married and Jenny was beginning to wonder if they ever would be. Maybe she made home too comfortable for them.

"When I saw the pictures of you and Jason together at your beach house, I knew he loved you a great deal. I told him to marry you and quickly, not to analyze the situation too much. This is one of his faults, you know. Perhaps he gets this trait from me." Jenny seemed lost in her thoughts for a few moments and then continued.

"When I met John, his father, I had been engaged to someone else for about a year. One night I went to a party with my sister, who was not overjoyed with my fiancé, and John came over, introduced himself and then told my sister he'd take me home. My fiancé was away for several months on business at the time. John didn't take me home but instead took me to a little bar where they had music and dancing. That night I realized I really wasn't in love with my intended anymore. The vibes were so strong with this man I'd just met. John took me for a long drive and to a small roadside inn for another drink. We ended up at his place that night and made love." She paused for a breath and watched Rachel's reactions.

"I pondered our relationship and wanted to stop seeing him and discuss my feelings first with my fiancé and family before making any firm decision, even though I knew I was very much in love with John. He listened to my vacillations. His response was to ignore my questioning and continue to take me out and make love to me. I guess I was too weak to resist him. Two weeks later, we drove to Lake Tahoe and got married, thus ending any other decision. I've never regretted it, and we haven't been apart since that first night except when John's out of town on business. I still dearly love him and know our impetuous actions were right." She smiled at the memory and continued.

"Please pardon my being so forthright and perhaps venturing into something that isn't my business. But you must realize that I love my son very much and want nothing more for him than the happiness his father and I have had in our lives. I'm not the kind of mother who wants to hold on to her kids and keep them unmarried in the nest. I only ask that they find someone who'll love them and make them happy." Rachel was breathless just listening to her.

"I guess I'm telling you this for several reasons. I know my son well enough to know that he's very much in love with you and probably has been for several months. For weeks before the weekend he spent at the beach, he stormed around here ready to bit off anybody's head if they looked crosswise at him. This is very unlike Jason. He's usually a gentle person, perhaps a little restrained in his relationships and pigheaded at times. I think you love him, if your look in the pictures mean anything." While telling her story, Jenny was very animated.

She continued. "You and Jason are separated by a whole continent. When they say that absence makes the heart grow fonder, that's only after there's a legal commitment. I know it wasn't true in my case. And no commitment causes doubts to rise. When he telephones

The Purloined Encryption Caper

you and you don't answer, he'll wonder where you are, maybe thinking the worst. If you call him and he's not home, you'll think he's out somewhere and wonder with whom. And if doesn't call you, you'll think he doesn't care. None of this helps a relationship." She took a breath and then added.

"Second, why wait? If either of you is uncertain or feel that you must wait, it's better to talk about it now and clear the air. There's no substitute for honesty in any relationship. I realize I'm talking to you as I would talk to my daughter and hope you don't mind." She paused, thinking of her last statement. "Jason told me your parents were killed in an accident. It must be hard, especially at this time of year."

Rachel bowed her head and tears came to her eyes as she thought of her parents and their own holidays together. "Thank you, Jenny. Yes, I loved my parents very much and I miss them terribly. We were very close."

"I shocked Jason when I invited both him and you to come on Christmas Eve, stay through Christmas dinner, and suggested you both could sleep in his room. He felt you might be embarrassed. If that's the case, I have an extra room where you can stay, but it's ludicrous for two adults at your age very much in love not to want to sleep together. I want you to be natural with us and relaxed. We're really quite a nice group of people."

After lunch, Jenny drove Rachel around Palo Alto pointing out the various stores in the event she wanted to shop. And Jenny would love to take her shopping but realized Jason would want to occupy all of her time as soon as his office closed for the holidays.

When she dropped Rachel off she got out of the car to unlock the door, kissed Rachel on the cheek and told her how glad she was that Rachel had come into Jason's life. "Also Rachel, I already like you very much. I hope you'll reconsider and spend Christmas Eve with us. We always have such fun opening presents on Christmas morning. I guess we're all still kids at heart."

As she began to drive away, Jenny stopped and motioned Rachel back to the car. "Jason will find out that we had lunch together, but our conversation is just between us, unless you tell him what we said. I won't deny anything or, if you want, I'll confirm it." Jenny wanted Rachel to know that she could trust his mother not to take sides.

Rachel poured herself a large glass of ice water and went out on the deck to think. She liked Jason's mother. She was down to earth and definitely honest. Rachel thought about what Jenny had said. She didn't know how much she would tell Jason, but would have to tell him they had lunch together. She would also tell him that they should stay over on Christmas Eve. If she and Jason did get married, it may be the last one for a long time, especially if they had the child she knew Jason wanted. But this was a bit too much for Rachel to think about now. She had to get through this evening first.

CHAPTER 14

Shortly after four, Jason returned to pick up Rachel. "I hope you weren't too bored being here alone all day. I telephoned around noon to see if you were okay, but you must have been outside or didn't hear the phone ring."

"As a matter of fact, I wasn't here," she answered. "Your mother called and asked to take me to lunch. We had a good talk. You're very lucky to have such an understanding mother."

"Oh, my. I guess her curiosity got the better of her. Did she convince you I was a good prospect for a husband or question if you were suitable for her elder son?" Jason joked.

"On the contrary. She was open and kind and personally wanted to invite us to spend Christmas Eve with them as well as Christmas Day. She assumed we were sleeping together and said it'd be okay if we slept together there." Rachel paused before continuing. "Jason, I think we should stay over Christmas Eve since she wants us to so much. Will it shock your brother or sister?"

"Heavens no. I can assure you that my brother's no saint. He's rather a ladies' man and has women chasing him all the time. Caroline's just broken up with a guy she more or less lived with for over a year. So I don't think there are any virgins left in the Conrad household, unless my parents adopted a new kitten," he said with a smile as he kissed her lightly on the lips while walking her to his car.

"Will I know anyone at the party? I think I may have met one of your staff, but I can't remember who it was--Sam somebody or other. Will they be lying in wait to look over the boss's date?"

"The person really lying in wait will be my secretary and friend, May. She's very anxious to meet you. Several heads of other companies in the Valley have been invited, some of which are Warden clients. I don't know exactly what your practice has been in being nice to visiting male clients," he said half kidding, "other than Bill Worth."

"They haven't had the privileges you've had," she responded with a smirk.

When Rachel and Jason entered, most eyes turned to them.

May was first to come up. "Jason, there are several committee members who have already arrived. You may want to go talk with them," she suggested. "Rachel and I will get the drinks and meet you there. What will you have? Your usual gin and tonic?"

"Yes, thanks, May." He was grateful for May's ability to handle the social graces so professionally.

The Purloined Encryption Caper

"I'll have a scotch and water," Rachel said to the bartender. "May, I know now why Jason relies on you so heavily. I can learn a lot tonight watching you work the crowd. Our office parties aren't quite this elaborate."

May couldn't believe that a professional woman from Washington could be so kind to another woman. May was used to the snobbish yuppie women who were rather cutthroat and also considered answering a telephone beneath them. No one would be like that in Jason's office. May saw to that. She insisted on the administrative staff using proper titles in front of guests. Rachel was certainly a major improvement over Claire.

She delivered Rachel to Jason who, in turn, introduced her to his committee members. May observed that Rachel, unlike Claire, didn't thrust herself into the middle of the conversation but instead stood by Jason's side listening to their comments.

A few minutes later, Bill Worth saw Rachel and came over with his hand out and a broad smile.

"What are you doing here?" he asked. "Is Jason's company in trouble or are you here to see how your West Coast clients amuse themselves? Are you staying long?"

"Through New Year's. Since Washington is chilly this time of year and our office is closed, I thought I'd visit California for the holidays. Jason offered to show me around and serve as a tour guide."

"I hope he includes Electro-Systems as one of the stops." At this point, Jason joined them.

Rose Ameser Bannigan

"You see, I finally met Rachel Brown," Jason said to Bill with a smile on his face.

"You must let us host her one night and give you a break." Bill had recently heard rumors about Rachel and Jason as had most of the other Warden clients in California and was interested in their personal relationship. He vividly recalled uneasily his comments to Rachel about Claire.

"We'll be glad to accept if we can fit you in. However, I should let you know that her visit here is personal and I've spoken for all her time."

Then Jason drew Bill aside. "Bill, I'm hoping to use this time to convince Rachel that I'm a pretty good guy so she'll say yes when I ask her to marry me. Remember? You're the one who told me she was the kind of girl a guy marries. Also, don't mention Claire's name again."

Bill patted him on the shoulder. "Ouch. Good luck, old boy. Maybe we could have you both over for dinner some night. I thought Rachel could answer a few questions I have about her last newsletter."

"In that case, Rachel and I would be glad to accept. I'm sure she can answer any questions you have. She's been involved in getting the inside scoop on all the secret stealing that's going on. As a matter of fact, she may value talking with you about it."

Rachel enjoyed the party and getting to meet people she only knew by name. And she was especially glad to have met May.

"Are you up to dinner now or do you want to go to the house?" Jason asked.

The Purloined Encryption Caper

"I had enough at the party to substitute for dinner, so it's up to you," Rachel replied.

"I had enough as well. I didn't know if everyone talked to you so much they kept you away from the table. Why don't we just go home unless you want to do the town?"

"No, thanks. The house it is." Rachel was tired and wanted to relax. Tomorrow was Christmas Eve day and if they were going to spend the night at the Conrads, she wanted to have time to shop.

"Jason, I'll need some help buying presents for your family to put under the tree."

"That's not necessary. I've bought several presents for each and I'll just indicate they're from both of us."

"I'd prefer to have something under the tree from me personally. Then I'll feel more like part of the group." With this explanation, Jason agreed to help.

Jason fixed each a cup of coffee and took them upstairs to the bedroom. Rachel had already gone up and changed into something more comfortable. She was waiting for him on the deck in her dressing gown. Before he joined her, he took off his tie and hung up his jacket.

"Everyone was envious of me. They kept looking at us as if we were harboring a big secret. They may suspect that we're lovers. No one asked where you're staying."

"Are you telling me they think I'm a fallen woman?" Rachel asked, jokingly.

"Worse, they may think that you're a woman who's fallen in love with me." Jason paused before going on. "Are you really in love with me, Rachel? Enough to marry me?" Jason hadn't planned to ask her so soon, but he loved her so much he couldn't imagine that she wouldn't want the same as he did, especially since she now gave herself to him totally when they made love.

"Jason, I love you more than I thought it possible to love a man. I suppose that's one of the problems. Our relationship has happened so fast that I'm afraid you'll lose interest, or I'll get hurt again." She then paused for a moment. "Do I want to marry you? Yes, but I can't desert Jack or Phil and the project we're working on."

"I can assure you I'll never lose interest. I'm not insisting that we marry immediately, although nothing would make me happier than if you didn't go back East and stayed here. I understand your wanting to finish the project, but I assume it'll be over in a few months. That'd also give you time to train a replacement. After all, it's in my best interest as well to have Warden Associates continue to serve me efficiently." He paused. "If your answer is definitely yes, I'd like to tell my folks tomorrow night. It'd truly make this holiday a very special one." He had his arms around her waiting for her answer.

"Yes, Jason, I'll gladly marry you, but I'll need some time to get organized and make plans."

"Just so you manage to see me in the interim. It's not easy being away from you. Tomorrow, when we're shopping for presents, I want to show you a ring I hoped I could give you in the event I could charm you into a positive answer."

They went back into the bedroom and, before they undressed, Jason put his arms around her and kissed

The Purloined Encryption Caper

her. "Here's to the future Mrs. Jason Conrad," he said.

They then went to bed, into the arms of Eros and Morpheus.

Jason's family was delighted that they would stay over for Christmas Eve. After having met Rachel, Jenny phoned Jason and told him he was indeed a lucky man to have found her and hoped he would take his mother's advice. Jason didn't tell his mother about the marriage plans, wanting to keep it a surprise.

After the shopping expedition, Jason and Rachel returned to the house to pack.

"Mother asked me to buy some bread and pastries from a special shop near here," Jason said. "I'll be back in less than an hour."

Jason also wanted to pick up the engagement ring. The jeweler said it would be ready by the time he came back and Jason wanted to surprise Rachel with the ring under the tree. When he initially showed her the ring, she had remarked that it was too expensive and that he'd already spent too much money on her. He'd paid for her airline ticket to California and refused to let her reimburse him.

"You might as well get used to it, darling, since you're going to be my wife and a kept woman. Remember, you're marrying a successful businessman. I have to spend my money on something. Later, when we have children, you may have to be more frugal."

The Christmas Eve tradition in the Conrad household was to serve beef fondue for dinner with each person making a different sauce, a large Caesar salad and French bread. Dessert was usually crème caramel or cherries jubilee.

After dinner, Jason and his younger brother, Allen, who could have been his twin except for the five-year age discrepancy, disappeared from the room. Rachel helped Caroline and Jenny clear the table. Then the women went to the deck to join John who was taking orders for after dinner drinks. Suddenly, Jason and Allen joined them, carrying two bottles of champagne and six glasses.

"Tonight's a special night," Jason started, "so I think it requires a special drink." He walked over to where Rachel was standing. "We wanted you all to know that we're going to take the plunge. Rachel finally said yes." Everyone toasted and embraced Rachel and Jason. Many questions were asked and answered with Jenny insisting that they not have too long an engagement.

"I feel wicked making love to you in your parent's home, but I think our spending Christmas Eve here was a good decision. I feel like part of the family now," Rachel whispered as she snuggled close to Jason that night. She would have to call Jack and let him know before word got back from someone else, such as Bill Worth.

Rachel began thinking about all the things she would have to do and the decisions they would have to make about their wedding plans. At first, she thought of eloping. But after meeting his family, she didn't think that was the proper thing to do. She didn't want a big wedding with a white flowing dress, rather something

The Purloined Encryption Caper

simple. The major decisions would be location and date.

Jason had gone to sleep almost immediately. Rachel had not, since her mind was so crowded with thoughts of her future.

The next morning when Jason awakened, Rachel was still asleep. He crept out of bed, dressed and joined his parents, who were sitting at the kitchen counter enjoying their first cup of coffee.

"Rachel's still asleep so I decided to let her be until she wakes up. What did you think of the news? Were you really surprised?"

"No," his mother said. "All I know is that if you hadn't asked her, I would've sent her a letter with your forged signature. I think you're so well suited to each other. I only hope you don't wait too long before you produce grandchildren. I take it you both want children."

Jason assured his mother they did. "She wants at least two. I'd like four. Furthermore, I'd like to start a family immediately. I think Rachel agrees, but not until we're married and she moves to California."

"You know," his father suddenly said, "I've met Rachel before. I can't remember where or when, but I know I have. It's bothered me. Don't look askance, Jason. I don't mean that she's harboring any deep secrets. I just know I've met her someplace else. You don't care if I talk to her privately when she comes down, do you?" Jason said he didn't but had a worried frown on his face.

This reminded Jason that he hadn't yet confessed to Rachel that he probably knew the identity of her journalist ex-lover in Europe and that he and Frank were good friends. He wondered if Frank was the one who introduced his father to Rachel, but couldn't remember when his father and Frank would have been together.

He would have to find out if Frank had located Rachel through a detective agency or if she had seen him. Jason began to worry. If Frank reappeared in her life, would she break her engagement to him and be part of Frank's life again, now that Frank was no longer married? And wealthy.

Jason decided to take a cup of coffee to Rachel. How he wished they could drive to the Tahoe border and elope. That way when she returned to Washington, she'd be his wife.

"Hi, here's some coffee to give you a start. And merry Christmas." Jason put the coffee on the bedside table.

"Thanks. I need this," she replied, taking a large gulp. "I think I had too much champagne last night, but it was so good. What time is it? Is everybody up?"

"It's nine o'clock. Only my folks have stirred so far. Why don't you dress and come down. Nothing fancy. Jeans or slacks are fine until dinner."

By the time Rachel appeared, both Allen and Caroline had joined the family. "Dad's in the process of making bacon and pancakes. You'll soon find out, Rachel, that pancakes are another Conrad Christmas tradition. As soon as we finish breakfast, we can start opening our packages. When we were kids it was sheer torture to wait until after breakfast to start tearing the

The Purloined Encryption Caper

wrapping off gifts." Caroline had decided it was her job to explain her family's behavior pattern.

Rachel thought about her family traditions and what they did when she was young. They'd always gone to Christmas Eve church services and when they returned home, each was allowed to open two presents. The rest were opened as soon as she was near the Christmas tree in the morning and her parents had their first cup of coffee. After the excitement was over, her mother cooked breakfast.

The real surprise for her that day was the ring that Rachel had thought would not be ready until the following week. When she saw it, Jason went over and put it on the third finger of her left hand. "In front of God and family, I want all to know that I intend to marry this woman," he said, mockingly, in Shakespearean prose. She blushed becomingly.

CHAPTER 15

After all the presents were opened, Jason's father offered to show Rachel the garden. Their home, too, was a lovely redwood deck-style house, with several levels extending over lush greenery. It was strange for Rachel to see flowering shrubs at this time of year as well as geraniums and impatiens still in flower. It reminded her very much of Hong Kong.

"You know, I have the distinct impression we've met before." He watched Rachel for her reaction. "But I can't remember where or when. Tell me something about yourself and maybe it'll come to me." He made a conscious effort not to sound like an inquisitor.

"There's really nothing to tell. My father was a professor of electrical engineering at the University of Pittsburgh, and lectured at Carnegie-Mellon. I was an only child and, therefore, never had any competition with siblings or ever had any reason to fight my parents. We were very close and did a lot of things together. I went to college where my dad taught and lived at home until my senior year. He'd encouraged me to go away for college and get worldlier, however, I loved being at home with them. But he insisted. He felt I needed to expand my horizons and also wanted me to graduate from his alma mater. At the University of Pittsburgh, I studied engineering and technology development, and at Northwestern, added journalism as a minor. I'd always been good at writing and dad thought I should sharpen this talent." She paused, thinking back of her frequent conversations with her dad.

"He was a wonderful father. His whole life was focused on his family. When I was about ten, my folks built a cottage on the Outer Banks in North Carolina." She looked up at Jason's father. "That's where Jason stayed with me the other weekend. Mother and I would spend all of our summers there and Dad would join us when possible. You see, he did a lot of consulting with corporations during summer vacation to pay for the beach cottage and put money in the bank for my education."

"Rachel, now I remember where I met you. It all comes back to me. Was your father Hugh Brown?"

"Yes," she responded with some surprise.

"I knew him," John confessed. "We used to be on several engineering advisory panels together. About eight years ago, we were both consulting for a company in Ohio, near Cleveland. I was waiting for a taxi in front of our hotel to take me to the airport. Hugh was waiting there, too, so I asked him if he wanted to share a cab. He said he was waiting for his daughter to pick him up. She was coming from Chicago and they were driving home to Pennsylvania together. You suddenly arrived and he introduced us. Initially, he said he took

The Purloined Encryption Caper

the consultancies to save for your college education, but instead you went to his university where there was minimal tuition and lived at home. At Northwestern, you'd received a full scholarship."

"Yes. When I think of all the bad press fathers and husbands get now, I don't understand it." Rachel was almost in tears remembering her dad.

"Jason told me your parents were killed in an automobile crash. I was so sorry to hear that. Hugh was so good at his profession and had so much to offer. It must have been very difficult for you." He paused, realizing how emotional Rachel had become. "I know you and Jason aren't married yet, but I hope you'll look on me as a substitute father. If Jason ever mistreats you, remember he has me to answer to. Not that he will, but Jason can be very difficult and pig-headed at times. He's been single for a long time and used to having his own way. Don't give in too easily."

Jason watched Rachel and his father walk up the driveway toward the house and was curious why she suddenly turned to him, put her arm around his shoulder, and kissed him on the cheek. It took me a long time to get Rachel to put her arms around me and kiss me, he thought, but dad manages to do it in one day.

Caroline, Jason's sister, really liked Rachel, much as she was prepared not to, and initially was upset when she first heard Rachel would be spending the holidays with them. Caroline assumed Rachel would be like Claire, critical of Caroline and her unwillingness to embrace the current fashionable feminist ways. Rachel seemed much warmer and more interested in

Caroline as a person. After breakfast when she and Rachel were helping with dinner preparations, she told Rachel she hoped they would be able to spend some time together.

"Of course, Caroline. Why don't I ask Jason to invite you to lunch one day?"

"No," Caroline responded. "I mean just the two of us."

That opportunity presented itself several days after Christmas. "Something's come up, Rachel, and I need to spend today at the office. If you'll drop me off, you can keep the car," Jason remarked as he put down the phone.

"If you don't mind, Jason, I'll call Caroline and see if she'll join me. So, I probably won't need the car." He was impressed at how quickly she became one of the family.

"Caroline, I find that I'm going to be free most of the day, today. How about lunch or shopping at one of the local malls?" Rachel asked.

"Great," Caroline responded, "but instead of doing the local scene why don't I drive you to the city? Have you been in San Francisco yet?"

Rachel hadn't and was glad that the first time she would return to a town where she had been so unhappy would not be with Jason.

"I'll pick you up in about an hour. You'll love San Francisco," Caroline commented enthusiastically. Rachel knew that Caroline had a purpose for this outing, but wasn't quite sure what it was. She had asked Jason that question earlier.

The Purloined Encryption Caper

"Perhaps she wants to see how you got started in your career. Caro, my nickname for her, just got her master's in political science and international affairs this past quarter and she's beginning to wonder what she should do. Until recently, she was going with a guy and I'm sure she thought she'd marry him and that would take care of everything. But they broke up recently. Mom's told her to take her time, but Caro wants to begin a life of her own. She's twenty-four and most of her friends are either getting married or settling into a career." Jason thought before going on.

"Quite honestly, Rachel, I don't think she'll ever be a real career woman. She's very much like you, in some ways. If only she could find a good man to marry, as you did," he said, winking at her. "I think she'd be happy and make someone a good wife. I guess mom's right. We Conrad children take a long time to find the right mate." He took Rachel's hand and pressed it to his lips.

When they were heading along the freeway to San Francisco, Rachel started the conversation. "Caroline, I can't tell you how wonderful I think your family is and how lucky I am to get a sister like you. I've never really had one, so it'll be a new experience. As a matter of fact, I've never had a sibling, so entering your family with both a sister and brother will be fun. I hope you and Allen will be patient with me if I don't know how to act at times as a member of a larger family."

"You should realize that I've been very spoiled, being the youngest child with a doting father and two older brothers to look after me. I've always been very close to Jason, much closer to him actually than Allen, in a way. And he's always been there for me." Caroline was waiting to see if Rachel would respond.

"I'd never do anything to separate you and Jason, and you'll always be welcome to stay with us after we're married," Rachel assured her.

As they had arrived in "Baghdad by the Bay", Rachel was lost in her thoughts of the last time she had been here preparing to meet Jeff. She also thought about the days after the memorial service when she walked the streets trying to decide what she should do. It was something like Caroline was going through now, except she had Jason and his family to console her.

"What are you going to do now that you've graduated?" Rachel asked.

"That's the problem. I don't know. San Francisco doesn't hold much promise for someone interested in politics and international affairs. And I've never visited Washington or the East Coast, other than a few days as a tourist in New York, so I don't know what's available there. How did you get started, Rachel? I hear it's not easy to land a job in Washington."

Rachel thought before answering. "I was lucky. When I was about to graduate, I was hired to go to Europe right out of college, so I never had to pound the pavement for my first job. If you're interested in testing the waters in Washington, why don't you come for a visit? You can stay with me and see what's available. I have an extra bedroom with an easy commute to DC, and it'd give us a chance to get to know each other. I'll promise Jason and your folks that I'll take good care of you and keep you out of trouble."

The Purloined Encryption Caper

They were walking along Union Square at the time. Caroline stopped and took Rachel's arm. "That'd be such fun. You're sure I wouldn't be in the way?"

Rachel assured Caroline she wouldn't. As a matter of fact she'd be glad to have a roommate again, however briefly. Rachel had gotten used to having someone around, either Ruth or Jason, and it'd be lonely now without either.

They had a leisurely lunch and managed to find some bargains at Nordstrom's and some of the other up-scale department stores. They returned to Jason's house late in the afternoon as he was getting out of his car.

"You two look as if you swallowed a canary," Jason said, waiting at the door. "Come in for a drink, Sis, and, if you want, join us for dinner. We're going to a local place down the road." Caroline willingly accepted.

At dinner, Jason and Caroline talked about San Francisco and how it had changed and what things would interest Rachel once she moved here. After they finished, Caroline thanked Jason and Rachel and drove back to her home across the Bay.

"What did you two talk about today?" Jason asked as they were getting ready to call it a night.

"Caroline is trying to figure out what she wants to do now. She's interested in seeing what Washington has to offer, so I've invited her to stay with me. It'd give us a chance to get to know each other. By the way, she said your family really likes me and is looking forward to having me join the family. Even your brother agrees, who Caroline thinks is beginning to think seriously about marriage, too. All he has to do, she said, is find a girl who'll have him. She's really quite funny and adores you. I told her that she'd always be welcome to come over."

"You're really getting to know more about my family than I may want you to," said Jason half seriously, " but I do think it'd be good for Caroline to get away from here for awhile, as well as from mother. Not that I think we coddle her too much, but it'd be new territory and she'd be able to become less dependent and develop some self-confidence. We'd always be here for her, but maybe it'll help her decide what she wants out of life. And it might help her emotionally if she's still moaning over her last love."

By New Year's, Rachel was looking forward to moving to California. They decided to get married in Washington and, hopefully, Jason's family would fly East for the ceremony. Otherwise, his family would host a wedding reception for them when she came to live in California. The actual date would be determined by Jack's ability to recruit a replacement for Rachel and for Phil and Mark to release Rachel from the project.

Two heavy hearts said goodbye at San Francisco airport on a rainy Sunday in early January. As they parted, Rachel looked at Jason. "I'm glad that I no longer doubt you. Before, I didn't really trust you and was afraid you'd just use me and I'd get hurt again. I guess I'm getting over my insecurity in relationships."

As her plane soared into the clouds, Jason realized he hadn't told Rachel about Frank. It had really slipped his mind until she mentioned her earlier distrust and her insecurity. As soon as he arrived in the office the next day, he would determine how soon he could go

The Purloined Encryption Caper

to Washington, even if it were strictly for personal reasons. Or perhaps, he could persuade Rachel to return to California in a few weeks. He didn't think he could go too long without seeing her.

He knew he also had to tell Claire about his engagement although she may have already heard about it. He was glad he had mentioned Rachel to Claire earlier. It would make the final break much easier.

He tried to phone Claire that afternoon but there was no answer. He then decided to write her a note informing her about his wedding plans and hoping the note arrived before she heard it through friends.

Indeed, Claire had heard about Jason's engagement to Rachel. Little did Jason realize that Claire had no intention of letting him go so easily or bowing out of his life gracefully. She had her heart set on becoming Mrs. Jason Conrad and would now do anything within her power to break up Jason's relationship with Rachel. In Claire's world, engagement rings didn't mean much-- the end justified the means.

Claire wasn't exactly sure what her tactics would be but she definitely had to develop a plan. She decided she would try to woo Jason's mother to her side. They always seemed to get along, and Claire couldn't imagine that Jenny would be taken in by someone who was an interloper in the California scene. As a locally-established professional woman, Claire felt she was far better suited to be Jason's wife. Also, she would send a box of candy to May, even though she didn't think May much liked her. But Claire had to develop allies quickly, something she had never bothered about before. She thought that Jason was a done deal and even when he first mentioned Rachel, Claire thought her a passing fancy that wouldn't last. Her feminine wiles reverted to basic drives.

To initiate her plan, Claire telephoned Jenny and invited her for lunch the next day. Claire would be very sweet and caring about Jason and express her concern that Jason needed a good woman to assist him in his business and Claire was just that person. She would pretend that she didn't know Jason was engaged since he himself hadn't yet told her. Sympathy was a good way to get someone to come to your side. Also, she sent a very large box of candy to May for the office staff. She wanted to wish them all a happy New Year, her card said.

This ploy didn't fool May, who immediately took it into Jason's office. "Here, have a piece," May said sarcastically. "It's from Claire. I hope it isn't poisoned."

Jason laughed. But he knew then that Claire was up to no good and decided there was no use in calling her now. He would await Claire's next step.

When he returned home from the office, there was a message on his answering machine from his mother. "Hi. What's up?"

"I thought maybe you could tell me," his mother said. "I got the sweetest call from Claire today asking me to have lunch with her, since she hadn't seen me over the holidays. Have you told her about your engagement to Rachel?"

"I tried to call her but couldn't reach her, so I dropped her a note. But she knows. It's a wonder she hasn't tried

The Purloined Encryption Caper

to be nice to Caro for a change. She sent a huge box of candy to May at the office, and you know how nasty Claire's been to her in the past. But May saw through her. I guess losing is not a word in Claire's vocabulary. Maybe I should forewarn Rachel. Who knows what she'll do next. Funny, I never thought she really cared that much for me, but I guess she really wants to be the wife of a promising business executive."

"I'll call you tomorrow evening and let you know what she says," his mother then added. "I'll tell her all about Rachel's visit and how delighted our family is with the marriage plans, especially since your dad met Rachel before and knew her father. You know what I'd recommend, my son? The next time you and Rachel are together, elope. I don't care if she takes months to settle her affairs back there. Make her your wife and then she'll plan to come to California earlier. Or get her pregnant and she couldn't delay."

When Jason hung up, he shook his head, amazed at his mother's forthrightness. But he decided he'd take her advice and the next time he went East or when Rachel came here again, he'd convince her to marry him then and there or elope.

The next day, Jason received a note from Claire, reminding him of his promise to accompany her to dinner that following Friday evening. It was the annual meeting of the professional lawyers association in California. Jason suddenly remembered the invitation she extended when they were out with Bill and his wife many weeks before.

"Claire, I got your note today and indeed I did forget."

"Jason, I guess congratulations are in order to you and Rachel. But I hope you can still accompany me to the association dinner. I've already listed you in the program. I'm sure that Rachel won't mind. As a matter of fact, I wrote her a note congratulating her on the engagement. I told her we've had a long-standing dinner engagement and that as an old and very close and dear friend, you'd certainly honor that commitment. I'm sure she wouldn't mind." Claire had been smug about her ploy. She hoped Rachel would begin to have doubts about Jason.

"Claire, I'm not going with you. I'm engaged to Rachel and love her very much. I won't do anything to hurt her and I don't appreciate your sending such a note." Jason slammed down the receiver, realizing what Rachel's attitude might be after her earlier doubts about him. "That bitch! I'm certainly lucky I never married her," Jason said aloud to himself.

Activity at Rainbow's End in Berkeley Springs was very hectic over the holidays. Carlo had convinced his girlfriend, Ellen, who worked at the CIA, not to go home to Rhode Island for Christmas, but to stay in Washington. They could share their time either at her apartment in McLean or at the cabin in the mountains. Carlo wanted to be able to utilize the cabin as often as possible since his video equipment was there. He wanted to compromise her completely. He was glad it hadn't started snowing yet.

She had willingly explained to him the CIA computer set up and its capabilities. He was amazed at how advanced they were at encryption technology, at

The Purloined Encryption Caper

intercepting electronic transfers, and how many money transfers the CIA had intercepted and were holding in a separate bank account. He didn't know whether that was legal in the U.S. or was the work of renegade CIA officers. Ellen told him that the officers joked that if Congress cut their budget for covert operations any more, the operations staff would have the confiscated money to continue with.

Carlo had also talked Julian into joining them for several days. Julian was dating a woman from the United Nations, temporarily assigned to Washington, to try to get Congress and the Administration to pay past dues to the United Nations. There was great pressure by the conservatives in the Congress to trim the UN staff and its activities. The Secretary General and his staff were trying to come up with devious ways to fund the United Nations on a continuing basis, so the UN staff wouldn't have to go with cap in hand to member nations annually. They felt it was demeaning, especially since they considered themselves saviors of the world and wanted to undertake their own activities without the need for Security Council agreement, especially the reluctant United States.

"A way has to be found," Moira said, "that would bring money directly in to the United Nations' coffers. We have tried to impose an international income tax on the developed countries, but it turned out to be totally unacceptable to the Western powers, especially the Americans."

Carlo was a dedicated socialist in his political thinking, but this didn't extend, of course, to his own pocketbook. He considered himself part of the governing elite, a key element in every socialist country. Ellen had recounted a conversation she overheard in their office. Apparently a West Coast company was on the verge of a breakthrough in software that had the capability of focusing on electronic transfers of large sums of money and could decode the electronic messages within a matter of nanoseconds. It could then intercept the message and transfer it to another account. This would permit someone to intercept an electronic transfer of drug money headed to a Swiss Bank Account and, as soon as it was received, transfer the funds to another account in a third country. Once this capability was finalized, the owner of this software could become rich. Not only could they trace someone's drug money but could appropriate those funds for their own purposes.

This is the key technology Lovenest hoped to steal. Carlo began to fantasize. Maybe what their group could do is make an arrangement with the United Nations' power brokers so that they could steal this technology and then, affect the transfer of funds to certain UN accounts which would serve to legitimate the funds and the process. The UN leadership would make an agreement to transfer a certain percentage of all money captured for the members of the group. It should be fairly easy because UN bank accounts and projects were never audited. His opium dreams seldom seemed so good since he knew most of the UN staff had no love for the Americans.

The more Carlo thought about this possibility, the better he liked it. It would ensure a steady income for them for the rest of their lives without their having to take extraordinary risks once the software was in their hands. He would discuss it further with Julian and then present the idea to Clive, Hans, and Pierre after the first of the year. Through Moira, they had access to the highest levels of the United Nations Secretariat and, even if they were unmasked, they could leave the country. Their governments would compliment them for being so concerned for world peace and they could then live in the country of their choice and not be criminals on the run. His fantasies intoxicated him.

When Carlo or Julian weren't using the cabin, Clive would use it occasionally for his partying friends. What none of them knew was that everyone who had been in the cabin had been recorded, not only by the videotapes they planned to use for blackmail or coercion, but also by Miles and Jan on behalf of the FBI. Now that the CIA knew that Ellen had been compromised, her apartment had been bugged and she had been under constant surveillance.

The willingness to compromise one's government and provide information to the enemy infuriated Mark but he was glad that they were going to close in on the group soon. He would have to contact Phil and find out how soon Jason's company anticipated completion of their new software and tell Jason he planned to have the FBI keep a close watch on his company. He now felt Jason would be the primary target of the dirty group of five.

Mark would assign extra people to watch Rachel's apartment building, not only for her sake but for Ruth's as well. He was afraid that kidnapping would not be alien to this group considering they were playing for high stakes.

When Mark got to his office he would determine how the UN received, banked and audited their accounts. He understood that it was done in a very sloppy manner, but he wanted to know if it was sloppy enough to launder millions of dollars of drug money, as well as money from terrorists or from Middle Eastern countries.

The FBI informant they fingered through pictures taken at Rainbow's End was already under watch and a telephone tap had been placed on the informant's office phone as well as her apartment. Mark was looking forward to throwing her in jail personally, if he could.

But first, Mark had to see what happened to Mary O'Bryan, a young intern at the Department of Commerce, who had contacted him regarding something "funny" she said was going on in her office at Commerce. Worried, she had talked with an uncle who told her to contact Mark, someone whom he had met several years ago. Mary had agreed to meet Mark for coffee that morning but never kept the appointment. She wouldn't give Mark her office phone number and insinuated that she didn't want anyone at her office or her apartment to suspect she was checking up on them.

For the moment, Mark would wait and see if she called him. If he didn't hear from her by the end of the next day, he would try to locate her either through his contacts at Commerce or through her uncle.

CHAPTER 16

"Oh, how wonderful," both Cindy and Susan gushed when Rachel returned to her office and told them about her engagement. "But what is Jack going to do without you? How soon will you leave?"

These questions were left unanswered when the door opened and Jack bounced into the office. He went directly to Rachel and embraced her. "I'm happy as hell for you and Jason, but I can't say as much for myself."

"Don't worry. I'm not leaving tomorrow. You can't get rid of me that easily," Rachel beamed.

"Well, maybe we should start talking about a replacement before the mail arrives and the phone starts ringing off the hook. The office has been closed for the holidays but the government and some of our clients haven't been so it's liable to be a hectic week. I anticipate we'll have a sack full of mail," he added. "I know we have a stack of faxes which Cindy is sorting now and I have hundreds of e-mails. Get a cup of coffee and come into my office."

As Jack and Rachel reviewed the faxes, they were both struck by a series of unsolicited messages from staff at the Commerce and Defense Departments, describing their departments' views on strengthening legislation affecting the sale of encryption technology and related technology and patent bills. They were espousing a policy whereby the government could take total control of all encryption systems in the name of national security, and detailed patent information would be made available to individuals around the world within eighteen months of an initial application, thus announcing to any interested parties new ideas being considered by private companies.

"Wow," Jack said. "Do you know these individuals, Rachel? They're crazy."

"Remember Tom took me to a party at Joe's shortly after I arrived? That's where I met many of these political appointees in the technology loop as well as Pierre Ledent and Hans Schmidt. I have their names in my card file, I believe, and they have my business card, hence the reason for faxing me these memos." Rachel went to her office and brought back her file.

"Yes. These are the same people. The thing for us is to determine whether their departments' views are in our clients' best interests. If they are, which I doubt, then there doesn't seem to be anything wrong, I suppose. If they aren't, then I think we have our work cut out for us." She frowned.

"But you see, Rachel," Jack explained, "I don't think the legislation these individuals are promoting is that of the administration or of the Congress. First, perhaps you could get a reading from the Hill staffers,

The Purloined Encryption Caper

such as Tom, or someone you can totally rely on." He began to sound conspiratorial.

"You might also want to check with Phil. If these individuals are promoting a certain line, let's see if they're being swayed by the same foreign elements you also met at Joe's place. Ask him if any political parties are getting payoffs from foreign countries, especially those in Asia. Foreign countries couldn't give them money outright, but might have made large contributions indirectly to certain re-election campaigns. See whether your Hill buddies are aware of any schemes and what the CIA thinks.

"And," he continued, "if we find that there's an all out information attack aimed at associations and firms representing technology companies, especially the smaller ones, that would be to their detriment, then I think it's time we try to get someone like Jason to testify before some congressional committees currently considering the subject. I think we'll have to act quickly, though. Do you think Jason would be willing to come East for this purpose? I know he's very busy with his company and his personal life and it'd probably take several days. I'm sure you wouldn't mind having him here for a few days, would you?" Jack said with a smile on his face.

"Not at all," she commented, smiling.

"There are other matters we have to talk about, but I think this is of critical importance. I'd like you to make some appointments now. We can then talk further at lunch. I think Luigi's missed our business over the holidays."

Rose Ameser Bannigan

Back in her own office, Rachel arranged to see Tom after lunch and Phil that evening. She hadn't yet told Phil and Mary about her marriage plans and this presented a good opportunity. She then looked at her mail to see if there were other letters promoting this unusual point of view on current legislation.

Tom was waiting at his office building entrance. "Let's go to the local coffee house. I feel like having a latte. Hope you don't mind. It'll be easier to talk and definitely quieter."

Tom had never done this before and Rachel was curious.

"Our office quarters are very cramped and the coffee shop will give us more privacy." He didn't want any of his colleagues to overhear their conversation. At this point, he wasn't sure whom he could trust.

They were seated in a booth in the back sipping their latte when Rachel told him about the faxes. "I brought you copies to help explain the situation."

"Thanks," he said, startled by their contents. "Do you mind if I keep these? I won't pass them on without asking your permission."

"Be my guest," Rachel said. "I didn't ask for them, so they're yours. What Jack and I wanted to know is if this is the position of the majority in Congress, or are evil forces, as Sherlock Holmes would say, at work here?" She paused to see his reaction. "Neither Jack nor I feel these policies are in the best interest of private American companies, especially the smaller ones such as our clients. As a matter of fact, it might even help the larger corporations, especially now that they're so involved internationally. Do you agree?"

The Purloined Encryption Caper

He nodded in the affirmative.

"Is there a possibility that we can get someone from the small business community to testify at the hearings, like Jason, for example, to put forth its point of view? Congress normally only asks executives from the Fortune 500 companies with a lot of political clout."

"This is very disturbing," Tom replied. "I knew something was up with some politicos and, I agree, I don't think this is in the best long-term interest of the U.S. To preclude U.S. companies from selling their technologies abroad is sheer industrial suicide. We can't restrict rights for government use only and then have the government sell or give these technologies to countries that they think are important, or might be important, or are making a lot of money for themselves or their friends." Tom again reread the faxes.

"Did you know that we gave super sensitive computer technology to China which we wouldn't even sell to France, one of our NATO buddies? China, in turn, will probably sell it for big bucks to whomever they wish, such as North Korea and Iran, and the people left out in the cold, of course, is U.S. industry. Let me run this by some friendly Congressional committee members who I know can keep their mouth shut. I'll get back to you." He hesitated before continuing.

"You realize, Rachel, if the legislation goes through as these people want, our dirty little group could easily grab the technology, produce it overseas and make a bundle. They wouldn't have any competition from U.S. industry since it would be illegal for them to sell it abroad, and our companies would be left holding

Rose Ameser Bannigan

the bag on R&D and start-up costs. I'm beginning to understand part of the reason for the dirty five's purpose here." Tom seemed to hesitate before continuing.

"I'm also going to share this with Mark, probably through Ruth, whom I plan to see tonight," Tom added with a smile. "I think she understands me and we've been seeing a lot of each other. Also, do you think Jason would be willing to come back for a few days to testify, if I can wangle an invitation? I'm not sure we could help him with travel costs, but I assume his lodging would not be expensive," he said with a wink.

She responded quickly, "I hope he'd jump at the opportunity. After all it would be in his interest. I didn't know whether you heard that Jason and I plan on getting married sometime this year after I hire someone new for Jack."

"Yes, I did. From Ruth, and I'm happy for you both. I don't like the idea of your leaving, but Washington is usually a very temporary stopover for most people." Tom got up to leave. "I'll be in touch."

That evening, after Rachel told Mary and Phil about her engagement to Jason, she gave a copy of the faxes to Phil and asked him what the CIA position would be.

"We haven't changed, Rachel," Phil commented. "We don't take a stand at the Agency on proposed domestic laws. We support the Administration's role and policies. However, the only concern we'd have would be if the technology reached foreign parties that could pose a security threat to the U.S. Also, we're interested in having available the best encryption systems for maintaining our secret communications.

The Purloined Encryption Caper

And other more sophisticated systems being developed to track down transfers of drug monies or illegal transfers would be of key interest to us. We don't want them to fall into foreign hands." He mentally tensed at the damage a determined enemy could do.

"I understand we've had software that's been very effective. However, we think that software has been exposed. I read that when the Justice Department disposed of outdated computers, they left information on the hard drives that should have been deleted. There are techies now trying to retrofit the system for their purposes. What is worse is that they'll use that software as a starting point and refine it. Our problem is that it doesn't seem to be illegal. I know that Jason's systems engineers have come a long way in developing interceptions of electronic transfers." Phil paused.

"We're anxious to see where the whole elaborate information highway system takes us. What's worse is that the people best at penetrating the system, the cyber-hackers, are sometimes only teenagers who break into systems and penetrate codes and passwords for kicks. That's why cryptology of the highest order is required to secure the functioning of an information society. Breaking into individuals' personal computers, breaking their keys and stealing credit card and bank account numbers is duck soup to these people and using this information for personal gain is rather common. It's like stealing a checkbook in the old days. But I don't need to tell you about this. It's Jason's company's forte."

She thought for a minute before replying. "Quite honestly, Jason never talks to me much about the details of his company or its products, except in general terms. But I think there are forces around, other than the dirty five, who I don't understand. I'm not sure others do either. Jack's concern is to make sure that legislation isn't made that's detrimental to our clients and to the U.S. business community in general. I'm not sure at this point who speaks for the government or the country for that matter. There are so many different political angles in this." Rachel then explained.

"I've talked to Tom about this and he's going to give Mark copies. Congress is going to have hearings, and I thought it was important that the smaller companies give their side of the story. Normally, only the larger companies, usually multinationals, are asked to testify. Tom then asked me whether Jason would be willing to come East for this purpose if he can get him on the calendar. I have to telephone Jason tonight and will ask him then."

Over dinner Mary asked Rachel if she was looking forward to her marriage and moving to the West Coast.

Rachel hesitated. "I really love Jason and want to marry him. My main concern is that I'm not sure what'll keep me busy in California. When I was going to marry Jeff, I knew that a military officer's wife is expected to carry out certain duties and I'd be busy moving a household every few years. But it'll be different in California married to Jason. I don't want to pursue a full-time career. We both want kids and I believe it's best for a mother to stay home with them, at least until they're in school. But I also don't want to be bored. I thought maybe I could talk Jack into using me

The Purloined Encryption Caper

on a part-time basis as an extension of his office, but I'm not sure he'll buy it."

Phil hesitated a moment and then said, "What if I wanted to set you up as a consultant working under contract in California as part of my group? Would that interest you? If there continues to be an increase in cyber-terrorism or industrial espionage the way we anticipate, we'll need eyes and ears within the camp. Laws and penalties are fine, and I know the bureaucrats think they scare the hell out of people bent on stealing secrets, flouting intellectual property rights and other similar offenses. But have you noticed any decrease in robberies or car stealing just because the FBI or Justice or the local gendarmes say lawbreakers will be thrown in jail? You're right, Rachel, regardless of the rights and wrongs in selling our technology, the people we're really penalizing are the companies whose people have the brains and guts to develop them." He paused.

"Keep in touch, Rachel, and let us know when Jason comes. This time we want to have you over, either here or in the mountains. We'll then toast the prospective bride and groom."

As she was preparing to leave, she removed a piece of paper from her purse. "By the way, Phil, while I was at the beach I rummaged through Steve's beach cottage to see if I could find any information that might indicate why he was murdered. I found this. I've asked Tom to get a copy of Steve's last draft and see whether these sentences were included in it. I'll let you know."

Phil read them and looked up at her. "Please do. I'll also ask one of my contacts at the Paris station to see if the French police checked out the hotels in

Rose Ameser Bannigan

Nice, Marseilles or on Corsica to see if Steve had been staying there."

When she got home, she faxed copies of the information to Jason's home fax machine with a covering note to phone her. She mentioned that Tom was going to see if he could add Jason's name to the list of people being asked to testify and wondered if Jason could make it.

When he telephoned, Jason sounded angry. "Those bums. They're really trying to kill us, aren't they? Don't they realize how much research and scale-up money goes into creating new technologies as well as the marketing costs before they actually return a profit? Of course, I'd be willing to testify. When do you think the hearings will be?"

"Tom thought maybe next week, starting Tuesday or Wednesday. You could come in the night before and I'd be only too happy to reciprocate with lodging," she said smiling to herself. "If you like, I'll ask Tom for dinner that night so he can brief you on questions that most likely will be asked."

"I'd expect to stay with you--*su casa, mi casa*--but don't invite Tom over. Perhaps I can phone him or he could give you what information I may need. Things are hectic here and now I'll have to work over the weekend."

When Jason arrived at Dulles airport the following Monday, Rachel was there to meet him and drive him back to her apartment. She was glad they could go in through the garage of her apartment building. Occasionally, strange men were still lurking outside

The Purloined Encryption Caper

her apartment building. She wasn't sure now whether they were good guys or bad guys.

"I've missed you so much," Jason said as he put his arms around her. "I can't believe that we'll have almost a week together. Where shall we have dinner tonight?"

"I've fixed dinner here so we can retire early. While I finalize dinner, you should call Tom. Then, I'll give you two options. First, we go for a walk and have a nightcap at Jacques or else we stay here and I put you to bed."

"I'll take option two. I need to sleep, but first I need to hold you and let you know how much I've missed you."

"By the way, Jason, how was your evening with Claire?" Rachel hadn't mentioned her letter from Claire to Jason on the telephone and had been hurt badly when she read it.

"I didn't go with her as a date. She really is a bitch for having written you. To be honest, I forgot about the dinner engagement until I heard from her after you left. You have to believe me. But I did make the presentation since my name was on the program and it wouldn't look good for me or my company to renege on a promise."

Rachel wasn't as sure of Jason's fidelity as she was in San Francisco and again questioned why he hadn't forewarned her about Claire's note. She had spent a rather restless evening the previous Friday, thinking about Jason and Claire together.

When they went to bed, they did make love, but Rachel couldn't get the notion of Jason with Claire out of her mind and wondered if Jason had been honest with her. Jason sensed the difference in Rachel. He resolved to take his mother's advice and marry her as soon as he could. He couldn't let mistrust enter their relationship again.

Jason attended all of the congressional committee hearings. At times, he was shocked at the restrictions the lawmakers might impose on U.S. companies to prevent them from benefiting from their patents.

Rachel managed to attend most of the hearings, but had to return to her office as soon as Jason finished his testimony. She didn't know how long it would take to draft her newsletter so she could get Jack's approval before he left on a business trip to Houston. Rachel promised to meet Jason at the Hilton's bar in Ballston at seven that evening.

As she approached the bar, she saw Jason through the window talking with a man who looked vaguely familiar and was stunned when she realized it was Frank Avery. She walked to the other entrance and quietly stood far enough behind them so they couldn't see her, yet close enough to overhear. They were boisterously reminiscing about college days and how they liked to taunt girls, making believe they were serious when they were only trying to make out..

"Yes," Jason replied. "We lost several fraternity pins that way. Finally, mother said I couldn't bring any more girls home under false pretenses." He was still laughing as he shook his head.

This was a cruel side of Jason that Rachel had never seen before and felt a cold chill grab her body. Why hadn't Jason mentioned that he knew Frank? She

The Purloined Encryption Caper

had finally come to trust Jason and now wondered if he really loved her or was only playing games with her, too?

It brought to mind a trick someone played on a fiancé in Germany. When one of the men was planning to get married, his fiancée invited all of the women he had ever dated to his house for a party to see his reaction. Fortunately, Rachel had not been on that list. It turned out that his fiancée never intended to marry him but wanted to get even with him for being so cavalier with the affections of so many women and for stepping out on her during their engagement.

Rachel had to get away and think, so she ducked into the small Italian restaurant she had gone to her first night in the Washington area. She sat at the bar and ordered a double vodka martini on the rocks. Then, she pulled out her cell phone and left a message on the Howards' answering machine.

"Phil, I accept the assignment we discussed this afternoon if it's still okay with you and Jack." She returned to the bar, took a gulp of her martini, and took off her engagement ring and put it in her purse. When she had almost finished her drink, she looked up and saw Jason entering the restaurant. He led her to a small table in the corner.

"Why did you run away?" he asked, holding both of her hands and looking directly at her.

Rachel decided she wouldn't say anything about seeing him with Frank but would await his explanation.

"Is this what they call the silent treatment?" Jason asked, coldly.

Rose Ameser Bannigan

Rachel shrugged her shoulders but still didn't say anything, afraid she would lose her composure.

Jason ordered himself a gin martini and Rachel asked for her second. Jason told the bartender no.

"I think I'd better get some food in you first," Jason said rather sternly. "What'll you have?"

Rachel ordered ravioli and a small house salad. Jason ordered the same.

"I think we'd better clear the air, Rachel, but first, I'd appreciate your putting the ring back on or do you want me to do it?" he asked authoritatively. Rachel reached into her purse and put the ring back on her finger. She then took the last remaining sip of her drink.

"I didn't know for sure until today that the journalist you were in love with in Europe was Frank Avery. You see, Frank and I were classmates at Stanford and very good friends." He then explained about the time he had drinks with Frank during his visit to Washington when he first met Rachel. At the beach, when Rachel told him about her experience in Europe, he thought the story was almost the same as Frank's, but since neither used the other's name, he wasn't sure.

"I didn't want to begin questioning you at that time to see if it was indeed Frank. You and I were just becoming very good friends again, or should I say lovers, and I didn't want to do or say anything that might cause any problems. I'd had a note from him that he was getting a divorce and was going to track you down, using a private investigator, if necessary. Frank only referred to you as 'Monk' until tonight, when he told me he had found you and that you lived nearby." Jason paused and took another sip of his drink. "He

The Purloined Encryption Caper

said he had tried calling you several times today. I assume you never did get the message by your reaction when you saw us together. I accidentally ran into him at the bar." He was studying her response as she took a deep breath

"No. I saw that there was a message, but I didn't check to see who'd called. For all I know, it may have been Claire trying to reach you." Rachel wanted to be as bitchy and hurtful as she could. "It was a shock to see him with you when I approached the bar, and I thought the worst. And I overheard some of your conversation. It was very painful." She was fighting back tears.

"What was so painful? Seeing him again, or knowing that we were friends?" Jason had been stern in his questioning. "And I don't know what else I can say or do to convince you that I am through with Claire." His exasperation was beginning to show.

Their food arrived and Rachel began to try to get some food down. The martini was beginning to make her a little light-headed.

When she didn't answer his question, Jason looked at her. "Rachel, there is one answer I must have. Are you still in love with Frank and, if so, is that why you ran away and took off my ring?" Rachel didn't respond and looked at Jason, wondering if she really knew him well enough to go through with the marriage.

"He plans to get in touch with you," Jason said. "He's determined to see if he can get you to go back to him. His last words to me at the bar were *'may the best man win!'* And he said that he would go to any length to win. By that, I assume anything goes in his book."

Rachel paused before answering. "Jason, how could you think I still love him after he lied to me," she said hesitantly. "I guess my insecurity in matters of the heart is showing. I love you or I'd never have slept with you or consented to marry you. If you doubt my feeling toward Frank, perhaps we should call the whole thing off."

She was ready to return his ring. "I thought both you and Frank were discussing me and playing a very mean joke on me, especially after the note from Claire."

"You must not think very highly of me," Jason said, feeling a little taken aback. "And why does he call you Monk?"

"My father gave me a carved wooden figure of the three monkeys--hear no evil, speak no evil and see no evil. I considered it good luck and had taken the figure to Europe with me. Frank saw it in my apartment the first night he came over."

On their walk home, Rachel said, "By the way, Phil asked me to go to Paris on his behalf to attend an international meeting on technology transfer and intellectual property rights. I was going to talk to you about it, but after I saw you and Frank together, I was so angry and hurt that I phoned Phil and accepted the assignment. I'll be in Paris part of next week. Jack already gave Phil his blessing before Phil asked me." The matter seemed closed to Jason. So he decided to fill her in on his conversation with Frank.

"Then you should know that Frank will be attending the same conference. He told me so at the bar, but I'm not sure I trust him there with you, even though

The Purloined Encryption Caper

you say you no longer care for him." Half-jokingly, he added, "He always got any woman he wanted at college and he's now obviously willing to go to any length to get you back." Jason put his arm around Rachel's shoulder.

"Rachel, tomorrow is Friday and I have several meetings in Washington, but will be finished early. I know tomorrow will be a busy day for you but let's go to Berkeley Springs for the weekend. I'll make reservations at the Country Inn. I don't want to stay with the Howard's, but, if you insist, we can have them join us for dinner on Saturday night."

CHAPTER 17

On Friday, Rachel not only had to make plans to be away the following week but also had to respond to a number of clients' requests asking about the Congressional hearings. Rachel arranged for Cindy to get copies of testimony given during the week. Cindy quickly duplicated copies and express mailed them to all of their clients. She also e-mailed a synopsis of possible outcomes to give a sense of the direction of the Hill discussions. Rachel took a set of papers back to Jason, and a set she could read en route to Paris.

She didn't have to worry about trip arrangements. Phil had made the airline and hotel reservations in Paris and had arranged for her to have appropriate press credentials. He felt it was important that she not be listed as representing the government but be a free agent, mixing freely with the international as well as American participants. Her newsletter editorship for a private lobbying firm gave her the creditability.

Rachel would be in an excellent position to judge the tenor of the meetings and see who was courting whom. Because of her language capabilities, she could easily listen in on conversations. There would be plenty of press people since this topic was growing in importance to both the international and American business circles. Critical articles on economic espionage and the economic counter intelligence activities were beginning to hit major front pages, both abroad and in the United States.

The drive to Berkeley Springs was restful, even though the January scene was bleak and barren. That tiny town always has a charm, regardless of the season. Jason didn't have the opportunity to really see anything during his previous hurried trip and was enchanted with it. He could understand completely why the Howard's spent so much time there.

After checking into the Country Inn, they strolled around town, had a drink at a local pub and later had dinner at the Inn. It was very romantic and Jason managed to cajole Rachel into putting their relationship back on track.

"Why don't we get married now? I'd feel so much better having you go to Paris as my wife rather than my fiancée," Jason said the next morning over breakfast. "Before meeting you, I never thought I had a jealous bone in my body, but I realize I do and I just don't trust Frank."

"Maybe you don't trust me," she replied, realizing that the topic of marriage was again surfacing. "I wouldn't be averse to eloping," she said hesitatingly. "Somehow, making wedding plans seems overwhelming. But it takes time to get a marriage

The Purloined Encryption Caper

license in Virginia or West Virginia and we don't have enough time. Also, today is Saturday and government offices are closed," she said, almost relieved that she'd have more time to reconsider her marriage.

"Why don't you get married nearby in Maryland?" volunteered the waitress who had been standing near their table. "You can drive there, about ten miles or so, and a Justice of the Peace can get you hitched. It wouldn't take more than an hour or so and probably cost no more than fifty to a hundred bucks. I could see if anyone here knows someone we can call if you're really interested." She obviously was a frustrated matchmaker who had discovered likely victims.

That waitress earned a very large tip for her information that morning from Jason. She made an appointment for them that afternoon with a Justice of the Peace in a small town across the Potomac near Hancock, Maryland. Since Jason didn't have the matching wedding ring with him, they went to a local jewelry store and bought matching gold bands.

They returned to the Inn, made arrangements for a photographer and called the Howards to see if they could join them for drinks and dinner that evening. There was no answer at the cabin so Rachel assumed they were not up this weekend. She then called them at their Virginia house and left a message to telephone Jason and Rachel at the Country Inn, saying they had news for them. They then drove to Maryland and Rachel became Mrs. Jason Conrad, in a simple but official ceremony. Other than Jack, the Howard's and Jason's family, they agreed not to tell anyone else, but

Rose Ameser Bannigan

to keep their marriage secret until Rachel's return from Paris.

When they returned to the Inn, they saw the Howard's driving away. They had stopped by to leave a message for Jason and Rachel, suggesting they join them for dinner at their cabin. Jason reversed the invitation and when the elopement was revealed, they quickly agreed. Both Mary and Phil were delighted with the news--it would encourage Rachel to join Jason sooner in California. Before, they felt she had been wrong when she didn't marry Jeff in Hong Kong.

Jason's family was also delighted. "I had lunch with Claire while you were away. She's determined to get you back," his mother warned him. "She's sure that Rachel is a passing fancy and that you will tire of her. But I assured her that Rachel had indeed stolen your heart. I can't wait to see her face when she finds out you're already married. She also telephoned Caroline and offered to set up appointments with friends for an office job. I thought Caroline was going to hang up on her but, much to my surprise, Caroline accepted an invitation to meet her for dinner next week."

Almost as an afterthought, his mother said, "Oh, by the way, Sam Penderton telephoned to see if I knew how he could reach you. Apparently, May is not giving out your telephone number at Rachel's place. He said it was rather urgent. Can I tell May you're married?"

"No. I'll tell her Monday. Did Sam leave a telephone number with you perchance, since I assume he didn't phone from the office?" Jason asked.

"As a matter of fact, he did." His mother gave him the number with a message that Jason shouldn't discuss

The Purloined Encryption Caper

anything with his wife should she answer the phone. With that bit of information, Jason knew why Sam called.

"Jason, the worst has happened," Sam explained. "I received an e-mail from Miriam. She plans to accept an invitation she said I extended to visit California and is arriving this coming weekend. Is it okay with you if I leave on a vacation with my wife so I won't be here? I'm not sure that I can face her at this time." Sam was obviously very upset.

"Sam, sit still and don't make any plans yet. Let me think. I'll phone you tomorrow and we can talk about it again." Jason wasn't going to let this problem spoil his evening which was soon filled with champagne and dancing.

When Mary and Rachel went to the ladies room, Jason told Phil he had to talk with him. Phil listened intently as Jason told him about Miriam and Sam and he was glad to have another piece of the puzzle to fit into Mark's scenario.

"Did Sam tell you whether he had divulged any information to Miriam?" Phil asked.

"He didn't think he had," Jason said, "other than what she got from his presentation, which, by the way, was on encryption. You know, Sam is one of the best computer systems engineers I have and is very valuable to me."

Phil thought about it for awhile. "Jason, how strong a person is Sam? Could he be used by the FBI to set a trap for Miriam and her gang? I would have to think this through and talk with Mark. But if we could get Sam to give or sell plans to her and compromise her in the process, we might be able to break up their ring, throw them in jail, or at least make them *persona non grata* in the U.S.

"I told Sam I would telephone him tomorrow. When I call, I'll set up a Monday appointment. What should I tell him? As far as I know, he may have already asked his wife where she'd like to go for a short vacation."

"I'll try to reach Mark and see what he says. Did Sam say when Miriam plans to go to California or did she ask Sam when he would be available?"

"Miriam proposed the following weekend but Sam plans to confirm the dates with her."

"By the way, Jason, have you mentioned your evenings with Miriam to Rachel? If not, you should be prepared to answer questions when she returns from Paris. I'm positive that Miriam will be at the meetings as well as Pierre and his partners in crime."

At that moment Rachel and Mary returned to the table. When Rachel saw Jason shaking his head, she said, "My, you both look as if you're hiding a big secret," she said teasingly.

"We were only marveling at how lovely our ladies are," Phil quipped to squelch her inquisitiveness. When Jason and Rachel went to dance, Phil told Mary that he needed some time to talk with Jason alone the next day. "Could you invite the newlyweds to lunch and occupy Rachel for a while so that Jason and I can talk?"

Mary agreed but wondered what was so important and secret that Rachel couldn't hear.

Phil took out his cell phone and tried to reach Mark in Washington. Since Mark wasn't there, Phil left a

The Purloined Encryption Caper

message on his answering machine to phone Phil at his West Virginia cabin. It was urgent.

It turned out that Mark was staying overnight at the FBI safe house with the Hanson's. Pierre had returned from Paris and Mark wanted to see if any meetings at Rainbow's End were arranged this weekend. There had been no activity there since New Year's Day. Mark assumed that Carlo, Julian and Clive would stop their amorous assignations once Pierre returned.

The German government felt Hans had spent enough time in the U.S. without any obvious benefit to them so withdrew him from the State Department program. So, when Hans called Pierre over the holidays with the news, Pierre told him he could serve as their transfer point for selling whatever technology or information they could get and Hans had readily agreed. But what neither Hans nor Pierre knew, however, was that through the CIA liaison with the German government, information had been leaked to the BND, the German intelligence organization, about Hans and the group's double-cross plan.

The BND didn't want an embarrassing international incident so ordered Hans back to Germany in order to keep him under surveillance. If or when they caught him in a compromising situation, they would arrest him. This way they would gain a lot of brownie points with a friendly intelligence organization and get rid of a troublesome employee at the same time.

Mark was sure the group would soon have to develop an action plan since their U.S. stay would end sometime within the next six months. He had heard rumors that the regular embassy staffs were anxious

Rose Ameser Bannigan

for them to leave and putting pressure on their foreign ministries to have them recalled. They had heard that the U.S. government was watching the visitors and didn't want these interlopers to compromise their own undercover activities. Also, there was gossip about their varied sexual affairs and attempts to penetrate the CIA, FBI and Commerce Departments as well as the White House. If this information ever hit the front pages of the *Washington Post* or more likely the *Washington Times*, their Embassies would be open to criticism not only by the U.S. government but by other diplomatic missions as well, since this would give the FBI an excuse to monitor diplomatic activities more closely.

Additionally, Mark had not yet managed to meet with Mary O'Bryan, the intern at Commerce. Her uncle was reluctant to share any information she had given him about activities at Commerce but gave Mark her phone number. All he could do was leave a message on her answering machine. She was never home when he phoned. He tried to reach her at Commerce but was told she was a "roving" intern and had no specific office assignment so no one at Commerce could provide definitive information.

When Phil and Mary returned to their cabin after dinner, their answering machine was beeping with a message from Mark indicating that he was at the Hanson's cabin and could be reached there.

"I need to talk with you," Phil said, "if possible, before noon tomorrow."

"How about meeting now? Are you up to having a visitor?" Mark asked.

The Purloined Encryption Caper

Phil agreed and in less than ten minutes, Mark was there. Mary had gone to bed, but had set out some sandwich makings in the event Mark was hungry.

"Mark, it's apparent now that Miriam is up to her stinking earlobes in this and plans to blackmail Sam. I think Sam told Miriam far more than he should have. God help us if he did the same regarding the new products that are about to emerge from Jason's company. I want to see if we can possibly use Sam to get Miriam." Mark showed his interest immediately and Phil continued.

"Jason's not sure how strong Sam would be in dealing with her. So, before we even approach Sam, I wanted to talk with you first. It would support our effort to silence this group one by one without having to go public. If the latter happened, I'm afraid the CEO's of high tech companies as well as the American people in general will be up in arms about our continuing involvement with both NATO and the United Nations. There's a lot of resentment anyway, especially since we signed both the GATT and NAFTA trade agreements." Phil thought about this before continuing and realized it would not bode well for the CIA or FBI either. Phil then produced a hand-written document.

"Mark, in reviewing the situation tonight, I jotted down the players and our progress thus far. The group consists of Hans Schmidt from Germany, Pierre Ledent and Miriam Gauthier from France, Clive Fyffe from England, Carlo Vecchio from Italy and Julian Vanderhaag from Belgium. Schmidt no longer is a problem. We have compromised him and he's being watched by the German intelligence. I have stressed to our BND friends there that once he knows he's been compromised, they should make sure he doesn't get the opportunity to communicate with the rest of the group here." Phil then continued as Mark nodded in agreement.

"Carlo is about to be compromised. We approached Ellen and gave her two options. First, she could cooperate with us to incriminate Carlo. If she doesn't, she might consider spending the next ten years in a federal prison for conspiring with an enemy agent since we could prosecute her under the Espionage Act. She saw the light." Phil filled his pipe before he continued.

"So, after New Year's, whenever she met Carlo, she's been wired. That bastard, Carlo, videotaped their love-making and then showed her the pictures. She thought it was rather humorous until he told her why he did it. That encouraged her to cooperate. Poor kid, she almost had a mental breakdown. She really believed Carlo cared for her and was going to marry her. Once we are able to compromise Carlo with his government, Ellen will quietly resign from the CIA for personal reasons and we'll wipe her record clean. A notation will be placed in her FBI file that she should never be authorized another security clearance since she is no longer suitable for any government position." Phil paused to relight his pipe, letting Mark absorb the details.

"Next, I'll see how soon we can compromise Julian Vanderhaag. Ellen told us he was seeing a high-level female UN official. He and Carlo talked to her about having electronic transfers of drug money deposited to

The Purloined Encryption Caper

UN organizational bank accounts or bank accounts of sympathetic UN officials. They hadn't yet talked to Pierre about their money laundering scheme. We've contacted the UN office where she works in New York and intend to see how we can get her to incriminate Julian. The FBI will be brought in once we hear from this woman. I don't know if you got the secure message I sent you yesterday afternoon." Mark hadn't.

"According to Ellen," Phil went on, "Julian set up a computer hacker network in their cabin and hired a number of young nerds to break into systems. I think he's only hired seven or eight thus far, but Julian outlined the targets and data they wanted. I thought maybe your people at the FBI could set up some counter intercepts to locate and identify these people." Phil paused again and then summed up.

"So we have only the Brit and the French to worry about. If we can trap Miriam by using Sam Penderton in California, we might be able to make a deal with our French friends. Jason returns to California tomorrow night and will meet with Sam on Monday. Is there any way that a local FBI agent can meet with Sam, or Jason and Sam, to determine whether Sam is interested and suitable to go along with our scheme? The payback, of course, would be some sort of cover story for Sam to clear his name with his wife, should the need arise."

"Perhaps I should go out myself," Mark suggested. "I'm scheduled to attend the international technology meeting in Paris, but I could take the red-eye special to California tomorrow night depending upon the activity at their cabin tomorrow afternoon. I could then fly to Paris over the Pole on Tuesday night. I should get there in time to case the meeting. By the way, is Rachel all set?"

"Yes, I think so," Phil assured him.. "I managed to get her press credentials. She should be able to overhear a lot of conversations since she's fluent in the principal conference languages. I assume you'll keep an eye on her. She looks so innocent people might try to take advantage of her and that could spell trouble, although I don't anticipate any. I have her tickets and made accommodations for her at the Pont Royale Hotel on the Left Bank. She said it wouldn't be as expensive as staying at the Hilton where the conference is and would also fit her press cover. She's leaving Monday night so she'd have most of Tuesday to rest up and get copies of papers available before the meeting. Where are you staying Mark?"

"I haven't made any reservations yet so maybe I'll stay at the Pont Royale, too. It will give me an opportunity to look after Rachel. Have you asked anyone from your Paris Station to talk with her or brief her?" Mark asked.

"No, I thought it'd be best for her to arrive at the conference cold. One of our people, Paul Westley, a good man, whom I trust, will be there and also will keep a watchful eye on her. He'll casually introduce himself to her at the conference so it doesn't raise any suspicions. Somehow, I don't think that this is much of a technical meeting, more likely a political one. I'm sure they'll discuss all the ramifications of the new patent procedures that arise from the trade agreements and the World Trade Organization but you can rest assured,

The Purloined Encryption Caper

they'll all be slanted against the *imperial government* of the United States."

"You'd better call it a night, Mark, if you plan to be awake tomorrow should any of the dirty five arrive. I understand Pierre is back in the States so he may have arranged a meeting. I can't imagine that he would forego the meeting in Paris, but maybe he'll fly back again for it."

Pierre did indeed return to Washington and was furious when he found that the other members of Lovenest had used the cabin for spurious sexual purposes while he was away. He had telephoned the other members when he returned, almost ten days earlier, and Carlo accidentally leaked the information when he was trying to impress Pierre with their videotapes. Consequently, Pierre felt it best not to use the cabin for a few weeks, and scheduled a meeting at a small restaurant nearby in rural Maryland. There, he told them that Hans had been recalled to Germany and would not return to Washington. He would, however, operate on their behalf with individuals in the Middle East and Europe.

The others revealed their current gains. Clive had harvested a large amount of information from Patent Office and Commerce Department computers through his friends there. Also, he was working with several Pentagon officials to try to influence the policies and legislation regarding the sharing of restricted technologies with NATO members.

Through the material obtained from the Patent Office, Clive was able to verify that the two key companies to penetrate which promised the largest payoff were Techno-Electronics & Systems, headed by Jason Conrad, and Electro-Systems headed by Bill Worth, both headquartered in Palo Alto. They were the major companies working on advanced encryption technologies and biometrics. He told Pierre that it was easy to pay off Commerce Department officials for information, sometimes through contributions to political campaigns. Also, the intern who was questioning certain matters at Commerce has been dealt with. They threatened to give her a bad review which would reflect badly on her college records. After that, she no longer asked any questions and finally returned home, promising to forget about her Washington assignment.

Julian briefed Pierre on his computer networking station in the West Virginia cabin. He had been able to recruit a number of teen-aged cyber-hackers willing to try to break into a network the group identified as well as get passwords for high-level defense and intelligence officials. They told Julian that getting general information would probably be easy, but getting technical details on software or hardware still being developed would certainly prove more difficult.

Julian found out that most of the smaller companies, such as Jason's or Bill Worth's, used stand-alone computers for development purposes and were only networked for information-seeking purposes or communicating with individuals through e-mail or the Internet. Many of the computers didn't even have hard drives. Also, their staff had been warned not to use e-mail for any confidential communications It was too

The Purloined Encryption Caper

easy to be read and the companies didn't want to have any paper trail.

This information interested Pierre but he knew now that he would have to find other ways to penetrate Jason's firm. Perhaps he could find out from Miriam whether she could compromise Penderton or else again try to seduce Jason. He would love to impart this information, possibly with photos, to Rachel. He planned to discuss this possibility with Miriam at the international conference in Paris.

CHAPTER 18

The overnight flight to Paris gave Rachel time to review everything that had happened recently. She hadn't yet floated the idea with Jack about being his West Coast representative. Phil said he might also be able to use her there and an affiliation with a public relations/lobbying firm would be perfect cover, provided, of course, that Jason approved.

She looked at her engagement ring and the gold band that Jason had bought so hastily and put it in her purse. Jason would put the matching wedding band when he carried her over the threshold in California.

The concierge looked at her strangely as she checked into the hotel. "Only for one, madam?" he asked.

"Yes," Rachel said, certain he recognized her from her previous stays and, for a moment, thought he was about to give her a key to another room.

"We have your reservation on the sixth floor as requested," he said after thumbing through the reservation list. The view from her room was the same as she remembered. You could see the Arc de Triumph, the Eiffel Tower and Sacre Coeur on Montmarte in the distance. She again realized how beautiful Paris was even on a cold wintry gray January day

It would be strange staying at the Pont Royale Hotel alone--it had so many memories. She wondered whether her feelings for Frank would really be as negative as she told Jason.

She showered, put on slacks, walking shoes and a warm jacket and decided to stroll across the bridge over the Seine to the Tuilieries. If jet lag didn't catch up with her, she wanted to revisit the Louvre, her favorite art museum. It was here that she first began to appreciate art. For her sixteenth birthday, her parents had taken her on a tour of all the famous European art galleries, starting with Paris.

The walk through the Tuileries brought a flood of memories. She noticed that French families still gathered, sitting on benches chatting while the children played and old men playing chess, never uttering a word. How she used to love strolling through these gardens and looking over the Place de la Concorde. Today, it made her feel young again.

By mid-afternoon, jet lag began to set in. Before returning to her hotel, she decided to visit the Cafe Flores for a cafe noir, much as she did years ago when she had spent so much time with Frank. The Cafe now had a warmed glassed-in front enclosure that made sitting there even in cold weather seem as if you were at a sidewalk cafe on a spring day. How she wished it were summer so it would be a real open air sidewalk cafe. This was where Ernest Hemingway and F. Scott Fitzgerald used to hang out during their youthful Paris

The Purloined Encryption Caper

days before meandering to Deux Magots, across the Boulevard. "Had it changed much since those days?" she wondered. It certainly hadn't changed much in four years since her last visit.

She sat down at the nearest empty table, but looking up, she saw the reflection of Frank's face. He immediately got up from the table where he was and came over.

"May I join you," he asked, "or are you waiting for someone?"

"No. Please join me, Frank. It's been a long time." Rachel acted nonchalantly, hoping that her nervousness wasn't showing. "Jason said you'd probably be here, getting information for an article. Do you think the folks here will 'fess up to their modus operandi against the imperial U.S. monsters?"

Frank was somewhat taken aback, not only by her mention of Jason but also her rather aloof, sophisticated, almost cynical attitude. This was not the Rachel he remembered.

"Yes. I told him I'd be here. By the way, how did you meet Jason?" he asked.

"His company's a client of ours, or I should say of the firm I work with. We met in Washington when he was on a business trip."

Frank decided to change the subject. "How have you been, Rachel?" he asked warmly. "I've thought of you so often and tried to find you. But if you were in Washington, you obviously had an unlisted phone. All the letters I sent to your Pennsylvania address were returned 'address unknown'. It seemed like you disappeared from the face of the earth."

Rose Ameser Bannigan

He looked at her left hand. "I see you're wearing an engagement ring. Jason mentioned that you're now his girl, but didn't say you were engaged. I see you don't have a wedding band yet, although 90's women don't necessarily wear wedding bands."

Rachel stared at him and said acidly, "No. I guess we women have taken a chapter from the book previously reserved only for men. For example, I see you're not wearing a wedding band either." She knew the answer to that question, but wanted to hurt him, and hurt him badly. She hoped that he still loved her so the pain he might feel would be that much more satisfying.

"Ouch. Perhaps I deserve that but I hope you won't spend all the time we may be together in Paris sniping at me. I assume the ring on your left hand is from Jason." Rachel nodded affirmatively.

"When you saw us at the Metro Bar in Arlington, I told him I was going to try to win you back if there was a chance. If he hadn't seen you, I think he'd have hit me." Rachel didn't say anything but continued to stare at Frank in disbelief.

"Who are with in Washington? I assume it's not the government," Frank said trying to change the conversation.

"No, I resigned last year. I now work for a lobbying and public relations firm called Jack Warden Associates. We represent the interests of small high tech companies and also provide office space and assistance while their executives visit Washington. I write a weekly clients' newsletter, so my purpose here is to send them whatever information that'll be useful." She didn't think it necessary to mention her contacts

The Purloined Encryption Caper

on the Hill or elaborate any further regarding her work for Phil.

"I'd better go," Rachel said as she got up to leave. She asked the waiter for her bill, but Frank insisted that he pay, for old time sake. She smiled.

"Where are you staying?" Frank asked.

"At the Pont Royale," she admitted.

This time he smiled and asked, "For old times sake?"

He walked her back to the hotel and when he asked for his key, she saw that he was in a sixth floor room as well.

Rachel was glad that she'd taken the offensive in their conversation. She didn't want him to think he had another chance. Subconsciously, she knew that if it weren't for her commitment to Jason, she might be tempted to renew their relationship. While she didn't respect him, she was still physically attracted. Was this always the way it would be, she wondered? Even if you're in love or married to someone, could feelings of physical attraction toward other men happen? Or was it that with Frank, there were so many good memories as well as bad ones. She desperately wished Jason were here.

Frank had wanted to invite her for dinner but changed his mind after he noticed her antagonistic attitude. Perhaps it would mellow as the week wore on. Even though she was engaged to Jason, he had no intention of letting that fact interfere with his plan to win her back. In his letter to her shortly before she left Frankfurt, he told her that if he couldn't have her, he'd do whatever was necessary to see that no other man did. Frank didn't realize that this was the reason she always had an unlisted telephone number.

That evening Rachel telephoned Jason. "I ran into Frank Avery at a local cafe and we had coffee together."

There was a long pause before Jason asked her how it went.

"Fine," she told him. "Frank noticed my engagement ring and said he assumed you gave it to me. I said yes."

"Only engaged? God, Rachel, why didn't you tell him that we're already married?" Jason seemed very upset.

"Darling, I thought we agreed to keep our marriage secret for the time being. Also, I didn't think I should break the news that one of his best friends was married to someone he thought he was still in love with. By the way, he's staying in this hotel, just down the hall. I thought I should tell you in the event you hear it from someone else. I'm never sure who has spies around." Her thoughts went back to the private conversation between Jason and Phil in Berkeley Springs when she and Mary had returned to the table the night of their wedding.

"I have no spies there," he said, "although I wish I did. I do trust you, my darling. I'll have to or else spend my whole life feeling challenged. Mark was here yesterday for a meeting with us and said he'll also be at the same hotel. He really is a nice guy and very helpful, even though I do get jealous of him when he's with you."

The Purloined Encryption Caper

"Darling, there's no need to. I miss you and love you, but I'd better sign off before jet lag destroys me. And I want to get a good night's rest so I'll be alert at the meetings."

At first she couldn't sleep thinking about her encounter with Frank. Now, she was glad the ice had been broken and she could be in control of the relationship.

The next morning Rachel arrived early at the Hilton meeting room, hoping to get an attendees' list. She had promised to fax it to Phil as soon as she could. She wondered why the Paris station hadn't arranged to do it. As she sipped her coffee, she saw Mark coming toward her.

"I see you made it," he said. "It's good to see you. Perhaps we can spend some time together."

"I talked with Jason last night and he said you'd gotten together in San Francisco. Is this regarding his company?" she asked.

Just then, Frank walked up and Rachel introduced him to Mark. As she watched them together, it was obvious that they already knew each other. Their conversation about the conference and their specific interests in attending seemed strange to Rachel. Also, Frank acted startled to find out that Mark was open about being with the FBI, which intrigued Rachel. She wondered if Frank expected Mark to be wearing an FBI flak jacket rather than a suit and tie. Still their conversation seemed strained.

The meetings were interesting to a point, but the main attraction was in seeing who was there and which organizations or European companies were represented. Many U.S. companies were represented by PR firms, not their officials, with the exception of the larger corporations who were usually represented by an appropriate vice president.

Rachel was much sought after since she was an unattached and pretty young American woman. Several of the U.S. representatives wanted to talk with her about Warden Associates and find out what they did. She wasn't quite sure of their motives but met with several during the coffee breaks. She didn't know whether Jack would welcome their business. She had never had any marketing role, since Jack always took care of that.

On the second evening, there was a reception in the Grand Ballroom of the French President's mansion. Rachel had ducked out of the last afternoon meeting to get her hair done and have a professional beautician apply her makeup. She had bought a special dress for the occasion and wanted to look her best. One of the women she met, a native Parisian, had recommended a good salon near her hotel. "Tell her to make you look *ravissante*," the woman said.

The salon did an excellent job. When she entered the ballroom, she had never felt or looked so beautiful. Her provocative steel blue silk dress had a semi-halter top, with a deep cleavage, yet still managed to cover the principal parts. She wore a large blue sapphire pendant, which Jeff had given her, resting just above the deepest part of her cleavage. Although she had butterflies in her stomach, she really enjoyed playing this role and having the eyes of so many men follow her as she entered the room.

The Purloined Encryption Caper

A young man in his mid-thirties approached. "You're Rachel Brown, I presume. I'm Paul Westley, a friend of Phil's. I was hoping I'd meet you here, but didn't realize what a pleasure it'd be."

"It's very nice meeting you," she responded. "I was hoping I'd meet a friend of Phil's in Paris." In a way, he reminded her of Jason. He had the same kind of masculine good looks. She wondered if he was married since he wore no wedding ring.

"Perhaps after the reception, we could have dinner together," Paul suggested. "I don't have a date or wife waiting for me at home and we both have to eat, that is unless you already have a date."

Rachel didn't know whether the invitation was an honest one or an excuse for them to talk since she was here at Phil's request. "I'd love to. I don't have any dinner plans. Normally, I figure there's enough to eat at receptions that dinner is not necessary. However, this one is so large that getting close to the hors d'oeuvres table may be quite a feat." Rachel noticed that the Europeans, especially the younger men, had a certain knack for hitting the food early and often.

She also noticed a very sexy French woman staring at her. Rachel smiled and turned away. Soon, the woman was at her side.

"You're Rachel Brown from America, aren't you? I believe we have a close friend in common, Jason Conrad," she said in a saccharine voice. "I'm Miriam Gauthier. I met Jason when he was in Europe a few months ago. We became close, or should I say, *intimate* friends."

Rachel felt a cold chill. What did this woman mean? Did he have an affair with her and, hence, the reason Jason hadn't telephoned when he returned from Europe? Rachel vaguely remembered seeing her name as one listed on Jason's second appointment schedule.

"That's nice," Rachel responded in a sugary tone. "Yes, Mr. Conrad is a client of ours." Rachel didn't want to admit that Jason was the one attached to the beautiful diamond ring on her left hand. She noticed that Miriam's eyes had hit it like magnets.

Fortunately, at that moment Mark came up and rescued her. Rachel introduced Mark to Miriam and then Mark steered Rachel away.

"I thought I'd better get you away from that barracuda," Mark said. "She's on Phil's 'watch' list. She and her boss, Francois, are close friends of Pierre's and are after certain U.S. technologies, including several being developed by Jason's company. Don't worry about Jason," he continued as if reading her mind. "He's very well aware of her game," he assured her.

"According to Phil, she tried to seduce Jason while he was here, asking him over to her apartment for dinner. The only thing she managed to do was let him know that she knew one of his associates, Sam Penderton. That's the reason I met with Jason on Monday. Sam's married, but apparently during a period of marital strife, he succumbed to her charms during a conference in New York. We're sure she has pictures of them *in flagrante*, so to speak. Jason's afraid she'll threaten to blackmail Sam to get classified information. She plans to visit California next week, after the meeting, since

The Purloined Encryption Caper

Sam stupidly invited her to California. I wasn't going to tell you this but I didn't want you to think badly of Jason. She'd do anything to cause trouble between you two." Rachel watched him as she replied.

"She told me she and Jason had become close, or as she said, she was on *intimate terms* with him. Naturally, Mark, I was startled, since as you know, Jason and I are engaged."

"Actually Jason confided to me in San Francisco that you're already married but are keeping it secret for the time being." Mark then smiled at Rachel adding, "I've never seen you look so lovely, Rachel. If I were Jason, I'd never let you come to this conference alone, and definitely not let you wear such a sexy and seductive dress."

Rachel mingled with the other participants, listening in discretely on conversations when she could. No one there, with perhaps the exception of Frank or Phil's friends, knew about her command of languages and so didn't stop talking in their native tongue when Rachel approached. She surmised by the comments being made that most Europeans felt that the United States was not being fair in holding back technologies that could be of major assistance to them. They seemed most irritated especially about those which give the U.S. a clear superiority in both information technology and communications systems and in their data scrambling ability to monitor or disrupt any electronic transfers.

She noted which individuals talked together and heard them discuss forming a group to try to undercut or boycott certain American companies, or agree to share whatever information they could steal from the

Rose Ameser Bannigan

U.S. utilizing whatever means necessary. They all confessed they had no love for the arrogance of the United States. Rachel almost giggled when she thought of walking up to some pompous French official and saying in her impeccable French, "I don't think that's a very honorable thing to do."

As the reception end neared, Paul Westley appeared by her side. "Ready for dinner yet?"

"I'm starved," she replied as she moved toward the foyer to get her coat.

"I see you're the lucky man tonight, Paul," Mark said, as they were leaving.

"Yes," Paul replied. "On instructions from Phil. But for once his orders are delightful to follow."

"You look so lovely, Rachel, that we must go to an elegant place. How about Maxim's or the Ritz?" Paul asked.

"It's your town and I'm your date, so either is fine by me."

Paul had already made reservations at Maxim's. Although he had been there a few times, he had never been there on an expense account. He was really looking forward to it and planned to show Rachel a good time, too. He was sorry she sported a large diamond ring on her left hand.

CHAPTER 19

The dinner and wine were excellent and Rachel realized that Paul was indeed a sophisticated, charming man who knew how to entertain and charm a woman. He's probably the favorite escort of the wives of congressional or government officials, she thought. He seemed to comprehend everything she was telling him about conversations she had overheard.

"No wonder Phil sent you. Apparently these old codgers thought you were some good looking chick who's put on the list as a payoff or that you were a mistress of some government official. Little do they know." He smiled.

Paul invited her to a meeting at the American Embassy on Friday to review the outcome of these sessions. "I'll pick you up Friday morning and take you directly into the Embassy so you won't have any trouble."

"Don't worry about me. I can meet you there. I don't want to create difficulties for you."

Rose Ameser Bannigan

"This kind of trouble, my dear, I enjoy," Paul said as he took Rachel's hand. "You know, Rachel, I can't believe that a woman as nice, bright and beautiful as you isn't married. Normally, the unmarried women who come through here, the friends or daughters of high level bureaucrats or politicos, are either ugly or plain looking or just plain dumb. Or am I wrong in assuming you're not married?"

"No, I'm not married," Rachel lied. "I guess I hadn't met the right person before, but I'm engaged to someone now and we'll be married shortly. How about you? I don't see a ring on your finger."

"I was once. But being married to an Agency man under diplomatic cover and therefore loaded with Foreign Service duties too, doesn't provide much time for marriage, especially a new marriage. So my wife packed up and went home. That was from my last post in Indonesia." Paul wondered why he was so forthcoming with Rachel. He usually didn't talk about himself. "Phil said you had also served in Asia. Did you enjoy it?"

"Yes," Rachel said. "Very much. I also enjoyed my short visit to Indonesia. It's such a fascinating country. I loved the Indonesians I met, although I understand the government leaves much to be desired. As a matter of fact, in Indonesia I met an American I almost married."

"What happened," Paul questioned, "or shouldn't I ask?"

"He was a Navy pilot and his plane crashed in the Pacific Ocean en route to meeting me in San Francisco to get married. I guess he was willing to do anything

The Purloined Encryption Caper

not to marry me," she said, trying to put a light tone to the conversation.

"I can't believe that. What was his name? Maybe I met him if he visited Indonesia often." The story had a vaguely familiar edge to it.

"Jeff Singleton," Rachel replied with her eyes lowered.

"So *you're* the girl he was in love with." Paul shook his head in disbelief. "He was assigned to the Agency for awhile and flew some of our people around Asia, including me, and he spoke of you often. I'm so sorry. He really was one of the nicest guys I ever met. We became friends immediately."

Paul had wondered whatever happened to Jeff's fiancée and had written to Jeff's parents expressing his sympathy and asked for the fiancee's name and address. He never got a reply. He told Rachel this.

She laughed and told Paul of her encounter with Jeff's family.

"I myself was going through a painful divorce at the time and felt that perhaps Jeff's girl was also hurting." Rachel looked at him, smiled and nodded her head. A certain bond developed that night between Rachel and Paul, not a romantic one, but one that could be a solid friendship if they ever lived in the same town.

Every evening when Rachel returned to her room, it was her habit to add whatever information she had acquired to a report she would eventually submit to Phil. She wanted to keep it current so it wouldn't be one horrible chore at the end of the meeting and also so she wouldn't forget important details. Because she was nervous about security and the possibility of somebody entering her room in her absence, every morning she would put her evening's addition in her safety deposit box kept by the hotel cashier. It was Wednesday evening and she wanted to review her total report so she went to the lobby to get her previous pages. There she ran into Frank.

"Where have you been keeping yourself?" he asked. "Have a drink with me in the bar downstairs for old times sake."

She consented and they took the elevator to the downstairs bar. It was fairly empty.

"You know, Rachel, I can't believe that we're together in Paris but not really together. I've thought so many times about our visits here and how much we loved each other. Have you really forgotten?" He paused. "I haven't. It's not that long ago." Frank looked at her adoringly.

"Perhaps to you it isn't, Frank, but to me it's several lifetimes ago," she replied with some acid in her tone. "I didn't forget it for a long time and I really didn't forgive you until this visit and my being in Paris again, alone. I hated you at first and felt betrayed, and for money, the biggest hurt of all. Then, when I was processing out of the Agency after my tour in Asia, one of my former colleagues in Europe told me how you used me to get information, and how he had fed info to me to give you items they wanted to appear in the press. I soon realized that the people I trusted the most were the people I should have trusted the least. It was a damned good lesson," she said bitterly. "I've found it hard to trust people, especially men, after that

The Purloined Encryption Caper

experience." She looked at him with scarcely veiled contempt. She decided to let it all hang out.

"Luckily at the time I learned this bit of information," she continued, "I was going to marry someone who was really a decent, wonderful man but he was killed in a plane crash so don't bother asking about the details. But he proved to me that there still are really good men around. I've met a few others in Washington since I've reentered the workforce. Jason, for example."

"I was sorry to hear about your folks," Frank finally said. "I tried to reach you, but couldn't locate you at the time. You know I still care for you or you wouldn't be avoiding me so much, or do you think I'd use you again for information? It occurred to me earlier, since apparently your office publishes a weekly newsletter that seems to be much sought after in Europe. But you should know that copies are floating around here with certain officials, some of them very unsavory. Luckily, I didn't have to ask you. I got copies myself from one such person, a Miriam Gauthier. Do you know her?"

Well, so Miriam was at work on Frank as well. "Yes, I've met her. But how did she get a copy of my newsletter?"

"You should say 'copies'. I think she has almost every issue you produced. Why not ask Jason?" Again, Rachel went cold but decided to ignore his comment.

"Frank, would you let me see the copies she gave you? Our newsletter is confidential and only for clients who pay a lot of money to have us represent them in Washington. It's not to be distributed to anyone else nor is it available to non-paying customers. Perhaps if I see them, I can figure out where the leak is."

"Would you care to come to my room for a nightcap, or don't you trust me?" He asked, noting that she didn't react to his statement about Jason.

"I'd prefer to wait here, if you don't mind."

When Frank returned, Rachel noted that it was an unaddressed copy and didn't have the last page, normally specific to each company. Therefore, it would seem it had to come from someone in her office. Was it Jack, Cindy, Susan, or was it taken by someone else privy to their files? Or had someone broken into their network and merely unloaded the information?

She noticed a fax number and realized with some relief that while the sender had a Washington, DC area code, it was not sent from her office. She copied the fax number and returned the copies of the newsletter to Frank. It should be easy for Phil or Mark to identify the sender for her.

"I appreciate this bit of information, Frank. Jason asked me whether we had any European clients. He said he saw a copy in one of the offices during his European visits."

Frank smiled inwardly. He was certain Jason had seen the newsletter in Miriam's apartment but didn't want to mention it again.

Rachel made movements to go. "Please, don't go," Frank said. "I've just ordered another round of drinks for us." He then reached for her hand and held it for a long moment. "Rachel, is there any chance of our getting together again? I know you're engaged to Jason, but engagements can be broken. I'm not married anymore, so we could get married. It was what you wanted at one time."

The Purloined Encryption Caper

Rachel laughed as she withdrew her hand. "You'll never change, Frank. Now, that you've arranged your life to suit yourself, you think you can take people and put them into the boxes you've designed to suit your needs and feelings." Rachel paused. "No, I don't love you any more, Frank, and I could never have the same feelings I once had. Am I still physically attracted to you? Perhaps a little, but I could never trust you as one should trust a husband. I hope we can be friends since you and Jason are or were good friends, but that's between the two of you. I don't know how men feel about being a buddy with someone who's been his wife's ex-lover," she said, enjoying the verbal needle she'd shot.

Frank winced as he responded. "To say that I don't envy Jason would be lying and you know it. Congratulations. He's a fine fellow. You know he turned pale when I mentioned your name to him last week. He then told me you were his fiancée and left the bar. I said may the best man win. I guess he wins." He paused. "But, I warn you," he said cynically, "as I wrote you several years ago, if I can't have you, no one else will either."

Frank knew he would never give up on the possibility of making Rachel his. He wondered if he told her about Jason's visits to Miriam's apartment, whether it would change her mind about Jason. Perhaps sometime he would use this bit of information against Jason, but not yet.

That night after adding the day's comments to her report, Rachel phoned Jason. It was good to hear his voice again, a bit of reality in the week's crazy happenings.

"I miss you, darling," Jason said. "How soon will you be on my side of the ocean?" His daily phone call had become a habit.

"I plan to leave Sunday," Rachel said. "This gives me time to visit museums and do some shopping."

"Don't see too many places without me. Save some for our future trips together," he quipped.

"You should have seen me the other night. I wore my new blue dress, had my hair done and makeup applied. I wanted to come close to the sophistication and sexiness of these French women."

"I don't think you have much competition, if I remember the French women I met."

"Including Miriam Gauthier?" Rachel questioned. There was a short pause.

"My God! Did you meet her? She tried to seduce me and lure me to her bed but without much success, I may add. I found out she had an affair with one of my associates. What else happened? Did you see Frank anymore?"

"Yes. He spotted me in the hotel lobby and we had a drink together. He seemed upset with the news that we'd marry soon, and that he didn't have a chance of changing my mind. I really enjoyed telling him that, but I'm grateful to him for the information about the newsletter. I think he's leaving as soon as the conference ends tomorrow. I have to stay for an Embassy meeting Friday morning and then finalize my report that afternoon. They'll fax or e-mail it by secure line to Phil. I'm sure Phil will give me a copy when I

The Purloined Encryption Caper

return to Washington and I can show it to you when we see each other."

"Jason, the strangest coincidence happened. The individual Phil nominated as my Agency contact knew Jeff in Indonesia. Talk about a small world."

They chatted a few more minutes and then said goodnight.

Before he hung up, he said, "Rachel, come back, get yourself organized and move to California. I'm not very good at waiting."

Rachel laughed, said she loved him and hung up. She was looking forward to seeing Jason again soon, but since this latest foray into the business world on her own, she wondered if she would be happy being only a housewife and mother.

Jason pondered about the information from Rachel's call. It was apparent that she had seen Frank and enjoyed telling him she was engaged to Jason. This was out of character for Rachel and closer to how Claire would act.

Also, her mentioning that her official contact had been a friend of Jeff's perplexed him. Would he ever be able to accept Rachel's past, especially her male relationships, without feeling a pang of jealousy? While he had many liaisons with women, other than Terry or Claire, his were more fleeting, while Rachel's relationships were more intense, or perhaps this was only his selfish point of view.

He also realized that she was truly enjoying her new found freedom and importance in the business world. Would she be happy as his wife? If not, would he be willing to share her with a professional job? Perhaps he would have to compromise. Why was it, Jason wondered, that love could sometimes be so disquieting. It was with a questioning heart that Jason slept that night.

The next day's meeting went quickly and Rachel spent Thursday evening wrapping up her report. She wanted to review it with the Embassy people the next morning, especially to verify names and titles before it was forwarded to Phil.

She had made serious decisions about her own life as well. She no longer feared running into Frank and if Jason wanted to continue his relationship with Frank, she felt she could tolerate their friendship. She realized she missed Jason more than she thought she would and wanted to move to California as quickly as possible without leaving Jack and Phil in the lurch.

But she also realized that she couldn't just sit home and wait for Jason to return from the office, at least until they had children. She wondered how her mother put up with it for all those years.

The next morning, Mark was at the Embassy meeting along with Paul and a handful of others. The CIA station wanted to finalize an overall report, one that could be shared with State and Commerce Department, as well as the more detailed, sensitive one that would go only to the CIA and FBI.

At the meeting's end, Paul asked Rachel what her plans were for Saturday. "I'm free and an excellent tour guide. It's one of my functions for visiting firemen and spouses."

The Purloined Encryption Caper

"I'm going shopping," Rachel said.

"I'm also excellent at recommending the best shops to go to, where top quality merchandise is sold at the best prices. What are you interested in?" he asked.

"It may shock you to know that I plan to load up on attractive, sexy lingerie. Remember, I'm going to be a bride and I need a trousseau," Rachel said smiling.

"I know the perfect place," he said, "and I'd be glad to escort you there. As a matter of fact, I promised my mother and sister to buy them some things the first chance I got. Perhaps you can even help me."

"Great," Rachel responded, "and if you want, I'll be happy to take them back to the States with me and mail them from Washington. They'll get them quicker that way."

It was decided that Paul would meet Rachel at the hotel at ten o'clock the next morning. They could shop, have lunch and then shop some more if necessary.

Friday afternoon when she returned to the hotel, Rachel accepted Mark's dinner invitation. They went to a charming restaurant near Notre Dame that resembled the catacombs and were seated at a table in the back, hidden from most other diners. Shortly after they had ordered drinks, Mark noticed Pierre and Miriam sitting at a table in the front of the room. He was surprised to see Pierre in Paris since he hadn't attended any of the meetings.

It was hard for Mark to concentrate on his dinner and Rachel with this development. Since Mark was leaving the next day and Rachel was staying on until Sunday, he decided to tell Rachel about the latest plans to neutralize the group of five. He also decided to contact Paul and ask him to keep a special watch over her. Rachel's back was to the table where Pierre and Miriam sat so she couldn't see them, and they, in turn, couldn't see her.

That the FBI decided to neutralize the foreigners one by one not to cause any public furor or unhappiness within the private U.S. business community surprised Rachel. "The NATO alliance is too important," Mark said, "to be challenged by two-bit hoodlums, such as these people, especially if the respective NATO countries are willing to take action themselves against these low-lives. We realize that the countries' intelligence leaders probably were in on the original plot to penetrate our companies and government to steal industrial secrets, but I don't think they were aware that this group planned to do it for their own personal greed."

"Politics," Rachel remarked, shaking her head.

When Rachel and Mark were about half way through dinner, Mark noticed that Miriam and Pierre were joined by two men he knew he had seen before in the States. He wanted to ask Rachel to turn around and look but was afraid it might attract unwanted attention.

Ten minutes later, the two men left, and shortly thereafter, Miriam and Pierre followed. Mark was sure they were up to no good and considered delaying his departure from Paris, but he couldn't do more than Paul could. And Paul knew Paris better.

Rachel had insisted on walking back to the hotel. While they were talking, it struck Mark who the men were--the thugs who had been watching Rachel's

The Purloined Encryption Caper

apartment building in Arlington. He would telephone Washington and get faxed pictures sent to Paul's embassy office.

He escorted Rachel to her room and told her to lock her door and not admit anyone. "If someone knocks and says they're from the hotel, check with the front desk first before you let anyone in." She promised she would, but was curious about his instructions.

Mark went to the Embassy and phoned Paul to meet him there within the hour. Paul was fully briefed about their project, first by Phil and then by Mark.

"Look, Paul," Mark said, as he showed him the faxed pictures from Washington, "these goons have been watching Rachel's apartment in Arlington off and on for the past few months. Tonight, I saw Miriam Gauthier and Pierre Ledent together at the restaurant you recommended. Shortly before they left, they were joined by these two creeps. I feel they're up to something, but I'm not sure what. They may be getting desperate enough about this time to try a coup." He paused for effect and continued.

"They know we've neutralized Hans and that Carlo is being recalled. Our colleagues at Rome Station went to the Italian intelligence service and threatened to expose his attempted penetration of the CIA unless the Italians promised to prosecute him. Julian is up to his eyeballs in trouble because of his attempts to subvert the United Nations people. The woman he propositioned got very nervous and went to the authorities at the U.S. mission. They're currently in conversations with the Belgians at NATO headquarters. It leaves only Clive and of course our good French friends.

"Clive is a lightweight in this operation and only follows instructions," Mark added. "He's done his good deed by identifying companies of interest as well as getting detailed patent application information and pinpointing Commerce staff who could be bought off. He's now enjoying himself as part of the gay political high life in Washington." Mark then continued.

"Our London station chaps will be talking to our cousins there early next week, as soon as we can send them some good photos or to a good friend of his wife's at the British Embassy in Washington. We understand Clive's wife doesn't know he's bisexual and can't understand why she wasn't able to accompany him to Washington. His wife is a distant relative of the Queen and Clive got his position in MI-6 through his wife. We think it will be easy now to quietly compromise him."

"This has been a hell of an operation," Paul observed. "I hope we don't have too many of them. But with the recent talks, it seems there may be many more in the future. You have to be congratulated for handling it without creating an international embarrassment. Hell, NATO is weak enough as it is and many Americans are wondering why we still have to prop up the European members now that the Soviet Union no longer exists, much less continue to add new members to NATO."

"We really only came across this den of thieves serendipitously." Mark then told Paul about the sequence of events involving Rachel, Phil, Jason, Jack and lastly seeing Pierre and Hans in Berkeley Springs.

"My main concern now is Rachel," he confided. "I have a gut feeling they'll try to waylay her or try to

The Purloined Encryption Caper

kidnap her here to trade her for Jason's new technologies. The $64,000 question is what will Jason give to have her back? The French aren't as sticky about this as we are. In America, you can fry for kidnapping and they know it. For example, did the French do anything about the businessman who was kidnapped and then released thirty-six hours later? No. They just told the press that they were searching for the perpetrators and would prosecute them once they were found. Thus far, nothing has been done."

That night Paul thought long and hard on how he could ensure that nothing happened to Rachel during the rest of her Paris stay. Before he went to sleep, he left a message on the answering service of two colleagues to telephone him as soon as they came home, but no later than seven-thirty the next morning. It was very urgent.

CHAPTER 20

Earlier that week, Pierre was packing to leave for the international technology meeting in Paris when he received bad news from Ingrid, Han's German proxy.

"Hans is being interrogated by the BND. They hadn't realized that what he was going to do in the States might embarrass the German government. There's going to be a critical NATO meeting within the next six weeks so they plan to throw him to the wolves and imprison him for insubordination to appease CIA," she informed Pierre in a state of near panic.

Ingrid had tried unsuccessfully to get more details but didn't want to get deeply involved or implicated. Hans hadn't made her privy to many details of his assignment in Washington, but told her to contact Pierre if there were any difficulties. If possible, she would try to learn if Hans had confessed the whole plot or where he was being held since he wasn't at his apartment. She would then let Pierre know.

"If he talks, everyone involved in your project will be blown. The Germans would like nothing more

than to reveal how the French spooks are trying to use their people for the financial gain of the French government--and against the Americans." Pierre was rather shaken by this news and by Ingrid's information regarding the French.

Also, there was a message on his answering machine to phone Sophia in Rome as quickly as possible. When he reached her, she was equally upset. "Please tell Carlo he's in deep trouble. I can't telephone him directly since I'm afraid his telephone is tapped. Our government has been informed about Carlo's attempt to penetrate the CIA by seducing one of the Agency's secretaries. I understand the CIA has threatened not to share any more data if they didn't recall Carlo immediately and prosecute him. And the Italian government plans to blame it on the French for trying to subvert their staff."

Pierre had to act fast. He decided to take an earlier flight to Paris and meet with Miriam. He was very angry. None of these problems would have happened if the members hadn't disobeyed his orders and used the cabin as a bordello over the holidays. Somehow, someone knew about their group and had followed them. He would have to find out how and by whom. He didn't care what happened to his partners but didn't want to get in trouble himself.

No doubt it was the CIA or the FBI, or both. But how did they do it? He decided to drive to Berkeley Springs that evening and see what he could discover. He took his luggage with him in case he had to go directly to the airport the next morning. Also, he would use the French Embassy car since it was easier to park

The Purloined Encryption Caper

at the airport using diplomatic parking privileges.

Everything has happened so quickly, he told himself. If the U.S. government's intelligence organizations were aware of their project, they obviously had no intention of leaking it to the press. They obviously wanted to do it discreetly and not anger either the U.S. public or the U.S. business community this close to the next NATO meeting. The American people would be furious if they felt that their European allies were trying to snooker American government personnel and steal from private businesses. Both the NAFTA and GATT agreements and the WTO were already very sore points with American workers, labor unions and some U.S. businesses. This would just add to the public uproar. The telephones of U.S. congressional representatives and the White House would ring off the hook.

Now he and Miriam would have to make one big coup to provide them enough money to live comfortably for the foreseeable future. They had to bet everything on getting the plans for the encryption systems and biometric technologies being developed by Jason Conrad's firm. He heard earlier that Rachel and Jason became engaged over Christmas and that Jason had recently spent a week in Washington testifying in front of Congress. At that time, he and Rachel had eloped. How much does Jason really love her, he wondered.

Two approaches were necessary: Miriam would proceed with her plan to blackmail Sam Penderton and they would also try to kidnap Rachel. This would put extra pressure on Jason to part with his cherished technologies.

Pierre was sure that Rachel knew more about

Jason's technology systems than she let on. When he checked her credentials, he found out she had an engineering and technology background and had previously worked for the CIA. She wasn't the Miss Innocent she pretended to be.

Pierre had been furious with himself for treating her with such kid gloves and wondered whether the Hill staffers and her boss knew of her past. Perhaps Pierre himself could have benefited from exposing her. Perhaps he still could when he returned from Paris.

He arrived at Rainbow's End late in the evening but turned off the headlights as he entered the driveway so he wouldn't alert anyone of his arrival. With no leaves on the trees, he noticed that a cabin several hundred yards away had lights on and smoke coming from its chimney. Apparently someone lived there. He wondered who it was. He hadn't paid any attention to it in the past or checked to see if it was occupied.

He silently opened his cabin door, put his briefcase on the table near the entrance and made sure everything was in order. He checked the computer system and changed the diskettes, putting the old ones in his pocket. He then started checking the wooded area surrounding his place. He didn't lock his door so he could get back in quickly if necessary. Could he get close enough to look into the window of the nearby cabin to see if there was any visible evidence that it was being used by the CIA or FBI? If they caught him, what would he say?

He couldn't worry about that now. He had to find out as much as he could about who lived there. It might provide him with valuable information.

He crept through the woods, careful not to make

The Purloined Encryption Caper

a sound, until he was within five feet of the other cabin's windows. There, he saw sitting at a table in the kitchen an older couple playing cards. There was no high powered equipment visible, so he decided to look into another window on the other side of the cabin. However, his foot slipped and he fell with a thud.

The noise brought the man sitting at the table out of the cabin in a flash. When Pierre tried to get up, he found himself staring into the barrel of a .38 automatic.

"Don't move. Raise your arms and walk slowly into the house, or I'll blow your head off," Miles Hanson ordered. "And tell me who the hell you are and what the hell you're doing here?"

His wife, Jan, had quietly left the kitchen, phoned the local sheriff and went to get her gun so she could cover Pierre from another room in the event he tried to attack Miles. She motioned to their house guest in the next room to be quiet and stay where she was. The guest happened to be Ruth Brennan.

"I must have gotten lost in the woods," Pierre said to Miles, a little shaken by the appearance of a gun in his face. He himself had a revolver but was unable to reach it without fearing a blast from the .38.

"That's a shitty excuse," Miles said. "I suggest you get inside where we can have a little talk and see what you're about."

Pierre obliged and preceded Miles into the cabin. Pierre took the opportunity to look around to see if he could identify any surveillance or recording equipment.

Rose Ameser Bannigan

The place looked like an average house in this part of West Virginia.

"Again, who are you, where are you from and how the hell did you get here?" Miles asked, knowing the answers to his questions, but waiting for Pierre's explanation.

"My name is Pierre Ledent, an official of the French Embassy. I am spending the evening next door at the cabin of a friend. I decided to take a walk in the woods and got lost. I saw the light and thought it was the cabin where I was staying." Pierre was grasping for any explanation he thought this man would accept. "I am new in this country and I don't know the area very well. Being greeted by a neighbor with a gun in hand is hardly what I'd consider American hospitality." He said it in a very haughty manner, which angered Miles further.

"And lying to neighbors is not what I'd consider very smart. You entered your driveway without using your headlights, so you must know your way around here. You see, sound travels far in the quiet of our nights. We thought we heard the motor of a car, but saw no lights. You must've had a reason. If you were heading for your friend's cabin, why didn't you go to the front door rather than peering through our windows? I think you're up to no good and I aim to find out why. The sheriff's on his way and you can explain your actions to both of us." Miles had become quite good at feigning a West Virginia accent and looking like a local.

"Please don't call the police," Pierre begged. "I have done nothing wrong and I must be back at my Embassy by morning." Miles ignored his comments.

The Purloined Encryption Caper

"Also, you can tell me what the hell goes on next door. We're law abiding, God-fearing mountain folk and the shenanigans that have taken place have been a disgrace. The local boys have witnessed some sex orgies with both male and females. We don't like that stuff happening around here, especially since you all seem to be a bunch of foreigners. U.S. country folk feel that if you want to carry on like animals, you can go back and screw in your own country, not in West Virginia. Don't corrupt our young folks here." His anger sounded authentic.

Miles felt he was on a roll and wanted to make Pierre squirm as much as he could. Hence, he played up his anger. This was easy for Miles, since he had developed a great dislike for the French in Europe, especially the Parisians. They were usually so arrogant, insisting their language take precedence over all others at international meetings, especially English, and they looked down their noses at what they considered crude Americans or Germans or Brits.

Of course, he remembered, they were always there for a handout when it came to asking the U.S. for money to cover costs associated with NATO or the UN or some other such purpose. And this bastard is trying to steal U.S. technologies to make money for both himself and his parasitic government, Miles thought. He had wished that Pierre had tried to run. It would have given him an excuse to rough him up a bit.

This was the opportunity Ruth needed to go next door and look inside the cabin. They didn't want to break in earlier, but Ruth knew he had not taken time to lock the door before he left. As she entered the driveway she saw he had driven his Embassy car and wrote down the license number. Also, she looked inside the car and saw that there were two pieces of luggage as well as a shopping bag of gifts. She wondered who they were for, but decided to investigate the cabin first. Before entering, she checked to see if anyone else had come with him. She doubted it, since the shopping bag was on the passenger's seat in the front.

She was right. The front door was unlocked. Fortunately, she was wearing gloves so she wouldn't leave any fingerprints. She rifled through his briefcase and found airline tickets for Paris the next day as well as $5,000 in dollars and a goodly sum of French francs. And many papers. She didn't want to take them, but glanced at them hurriedly. It was apparent that Pierre had become aware that both Hans and Carlo were compromised. There was someone named Ingrid and Sophia on the notes. Obviously he didn't know yet about Julian. Would he try to contact Clive before he left? She doubted it. He'll just up and run leaving Clive to hold the bag for the others' actions.

She saw two other doors in the back. She unlocked both of them, hoping that when Pierre left, he would be in such a hurry he would not bother to check. This would give her further access when Pierre was safely on the plane to Paris. In a small room in the back, she noticed the computer setup. It was beeping. She was afraid to open the computer for fear she would lose messages, but decided that tomorrow she would ask for one of the FBI computer jocks to break into the system.

The Purloined Encryption Caper

Was this how they were getting some of the technology that the FBI heard had been stolen from several of the smaller high tech companies? She also had heard that there were hacker attempts at breaking into the NSC and other intelligence organizations and Commerce Department networks. No one knew who it was or if they had succeeded. They only knew that it was from somewhere in the Blue Ridge area.

Ruth delved further into Pierre's briefcase. She found his address in Paris as well as a fax from Miriam which said he would not be able to attend the international technology transfer meeting in Paris since his office hadn't registered him in time. But she hoped he would still come to Paris.

Ruth copied the telephone number and was tempted to listen to the messages on the answering machine. If she could get in tomorrow, she would. At the moment she wanted to get out before Pierre returned or before someone else arrived.

When Ruth returned to the Hanson cabin, Pierre had already been taken by the local sheriff to Berkeley Springs to be booked as a trespasser. Miles was amused that Pierre had finally claimed exemption from U.S. laws because of his diplomatic status. The sheriff said he would release him only after the State Department confirmed it. Pierre was obviously agitated and insisted that he be freed to catch his morning flight.

When the sheriff found that Pierre could still reach the airport in time to catch his flight if he were kept overnight in the local jail, the sheriff decided to take Pierre to Berkeley Springs and book him. As the sheriff left, he turned around and winked at Miles, as much as to say, "Don't worry. We're not going to let these frogs threaten us with diplomatic mumbo jumbo. This is still our land."

Ruth and Miles went back to Rainbow's End and began to take pictures of the material in Pierre's briefcase. Ruth had already called the Bureau to get an emergency search warrant and arrange to have a good computer and electronics geek come to Berkeley Springs the next morning.

The one telephone call which Pierre was permitted to make from the Berkeley Springs sheriff's office was to Clive, the one remaining member of the group still resident in the United States. He asked Clive to get someone to the mountain cabin to download any information on the computer and insert a virus to confuse anyone else who might want to tamper with their setup. Clive told Pierre not to worry. He had all the necessary passwords which Julian had given him before he had left. Clive could take care of matters from a friend's computer in Washington and wouldn't need to travel to West Virginia. This Clive did and immediately faxed it to a number which Pierre had given him in Paris. Ironically, his friend with the computer was a U.S. government employee.

Meanwhile in Paris, Miriam was anxious. She already had word from Pierre about the disaster that had befallen, since Pierre phoned her shortly before he headed for the cabin. They had an agreement that he would phone her as soon as he arrived at Rainbow's End and he knew all was safe there. But that call never came.

The Purloined Encryption Caper

Had he arrived safely? Were there any problems? These were the concerns that plagued Miriam. She had already booked her flight over the Pole to San Francisco for Saturday evening, but she needed to know definitely whether she was to proceed with her plans to waylay Rachel. She and Pierre were to meet for dinner Friday evening at the restaurant near Notre Dame. Would he still come?

She decided she would proceed on her own, faxed Sam Penderton about her arrival and asked him to meet her at the San Francisco airport. If she could not stay with him, she hoped he would make suitable hotel accommodations. Remembering their nights together, she wanted to relive them again in San Francisco, continue their relationship and begin where they left off, she assured him in her message. She wondered if he were still married. She hoped so.

When Sam received the fax, he turned pale. Mark warned him that this would probably happen but Sam had hoped that it wouldn't. He hadn't mentioned his indiscretion with Miriam to his wife and knew that if she found out, she would immediately seek a divorce. Mark had assured him when they met in San Francisco that if Miriam did visit San Francisco, the FBI would do all within its power to intercede on his behalf with his wife. Sam next told Jason who, in turn, phoned Phil in Washington. Phil then called Mark in Paris and told him about this latest development.

"I'll catch the flight from Paris directly to San Francisco on Saturday morning, if possible. Otherwise, I'll fly to Washington and then on to San Francisco to help Jason and Sam. Phil, I have a gut feeling that Rachel might be waylaid or worse, kidnapped, by Pierre's group on Saturday. I think Paul has the situation in hand and will be with her all day to ensure that she gets on the plane Sunday morning." Mark tried to sound as reassuring as possible so Phil wouldn't worry.

Phil debated whether to tell Jason. He was afraid that knowing this might weaken Jason's resolve to play along with the FBI and CIA to confuse the French conspirators. However, he had to find out exactly how much Rachel knew about the new technologies Jason's company was developing and also, for his own satisfaction, how far Jason was willing to go to protect Rachel. Were his company and the potential business its development could bring more important to him than Rachel's safety? Phil decided to call Miles in West Virginia.

CHAPTER 21

"What's new, Miles? Anything happening up there?" Phil asked.

"Boy is it ever! Pierre was snooping outside our window when I shook him with a gun in his face. He's currently being questioned by the Berkeley Springs county sheriff and will probably be held overnight. While I had Pierre in my gun sight, Ruth went over to Rainbow's End and found plenty. Pierre plans to return to Paris tomorrow morning so had all of his luggage and his briefcase with him. Ruth and I returned to the cabin when we knew Pierre was safely jailed in Berkeley Springs and photographed all his material. Ruth will bring the film back with her tomorrow. We found out that he knows about Hans and Carlo. Ruth also asked her office to have FBI specialists come here tomorrow to check out the computer setup and telephones. Don't worry about the legality. Ruth got a FISA emergency search warrant from Washington."

Instead of waiting until Friday morning, Ruth decided to return to Washington late Thursday evening and talk to several of her colleagues the next morning before they left for the mountains to meet Miles. She had just entered her apartment when the telephone started ringing.

"Ruth, this is Phil Howard. Is it possible for you to catch a flight first thing tomorrow for Paris? I just may need a double for Rachel there. I assume you have a key to Rachel's apartment. Could you borrow a few of her clothes to take with you and be ready to leave at a moment's notice? I'll have to find out how quickly I can get you there." His voice betrayed his anxiety about Rachel.

"What's happened to Rachel?" Ruth questioned. Phil told her about their hunches. "Perhaps a double may come in handy and confuse the French or the hoods."

"It's strange," Ruth said. "The thugs who have been outside the building were still here even though Rachel left. But I noticed the day before yesterday they were no longer here." Ruth became concerned. She knew she had fooled them into thinking she was Rachel several times. Perhaps that's why they had stayed around. But why had they disappeared all of a sudden?

On Saturday morning, Mark caught his flight back to the States. He had been lucky and gotten a flight over the Pole and would get to San Francisco before Miriam arrived.

At ten that morning, Paul picked up Rachel to begin their shopping adventure.

"If you're interested in fine lingerie, mademoiselle, you must not miss Lili's on the Rue St. Honore. It has the

The Purloined Encryption Caper

finest lingerie in Paris." This advice was volunteered by an elegantly dressed French woman standing at the concierge's desk.

"I promise I shall go there," Rachel said with a smile.

Since it was such a nice day, she and Paul decided to walk. They stopped at a few small shops where Rachel purchased gifts for Cindy and Susan and then continued on to the shopping district around the Rue St. Honore.

"I'm ready for a bite of lunch. It's already 12:30. How about you, Rachel?" Paul asked. She agreed. They stopped at a small cafe where Paul signaled to his two office colleagues surreptitiously so Rachel wouldn't notice. He had prearranged this stop with his fellow case officers in order that they would follow him and Rachel to make sure they would be able to identify Rachel in the event they needed to find her without Paul along.

Paul and Rachel enjoyed lunch as well as the excellent wine.

"By the way, Paul, I know that Phil was checking with someone in your office about the circumstances surrounding the death of Steve Holliday. You may remember he was the Hill staffer with the Senate Intelligence Committee whose body washed up on the Riviera beach several months ago. Has the station found out anything new?" Paul shook his head.

"I never believed it was an accident. Steve was too good a swimmer. He was a pal from my younger days when we both spent our summers on the Outer Banks in North Carolina. The rip tides and undertow there are fierce, and yet Steve was never daunted by them." She did not mention the sheet of paper she found at Steve's cottage mentioning Nice, Marseilles and Corsica, and that those sentences were not contained in the latest draft of Steve's report that Tom managed to get.

"Rachel, I don't know the latest on that. My colleague, Jim Corbett, is supposed to be following up on the case. I'll ask him about it when I get back to the office and let you know. I don't think he's found out anything new since the French police have quietly closed the case. But what makes you think it wasn't an accident?"

"While we were at the beach last year," she explained, "he had almost finished a report on industrial and computer espionage. He only needed to verify some data from a confidential source. But then he was killed--yes, killed, I'm certain--before he was able to present it to his committee chairman."

Paul shrugged, paid the bill and they both started walking toward the lingerie shops. What they didn't notice was Miriam also watching Rachel and accompanied by the two French hoods who earlier had been watching Rachel's Virginia apartment. Soon Paul and Rachel were standing in front of an elegant window display.

"Look," Rachel said, "here's Lili's. Let's go in so I can tell the woman at the hotel that I actually did shop here." Paul agreed and they entered the store. It was a swank boutique, a little expensive, but since Rachel was buying a honeymoon trousseau, Paul didn't think she would mind the cost.

The Purloined Encryption Caper

"This set is lovely," Rachel said, holding up a diaphanous peignoir set. "I'll take it."

"You must try it on," the saleslady insisted. "It will only take a minute and if you don't like how it looks on you, I can always bring in others for you to try."

Rachel agreed and followed the saleslady to the back of the store toward the dressing rooms. Paul sat down on a small divan in front and prepared to wait until Rachel made up her mind. A few minutes later, the saleslady came back to the front of the shop and said that Rachel hadn't liked the original set so she was taking different sets to madam and hoped monsieur wouldn't mind waiting.

Rachel was gone for over thirty minutes when Paul began to be concerned. He went to the back of the store and called Rachel's name. When there was no response, he entered the dressing room area to look for Rachel. She wasn't there.

"Damn," he said to himself, "what a clever ploy." He went to an exit in the back of the store and saw that it opened on to a narrow alley. He was only glad that he had been able to slip a tracking device in Rachel's purse at lunch. At least they might be able to find her through the beep. He returned to the store and grabbed the saleslady by the shoulders.

"Where have they taken her?" The saleslady pretended she didn't understand but, after a few more hard shakes, confessed that a woman had given her 1,000 francs to play her role. Paul ran out of the store and looked for his colleagues. One was still out front waiting.

"Where's Jim?" Paul asked.

"He decided that someone should watch the back door, just in case. What's happened?"

"I think they managed to sneak her out the back, probably around forty minutes ago. I put the beeper in her purse. Do you think Jim was able to follow them?"

"I think so. I don't know what their transportation is, but Jim's driving a motor scooter. Depending on how far they take her, he should be able to keep up with them, especially since he can manage the narrow streets and even use the sidewalks if the streets are jammed. He has his cell phone with him. Should I try to reach him?"

"Please, and then call Inspector Dumont at Surete headquarters and the CIA station and have them fax pictures of Miriam, Pierre and the two French hoods to the Inspector. I have a feeling this is a desperate move and they're pulling out all the stops to blackmail Jason. Also, call Phil in Washington. He'll be upset and may want to notify Jason, but that's his call. Be sure to tell him we think one of our men is following Rachel."

"I tried to call Jim. There isn't any response, but he may not be able to hear it ring streaking down the noisy Paris streets."

Jim had indeed followed Rachel and her abductors and they were now approaching the Gare du Nord area. He ignored his telephone's buzz. Suddenly, the abductors stopped and with Rachel between them entered a deserted rundown building. Jim wasn't sure whether it was an old warehouse or an unoccupied residence. He noticed that Rachel wasn't struggling

The Purloined Encryption Caper

very much, so assumed they had either drugged her or she decided to save her strength for a more worthwhile effort. There were only two of them now. The woman had been dropped off at a Metro stop shortly after they left Lili's.

When he stopped and was alone, Jim heard his cell phone ring again. "I've followed them to a side street off Rue Lafayette near Gare du Nord. They've taken her into a deserted old building. I'll stay and watch. No lights have been turned on, so they're either in a basement room or they're purposely keeping themselves inconspicuous. There are only the two heavies. The woman who was with them was dropped at a Metro station. When she got out, she looked at her watch as if she were hurrying to go somewhere." He failed to identify the woman as Miriam.

"Keep watch," Paul said. "I'll try to get someone else there as quickly as I can. It will probably be French undercover men but I'll describe you to them so they know who to look for. We shouldn't try to do anything hasty. We don't want the goons to hurt Rachel. She won't be any use to them dead, so I'm sure they'll not harm her intentionally if they don't think they're under suspicion."

"I'm able to pick up the beeping sound from her device so I know she's still in there, or at least her purse is. In the event they move her, I'll follow and try to call you. I just don't want to lose her."

Rachel was at a loss to know what happened. When they first grabbed her, they had put a handkerchief over her mouth and nose. When she came to, she realized she was in a strange car with the two men who had watched her Arlington apartment. She thought she had heard the voice of a woman, but since there was no woman in the car now, she felt it must have been a dream. She had a vague memory of seeing Miriam in the lingerie shop. Why are they taking me Rachel wondered. There's no use fighting at this point. If there were only one man, I think I could handle him unless he knows martial arts, however, two are out of the question.

In French, they asked if she would like a drink of water. She felt her salvation was in not letting them know she spoke or understood French.

"I'm sorry, but I don't speak French," Rachel said in English. In broken English, they then asked her if she wanted water. She shook her head no.

Rachel sat with the two men for over an hour, waiting. The men talked freely about their assignment and wondered where their *patrone* was. Their job was over, and they wanted to be paid so they could go home to their families and be rid of this woman. They did not live in Paris but in a small town in southern France near Marseilles. If perchance they were caught, it would have grave consequences for them as well as their families, especially since the woman was an American. "We don't want to have to liquidate her as our friends had to do with that American man in Cannes," the larger man said.

It occurred to Rachel that these men were probably talking about Steve, and his death was somehow connected to this group.

The larger of the two men asked the other if he could guard Rachel while he went for some food. "Of

The Purloined Encryption Caper

course," the other man sneered. The larger man then left and said he would be back within the hour.

If she did manage to overcome the remaining man, what would she do? Could she find a taxi to take her back to her hotel or could she find a policeman? The larger man said he was taking the car.

Jim noticed that one of the abductors got in the car and drove away. Jim informed Paul and said he was going to try to get in and see what was what. Jim waited about ten minutes to see if the other man returned, and then entered the building quietly. He heard Rachel ask what they intended to do with her and why they had kidnapped her. Jim could tell where they were from the direction of her voice and quietly crept toward the sound.

Now that his eyes were accustomed to the dark, he saw he was facing Rachel. The other man's back was toward him. Jim came crashing down with a karate chop on the back of the man's neck and the man crumbled.

"As soon as I move this creep and tie him up, we'd better get you the hell out of here, Rachel. By the way, let me introduce myself. My name is Jim Corbett, a friend of Paul's."

"Are you a welcome sight," Rachel said with visible relief..

"We have to be careful since his buddy may return anytime now. I think they're waiting for someone, although I'm not sure who."

Jim began dragging the man's body into a room at the end of the hall. He put the body in a closet and locked the door.

Jim then managed to reach Paul on his cell phone. "I just managed to find Rachel and am about to take her away from this building. The man who left to get some food, might return shortly. They were obviously waiting for someone, but they didn't mention who. I'll take Rachel to safe house number ten which isn't far from here. I should get there in about thirty to forty-five minutes. By the way, I can't hear my cell phone ring while I'm on the scooter so don't bother calling me. Also, Rachel asked that you notify both Phil and Jason that she's okay, in the event you told them otherwise." Jim paused. "I put the man I chopped in a locked closet in a room at the end of the hall. I left the key in the door."

Meanwhile in the other room, Rachel was combing her hair when she heard another voice.

"Monk, over here. Did my friend manage to outwit your kidnappers?"

"Frank! Did you help Jim find me? I'll be forever in your debt for this. It's been gruesome."

"Quickly, get in my car so we can get out of here." Obediently, Rachel climbed into Frank's car. She sighed as she settled back and rubbed her head. Frank returned to the building.

When Frank reentered the building, he met Jim coming out of the other room. "I've got her, Jim. But to continue our plan, I'll have to hit you slightly. Just lie there until the police or your fellow colleagues arrive. I'll take Rachel to my place. You can tell them that the man in the closet's partner returned and hit you. Be careful that he doesn't. Also, if you can reach

The Purloined Encryption Caper

Miriam before she leaves for the States, tell her I'll contact her at her apartment on Tuesday afternoon. Okay? Otherwise, let's go our different ways not to compromise our situation. I'll be in touch later." Jim agreed to the plan.

The larger man returned approximately twenty minutes later, and found a young American man lying unconscious on the floor. The woman they had kidnapped was missing. *"Merde!"* he said aloud. Somehow, they had found out where they were hiding and had come to rescue her. His friend probably hid and then managed to incapacitate the American and left. Hopefully, his friend still had the woman. He decided his best move was to get the hell out of there and meet his *copain* in their village in southern France. Before he left, he put a large brown box in the window.

"Frank, I never thought I'd be so glad to see you again. I don't know who these men are working for and why they bothered to kidnap me."

"Probably for money," Frank responded.
"I don't understand why people do such hideous things. Does money mean that much to people?"

"Yes, Rachel, it does. People will do a lot for money. Or love."
They rode on for another ten minutes when Rachel looked out the window and realized they were heading away from Paris.

Rose Ameser Bannigan

"Where are we going, Frank? This isn't the way to the hotel."

"No, it isn't. I said people would do a lot for money or love, and I guess I'm one of those people. So is Jim. That's how I knew where you were."

CHAPTER 22

"But why?" Rachel asked, shocked. "How much money do you need? I understood from Jason that you inherited enough money to be very comfortable for the rest of your life."

"My mother was very rich. But she didn't leave me any money at all, just the large family estate, which is impressive, but badly in need of upkeep. Betty and I thought we had the old woman fooled but she had the last laugh. I told Jason I had inherited the money as I thought at the time. Later when the lawyer read the will, we discovered that she had disinherited both of us. She knew about my affair with you and others, Rachel, but she also found out about Betty's affair with the man she recently married."

Frank looked at Rachel to see if she believed his story. Then he continued.

"The money and estate, according to the will, now pass on to my issue, which must be legitimate. Since you're one woman I've always loved and wanted and couldn't shake from my mind, I planned to find you, marry you and then immediately get you pregnant. As soon as I had a child, I would become rich or, I should say, we would become rich. So, I am carrying out my plan. We're heading for a quiet town in northern Europe where a friendly man will perform the marriage ceremony." Rachel couldn't believe what she was hearing.

"I won't be such a bad husband and we did have fun in bed," he said as he started caressing her thigh. "And I said that people will do anything for either money or love. My reason is for both. I'd do anything to get you and I told Jason as much the last time we met. In my letter, I also wrote you that I'd never let another man have you."

Rachel moved as far away from Frank as she could. "You forget, Frank, that I'm engaged to Jason and I love him very much." She thought for a few minutes. If she angered him and told him they were already married, she wasn't sure what he would do, especially since she knew Frank always carried a gun.

"My darling Rachel. I'd never let Jason stand in the way of getting what I want. And after a while, you'll forget about him, learn to love me again and realize that we were meant to be together." Jason kept his hand grasped firmly on her knee and near his jacket pocket that held his gun.

"I could never love you again," Rachel said with disgust in her voice. "You must realize that. And if you really love me, I don't understand how you could do this or even want me on those terms." She hesitated and then looked at Frank. "I get sick to my stomach to think of the time I wasted on you and later thinking

The Purloined Encryption Caper

about you. How could I have been so stupid? Are you planning to use me against Jason, too?"

Frank didn't respond but quietly drove on. Rachel was sick, thinking of what could happen. She had thought that Frank had accompanied Jim to rescue her. Now she found that Frank had been waiting for an opportunity to kidnap her himself. She wondered how Frank knew where she would be held unless he was working in tandem with Miriam and Pierre. He must know Miriam since he got a copy of Rachel's newsletter from her. Also, he mentioned that Jim was involved with them as well. She would have to try to get word to Paul or was he in on the plot as well?

"Is Miriam one of your lovers, too, Frank? Or are you and Pierre partners in crime?"

"Did I have sex with Miriam? Yes, whenever I came through Paris, and she was available. She's very good in bed. I told her once she should give lessons to young American women. But, do I love her? No. She's not the type of woman a man falls in love with or marries. And she would make a horrible mother. She believes, however, that I love her, at least a little, and because she's anxious to become an American citizen, she told me she's in love with me." He seemed to be enjoying his confession and continued.

"She's willing to sell Pierre down the river and leave him hanging out to dry in order to get me. I was never in on the plot to sell technology. That is something she and Pierre and their Europeans buddies designed. I came in at the end. When I saw your newsletter at her apartment and read it, I cut myself in. Not to hurt you, but to find you, get you back and use you for my own purposes."

"Why don't you marry Miriam? She's really more your type, regardless of what you think or say. Or is she already married?"

"No, she's not married. She manages to string a lot of men along and keep them under her spell or in her bed. Even Jim. But I'm not so sure how many would be willing to take her as a wife. As I said before, she's not the kind men want to marry, especially American men. She's rather worn." Rachel jerked her head up and looked at Frank.

"Don't pretend to be so shocked. Even your dearly beloved Jason succumbed to her embraces. Or didn't he tell you? Where do you think he saw a copy of your newsletter? Certainly not in a French businessman's office," Frank said sarcastically.

"Yes, he told me she tried to seduce him, but he didn't give in to her."

"And you believed him? You're really still very naive, Rachel. I thought by now you would have grown up and realized that all men are susceptible to sexy women, especially those willing to provide them with what men really want from most women--a good lay. Remember, I know Jason very well. I know his appetites from his college days. You can't possibly believe that Jason is a saint and wouldn't sleep with other women while he was sleeping with you."

Rachel felt as if she couldn't breathe and was unable to speak, afraid she might begin sobbing. Why had Jeff died? He was the one decent person she had

The Purloined Encryption Caper

known who could have saved her from this turmoil and unhappiness. And now she was already married to Jason and very much in love with him, but again beginning to question his faithfulness and honesty.

Was Frank right about Jason? Did he have an affair with Miriam? Miriam was such a horrid person and the thought of Jason making love to Miriam revolted her.

She suddenly felt like running and wished she could go back to her beach house. But that place was spoiled for her now since she and Jason had spent time there together and it would bring back too many memories.

Frank rambled on about their future life together as he drove toward the Belgian border. "If you do find that later on you can't stand being married to me, I'll consent to a divorce but by then I'll have my money. I'd never let you take my child though and, knowing you as I do, Rachel, you'd never desert a child." He paused and changed his almost sarcastic tone. "With money, Rachel dear, we can live a very comfortable life."

Rachel felt nauseous and could barely manage to keep from showing it. She turned away from him and rested her head against the corner of the car window. She finally fell asleep.

It was pitch black outside when she awakened and found they were in a small city somewhere in northern France or possibly Belgium. She couldn't figure out where, only that she saw several signs in French.

Frank stopped the car in front of a rather tall sterile-looking concrete apartment building, fairly new by European standards. Frank opened the door to an unguarded, simple small lobby, led her to an elevator

Rose Ameser Bannigan

and pushed the button for the sixth floor. When they entered the apartment, Rachel was thankful that it at least looked clean.

"Here we are, my love," he said. "Make yourself comfortable since you'll be here for a few days. And don't try to scream or escape. The windows are sealed and the place is quite soundproof. There's food in the refrigerator and you'll find some of your things in the bedroom. I convinced the hotel cleaning lady to bring me some items of yours, for a small fee of course. I hope I chose correctly. The bathroom is beyond the bedroom and quite Western. I hope you'll consider sharing the same bed with me. But if you prefer to wait another day, I'll sleep in the other bedroom for the time being. But rest assured, my wait won't be long."

She did not doubt his threat, as he suddenly embraced her and forcefully kissed her and felt her breasts. She pushed him away and was about to knee him in the groin when he pulled back and let her go.

Rachel went into the bedroom and realized she had to use the bathroom. While there, she heard the outside door close and then locked. "I'll wait ten minutes," she thought, "and then I'll make a break for it." Where she would go didn't matter as long as she could get away.

When she tried the door, she found Frank had locked her in from the outside. What if there was a fire? Frank was right. None of the windows would open. He had also gone through her wallet and taken most of her money so that even if she did escape, she wouldn't have enough to buy a train ticket back to Paris.

The Purloined Encryption Caper

When the French police arrived at the deserted building near the Gare du Nord, they were surprised to find a young American male lying on the floor, just regaining consciousness. They rushed to the closet in the back room, unlocked it, and found one of the kidnappers sitting in silence, still a little stunned from the karate chop. They handcuffed him and put him in their police van. Then, they telephoned headquarters to report their findings.

"My God," Paul said as he hung up. "We lost Rachel again. The French police found Jim unconscious as well as the French thug in the closet. But Rachel was gone. Apparently, the other thug returned, found Jim, knocked him out and took her. Where she is now, heaven only knows. They're presently interrogating the hood they have, hoping he'll lead them to his comrade. I wouldn't want to be in his shoes. The French police can be unpleasantly persuasive when they want to be and taking an American hostage, especially a woman, doesn't sit very well with them."

"What about the woman at the shop who insisted Rachel try on the clothes?" the other CIA case officer asked. "Do you think she can shed any light?"

"Probably not. She doesn't know any of the details. I assume she's a friend of the woman who helped those two hoods kidnap Rachel. According to information we managed to get from Jim, they dropped the woman at a Metro stop. I'll give you even money she's across the border by now, possibly on a plane bound for another country. I'm assuming it was Miriam who arranged the kidnapping plot. The saleslady said the name of the woman who bribed her was Miriam."

Paul and the other CIA officer went back to his office to meet Jim. When they arrived, Paul briefed the others about the overall operation against Jason Conrad. They had all met Mark earlier, but didn't know his exact role until this moment.

"You know, Mark mentioned that Miriam might try to blackmail Sam Penderton, one of Jason's key staff associates. I wonder if she's on her way to San Francisco. Also, I wonder where Pierre is. He might have been the *patrone* they were waiting for. There would be no reason to kidnap Rachel unless they tried to either get information from her or use her as bait to blackmail Jason."

"Have you called Phil in Washington to let him know the latest or tried to reach Jason?" Jim asked.

"I've been putting off calling Phil," Paul replied, "hoping the French police might get lucky. God only knows we need it. But I guess I can't wait much longer. No one here called Jason but left it up to Phil. He may not have been able to reach Jason, since it's Saturday unless he carries a beeper or cell around with him on weekends. Perhaps it's better that Jason not be told yet," Paul mused. He then continued with his briefing.

"Also, I understand Mark is currently en route or has already landed in San Francisco to be there if Madam Miriam arrives. We figure they planned a two-pronged approach. Miriam would try to blackmail Sam and, at the same time, they would kidnap Rachel. This way they would have both Sam and Jason under the gun to give them the information they want. They would exchange Rachel and not expose Sam if Jason handed

The Purloined Encryption Caper

over the data they want." Paul paused to get a cup of coffee.

"Quite a plot. I think they're rather desperate now since their whole project has collapsed. They don't even get the satisfaction of disrupting the NATO meeting or getting the Americans upset since the FBI and CIA have managed to disrupt their little game by picking off the players individually. What we don't know is where Pierre is." Paul then told them about the incident at the Hanson's cabin in West Virginia and Ruth Brennan's actions.

"Mark didn't tell Rachel much about this part of the operation to protect her should anyone try to question her. People like Pierre, Hans and the others are trained to be very good at detecting if someone is lying and they don't act kindly toward them.

"You know," Paul continued, "Rachel is really Mrs. Jason Conrad. She didn't tell anyone they eloped over the past weekend but Pierre found out about it accidentally when he was having dinner in Berkeley Springs. Apparently, the waitress told him about this nice young couple who decided to elope at her suggestion. Pierre or one his friends checked and found out indeed it was Jason and Rachel who had tied the knot. So when they decided to kidnap her, they knew she was already Mrs. Jason Conrad."

After another hour went by and the police still weren't able to locate Rachel or get more information from the kidnapper, Paul decided to bite the bullet and phone Phil. While it was midnight in Paris, it was only late Saturday afternoon in Washington. With a little luck, they wouldn't be able to reach him and it would give Paul and the police more time to find Rachel.

Paul wondered if the trap the FBI was setting for Miriam in California would really work. If they were going to protect Sam from publicity as well as Jason's company, they would do whatever was necessary not to make their scam public. Could they get information on Rachel's whereabouts from Miriam?

Paul wondered why Jim had all of a sudden become so quiet and looked distressed when he heard they were trying to incriminate Miriam.

Earlier that day, Pierre was waiting for Miriam at her apartment. That was their plan if the kidnapping went off as anticipated. She opened the door and embraced him.

"She's all yours now, mon amie," Miriam said. "Our two friends are either en route to the Gare du Nord building or they're already there waiting for you. Now, I must pack my suitcase in order to catch my San Francisco flight. Are our contact points still the same and do we still rendezvous in Amman?" Pierre smiled at her and nodded his head.

"Then, I assume we can have our Syrian friends meet us there with confirmation that the five million dollars has been deposited to our Swiss bank account, with a promise of more to come if the software is as good as we anticipate. From Amman we can go somewhere that won't give in to pressures from either the Americans or the French. I'll be in Amman, hopefully by Wednesday or Thursday. Then we'll have time to celebrate."

The Purloined Encryption Caper

What Pierre didn't realize was the arrangement Miriam had worked out with Frank and Jim. If her plans with Frank materialized, she had no intention of meeting Pierre. She would sell the technology to another buyer she had found. Several dissident Saudis in exile had expressed great interest in it and even offered her more than the Syrians. She could then blame the scam on Pierre and perhaps even tell the officials where they could find him. Miriam had no scruples in double or triple dealing with people as long as it suited her and promised greater financial awards or gave her what she wanted.

Pierre left her apartment, but first wanted to make sure that he had taken all of his treasured possessions from his own place. He wasn't sure how soon he would be able to return, if ever. He taxied to his residence, packed several trunks which he took to the Gare du Nord, and made arrangements to send them to Geneva where he planned to eventually claim them. With his diplomatic passport, he was able to clear customs quickly.

With only his briefcase and one suitcase, he headed on foot toward the building where Rachel had been taken, only a few blocks away. He was glad the suitcase wasn't heavy. It contained only enough clothes to last him until they could tap into their Swiss bank account. He looked at the building where Rachel was supposed to be held. In the window facing the small alley way was a large brown box, the signal that something had gone awry.

Pierre stopped and went around to the back of the building to see if he could hear any voices. He didn't hear anything, so he left his suitcase, but not his briefcase, by the back door and quietly entered the building. What he saw displeased and frightened him. There were two French policemen as well as an American man waiting, watching the front entrance to the building, getting ready to pounce should anyone enter. They had not thought of checking for a back entrance.

Pierre quietly left the building, took his suitcase and went back to the Gare du Nord. There he took a Metro to the far side of the city as close as he could get to Orly Airport and then found a taxi to take him the rest of the way. He was sure that the French police would be covering DeGaulle International airport.

Arriving by taxi, Pierre noticed that a flight was leaving within the hour for Marseilles. That was perfect. If necessary, he could always take a boat to Tunis or perhaps Egypt and, from there, travel to Amman in the event the airports were being watched.

By nightfall, Pierre was checking into a small pension near the Marseilles waterfront. He was tired and hungry but decided not to wait until the next day to make his onward plans.

His decision was wise. At midnight, a freighter was leaving Marseilles for Alexandria, Egypt where it would unload and then move on to Haifa. This would give him the option of getting in touch with Miriam and having her meet him in Haifa or Alexandria rather than Amman. He would leave a message at the Amman hotel for her to be sure.

While the freighter accommodations were not luxurious, they were adequate and Pierre settled in

The Purloined Encryption Caper

for his three-day trip to Alexandria, and then another day to Haifa. He figured that he would reach Haifa by Thursday, assuming the unloading at Alexandria took only one day.

"This may work out just fine," Pierre thought, as he secretly smiled to himself. Now he and Miriam could find a place and spend the rest of their life enjoying their millions. Or else, they could split the money and go their separate ways. He didn't know precisely what Miriam had in mind since she was not the type of woman who made commitments to men, although she had once indicated to him that she had really been taken by a certain American gentleman. Thank goodness she didn't let this stop her from making love with him, but Miriam's love never included being faithful.

Merde, he was glad he no longer had to take orders from those idiot officials at his Bureau. He was also tired of smiling at all of the bumbling and crude diplomats he had to deal with, especially the Americans. "That's all in the past," he mused. He couldn't understand Miriam's obsession with America and her hopes to some day become a citizen of that country.

CHAPTER 23

Ruth was about to leave her apartment to catch the plane to Paris when the telephone rang.

"Forget Paris," Phil said. "There's a change of plans. Rachel's safe. One of our guys managed to rescue her from the two thugs and will put her on a plane for the States tomorrow. But Ruth, I'd like you to go to San Francisco in the event Mark needs you there." Phil then told her about his plan. "If Miriam sees you with Jason, we hope she'll think their kidnapping ploy backfired. We can't get Rachel there in time." Phil paused to see if Ruth had any questions.

"We'll ask Jason to meet you at the airport and take you to his house," he continued. "Mark's flying there direct from Paris and will go to Jason's place when he arrives. Sam is meeting Miriam's plane and taking her to a motel near the airport and will arrange to meet her for drinks and dinner when we assume she'll make her pitch. We've been able to confirm that she's booked on flights from San Francisco to London and thence to Amman, Jordan, for both Monday and Tuesday evenings. She plans to get what she came for by then, and the sooner she does, the quicker she'll leave." Phil hesitated to catch his breath.

"Mark will telephone me as soon as he gets to Jason's place and we'll then coordinate the rest of the plot. I'm sure Miriam plans to meet up with Pierre but we know that Pierre didn't fly to Amman. The French police are checking all airline manifests since he was last seen in Paris. They've already checked all outbound flights from DeGaulle and found nothing so they're now checking Orly, but that'll be more difficult. If he left from there, he probably flew to a place within France where he could leave the country surreptitiously, possibly under an assumed name. But they'll find him. The French government is very embarrassed. They don't like kidnappings happening on their turf, especially when the CIA is involved. They're still embarrassed over the kidnapping of the businessman several months ago."

As Ruth headed to the airport, Phil realized that he hadn't told Jason about Rachel's kidnapping adventures in Paris and decided to rectify that situation. He also wanted to make sure that Jason would meet Ruth at the airport.

"Jason? Phil Howard here. Hope I didn't waken you." Jason assured Phil that he hadn't.

"I have good news--and bad news." Jason began to get a sinking feeling. "First the bad news. I didn't want to worry you and you couldn't have done anything anyway, but Pierre and his group tried to kidnap Rachel in Paris. The good news is that Paul was with her. Rachel was determined to buy some sexy lingerie

The Purloined Encryption Caper

for her trousseau to try to seduce you, I assume." Phil wanted to add a touch of humor, if he could.

"One of our guys was able to follow her. When the opportunity arose, he karate chopped the French thug and removed Rachel. The two guys who took her were the same ones that were watching her Arlington apartment building."

Jason tried to interrupt Phil as he talked, but Phil continued. "She's fine and safe now. I assume they've taken her back to her hotel. Paul will put her on the plane tomorrow morning. I know you're probably mad as hell at us but I'd have called you earlier if anything had gone wrong or if there was anything you could have done." He wanted to sound more reassuring than he felt.

"Thank God, Phil, she's all right. I've got to get her away from all those creeps. You're right. I'm a little pissed off I wasn't told earlier. I'd have caught the first plane to Paris to see what I could do."

"Jason, that's the reason we didn't tell you. We didn't want to keep track of you as well. Our CIA station isn't that large so we don't have any bodies to spare. Will you be able to meet Ruth?" Phil said, changing the subject.

"Of course. But I'm not sure why she's coming," Jason said. "Do you think Ruth can pretend she's Rachel?" Jason seemed skeptical.

"Something like that. Sam will meet Miriam at the airport and take her to a nearby motel. This evening, he'll take her to dinner. I want you and Ruth to go to the same restaurant and sit at a table close to them, near enough for Sam to look over and greet both you and Rachel by name, but not close enough for Miriam to realize that Ruth is not Rachel. This should unnerve her since she thinks Rachel is still being held by Pierre in Paris or wherever he planned to take her. I've a feeling Rachel was also scheduled to end up in Amman, to be released only after they verified that the stolen technologies were authentic. That ace in the hole has now vanished." He hesitated a moment to let it all soak in, then continued.

"When Miriam sees you with Rachel, or rather Ruth pretending to be Rachel, I think she'll put pressure on Sam to give her the data quickly. She'll be afraid to hang around." Phil paused and then asked. "Did Sam manage to convince his wife to be out of town for a few days?"

"Yes. She's not here, so Miriam won't be able to telephone her. Will the FBI keep track of Miriam and see where she goes?" Jason questioned.

"Yes. Mark is en route to San Francisco from Paris. He took a United flight over the Pole and will meet you at your place this afternoon. I'm not sure exactly when he's due to arrive, but maybe you can check at the airport. He has your address but doesn't know that Ruth will be there, too. As a matter of fact, he left Paris before Rachel was taken so he doesn't know anything about that episode either." Phil hesitated, waiting to give Jason time to digest the information.

"Once both Ruth and Mark arrive, give me a call at home. We have several strategies to work out. First, we can scare the hell out of Miriam so she leaves the States in a hurry and, hopefully, doesn't ever come back. Second, we could call the French Embassy here

The Purloined Encryption Caper

in Washington and have them take her in. I'd rather not do this, since the press is liable to get wind of it. Then the project would be front page news, something we've been trying to avoid." He knew Jason would understand and agree.

"Our last option is to give her phony software and let her proceed to her rendezvous with Pierre for the sale of the goods to their buyers. I'm sure the deal is with some Middle Eastern country. Syria or Iran is my guess. When the buyers realize the software is phony, probably only after they've deposited a huge sum of money in an unnumbered bank account, I wouldn't give a plug nickel for the life of either Pierre or Miriam. You've talked with Miriam, Jason. Do you think she's smart enough to know whether the stuff you would give her is authentic?"

"Actually, Phil, I don't know her that well. Sam may. I'll phone and ask him now. Do you want to hold? Better yet, why don't I find out, and let you know. Then we can plot our action after Ruth and Mark arrive. I'll also think about what kind of package we can give her that wouldn't make her suspicious."

After Jason hung up, he sat down and thought about Phil's call. He wondered if Rachel was really okay. Phil didn't go into much detail and Jason knew he wouldn't get any more information from either Ruth or Mark. He decided to try to phone Rachel at her hotel in Paris, but she wasn't in her room. Jason left a message for her to phone him as soon as she returned, saying it was urgent.

Jason decided he had better buy some food if he was going to have house guests. He quickly finished his second cup of coffee and got ready to leave for the store. He turned on his answering machine in the event Rachel telephoned and made sure he had his cell phone with him.

When he returned there wasn't any message from Rachel but there was a message from Ruth. Her plane was scheduled to arrive earlier than anticipated, so she would be waiting outside the airport at three o'clock that afternoon.

He readied everything, phoned Sam and arranged to meet at the office to see what they could do about faking something to give to Miriam should the need arise.

"Sam, I don't know how we found ourselves in this mess, but I'm certainly going to put in more stringent security controls. I knew that the whole economic espionage situation was bad, but I didn't think our so-called allies were so desperate. I think I'm going to tell my congressman to get us the hell out of NATO and the UN. These people aren't our friends and I'm tired of my tax dollars being used to support them. They try to screw us at every turn."

"Well, Jason, I know one thing. In the future, I'm going to be the most faithful husband in the world. And I'm most grateful to you for helping me out of this. These people or so-called foreign friends are really bastards, with a real bitch thrown in for kicks. But maybe we can screw them for a change. Miriam really doesn't know much about technology, so she won't know whether the stuff we give her is authentic. I don't know about Pierre, though. I understand he's an engineer and very bright. He might be able to check

The Purloined Encryption Caper

whether it's the real stuff. Hopefully they'll be able to stop him before he can test it, or at least he'll be far away from the United States and France. I shudder to think what our options would be if they still had Rachel."

Jason thought about the coming week. He or someone from his firm had to attend meetings in New York on Thursday or Friday. He decided he would go himself and fly to Washington on Friday afternoon so he could spend the weekend with Rachel. It was only a week since he had last been with her, but it seemed an eternity.

"Now that we're married, you might want to consider leaving some clothes at the apartment, so you don't have so much to carry back and forth," Rachel had suggested the last time they were together.

He looked at her and shook his head. "Now that we're married, dear girl, I think it's about time we think about sharing the same house, on the same side of the continent permanently. In other words, I hope you can move to California instead of our always making plans to meet somewhere."

Recently, Jack told Jason that the office had already received a number of resumes from highly qualified people so Jack would be able to release Rachel rather quickly. Jack realized how much Jason loved Rachel and how much he missed her. He knew how he would feel if he had to be separated from Jean for any length of time.

After a few hours of sleep, Rachel awakened in Frank's apartment. At first, she couldn't grasp where she was but then remembered. She was also famished. She hadn't had anything to eat since her lunch with Paul. She went to the kitchen and poured a glass of juice and sliced off some French bread and cheese. As she ate, she thought about the last several hours and the comments Frank made about Jason.

She didn't really care what Jason did before they met. What troubled her most was the thought that he had slept with Miriam after she and Jason had made love. She found this hard to accept. If true, she might even consider having her marriage annulled.

She also thought about her few days in Paris and her venture into the world of big international business. She was entranced with her role at first but the kidnapping episode unsettled her. She now wanted to be taken care of and not be in the world alone. If she still stayed married to Jason, she would like to work, at least at first, and would explore with Jack and Phil about the possibilities if she got back to the real world..

She prayed that she could escape from her current predicament and that Frank's comments about Jason were made only to upset her. "When," she mused, "should I tell him that Jason and I are already married?"

CHAPTER 24

After Pierre left, Miriam packed clothes and items she needed and treasured in several trunks to be sent to the Geneva address Pierre had given her. Miriam left a note for her sister to keep the apartment and use it if she wished and warned that she planned to be out of France for an extended period. She also promised to send money every month to pay her lease and apartment expenses and any other bills she might receive.

Miriam made her flight to San Francisco with time to spare. When comfortably settled, she leaned back and was relieved at how well everything had gone. She wondered if Pierre had found Rachel and managed to get her on the plane to Amman. Miriam had arranged for a French passport for Rachel in the name of Mrs. Ledent in the event there was an all out search.

She was somewhat jealous that Jason had refused her for Rachel and couldn't understand it. She felt she was far more desirable and certainly had more animal sex appeal. She would try again to seduce Jason in San Francisco. He was one of very few men who had not succumbed to her charms. But she did not want to be distracted from her major goal--to get his unbreakable encryption system and other valuable technologies. Those would bring both her and Pierre a lifetime of luxury, either together or apart.

Would Pierre propose marriage to her and would she accept? Yes, possibly, unless she could get Frank to marry her. She and Pierre were already in bed together in this plot and, in bed together otherwise, which was always very enjoyable. But, she really wanted to become an American citizen. At the moment, only Frank could give her access to a green card, except for Jim, who would never marry her. He had used her only for sex and extra money, and she knew the girl he probably would marry was in Washington, working at CIA headquarters.

When the plane landed and she was waiting in line to clear customs and passport control, she realized how little she managed to sleep on the plane and how exhausted she was. When she emerged with her luggage, she spotted Sam Penderton, who waved and came over to meet her. She imagined that he would take her in his arms and kiss her but he didn't. She realized this was a public place and his home turf and he might not want to risk being seen. She would have her chance later but privately hoped she wasn't staying with him. She needed time to rest and get refreshed before she proceeded with her plans to lure some secrets from him. She also might need to make a fast escape. In addition, she wanted to contact Jason. She still could not believe she was bested by that cold looking American woman. It might be necessary to try

The Purloined Encryption Caper

to blackmail both Sam or Jason, especially since Jason was now married to Rachel.

After Frank left Rachel, he drove to a nearby hotel to spend the night. He did not want to spend the evening arguing with Rachel. If he stayed in the apartment, he knew he would try to make love to her, perhaps forcing her.

When he discovered that Rachel was engaged to Jason, one of his prime rivals in college, he was shaken. Frank had always been able to get any girl he wanted, many times luring dates away from Jason. Not that Frank was necessarily interested in the women, but he wanted to show the other guys, and Jason in particular, that he could do it. He did not plan to let Rachel break his record, especially since he had been her first lover and he was still in love with her.

Frank had much to do the next day and wanted to line up an appointment with his Belgian friend who had promised to perform the ceremony. He wondered whether Rachel would ever come around and love him again, or if she would balk in front of the *prefect*, the Belgian equivalent of a justice of the peace, and say she didn't want to marry him. If so, would the *prefect* go through with the marriage ceremony?

The *prefect* couldn't speak English but, as Frank remembered, Rachel was fluent in French and knew German. Frank had a fairly good grasp of French so would be aware of any difficulty that Rachel might cause. But German was a different matter. The Belgian *prefect* was also arranging for the necessary witnesses.

Frank telephoned Miriam at her apartment but there was no response. She promised to wait at her Paris apartment after returning from the States. Frank knew she and Pierre were ultimately going to Jordan but little else other than that they had planned to obtain technology from Jason's company to sell to a Middle Eastern buyer. They would then cut Frank in on his share, a pittance compared to what they hoped to get.

Frank didn't care. What had concerned him was that Pierre planned to take Rachel to Amman with him, if necessary. That Frank could not tolerate. He wanted Rachel for himself, regardless of how he had to get her. The thought of Pierre taking advantage of Rachel and, yes, raping her, which Pierre was very capable of doing, was more than Frank could tolerate.

He telephoned the Belgian *prefect* and set up an appointment for Tuesday morning at nine. The Belgian would take care of everything and could even make arrangements for a honeymoon trip if Frank wanted, perhaps a nice cruise somewhere in the Mediterranean or around the Greek Isles. Frank said, yes, a month's cruise among the Greek Isles would be good. Also, possibly the *prefect* could arrange a month's stay on one of the smaller, lesser known Greek Islands where he could finish his book.

"I've arranged everything," the *prefect* said later when Frank called him. Frank would drive Rachel to Marseilles after they married where they would board the Mediterranean cruise ship.

Frank also telephoned the cleaning woman at the Pont Royale Hotel and had her pack the rest of Rachel's clothes and put them in a postal box where he had

The Purloined Encryption Caper

stashed an envelope with some money to pay for her services. He didn't want to risk going back to the hotel himself. Someone might be watching. He then faxed his New York bank to wire money to a bank in Marseilles instructing them to pay a travel agency in Brussels for two cruise tickets. Within the next few weeks, he would contact them requesting money be wired to him in Athens.

When Phil received the call from Paul telling him that Rachel had been kidnapped again, he was shaken. When was he going to tell Jason? If he told Jason before his dinner with Ruth, he knew Jason would scrub his role in tonight's operation and take the first plane to Paris.

Paul said that the French police had one of the original kidnappers in custody and were currently arresting the other one. But the original kidnappers denied any role in the second kidnapping. The police were almost certain now that Rachel had purposely disappeared and were checking all airline manifests. They learned that Pierre was on a freighter en route to Alexandria and Haifa but there was no mention of a woman with him.

The French police had notified the police in Egypt and Israel to arrest him when he disembarked. Two CIA officials from the Cairo station would go to Alexandria to question Pierre but wanted the Egyptian police to be with them during the interrogation in the event some hard questioning was needed. The Americans were prohibited from using physical force since the U.S. Congress didn't think it was polite for its officials to act discourteously. The Egyptian police had no such qualms, especially with a French citizen. They had not forgotten Napoleon's brief visit.

Earlier when Paul had gone to Rachel's room at the Pont Royale Hotel, he found the cleaning woman packing some of her things. He considered having the woman arrested but, instead, decided to follow her. She deposited the suitcase in a large postal box and took from it an envelope, obviously payment for her services. Paul asked to have a French inspector assign someone to see who retrieved the suitcase.

They didn't have to wait long before Frank appeared. The police were asked not to accost him but to follow to see where he was going. When they came to the Belgian border, the French police had to negotiate with the Belgian police to take up their quarry. While they were negotiating, Frank managed to lose them. The gendarmes telephoned Inspector Dupont at Surete headquarters to inform them about their bungle. He in turn immediately passed this information on to the CIA station, identifying the individual as an American.

"Damn," Paul said. "Which American would be interested in kidnapping Rachel or did she go willingly with someone?" On a hunch, he asked the concierge at the hotel whether any Americans were staying or had stayed there who were friendly with Miss Brown.

"Oh yes," they said. "Two Americans were here. One was Monsieur Mark Strait, with the U.S. Government. He checked out early Saturday morning. The other was a journalist, Monsieur Frank Avery, who had drinks with Miss Brown several times. You know," the concierge whispered discreetly, "I remember them

The Purloined Encryption Caper

both being here together several years ago when they were having an affair, although I don't want to be quoted. But I don't think he would do anything to hurt her. I think he's still in love with her."

"Is he still registered?" Paul asked.

"No, he checked out Thursday evening. He said he was returning to the States," the concierge responded.

"Thanks," Paul said. "In the event he shows up again, would you please call me at the Embassy, or notify Inspector Dupont at the Surete. It's very important." The concierge said he would, but was mystified at the request.

Paul next called Phil in Washington. "Have you telephoned Jason yet regarding Rachel?" Paul asked.

"I've been sitting here wondering whether I should," Phil answered. "I was hoping Mark would telephone so I could get advice from him. I'm afraid that if I tell Jason, he'll refuse to go along with our scam against Miriam tonight and take the first flight to Paris."

"That's your decision, but I have a request for some information and you might have to talk to Jason to get it. Do you know a Frank Avery, a journalist who covers Europe for some New York paper? I believe he was once a very close or shall we say intimate friend of Rachel's when she lived in Europe." There was a long pause.

"Paul, I don't think I can ask Jason that kind of question. Why do you want to know?"

"Well, we understand that an American man telephoned the hotel cleaning lady to get some of Rachel's clothes from her room, and deliver them to a postal box. They were retrieved by Frank Avery. The

French police followed him, but at the Belgian border they had to transfer the case to the Belgian police which took so much time that they lost him. However, the concierge at the hotel remembers Frank and Rachel had drinks together several times last week and, years ago, were lovers when they frequented the hotel. Frank just may be the key to her disappearance." Paul thought a few moments before continuing, realizing Phil and Rachel were close friends. He plunged on.

"He may have taken her by force or she may have gone with him willingly. Phil, if it was the latter, you'd think she would have retrieved all the clothes herself and not have Frank get them."

"Keep me posted," Phil said. "I don't think I'll tell Jason now in case she did go with Frank willingly. There's nothing he can do and I don't want anything to go wrong with our approach to Miriam tonight. If Mark calls, I'll confide in him."

When Frank returned to the apartment and unlocked the door, he found Rachel sitting in a chair in the living room. She had changed into clothes Frank had originally got from the cleaning woman and looked very enticing. He wanted to take her in his arms but her look told him that it would not be a welcome gesture.

"I hope you had a peaceful night's sleep and something to eat. You must've been very hungry."

"What do you want with me? Just let me walk out that door and I promise I won't say a word about this to anyone. You can go scot free without any possibility of a kidnapping charge."

The Purloined Encryption Caper

"Dear innocent Rachel. No one in this country would believe that as two former lovers, I'd be accused of kidnapping you. They'll think that you wanted to escape your current fiancé and had put your ex-lover up to this plot. This isn't the United States with all your feminist abuse laws, you know. Here in Europe, they are reasonable. You won't have much longer to wait. Early Tuesday morning, we'll be married and then go on an extended honeymoon." Ignoring her shocked reaction, he continued. "At the end of that time, you'll not only once again be madly in love with me but will be pregnant with my child. Remember? That is what we talked about at one time? You said you wanted to marry me and have my children." He even smiled as he said it.

"You absolutely disgust me, Frank. I can't imagine what I found so exciting about you." Her look emphasized her words.

"You'll change your mind, Rachel. I thought we should perhaps start our efforts tonight. I plan to spend the night here in the same bed with you."

"You'll have to rape me, Frank. I'll never agree to sleep with you."

"If you insist," he responded, with a leer on his face.

Rachel realized that Frank could easily overpower her and he would think nothing of putting her to sleep somehow and then raping her. But she knew she would not get pregnant. She was still on the pill.

"Frank, if I'm still your victim on Tuesday morning and we are officially married, I'll agree to your raping me. I can't call it making love. That doesn't exist between us anymore. Until then, please don't touch me. I'll try to kill you if you do and I'll call it self-defense."

CHAPTER 25

"Sam, how wonderful to see you," Miriam smiled coquettishly. "I thought you might have issued your invitation to me in a fit of momentary passion. But I see you really meant it," Miriam purred in a sexy voice. "I'm so tired after my long flight. I hope I'll have time for a short nap this afternoon."

"Miriam, it's good to see you, too. No, I hadn't forgotten my promise." Sam then paused. "Unfortunately, my wife is out of town or else she would show you the places here that are indeed important for ladies." Sam wanted to indicate to Miriam that he wasn't afraid of her contacting his wife, but she seemed to ignore the message..

"I've made reservations for you at a motel in Menlo Park, not far from my house, convenient to the airport. Also, there's good shopping nearby in the event you want to buy a few things before returning to Paris." Sam paused, waiting for her reaction. "I'll tell you what. I'll take you to your motel and pick you up at

Rose Ameser Bannigan

six-thirty for dinner. That should give you some time to get yourself settled and take a short nap. Okay?"

"Yes, Sam, I appreciate it. Do you have Jason Conrad's telephone number? I told him I might visit San Francisco and promised to phone him."

"You might want to congratulate Jason. He's become engaged." Miriam just looked at him and smiled. She knew from Pierre that Jason and Rachel were already married.

"How could he have been so stupid to let a woman like Miriam seduce him?" Sam opined silently. He knew now that all she wanted was to blackmail him. He was glad his wife was out of town since Miriam would obviously have had no qualms about calling his wife and telling her in great detail about their nights together.

Ruth arrived at the San Francisco International Airport on schedule. Jason greeted her with a hug and light kiss in the event one of Miriam's henchmen was watching. She only had carryon luggage so they left the airport immediately. As they were walking out the door, they ran into Mark.

"Ruth, what are you doing here?" Mark asked.

"Let's keep it down a little, Mark," Jason said. "We have a plan to follow and don't want anyone to overhear us. Come, and I'll give you a ride to the house and brief you."

"What gives?" Mark questioned as Jason started his car.

Jason related the story of Rachel's kidnapping. "They're holding Rachel hostage. That's their insurance

The Purloined Encryption Caper

in the event Miriam's plan to get the details from Sam doesn't work. Miriam doesn't know that Rachel's free, so we plan to frighten her by having Ruth appear as Rachel here while Miriam's having dinner with Sam."

Jason showed Mark and Ruth to the guest bedrooms on the lower floor and told them to come up to the living room when they were ready.

"Sam will take Miriam to dinner at a small secluded restaurant not far from here," Jason explained. "I plan to be there with Ruth. Since Miriam has only seen Rachel twice, we hope she'll think that Ruth is actually Rachel. Sam will look over at us--we have specific tables reserved--and say hello, using my name as well as Rachel's. He'll then tell Miriam about the attempt on Rachel's life and that she luckily got away. He'll mention that one of her abductors is in custody, and that the French police are about to arrest the second one." Jason continued.

"Also, Sam will tell Miriam that the French police are searching for a Pierre Ledent with a watch at all airports because they know he's involved, and a woman is involved, too, whom they're currently trying to identify." Jason smiled as he thought about the plot. Then he continued. "The French police questioned the lingerie shop sales lady about who bribed her to mislead Rachel. They've agreed to prosecute all persons involved. In the States, kidnapping is a federal offense as it may be in France so they'll probably throw the book at them." Jason paused to let them absorb the details.

"We feel that Miriam will be frightened. The first thing she'll probably do is try to reach Pierre. We're sure she and Pierre have plans to make contact while she's in San Francisco. Your office here, Mark, has put a tracer on her motel room phone so they can find out where Pierre is, or where they plan to meet. The FBI will follow her to see where she goes. Then they plan to arrest her at some point, depending upon what they can get on her. We'll have to play that part by ear."

The telephone rang interrupting Jason's tale. "Well hello, Miriam," Jason said in a warm voice. "I see you did manage to come to sunny California. How long will you be here? I assume that Sam will take care of you this evening. I have plans myself, but why don't you telephone me tomorrow? Great, I hope you like our fair city."

Jason smiled as he hung up. "Bitch. She not only wants to blackmail Sam but won't give up on seducing me. If she only knew what was in store for her." He relished the thought.

Jason looked at his watch. It was five-thirty local time and three hours later in Washington. Rachel should be back home by now. He decided to phone her but there was no answer. Thirty minutes later, he tried again but with the same results. He then tried Phil's number as well as on his cell phone, but there was no answer on either phone so he left a message.

Although he was concerned, Jason felt that if there had been any problem, he would have been told. He wanted to try again but noticed that it was after six and he and Ruth would have to leave soon for the restaurant. He would try phoning Rachel again when he returned.

Jason and Ruth entered the restaurant, going directly to their assigned table. Sam looked over and greeted

The Purloined Encryption Caper

them by name. Miriam turned pale as she listened to Sam's explanation of the kidnapping snafu.

Apparently, the trap worked. Shortly after she finished eating, she excused herself to use the ladies' room. She went straight to a public telephone near the rest rooms. She didn't notice a man nearby watching her who was able to determine what numbers she dialed. Three different ones, all international, but there seemed to be no answer. Fortunately, Miriam didn't have her cell phone with her.

As soon as she returned to the table, she and Sam left the restaurant abruptly. Mark followed them back to Miriam's motel. He could hear her feigning exhaustion to Sam, saying she would see him the next day and would he telephone her, but not too early. Sam drove off. Approximately fifteen minutes later, she exited the motel, hailed a taxi and headed for the airport. She booked a red-eye flight to Washington.

When she was safely boarded, Mark returned to Jason's house, gathered his luggage and arranged for the next plane to Washington. He also telephoned Phil to alert him to Miriam's movements and informed Jason that he thought the plan had succeeded. She didn't even have the opportunity to ask Sam for anything. It was obvious that now saving her own skin was uppermost in her mind.

Ruth had already retired but Mark awakened her and informed her they were returning to Washington. So by midnight, California time, Miriam, Mark and Ruth were all headed to Washington but on different flights.

After they left, Jason sat in his den, looking at the pictures he had taken of Rachel on the Outer Banks. He broke out in a cold sweat when he thought of the possibility of losing her.

Miriam had been so confident of her plan when she arrived in San Francisco and was positive she could convince Sam to share his company's secrets with her. If she couldn't seduce him into giving her what she wanted, she would resort to blackmail and threaten to tell his wife. But Sam hadn't been at all concerned when Miriam asked him about her and even volunteered to have them get together if Miriam planned to stay another week.

Miriam couldn't afford this waste of time, so realized her blackmail plan had failed. She was also startled to see that Rachel had been freed and obviously had taken a trans-polar flight to San Francisco as well.

What had gone wrong, she wondered. Had Pierre and his men lost their courage, or had someone discovered his plan and informed the police. Maybe Jim had been pressured and confessed. It wouldn't take the police long to figure out who the woman was working with Pierre. And where was he? She phoned his apartment and the hotel in Amman. The hotel in Amman had told her that Pierre had canceled his reservation.

She tried to call Frank at his Paris apartment but there was no answer. In the event Pierre didn't show up at the deserted building to take Rachel to Amman, why did her backup plan for Jim to take her fail?

Miriam didn't know what to do. Perhaps she

The Purloined Encryption Caper

should go to the house in West Virginia although Pierre may have blown that place after he was arrested for trespassing. Pierre told her that his other NATO colleagues, all but the Brit, had been exposed and recalled by their governments. She couldn't go back to Paris. As a matter of fact, she was sure that all of the airports in France would be alerted for her. But had they traced her to the States? Perhaps she shouldn't have left San Francisco so quickly.

When her plane landed in Memphis, she was tempted to hide out there for several days. Her connecting flight to Washington was delayed for two hours so she decided to take a taxi and see if she could find a motel near the airport. However, when she looked outside, there were six inches of snow and ice on the ground, making driving difficult. She quickly changed her mind and hurried to catch her connecting flight to Washington.

Luck was with her when she arrived at National Airport. What snow there had been in Washington had melted. She rented a car to drive to West Virginia, and decided to check into the Berkeley Springs motel she had stayed at earlier, about two miles from the cabin, so she could quietly check out the cabin the next day without luggage. Pierre had told her about Julian's hackers who were breaking into networks and stealing information and software. If there was any data there, she could retrieve it. Although it would not be as profitable as the technology she hoped to get from Jason's company, it might sell for enough money to live on until they decided on the future.

As Miriam drove along Route 522 heading for

Berkeley Springs, she thought she was being followed. However, the car pulled off on a side road before she reached the West Virginia border. She breathed a sigh of relief.

She also thought about Frank and what her chances with him might be. She didn't think Pierre loved her and she wasn't sure that Frank did either, but it really didn't matter. If she hadn't wrecked her chances, she wanted to come to the States and get her green card by marrying Frank. She would try telephoning him after she got settled, either from the cabin or from somewhere in Europe. If she did go to Amman to meet Pierre, she would ask Frank to meet her there, too. Maybe she and Frank could take their share and she could get Frank to marry her, at least temporarily until she could get her green card.

Frank had mentioned that his mother had cut him out of the will and her money had been bequeathed to his future offspring. But she knew this wasn't true. Once when she was in his Paris apartment alone, she looked through his desk and found a copy of the will. She didn't know why Frank was spreading this false information but, knowing Frank, he definitely had a purpose.

Mark and Ruth were waiting for Jerry, a fellow FBI agent, to pick them up at National Airport when Ruth looked over and saw Miriam get on a Hertz shuttle bus. They were in luck. They could get the license number from the Hertz rental agency and follow her. Ruth asked to be dropped off near a hotel where she could grab a cab. She gave Mark her cell phone number and

The Purloined Encryption Caper

headed for her apartment to pick up her car so they could both track Miriam.

Miriam headed for Route 7--Leesburg Pike--apparently heading west for Berkeley Springs. Mark telephoned Miles in the mountain lookout cabin on his cell phone and told him to watch for Miriam. He also gave directions to Ruth and told her that when they managed to see each other's car, they should stop for a moment and Mark would ask Jerry to join Ruth and drive. In the event Miriam noticed two cars following, she would be confused by the variable number of individuals in the cars and by the different drivers. Also, Mark was afraid Ruth might fall asleep at the wheel.

As Ruth and Jerry sped down Leesburg Pike, Jerry asked if she was familiar with this road.

"I've never gotten this far since I've been here," Ruth confessed.

"I've read that years ago this road probably began as an animal trail and subsequently used by American Indians. During colonial times, it became an important transportation route between Alexandria and Winchester when tobacco and other farm products were carried from the Virginia countryside to the port of Alexandria." Jerry continued to explain local history as a way of keeping Ruth from falling asleep.

About twenty-five miles from Berkeley Springs, Mark called Ruth and told her he was going to take an indirect route to the cabin. "It might make Miriam suspicious if both cars follow her all the way to Berkeley Springs," he said. So at Route 127, Mark

Rose Ameser Bannigan

turned off Route 522. Ruth and Jerry continued to follow Miriam.

Shortly after Miriam passed through Berkeley Springs, she turned west on to route 9, the mountain road to her cabin but quickly turned into a motel parking lot, got out of the car and went into the office. Ruth dropped Jerry about a block away and then headed for the Hanson cabin. Jerry walked back and checked in the same motel where Miriam had registered and watched out his window for her movements.

He flashed his FBI badge at the motel owner and told him not to mention to anyone that he was there, especially the woman who had just checked in.

"You mean the French woman? Strange, we've suddenly had a lot of foreigners around here, especially Frenchies. Are they going to be making trouble for us?"

"Yes, she's the one. We don't know what they're up to, but we're keeping an eye on them in case they try something," Jerry responded.

"Last week the sheriff dragged a Frenchman into town for questioning and kept him in jail all night," the clerk volunteered. "Said he was a French diplomat, but the sheriff didn't believe him until he checked his name with the State Department. Frenchie was mighty sore, I understand, but the sheriff caught him trespassing and didn't want to take no chances. Frenchie said a friend loaned him a cabin and he said he'd gotten lost. But no one believed him. As a matter of fact, I think I'll call the sheriff and let him know another Frenchie's here. He probably doesn't have much to do anyway."

The Purloined Encryption Caper

Shortly thereafter, the sheriff's car parked across the street from the motel. Jerry decided to go out and talk with him.

"Hello, Sheriff, my name is Jerry Coldwell," he said as he flashed his FBI badge. "I hear you've had some trouble with a visiting Frenchman." The sheriff nodded his head. "There's a French woman in the end room who may also be part of the same trouble, but I think we have the matter well in hand. I understand you know Miles Hanson. My fellow agents, Mark Strait and Ruth Brennan, are there waiting for a Miriam Gauthier to arrive. If I need a ride, can I count on you to get me there? I have directions to their cabin, but I'm not sure exactly where it is."

"Sure," the sheriff replied. "Happy to. I know Miles and where he lives. Here's my phone number. Give me a call and I'll be here quick as I can. Those French folk are certainly trying to cause problems for this town, aren't they?" The sheriff walked away, glad that he had been clued in for possible problems.

CHAPTER 26

In the southern Belgium border town, it was almost dark. Frank was getting anxious for the night to pass quietly so he could go to the *prefect* to marry Rachel. He had asked her to pack what few things she had because he planned to leave for Marseilles immediately after the ceremony.

He would love to see the expression on Jason's face when he heard that Rachel had married him, even if it was against her will. He would win and be the best man after all. How Frank will relish sending the huge diamond engagement ring back to Jason.

That evening Rachel didn't say a word to Frank. He told her of his plans and cautioned her not to speak out at the ceremony. "Very serious consequences would happen," he warned. Frank had managed to pay the *prefect* well for his role in undertaking the ceremony. He confided that Rachel was hesitant about getting married, but they should notice the engagement ring she was wearing. Once they were married, she would settle down, he assured the official.

Rachel slept little that night, even though she had locked her bedroom door and put a chair in front of it to keep Frank out. She was trying to figure out how she could escape. Earlier, she tried to break out but Frank had double locked it.

The next morning, Frank first took their luggage to the car and only then did he let Rachel come down. He even took the precaution of tying her hands behind her back so she wouldn't try to run away. He drove north, deeper inside Belgium and soon came to a small house with a sign outside advertising the residence/office of a *prefect*. Frank opened the door for Rachel, untied her hands, took her arm and led her into the house. It was exactly nine o'clock. The *prefect* asked Frank and Rachel to follow him into an office but, before they reached the door, Rachel asked the lady of the house if she could use the bathroom.

"Oui, madame," the woman said in broken French. It was obvious to Rachel that her principal language was not French but German. Rachel followed the woman up the stairs into a small bathroom that contained only a toilet. The woman indicated that she would wait for Rachel outside the door.

When Rachel reappeared, she asked for a basin to wash her hands and a mirror to comb her hair. The woman took her around the corner into a large bedroom. There was not only a basin there with a mirror, but Rachel noticed that there was a telephone by the bed.

Rachel pleaded with the woman in German to let her use the phone. She gave her a five hundred French franc note she had hidden from Frank in her shoe and told her it was very important. The woman agreed

The Purloined Encryption Caper

but couldn't understand why this crazy American woman was giving her so much money. Rachel asked the woman to stay and locked the door. She quickly contacted the CIA station in Paris and told the case officer who answered what had happened, where they were and what Frank's plans were. "Also, tell Paul not to trust Jim. I think he's been compromised and is involved in the plot with Frank and Miriam," she added.

There was a knock on the door and before she opened it, she turned to the woman, took her shoulder and said in German, "I don't want to marry this man. As a matter of fact, I'm already married. If the *prefect* marries us, he will get in trouble. Please tell the *prefect* to delay the ceremony on some pretext."

Another knock was heard. She opened the door and there stood Frank.

"I only wanted to wash my hands," Rachel said, "and there was no basin in the WC." She proceeded at Frank's side who looked at her very suspiciously.

"I don't trust you Rachel. I know you have something up your sleeve, but it won't work. Let's get on with the ceremony."

When they got back to the room where the *prefect* was, Frank asked him to start the ceremony. The *prefect* looked at both Frank and Rachel and began to mumble some words in Latin. Frank didn't pay much attention to what was being said but merely kept looking at his watch.

When the *prefect* asked in French if there was any reason the marriage should not take place, he looked straight at Frank.

"No," said Frank, "Let's finish the ceremony." The *prefect* then looked at Rachel.

"Yes, your honor," she said in French. "I'm already married." Frank was stunned in disbelief.

"Don't believe her," he said. However, the *prefect* was not so sure and began to speak in German to Rachel. She confirmed what his wife had told him earlier. Rachel then asked him in German not to continue with the ceremony and that she would match whatever amount of money Frank had already given them.

At this point, the telephone rang. It was the local police who had been called by the American Embassy in Brussels. They asked the *prefect* to hold both the man and the woman there until they arrived which would be a matter of minutes, but not to let anything happen to the woman. The *prefect* kept talking on the telephone, even though the party at the other end had already hung up. He wanted some way to delay until the police came. He thought he had spied a gun in the man's pocket.

Frank was getting very edgy. "Let's get on with it," he said sternly as he took the telephone from the *prefect* and hung it up. "We have a boat to catch, remember, and I'm anxious to have the service finalized."

The *prefect* continued with the ceremony and finally when it became apparent he couldn't delay any longer, he asked Rachel what she meant when she said she was already married.

"If you'll let me get my purse, I'll show you a copy of my marriage certificate, issued in Maryland earlier this month. And this man is not my husband." With

The Purloined Encryption Caper

this she got her purse and produced a duplicate wedding certificate.

"So you are not Miss Rachel Brown but instead Mrs. Jason Conrad?" the *prefect* asked as he looked at her marriage certificate. Frank had turned beet red.

"You bitch," he said angrily through clenched teeth, "and neither you nor Jason told me." He went to slap her, but she drew aside and grabbed his arm in mid-air. He then reached in his pocket, but before he could get what he may have been reaching for, Rachel grabbed his other arm and flipped him aside in a judo throw.

A gun flew from his pocket and Rachel dashed for it. Frank tackled her from his horizontal position, but probably wished he hadn't. The man who was to be a witness standing next to the *prefect* kicked him in the groin so hard that Frank screamed.

"You bastards!" he shouted as he clutched his groin, moaning. "You'll pay for this and plenty!"

Rachel wasn't quite sure they would, since at that moment the Belgian police entered the room. When they asked what happened and the *prefect* had related the occurrence, their only comment was "crazy Americans."

They took Frank away with them. They also gave Rachel the keys to his car and asked her to follow them to the police station.

She immediately got into the car and prepared to follow when she realized she hadn't paid the group the money she had promised. She didn't have very much money left, only what she had found in several of Frank's jacket pockets hanging in the car. However,

Rose Ameser Bannigan

she got their names and addresses and promised to mail or wire more to them.

The police asked her what happened. She carefully selected her words. She didn't want Frank to end up in a Belgian jail regardless of how evil he had acted.

"I was kidnapped by several French thugs," she started. "This man, Frank Avery, followed the thugs, entered the house where I was taken and asked me to go with him. Since I knew he wouldn't purposely hurt me, I agreed. I think he misinterpreted my action, since we at one time had une *affaire l'amour*, and he said he was still in love with me. But now I am married to someone else and it's very hard for him to accept this fact," she said with a wink.

"Why don't you let me talk to him and perhaps we can iron out the problem in a friendly manner so you won't have to get officially involved." Rachel said she didn't want to press charges if he agreed to her conditions.

The last thing the small town Belgian police officers wanted was to get involved in an international incident, especially since they found out that Frank Avery was a senior reporter for an important American newspaper. The police had talked with their head office in Brussels and the central office was hopeful that the incident could be handled diplomatically without any arrests or incidents. They agreed and brought Frank into the room where she was.

"Rachel, why didn't you tell me that you were already Jason's wife," he asked angrily when they were alone.

The Purloined Encryption Caper

"Because, Frank, we eloped the weekend before I came to Paris. We didn't have time to change my name legally or tell anyone about it, so we agreed to keep our marriage secret until I got back. Then after you kidnapped me, I felt it was the only ace I had. I wasn't sure what you would do if I told you."

"Tell me, Rachel. Would you have come back to me if Jason were not in the picture?" Frank asked, feeling a little sanguine.

"I don't know. I might have but not the way it would have been in the apartment. I might have taken your gun and killed you if you had tried to rape me." She paused before continuing. "You're right in saying I'm naive. I guess I still want to feel that I can trust people. But once someone has crossed me, Frank, I wouldn't hesitate to hurt that person any way I could. I'm no longer that innocent." One look at her eyes convinced him she was serious.

"By the way, where did you learn judo and karate well enough so you could toss me the way you did?" Frank asked.

"I have you to thank indirectly." Rachel smiled. "When I reached Hong Kong, the last thing I wanted to do was meet any men, so I took Chinese language lessons and self-defense training to get my mind off you and all the other unpleasant things that had happened. Actually, I got to be very good. With a few more lessons, I think I could earn my black belt. I knew you always used to carry a gun although I never could figure out how you got it through the airport security checks. But when I saw your hand go to your pocket at the *prefect*'s, I knew I had to act."

Frank looked at her. "I would have used it only to take you away with me. I'm still in love with you and could never hurt you. Actually, as tough as I act, I never could shoot anyone. That you have to believe."

He then changed his attitude and expressed a little fear. "What do you think they'll do with me?"

"If you promise to let me go, I'll tell them that I don't want to press charges. Just let me take your car and you can fly home directly from Brussels. I think you'll be PNG'd out of Belgium for a while, but you can probably even talk your way out of that. I don't think they'd want to have an international newspaper correspondent put in jail. If I were you, I'd get your editor to vouch for you, contact the Belgian Embassy in Washington or wire the Belgian police directly. Now might be a good time to write that book you always wanted to write. First, though, give me back all the money you took from my purse."

The police returned to the room and Rachel told them about their agreement. The police seemed pleased with the outcome. As they were taking Frank away, he turned around and looked at Rachel.

"The papers for the car are in the glove compartment." Frank then looked up at Rachel. "I have two tickets for a cruise through the Greek Islands. It would have been fun, Rachel. Remember we always talked about taking such a cruise."

"Maybe you can find another woman to go with you and have your child so you can finally get the money you crave so much." She then got into his car and drove away, anxious to get back to Paris and fly home.

The Purloined Encryption Caper

After she crossed the border into France, she pulled over to the side of the road and sat for ten minutes trying to calm her nerves. She was shaking and had broken out in a cold sweat as the events went through her mind. Then, she started the car again and headed straight for Paris. She thought about telephoning Jason but, at that moment, all she could think of was getting to the safety of her hotel.

After about an hour, she came upon an attractive cafe in a small French village. The sight of the restaurant made her realize how hungry she was. She stopped, went in and sat at a small table in the back.

While she ate, she again thought about the events of the last few days. She was glad that Frank would not end up in jail. After all, he had meant a lot to her once and she would have felt guilty if they had arrested and jailed him. She could not understand Frank's involvement in the plot. Money must be very important to him. He at one time said: "I could screw the wife of my best friend and not think much about it, but I could never betray my country." How then could he agree to work with Miriam and steal technology from Jason?

She also thought about the things Frank said about Jason. She was sure now that Jason had indeed succumbed to Miriam's charms. What would she do and how would she act when she next came face to face with him? These thoughts were still with her when she entered the outskirts of Paris, drove to the car rental agency to return the car and took a taxi to the Hotel Pont Royale.

When Jason again tried to telephone Rachel in Washington early Monday morning and received no answer, he got worried. He telephoned Phil but was told he had already left for the office and probably could not be reached since he had a number of meetings that morning. Jason next called Jack Warden's Washington office.

"Jack, is Rachel in?" he asked.

"No," Jack said. "I was expecting her back today, but so far haven't had any word. I thought maybe you'd gone to meet her in Paris and she decided to take an extra day."

"I think something is wrong and no one is leveling with me," Jason continued. "I've tried to reach Phil but he's already at his office and I don't have his number. Can you try to reach him for me or try to reach Mark? He should be back in Washington by now. I'll be in my office. When you call, tell May it's urgent and get me from wherever I am."

When Jack reached Phil, he learned the worst. Rachel had been kidnapped again, but this time they did not know by whom. She might have been taken by Pierre. Phil had hesitated calling Jason since Phil knew Jason would immediately fly to Paris and try to look for her. Then the CIA station would also have Jason to placate and complicate their job.

"Could you delay calling him, Jack? I hate to ask you to do this, but it will be best. If we don't hear anything by four this afternoon, I promise I'll call Jason and tell him myself." Jack promised, phoned Jason and told him that he hadn't been able to reach Phil either.

The Purloined Encryption Caper

Jack then became very concerned and phoned Mark's office and got Mark's number.

"Mark, I don't know if you're aware, but Rachel has been kidnapped again, and this time they don't know who did it. Jason's worried sick and Phil won't level with him. He's afraid that Jason will head for Paris and complicate matters worse. Do you have any suggestions?"

Mark didn't. "Honestly, Jack, what next. This little group is giving us no end of problems. We've got Miriam under surveillance in Berkeley Springs, waiting for her to make a misstep so we have grounds to detain her."

"We know it's neither of the two hoods who took Rachel initially," Jack added. "They're both under arrest and are being interrogated by the French police in such a fashion that they couldn't possibly hide anything. The creeps confessed that they were in the pay of Pierre to watch Rachel initially in Arlington and then kidnap her. I don't think those guys will see the light of day for a year or two. A few of the police think that Rachel might have left with someone on her own accord, a Frank Avery."

"Hmm, I wonder. It's possible, but I doubt Rachel would do such a thing," Mark said hesitantly. "Do you think that perhaps Miriam is considering taking over the whole operation? That doesn't seem likely, though, since she bolted so quickly from San Francisco and didn't even threaten Sam. Maybe Pierre took Rachel himself, although he usually has someone else do his dirty work. Has anyone heard where Pierre is? We know that Miriam couldn't reach him when she telephoned him from San Francisco, and we don't think she tried to call him from here, unless she used a public phone or bought a cell phone. Let me think about it, Jack, and I'll get back to you."

Mark never did call Jack back that day. He was too busy trying to cover Miriam's actions. Also, the mention of Frank Avery's name bothered him.

Late that afternoon, Phil decided to bite the bullet and call Jason. How he dreaded the call.

"Jason, I have bad news. We thought Rachel was safe, but we found out that after the CIA guy rescued her, he was clubbed himself and Rachel just disappeared." Phil could hear Jason's anguish in his response.

"It wasn't either of the low-lifes who took her initially since they're both in jail and don't know anything about it. It's as if she vanished in thin air. They don't think Pierre took her, but they're not certain. Some of the police think she may have disappeared voluntarily. There's an all points bulletin out for her. Why don't you sit tight and I'll let you know if anything turns up."

"Screw it, Phil, I won't," he said as he slammed down the receiver. He then telephoned United Airlines and within four hours, was on his way to Paris on a non-stop flight over the Pole. Before he left his house, he tried telephoning Frank at his house. Someone answered and told Jason that Frank had not returned from Europe and they didn't expect him back for several months.

He phoned Phil. "Sorry for being so rude earlier, but I can't sit here like a weak sister and wait for someone else to find my wife. I'm off to Paris on a transpolar flight. If your Paris office wants to do something for

The Purloined Encryption Caper

me, they can make hotel reservations at the same place where Rachel stayed and meet my plane. And, by the way, ask them to try to locate a Frank Avery. He may be the key to Rachel's disappearance, although I'm not sure of it." Jason dreaded the thought that he might arrive in Paris and find that Rachel decided to go away with Frank.

When Jason mentioned Frank's name, Phil, too, felt Rachel might have gone off with Frank. Maybe the concierge at the hotel was right. But this would be a much different Rachel than he had ever known.

CHAPTER 27

Miriam didn't leave her Berkeley Springs hotel room that evening, just phoned a local pizza parlor and had them deliver a mushroom-topped pizza and coffee. She would love to have had some wine but didn't want to risk going out and being seen. She also wanted to have a clear head the next day. She felt her chances were better for getting to the cabin undetected in daylight than at night considering what had happened to Pierre.

As soon as daylight broke, Miriam walked to a small breakfast diner and had a large American breakfast. The pizza wasn't very good the night before and she was starved. She drank a lot of hot black coffee to get her blood circulating. American coffee was always so weak, not like French cafe noir, but she decided not to ask for an espresso or cappuccino. Few West Virginians drank anything but good old American brew in the morning. She hadn't put on much makeup and wore a pair of slacks and a T-shirt with a warm jacket to look as local as possible.

After breakfast, she checked out of the motel. She didn't want to leave her luggage in the room since she might have to leave in a hurry, in case she encountered problems at the cabin.

She slowly drove up the road and pulled into their safe house driveway. Most of the snow had melted, but it was still slushy. She always had marveled at snow ever since she was a little girl in Paris. When she first met Frank, she told him she was still pure as the driven snow. He said, "You mean pure as the driven slush!" and laughed. She thought about that first night with him, smiled and wondered where he was now. She marveled at how much more considerate American men usually were than their European brothers and so much more relaxed with women.

She almost didn't bring her key to the cabin but was now grateful that she did. Mon Dieu, had her plans gone awry! Entering the cabin, she winced at the smell of stale cigarette smoke, beer, wine and whiskey. Cans and bottles were piled high in the closets and kitchen trash cans. Apparently her colleagues weren't very neat.

She went to the back of the cabin where Julian's computer setup was located. It was still intact and buzzing and it appeared that a number of messages were on the answering machine. She first checked the computer and then the phone messages. Were there any calls for Pierre from women? She didn't believe him when he said he hadn't found anyone in the States to sleep with. His sexual appetites were too demanding.

The Purloined Encryption Caper

She downloaded a number of diskettes. There was a great deal of information and she hoped it could bring in money for her and Pierre or Frank. If there were passwords for important programs and contacts at the National Security Council and the Defense Department, it would indeed be of interest to her Middle East clients.

There were e-mails from several hackers requesting payment for past activities. She promised to pay them within the next few weeks and asked them to hold on to any new data they might obtain. She told the group that they were moving their operation to Europe while they were on vacation, and would let them know the new address as soon as one was established.

A Middle East address might frighten the hackers so she didn't want to mention Amman. Sometimes these people get a twinge of patriotism and she didn't want them to report her to the authorities or put information on the Internet about their group, a practice becoming more and more common.

The telephone calls were from personal friends of both Clive and Carlo. There were calls to Pierre from Ingrid, Sophia and someone called Patrick from London. She was sure this had to do with Clive. She wondered where he was. Only Pierre knew what happened to Hans, Carlo and Julian.

Should she telephone Patrick? She took the number and planned to give it to Pierre when she saw him.

Then she decided she had better leave the area. She would drive to Pittsburgh and take a flight from there to Europe. In Pittsburgh she would try again to contact Pierre or Frank. If Frank had returned to New

York, she could visit him there. It was imperative that she reach either Pierre or Frank before she returned to France. Her last resort, of course, was Jim, but he was such an innocent that by now he might have confessed.

After wandering for three hours through parts of Maryland with a road map at her side, she entered the Pennsylvania Turnpike. She felt she had evaded anyone who might have tried to follow her. She hadn't noticed anyone at the cabin and decided not to look around as Pierre had done. Now, she was on her way with enough codes and information she hoped could keep her solvent for awhile.

Mark and Ruth had watched Miriam as she entered the cabin and downloaded the information from the computer and recorded the telephone messages. What Miriam hadn't realized was that the information she took had been put there not by the group's illegal hackers but by the FBI. Now they would be able to trace where she was and to whom she was selling the information. The passwords at the NSC and Pentagon had been changed, but a dummy computer had been maintained with the original passwords.

They had also put a chip and various cookies in the computer Julian had set up to facilitate monitoring the machine in the event someone else tried to contact Lovenest.

Jerry, who had the sheriff drive him to the Hanson's cabin, got in Ruth's car and followed Miriam. When her car entered the Pennsylvania Turnpike and headed toward Pittsburgh and the Ohio State line, he figured

The Purloined Encryption Caper

her destination was either Pittsburgh or Cleveland where she could get a flight to Europe.

The FBI offices in both cities were contacted and they in turn alerted all turnpike toll takers and turnpike police patrols to be on the lookout for Miriam's car and to inform them immediately as soon as it was spotted. It wasn't necessary for Jerry to follow her once she was trapped on the Turnpike.

It was noon when Jason arrived at DeGaulle airport in Paris. Paul was waiting and took him directly to the Embassy CIA station.

"Any news yet?" Jason asked as they were driving into the city.

"Nothing new," Paul lied. "We're still not sure who either took her or who she went with. Do you by chance know a Frank Avery?"

"Yes, very well. Don't tell me that son-of-a-bitch had anything to do with this," Jason asked. "He and Rachel at one time were an item, but I don't think she'd willingly go with him." At least he hoped she wouldn't.

Paul continued. "The only other possibility is that she might have been taken by Pierre and is on the freighter with him. But I doubt it, unless he paid off all the dock workers and boatmen in Marseilles to keep quiet. He's scheduled to hit Alexandria sometime tonight, I believe. The Egyptian police have been asked to go aboard and arrest him. He has a ticket to Haifa so, if he escapes the Egyptian police, we'll have to trust the Israelis to do the job, assuming, of course, that the Israelis are not among their prospective customers."

"Paul, is there anything I can do?" Jason asked, dejected and exasperated. "If not, I'm jet lagged. If you don't mind, I think I'll check into the hotel and take a nap. Also, I'd like to talk with the concierge and others at the hotel. Someone might have overheard something."

"Sure, Jason, I'll drop you off. It must be hell for you, but there's not much one can do, other than wait and hope the police come up with something. I'll contact Phil and see whether they've been able to trace Miriam's whereabouts and maybe she can lead them to Rachel. As far as our guys have been able to figure, Miriam won't be able to contact Pierre until Tuesday night. He might even try to contact her from the ship, although I doubt it. I think Pierre is now more concerned with saving his own skin. There's not much honor among this den of thieves."

Jason registered at the hotel, identified himself as Rachel's husband and asked about her. The concierge took Jason into his office to register but did not give him much information. He remembered Frank and Rachel from former days and didn't want to get involved in a *ménages a trois*. Also, he wasn't sure whether this man wasn't lying when he said he was Rachel Brown's husband.

Jason went to his room, took a hot bath and stretched out on the bed for a nap. He had some bad dreams, some involving Rachel, and awakened with a start. His memory refused to reveal his troubled dreams. "What will I do if they can't find her?" he asked himself. He couldn't just sit in the hotel and wait. It was nearly six.

The Purloined Encryption Caper

He called room service, ordered a gin and tonic and called Paul.

"Damn, Jason. I should have called you earlier but we've been busy as hell. I talked with Rachel. She called from a small town across the French-Belgium border. Apparently, she had been with Frank Avery. He was the one who took her when she got away from the two thugs. I'm not sure at this point whether he was her savior or kidnapper, but I do know that he tried to force her to marry him. She managed to telephone me from the *prefect's* house and we got the local police to arrest him and free her." He awaited an angry outcry from Jason, but none came. He resumed the saga.

"As I understand from our Brussels Embassy, she has Frank's rental car and is returning to Paris. She could show up at the hotel, although she may not want to return to the same hotel. We have the French gendarmerie on the lookout for her and the car, although we're not quite sure of its make and color. The Belgian police forgot to get that information, but at least we know she's okay."

"That's good news. Paul, I'm going to get something to eat and then I'll be back in the room, probably in about an hour. Leave a message if you learn anything or call me later. Thanks for the good news."

Meanwhile, late that afternoon Rachel returned to the hotel, asked for her key and went to her room. The concierge hesitated but decided not to mention that a man named Jason Conrad, who said he was her husband, had registered earlier.

She tried to phone Jason at his office. They told her he had left the day before and hadn't called his office today. Why didn't May know his whereabouts? It was very unlike Jason. She then tried phoning him at home, but no one answered. She left a message on his answering machine.

After she showered and dressed, she felt like having a very strong drink and some food, so she went to the little cafe near the hotel. They seated her at a corner table and brought her the vodka martini *Americain* she ordered. She quickly downed that and ordered another. She ordered the *carte de jour* and was halfway through when she spied someone at a table near the entrance that looked a lot like Jason.

Suddenly, he looked at his watch, asked the waiter for his check and left. The way he looked at his watch made Rachel realize it could indeed be Jason, but that was too much to hope for.

She paid her bill and left the restaurant in a hurry to follow this man, leaving half of her meal untouched. He seemed to be walking very fast.

"Jason!" The man turned around, and looked as if he had seen a ghost. "What are you doing in Paris?" Rachel asked.

"My God, Rachel, where did you come from?" he asked running to her. He took her in his arms and held her. She was sobbing and found it difficult to talk, so he held her close to him for several minutes.

"Come, let's go to my room, darling, where we can talk," Jason said.

"I was sitting in the back of the restaurant and thought it was you, but I'd just finished two martinis

The Purloined Encryption Caper

and wasn't quite sure. Then, by the way you looked at your watch and moved, I knew it was you. There couldn't be two people in the world that much alike. Are you staying here?" she asked as they entered the lobby of the Pont Royale Hotel.

"Of course," he said. They both retrieved their keys and walked arm in arm in the direction of the elevator, much to the amazement of the concierge.

Once in the room, he kissed her lovingly and passionately and held her so tightly she could hardly breathe. "You had us all so worried," he finally said. "I didn't know about your adventures until yesterday so I took the first flight to Paris to find you. Phil didn't want me to come, but I couldn't sit idly by. I was sick with worry. Are you really all right?"

"Yes, I am now, but I was terrified earlier. I didn't think I'd ever see you again," Rachel said, nuzzling against him. "Did they tell you everything that happened?"

"Yes. Most of the details, except the last chapter. Who took you from the house near the train station? I assume it was Frank."

"Yes, it was Frank. In a way, I think he tried to save me. It only got sticky when he tried to arrange for us to be married. He's really sick, you know, to try to pull off what he did. The funny thing is that I'm not sure he wanted to marry me as much as he wanted to one up you." Rachel was confused and the drinks were taking effect.

"Jason, I should call Paul and Phil, unless Paul calls him for us. His fellow CIA officer, Jim, is a friend of Miriam's and I think part of the cabal. Frank said

Rose Ameser Bannigan

Jim had no intention of taking me to Paul when he rescued me from the hoods but rather to another place to wait for Pierre or someone else designated by Pierre. Somehow Frank is involved, too, but not in their plan to sell technologies to our enemies. He once said that he'd have no qualms about screwing his best friend's wife, but would never betray his country. I know he certainly intended the former, but he didn't succeed."

They telephoned Paul and arranged to meet him for breakfast. Paul promised to telephone Phil and Mark.

"And now, my darling, I think we have some other business to attend to," Jason said as he gently led her to his bed.

While she was undressing, she suddenly stopped and looked at him. "Jason, there is a question that I must have answered and answered honestly. Frank mentioned that he had slept with Miriam. I think he was enjoying her charms even while we were going together. When I looked shocked, he told me not to be so naive. She was a very good lover and even you had succumbed to her charms. Is it true, Jason?"

"No, but she tried," Jason said with determination. "You must believe me. I couldn't, especially after we'd made love."

CHAPTER 28

The phone awakened Rachel early the next morning. It took her a minute to realize she was in Jason's room so she handed the receiver to him.

"Jason? This is Phil. I understand that Rachel's with you and that everything's okay. Is she there perchance? I'd like to talk with her before I talk further with Paul."

"Rachel, we're all so glad that you're safe and sound. We were worried about you. Has Jason filled you in on Miriam's visit to San Francisco?"

"No, he hasn't. I guess it wasn't uppermost in his mind last night," she said smiling.

"Sorry to bother you so early, but I need to know the answer to one question. Do you really believe Jim was involved in the second attempt to kidnap you?" If Jim were involved, Phil would have to begin the process of discovering if any other CIA staff might also be involved.

"I know he's one of your case officers, Phil, but, yes, I do. He seemed to know the arrangement of the rooms well in the house where they first took me. Frank also told me not to trust Jim. But coming from Frank, I'm not sure what to believe any more. Did Paul say anything to you?" Rachel didn't want to implicate anyone but, at the same time, felt she had to be honest with Phil.

"No, he just repeated what you had told him earlier. Well, thanks. I assume you and Jason will be back soon. I'll phone Jack to let him know you're okay." Rachel then hung up and looked at Jason.

"Now, Mr. Conrad, I want you to tell me exactly what happened in San Francisco with Miriam."

Jason described their ploy of having Ruth pretend she was Rachel. "At that time, none of us knew anything about your second kidnapping. Miriam really got spooked when she thought she saw you at the table with me. And we managed to save Sam from being blackmailed. We even had some phony software rigged up to give her in the event she didn't buy our scheme. She must not have seen you all that much or not enough to know the difference between you and Ruth."

Paul arrived alone for breakfast. Rachel was afraid he might have Jim with him. She didn't think he believed her the night before.

"God, Rachel, I really screwed up and I promised Mark that I'd take good care of you. At least it gave me the chance to meet Jason."

Rachel gave Paul a blow by blow description of her kidnappings, but omitted the part about Frank's wanting her to have his child. She hadn't even mentioned that to

The Purloined Encryption Caper

Jason, or about Frank's plans for a cruise to the Greek Islands.

"What I can't figure out is where Frank got the money to do all these things. He told Jason that when his mother died, he came into a large inheritance. But Frank told me that his mother had basically cut him out of her will until he produced an heir and the money would then go to the child."

Paul looked at her and said nothing.

"Tell me Paul," Rachel then asked, "does Jim know Miriam or has he had an affair with her?"

"I'm not sure, but I think he might have and we're looking into it now. You know, Rachel, Phil has suspected there's been a leak in our office for the past few months, ever since the first time Jason came to Paris. We couldn't figure out why Francois Descartes, whom you were supposed to see, Jason, all of a sudden wasn't available and Miriam was substituted in his place. In the office, I mentioned that Phil had checked out Jason's appointments and I assume that Jim then told Miriam. We now have Jim under surveillance and I hope you have no plans to meet with him. I know he'll try to call you. He's expressed concern." Paul was very cautious in his statements. It had appalled him to think that Jim would be willing to betray his organization and country.

"No one will see Rachel without me, Paul," Jason commented. "As a matter of fact, I plan to take Rachel back home on the first available flight. I have no intention of losing her again."

"Where is Miriam now, Paul? Do you know?" Rachel asked.

"As I understand, Mark's boys are keeping her under surveillance and she's heading for either New York or Europe." Paul then explained the computer setup in Berkeley Springs and Mark's efforts to compromise the members of the group individually to avoid an international incident.

"No one ever told me," Rachel said.

"No. I don't think Mark wanted you to know too much. You know, Phil asked Mark to keep an eye on you and Mark was the one who insisted that we not leave you alone. You weren't aware but, at your dinner with him on Friday night, he spied Miriam and Pierre with the two hit men at the same restaurant. He was grateful your back was to them so they didn't recognize you. They certainly didn't identify Mark." Paul paused, waiting, in the event Rachel had any questions.

"After Mark left you at your hotel, we met at my office, and he had the FBI fax pictures of Pierre and his goons to me. I'd already arranged for two of my colleagues to follow us on Saturday. I don't think it was just happenstance that Jim was at the back door of Lili's, but it's now obvious he was in on Miriam's plan from the beginning. I'd like to think that he wouldn't have let anything happen to you, that he'd just hold you for protection until they could get the material from Jason. Perhaps Miriam was using him. She has a way with men, I understand."

Rachel looked at Jason. He was quite aware of the reason why.

"I'll pass this on to Phil and Mark, whom I know are worried," Paul said. "By the way, in your purse in the side pocket is a small tracking device. Could I

The Purloined Encryption Caper

please have it back?" Rachel looked in her purse and saw what looked like a very small cigarette lighter.

"I never even knew I had this. When did you put it there? And what is it?"

"It's a tracking device that emits a beeping radio signal. In the event they did take you, we could've located you by this signal, that is if they didn't take you too far or that you didn't lose your purse," Paul confessed.

When they returned to the hotel, Jason insisted on her coming to his room while he made flight arrangements to Washington. He then accompanied her to her room. "I'm not taking any chances and won't leave you alone for a minute."

"They wouldn't be as interested in me now as they would be in you since you have all the technical secrets. Also, you'd have been proud of my defense ability. You should've seen me throw Frank when I thought he was reaching for his gun."

"Gun? You didn't mention anything about a gun." Jason was startled by her casual statement.

"I knew that Frank used to always carry a gun but for the life of me I never could figure out why. So when he started to put his hand in his pocket, I remembered this and gave him my judo throw. His gun went flying. When he went for it on the floor, the man who was to be our witness kicked him in the groin. Boy, did he scream. It must really have hurt," she said laughing.

"Ouch! But he deserved it." Jason was quiet for a moment and then said, hesitantly.

"You said that Frank told you he didn't inherit his mother's money? That's a lie. I know for sure that he did. Another college friend who lives in Chicago recently told me that Frank was on easy street. There was a big write-up in the Chicago papers about it with pictures of lawyers reading the will." Jason paused.

"Apparently, his mother was far wealthier than anyone knew. Frank inherited almost a hundred million dollars and all of the property. His ex-wife got a couple of million and all of the servants were remembered along with her favorite charities. See what you passed up? You could've been the wife of a multimillionaire instead of a struggling businessman." Jason was watching Rachel to see her expression.

"That bastard. You know what he told me? He wanted to marry me and get me pregnant because he didn't inherit anything. All the money was left in a trust to pass on to his child or children." She sighed. "Jason, I'm so glad that we eloped. Frank was really angry when I pulled out the duplicated copy of our marriage certificate. His exact words were 'you bitch, and neither you nor Jason told me'."

"What did they do to Frank? Do you know?" Jason asked suddenly.

"I probably did the wrong thing. I told the police I didn't want to press any charges. I thought I'd find myself involved in the middle of a police mess and be stuck in Belgium for weeks. Also, he did get me away from the first house. I don't think the police wanted to press charges either, especially when they found out that Frank was a senior U.S. newspaper correspondent. He's a very unhappy man who really doesn't know what he wants. Apparently, after he got his millions and more money than he needed, he found out that

The Purloined Encryption Caper

all that money didn't really make him as happy as he thought it would."

Since Jason couldn't get reservations back to Washington until the next day, Jason decided to move into Rachel's room so they could have a one-day honeymoon in Paris.

"Rachel, I want you to make an appointment at that salon and have them make you as glamorous as you were at that banquet. Then put on the new dress you wore to the banquet. I'll make reservations for dinner and dancing at the best place in town and we'll enjoy Paris as it should be enjoyed. But, I will walk you to your appointments and wait nearby so I don't lose you again."

It took Miriam almost five hours to reach the appropriate Pittsburgh exit for the airport. It was almost four in the afternoon. She parked the car in the rental agency lot, but told them she needed to go to the main part of the airport first to see if she could get flight arrangements to either New York or Europe. Also, she was anxious to have access to a telephone. Her cell phone was out of juice. If Frank were in New York, she'd go there for a few days. Otherwise, she would try to find Pierre and arrange to meet him.

There was no reply at Frank's apartments, either in New York or Paris. She also tried to telephone his office and was told the same information that was given to Jason. Miriam was puzzled. Since reaching Frank was out of the question, she attempted to telephone Pierre, first at his Paris apartment and then at the hotel in Amman where they were to meet. There was no answer in Paris and the only information the Jordanian hotel operator gave was the same as before: he had canceled his reservation.

Miriam decided her best course would be to fly to London and then to Amman, according to their original plans. Perhaps he was compromised by the French. When she reached London, she would telephone the hotel in Amman again, maybe by then Pierre would have left a message.

The hotel operator said there was indeed a fax for her from someone in Egypt. She asked her to read it to her. 'Dear Miriam: Our meeting has taken a change of course. I need to make a business meeting in Israel before joining you in Amman. You should proceed to Amman as originally planned and I will contact you there regarding my date of arrival. In the event of a further change in plans, we should meet to retrieve our trunks. Regards, PL'

She confirmed her planned hotel arrival and requested they keep her reservation and any other messages that might arrive for her. She then reconfirmed her plane reservations to Amman with a stopover in Rome. There, she would check again with the hotel in Amman.

"We just saw her car leave the Turnpike at the Pittsburgh airport exit. We have the local airport police on the lookout for her." The Pennsylvania highway patrol then signaled the Pittsburgh police to contact the airport to learn her destination. They gave this information to the local FBI officer who in turn informed Mark.

The Purloined Encryption Caper

Mark telephoned Phil. "Can we get together this afternoon? I need some advice."

"I think we should, Mark. I have a lot to tell you as well. How about a small bar near your office or a Metro, or we can meet at the nearby Sports Bar? I'm at my Rosslyn Office today. So take your pick."

"I'll meet you at the Bar in about 20 minutes."

They arrived at the bar within five minutes of each other. "What's up, Mark? Something big happen?" Phil was anxious for an update.

"I got word that Miriam left Pittsburgh on a flight to London and Amman via Rome. Can your office notify the CIA Amman Station to keep an eye out for her? I'd like to see where she goes, where she's staying and whom she meets. I have a feeling it'll be Pierre. However, we're trying to have Pierre arrested or picked up in Alexandria by the Egyptian police. If that fails, we hope to get him in Haifa when he docks on Thursday. And if *that* doesn't work, I think he may either go to Amman to meet Miriam or else have her meet him in Haifa. It also means, I think, that the final recipient of their data is possibly Syria or an al-Queda terrorist group. Maybe Iran, or possibly even Israel, although I hate to think what the political ramifications of that would be."

"I'll telephone our station chief as soon as we finish. I may have to get him out of bed, but I guess that goes with the territory." Phil then filled Mark in on the Rachel and Jason situation.

"Thank God that ended well," Mark said. "You know, Phil, there's one thing I hate to admit after all that's happened. You must promise not to tell anyone, especially Rachel or Jason." Phil nodded his agreement. "Frank Avery has really been working as an informant for the FBI for the past few years. In Paris when I had a hunch that they might try to kidnap Rachel, I asked Frank to keep an eye out for her. I didn't know about his past relationship with Jason and his love for Rachel." Mark was feeling very sheepish, but continued.

"At the technology conference in Paris, Frank told me that he'd become very close to Miriam--intimate seems to be her chosen word--and knew she was going to try to get the goods from Jason's company. He said she and her chums were determined to make one big killing before they finally disbanded. Each one was going to sell the same technology to a different rogue country for as much as they could. After that, Miriam wanted to marry Frank so she could get her green card. Can you imagine? Frank pretended that he could really use some money for the next year until he became a legal father." Mark paused and took a sip of his drink.

"During the conference, Frank said that earlier he told Miriam he didn't have access to his inheritance for some reason or another so if they would cut him in, he would be willing to help them. She then told him about their plans to kidnap Rachel and asked him to be available in case something went wrong. That's why I insisted that Paul accompany her shopping that Saturday. With Frank there as double protection for Rachel, I felt I could leave Paris." He paused again to let Phil get the full picture.

"I had no idea he would try such a trick with Rachel and I'm sorry now that I trusted him. I'll have to deal with him when he returns to the States. He's

The Purloined Encryption Caper

been an excellent source of information on economic intelligence activities in Europe, especially since he travels widely and has good access in most countries. I would hate to blow his cover, especially since he does everything *gratis*." Mark took another sip of his drink.

"We need him now more than ever. I'm deeply grateful to Rachel that she didn't press any charges in Belgium. It might have gotten sticky since I assume he would've contacted me." Phil looked incredulous at this bit of information. Then Mark continued.

"I didn't want to tell anyone at the Paris station about Frank after you expressed your concern about a leak. Please don't tell either Rachel or Jason. They don't need to know. I guess those two were just Frank's Achilles ' heel. Love and pride does that, I hear." They smiled at each other, shook their heads and left the bar.

As they parted, Mark looked at Phil. "Keep me informed, will you? I think the action is now in your court."

"Will do," Phil promised. "But I have a question. Whatever happened with the Department of Commerce intern who contacted you but never showed up for her appointment? Did you ever talk with her?"

"No," Mark replied. "When I couldn't locate her at Commerce, I contacted her uncle who originally asked her to phone me. He just said that his niece decided Washington was not for her and went home. It was a strange conversation and, apparently, he didn't want to go into any detail."

Rose Ameser Bannigan

Phil headed back towards his office to start the next and he hoped final phase of what his office file had labeled 'The Purloined Encryption Caper'.

CHAPTER 29

As Frank reviewed recent events, his scheme to save Rachel from her original kidnappers and then Jim had gone off as planned. He had promised Mark to be there for Rachel in the event Paul failed, but what he didn't tell Mark was his past competitive friendship with Jason and his continuing love for Rachel. Frank would have saved Rachel regardless, but he realized now that she would never come back to him. He wanted her more than anything else in the world, regardless of how he had to get her. Thus, when he managed to take her away from that building near the Gare du Nord, he remembered the *prefect* in Belgium who for a certain amount of money would perform a marriage for anyone.

It would have worked except for one thing--he hadn't counted on the honor of the *prefect's* wife who was to serve as a witness, who believed Rachel's story and demanded her husband listen to her. The final blow, of course, was when Rachel told him she and Jason were already married. He had expected Rachel to be more docile and go along with his plans and had also expected her to succumb again to his charms as she had always done earlier. Frank could not accept rejection. Would Rachel have left Jason and married him if she had known before she married Jason that he was a now a very rich man? He doubted it. He might do anything for money, but Rachel wouldn't.

The Belgian government insisted on his taking the next flight out of Brussels which happened to be headed for London. Frank thought that the London police might be on the lookout for him so he didn't go through immigration at the London airport but instead booked the first flight back to Paris.

After inheriting his money, Frank had bought a small apartment on the Rue de Bac, located almost across the street from the Hotel Pont Royale where he had gone the previous Thursday after checking out of the hotel. He only stayed at the hotel earlier that week because he learned that Rachel was registered there. Tonight he would go back to his apartment.

From his front window, he could see the hotel entrance and was stunned when he saw Jason enter. Jason must not know about Rachel's release, Frank thought, or why else would he come to Paris? Does that mean she didn't telephone him? With a vodka tonic in hand, Frank kept a close watch to see what would happen next. He was surprised to see Rachel enter several hours later. Does she know Jason is here? Does she still care? Perhaps he had succeeded in poisoning her mind against Jason when he mentioned that Jason had diddled Miriam, too.

The Purloined Encryption Caper

Frank left his apartment and walked up the Boulevard St. Germain to the Café Flores, realizing how badly he had screwed up his life. It had left him all alone: no wife, no mother and not even a woman he cared for. Only a bunch of easy money-seeking women who didn't mean a damn thing to him, flattering him for attention and expensive gifts.

If he really had any guts, he would have stood up to his mother earlier, married Rachel and lived his own life. But before, he always felt money was the most important thing in his life and was afraid of her threat to cut him out of her will. Now he knew his mother would never have done it but used this threat as a way to keep him under her thumb.

In returning to his apartment, he was startled to see Rachel and Jason walking arm in arm back to the hotel. They looked so happy and in love. He fell back so they wouldn't see him and then went to his apartment. He took out a sheet of paper and began to write.

"Monk,

"Can you ever forgive me? I never meant to harm you but thought you just might come around to love me again and agree to marry me of your own accord. I see I was very wrong and very selfish. Please forget the last few days, if you can. I lied when I said my inheritance had not come through. It has and I am indeed a very wealthy man--in dollars only, not in love. If you ever need anything and that goes for Jason as well, I'll always be there for you both. Jason is a lucky man and you are also lucky. We were all friends at one time and after awhile, I hope we can be again. It would mean so much to me. By the way, Miriam told me she didn't succeed in seducing Jason. I only said that to hurt you. Frank"

He than put the note in an envelope and addressed it to Rachel Brown, c/o Jason Conrad, walked to the hotel and asked the bellboy to deliver it. The concierge witnessed this and just shook his head. Crazy Americans, he thought.

The next day Rachel received Frank's letter and handed it to Jason. "You're right, Rachel. He is indeed very unhappy but he's in a stew of his own making, I may add."

Jason and Rachel walked around Paris, enjoying the small cafes. "You must show me Lili's lingerie shop before I drop you at the beauty shop. You never did get the peignoir set you wanted and I intend to see that you have it. If you won't take me, I'll ask Paul to buy it for me."

"I don't ever want to see that place again, Jason. I just might hit the saleslady over the head although it might be fun to see her face when I walk in."

She led Jason to Lili's. The woman who originally waited on Rachel was not behind the counter. When Rachel identified the set she originally wanted to buy, the new clerk asked her if she wanted to try it on.

"No thank you," Rachel replied emphatically. "I'll never make that mistake again." The clerk was mystified at her customer's strange reaction, unaware of the past happenings.

That evening even Jason was amazed at how beautiful Rachel looked after her beauty treatments, wearing the same dress she wore to the conference reception. She should do this more often, he thought,

The Purloined Encryption Caper

although he never wanted her to wear such a seductive dress without him around.

The concierge had made reservations at the best restaurant in town that also had dancing. Jason wanted the night to be perfect and it was. "I'm not sure you'll be content with Jacques Café after this," Jason joked as they whirled around the floor.

"No place will ever replace Jacques," Rachel said, kissing him on the cheek. "That hideout has too many pleasant memories."

As the freighter neared Alexandria, one of the ship's second mates approached Pierre and admonished him. "You must be a very famous or infamous person to have so many police waiting for you on the dock. Have you killed many people?"

"What do you mean that police are waiting for me?" Pierre questioned

"I've read the radio messages. The Americans have asked the Egyptian police to take you into custody and turn you over to the American Embassy for extradition to the United States. In the event you manage to evade the Egyptian officials in port and hide on the boat, they have requested that we inform the Israeli gendarmes so they can take you when you reach Haifa. Did you murder someone?" There seemed to be a touch of envy in his voice.

"No, I didn't murder anyone, but of course I don't want to go to the United States, especially at their invitation. My ultimate destination is Amman, Jordan, where I am to meet a beautiful woman. I guarantee you that I have not murdered anyone or even harmed

anyone in any way. What do you suggest I do?" Pierre asked, hesitantly.

"My friend," said the official, "I don't think it will be possible to escape the police anywhere in the Mediterranean, except perhaps Lebanon, especially if the Americans are anxious to get their hands on you. They may even have alerted Interpol, so I would recommend that you take a boat back go Greece or Italy. From there, you can contact your woman to meet you elsewhere. Was her husband a high U.S. government official?" the seaman questioned with an envious glint in his eye, sure that any Frenchman's problem revolved around murder, sex or a woman or most likely, all three.

"Something like that. Thank you for the advice. But how can I take a boat back to Italy or elsewhere if I can't land in any of the ports along the way?"

"My friend," the officer said, "we can transfer you by launch before we arrive in Alexandria. My brother is on a freighter registered in Liberia that we will pass soon on its way to Naples. I doubt whether it will stop in Piraeus but he can get you into Italy very easily, since he has many friends and a few Euros would ensure your easy entry. You'll have to decide quickly, however."

He winked as he rubbed his fingers together. "The cost will not be much and much cheaper than hiring an Egyptian or Israeli lawyer, I assure you. It will give both my brother and me great satisfaction to outsmart the Americans. Their support of Israel has angered us for many years. You see, we are members of the Muslim Brotherhood and the Americans have given the

The Purloined Encryption Caper

Egyptian government support to suppress our cause."

Pierre negotiated with the second mate and was amazed that the toll was surprisingly cheap. Several hours later he was settled in a small cabin on a freighter headed for Naples. Before he debarked, he gave the second mate a message to send to the Amman Hotel.

Meanwhile, Miriam's plane arrived in Rome. When she telephoned the hotel in Amman, they read the message they had just received for her sent from a boat somewhere in the Mediterranean. "Ma chere Miriam," it started. "My plans have changed altogether and I must now go to Italy. I suggest that you meet me to pick up our trunks and we can proceed from there. Regards, PL."

She immediately went to the airlines counter and changed her flight plans. Since she only had hand luggage, it presented no difficulty. She decided further that if they were trying to trace her, taking another plane to Geneva where both she and Pierre had sent their trunks wouldn't be wise. Therefore, she decided to stay overnight at a small pension she knew in Rome and go by train the next day to Geneva.

She was grateful their group had been able to sell some of the stolen software as well as various passwords via their computer network. They might be able to contact the agents in Amman from Switzerland to sell the rest of the information. Also, in the event she reached Geneva before Pierre, she would try to find somewhere they could re-establish their computer network.

Miriam would try to contact Frank again. Perhaps he was still in Paris or had returned to the States. If

Rose Ameser Bannigan

all else failed, she would phone Jim from Geneva. He still worked for the CIA and she was sure that he would help her, especially since she could incriminate him in their earlier activities. Jim also managed to involve his girlfriend who currently worked in CIA headquarters, the one who had helped Pierre identify Phil as CIA staff as well as pinpoint an appropriate lover for Carlo. Jim was Miriam's ace in the hole.

When the freighter arrived in Alexandria, there was indeed a contingent of Egyptian police waiting. They got permission to board the freighter but were dismayed when they found that Pierre was not aboard. They searched everywhere, delaying the unloading for several hours and then sent an all-out alert, certain that he managed to jump ship and was probably hiding somewhere in Alexandria. They also decided not to notify the American Embassy yet of their failure, believing they could locate Pierre within a matter of hours. They didn't want to suffer any embarrassment in the eyes of the Americans, especially since the USAID program had spent so much money training the Egyptian law enforcement officials.

CHAPTER 30

Jason returned to Washington with Rachel. "Before all this happened, I planned to attend a meeting in New York tomorrow but I didn't plan to get there via Paris," he said as they entered her Arlington apartment.

Rachel walked into her office the next day amid screams of 'welcome back' from the ladies. Jack heard the commotion and came out to join them.

"Well, our wandering girl is back. Grab a cup of coffee, Rachel, and come into my office and give me the gory details. I'd like to talk with you before my appointment," Jack said. Actually he didn't want her to share any details with either Cindy or Sue, since neither was aware of what had happened. As far as they knew, Jason had joined her in Paris and had decided to extend their stay.

"Jack, it's been pleasure, pain, and pleasure, in that order," she began. "I hope that Phil and Mark kept you better informed than they did Jason. He was really ticked off for while, but I told him not to be so hard on them. They were only trying to do their job and also protect us. I think he now agrees. What's happening here?"

"Nothing much. I'm sure you thought you were away for a long time but it's only been a little over a week. As I told Jason, my newspaper ad for your replacement brought in a lot of applications, some who might even be suitable. I interviewed several but haven't come to any decision. I want you to review this stack and mark the order of preference you think is best, based not only on their application form but also on my interview notes. But are you sure you're going to leave?" Jack asked half-jokingly.

"Yes, I am, that is if I intend to remain Mrs. Conrad. I think Jason is rather tired of trying to keep up with all my machinations and coast-to-coast commuting. But I've got to admit that I'll really miss the office and especially working for you."

"I've been meaning to talk with you about this and thought maybe lunch at Luigi's might be a good place." Rachel smiled and hugged him. "And did I tell you that I've been receiving several inquiries from companies around the country asking about our services? What did you do? Deal out your business cards in Paris like a game of cards?"

"A lot of guys there asked about our company. I told them about our capabilities generally and gave them a business card but suggested they contact you, that you handled marketing and I was only a researcher and writer. I'm glad you might get something for your money since I don't think that Phil has reimbursed you for my salary."

The Purloined Encryption Caper

"He offered but I turned him down," Jack confessed. "I think I've gotten full value."

At lunch, Jack again told her how much he was going to miss her. "You know, I was wondering whether you'd consider staying on my payroll and working out of an office in Palo Alto. Since we'll probably get more clients, I can afford to hire someone else for here and have you cover West Coast activities. Also, with fax machines and especially e-mail, we could communicate constantly and possibly issue the newsletter occasionally from there." Jack paused.

"It wouldn't be full time at first. I'd have to see what the cost would be to set up a small office there. Phil's offered to pay part of the tariff as long as you'd be willing to do some hush-hush work for him as well. I'm sure you'd want to talk to Jason about it first."

"You're right, but I'd love to continue to work for you as well as Phil. Possibly I could handle the job out of Jason's house. I'm sure he wouldn't mind if I turned an extra room into an office." Rachel didn't want to tell Jack that this is what she had wanted but didn't have the nerve to ask him. Now she felt that Phil had run interference for her and suggested the arrangement to Jack.

Rachel reviewed the applications but when she came upon one that had been faxed to Jack, she was startled. The originating fax number seemed familiar. It turned out to be the same one that originated Miriam's copies of her newsletter.

"Jack," she asked breathlessly. "Who sent this application? Is it from an applicant or was it as the recommendation of someone else?"

"Oh, that one. He's really not in the running. I interviewed him only as a courtesy to Cindy. He's her live-in or whatever you call someone you're sleeping with these days. Why do you ask?"

"Remember when I mentioned that Miriam had copies of our newsletter and it had been sent by someone from a 202 area code?" Rachel said. "Well, this is the number it was sent from. Do you think that Cindy is sharing our newsletter with her boyfriend and he, too, is involved with Miriam's gang?"

"Let's find out now." Jack buzzed and asked Cindy to join them. "Rachel, why don't you ask her about it in your usual diplomatic manner?" If Cindy were innocent, Jack didn't want to take the heat since he would need Cindy more than ever once Rachel left.

Cindy entered, looking a little anxious. "Is anything wrong?" she asked.

"You know, Cindy, when I was in Paris, I saw copies of our newsletter that had been sent to a French businesswoman and couldn't figure out how she got them. Then I noticed the fax number on the top of the newsletter was the same as your boyfriend's. Could he be involved with any French people?" Cindy look devastated. "Please Cindy be truthful. This is very important." Rachel tried to be very sympathetic, yet stern, in her approach.

"I don't think so. I showed him the first newsletter we did. I was so proud of my role and being listed on the masthead. He then asked if I would show him all future copies. I never thought he'd pass them on but he did say his boss found them very interesting and

The Purloined Encryption Caper

wanted to see them, too. Was this wrong?" Cindy was rather sheepish at this point.

"Can you give me the name of your boyfriend's boss and your boyfriend's full name, too? You see, these are copyrighted and if any copyright infringements occurred, it will be important for us to report them to our legal counsel." Rachel wanted to make it sound official.

Cindy proceeded to list the names and handed them to Jack. "Don't tell your boyfriend anything about this for the moment. Promise?" Cindy agreed but was on the verge of tears. After Cindy left Jack's office, he phoned Phil and told him that it was an official in the Department of Commerce who was faxing copies of their newsletter to Miriam.

"Can you or Mark check on this for us? I don't think any damage was done although I don't like people getting information gratis. But I think something is smelly in Commerce." Phil assured Jack that either he or Mark would.

"Can I talk with Phil before you hang up?" Rachel asked.

Rachel spent a few minutes of small talk with Phil before addressing her real concern. "Phil, I asked Paul whether they had any more information about Steve's death. He told me Jim was handling it, but in view of Jim's involvement with Miriam and the French, I don't think he did anything. She probably told him when they were between the sheets to forget about it. However, when I was being held by those two French low-lifes, they mentioned that they hoped they didn't have to snuff me out the way the Corsicans did with the

American man who later washed ashore near Cannes. Can you ask the French police to interrogate the two who kidnapped me and see what they know? I'm more than ever convinced that Steve was murdered. He was just too good a swimmer to have drowned."

Phil promised he would and then added. "One thing you should know, Rachel, which isn't public knowledge yet. Clive, the Brit involved in the scheme with Pierre, was found this morning at the base of the Winston Churchill statue, outside the British Embassy. Mark just told me. The ruling is suicide, but I'm not sure. If the press doesn't make an issue out of it, I think the FBI will just let the ruling stay. I don't think you'll see it on the front page of the papers since the Brits want to keep it quiet. The British Embassy has already flown the body home. Just thought you should know. You can tell Jack." Phil then hung up.

"You're not going to let go regarding Steve, are you Rachel?" Jack asked after she had hung up.

"No. It's one thing I have to clear up before I move to California or know that someone is looking into it. It's the least I can do for Steve."

When Rachel returned to her apartment that afternoon, Jason was on the phone talking to his family. "I don't know exactly when I can convince Rachel to move West," he said to his mother, "but rest assured, I won't let her stay in Washington too long." He paused. "She just walked in. Here, I'll let you talk with her."

Rachel took the phone and assured her new in-laws that she was safe and planned to settle in California as soon as she could finalize her work here. "I'll still be

The Purloined Encryption Caper

working part-time for the office though, unless Jason absolutely refuses to let me."

Jason looked up, a bit chagrined at the idea.

"Sure, I'd love to talk with Caroline." Rachel told Jason's mother.

Caroline told Rachel that she decided to take her up on her offer to visit Washington and stay with her and would plan to arrive as soon as Jason left. She didn't want to interfere. Caroline then asked to speak to Jason.

"You'd never guess what I went through. Just be prepared to pay a hefty bill for dinner for both Claire and me at that new ritzy restaurant that just opened," Caroline told Jason.

"Why?" he asked.

"Claire suggested we get together for dinner and then offered to introduce me to several individuals who might be interested in hiring me. The whole purpose I'm sure was to try to woo me to her side and get you to ditch Rachel, positive that she was just a passing fancy." Caroline giggled.

"She told me she'd make you a much better wife. I really enjoyed telling her that you were wildly in love with Rachel and the family was delighted with the marriage. I thought she would fall off the chair since she thought you were still only engaged." Caroline paused and dramatically continued with her narration. "Married? When did they get married? Claire asked. I enjoyed telling her about your elopement." Caroline was enjoying herself immensely.

"She then said that what you needed as a spouse was a professional woman not just an ordinary woman, making an ordinary woman sound like a prostitute or worse. Claire was so bitchy and all her niceness vanished. She got up and left the restaurant, sticking me with a hefty bill."

Jason wasn't sure he had wanted Claire to find out about his marriage this way but could see why Caroline enjoyed sticking it to her. Claire had always been so snobbish in dealing with Caroline.

"I'm leaving here Sunday, Caro, so if you want to visit with Rachel for awhile, please don't let me stop you. You might want to give her a breathing spell, however, Rachel told me she'd love to show you around and introduce you to people who might have entrée to the job market. Just let Rachel know in advance when you plan to come so she has time to get organized. But make it soon because I want her to move to the Coast as quick as she can. And send me the dinner bill. It's a charge I'll gladly pay."

Jason was rather pleased that his sister would be here with Rachel. He felt that Rachel would be a good influence on her.

After Jason hung up, he looked at Rachel sternly. "What's this about still working when you move to the West Coast? What would you do and who would you work for?" She just looked at him. "You didn't mention this earlier. Are you sorry now that you married me?"

"No, and you know better. I'm not a feminist with a desire for a career. We both want to start a family as soon as possible. However, it may take awhile until I get pregnant and I'd like to have something to do in the interim. Jack talked about the possibility of a branch office on the West Coast. Phil also mentioned using me if necessary to get information for him, especially since economic espionage still remains a major problem for both the CIA and FBI. It wouldn't be full time but would keep me busy and out of your hair. I'd be a consultant."

Rachel was beginning to get a little upset the more she thought about the conversation. "Look at it from my perspective, Jason. I'm not used to sitting home during the day. You said you'd insist on keeping your cleaning woman since you don't want me to waste time doing housework. I definitely agree. You'll be busy at the office but shopping until I drop has never been a great pastime for me. There'd be nothing much to shop for. Between us we have more furniture than we'll ever need." She paused, then continued.

"In talking with Jack, I even discussed the possibility of setting up an office at your house, at least initially, until we see how things go," Rachel said meekly.

"You mean 'our house', don't you?" he said caustically.

"I mean our house. However, at this point, having spent only a few days there, it's difficult to think of it as 'our' house. I guarantee that once I get there and start rearranging things, I'll feel more like an occupant and not a guest. Tell me, honestly, do you feel like this is 'our' apartment or do you think of it as Rachel's apartment?"

He smiled and had to agree with her logic. "Talking about your apartment, how long is the lease for? Should you be giving notice?"

Again Rachel hesitated in answering. "I thought that if it's okay with you, I'd keep the apartment for

Rose Ameser Bannigan

awhile, especially until I get established in California. You or any of your associates could use it for official visits. Who knows, maybe Caro will take a job here and then she'd have a furnished apartment to move into. But enough discussion about our life tonight," she said laughingly. "Why don't you fix us a drink and I'll make reservations at Jacques for dinner?"

"You win," he said, realizing that compromise would be an important part of his new relationship with Rachel. "Just one thing. Tomorrow we sit down together and plan our future. I'll agree to your keeping the apartment and you're right about Caro. I think it would be good for her to get away from California for awhile, even if she doesn't find the perfect job right away. But I want you to begin to think of the house in California as our house so when I talk about going home, we both know where home is." He paused, waiting for any comments. She smiled.

"Another thing," Jason continued, "since you won't have to worry about closing out an apartment and putting household effects away and things like that, I think we should throw away your birth control pills and start working on our future tonight after dinner. Agreed?"

He got his answer when Rachel went to her purse and handed him her pills. He immediately flushed them down the toilet. When he returned, she put her drink down and gave him a very passionate and wet kiss, nuzzling his neck and unbuttoning his shirt.

"Why wait?" Why not start before we go to Jacquest?" Rachel whispered as she led him into the bedroom.

EPILOGUE

The train departed Rome shortly after Miriam arrived at the station. She didn't see anyone following her so felt secure, at least for the moment. She had purchased a ticket only as far as Milan where she planned to try to contact Jim or Frank again. Perhaps Jim had heard from Frank and would have word for her.

She got off at Milan. The next train to Geneva was in four hours, so she checked the luggage she was carrying at the baggage counter and headed for a public phone. Her cell phone needed charging. Jim answered on the third ring. A click was heard after he picked up the phone. Obviously someone else was listening in

"Jim? This if your friend. How are you?"

"Fine," he responded in a stilted speech. "Where are you? I've been trying to reach you. Have you left the United States?" he asked, knowing full well that she had boarded a plane for London and had plans to go to Amman.

"Yes, I did," she responded, "but found I had some unfinished business, so I'm now en route back to San Francisco. Perhaps when I return to Paris, I'll call you and we can get together for dinner. Au revoir, until then." She hung up quickly.

Miriam didn't want to mention her whereabouts since she knew someone else was listening in and didn't want to stay on the line long enough so they could trace the call. Apparently, the CIA found out about Jim's betrayal. She wondered how long they would let him stay in Paris and whether it would be safe to phone his woman friend in Washington at CIA headquarters. She decided against it.

She next dialed Frank at his Rue de Bac apartment. There was no response, so she next tried to reach him in New York. Again, the same recording about being away for several months repeated itself.

Reclaiming her luggage, she boarded the train for Geneva. She was grateful that with the new European Union agreements, there were no customs or passport checks going from one major European country to the next.

In Geneva, she went immediately to a small pension, registering as Mrs. Pierre Ledent, and told them her husband would be checking in sometime soon. Next, she went to the major railway luggage claim building to search for the trunks she had sent from Paris. They were there. Also, she spotted Pierre's trunks waiting to be claimed and managed to attach a message to the smaller one letting him know where she was staying. She had signed it Mrs. PL, an indication they were registered as a couple.

After paying the storage charge, she returned to the pension. She then unpacked a few items, went to the small cafe next door for a bite to eat, and decided she would await Pierre.

The boat taking Pierre to Italy sailed slowly into Naples harbor. Before it arrived however, the ship's officers lowered a launch. "Here, my friend," the mate said, "it will be better for both of us not to have you on board when the customs officials arrive. You are not on the passenger list and they check the crew very carefully."

Pierre thanked him for his help, paid him for the passage, and waved goodbye from the launch. "It was good to have known you," the seaman said. "I will forget that we've ever met, and assume you will do the same."

Pierre climbed up the steep steps leading to the quay and walked quietly down a side street. It was dark and gloomy but Pierre was lucky he didn't run into anyone who might be looking for trouble. After about fifteen minutes, he saw a taxi waiting for a passenger in front of a cafe. He pulled out a $50 bill and asked the taxi driver to take him to the train station. The driver grinned broadly, saluted him and stepped on the gas as soon as he closed the door.

It took less than twenty minutes to reach a large ancient building. Pierre got out, went to the ticket counter and found that the next train going north would leave in two hours. He sat on a bench as far out of sight as possible and waited. He hoped there wasn't a search out for him but decided he would face that problem when and if it happened. Since no one had been hurt, he couldn't imagine that the French police would have issued an arrest warrant unless the Americans were pressing them. He also doubted that the Americans would make a major issue of it. They wouldn't want international publicity so close to the next NATO meeting.

The next morning he arrived in Geneva, tired, dirty and very hungry. He found a little brasserie where he enjoyed fresh croissants and strong French cafe noir. "Civilization," he said to himself. He next went to collect his trunks and found the note from Miriam. When he arrived at the pension, she was dozing on the bed.

"Well, cheri, here we are," she said. "You look a little haggard and tired. Was it that bad?"

He looked at her and decided to tell her about his escapades. "The food on freighters is not very good and the accommodations leave much to be desired." He began to undress, excused himself and took a shower.

"I feel like a new person," he said as he returned to the bedroom. "Come, let's go for a walk around town and see what the surrounding area is like. I normally don't stay in this part of town, but the major hotels usually are very concerned about reporting all visitors and checking passports. I would not like to surrender ours for awhile."

After a short walk in silence, Miriam told Pierre about her visit to California where she saw Rachel with Jason. "She must have been rescued shortly after I left the men although I don't know how. I'm sure no one saw us leave the lingerie shop."

Miriam didn't want to tell Pierre about Jim. *"After San Francisco, I visited the cabin and took the tapes and material that was on the computer. I left messages for the hackers Julian hired letting them know we were closing our base in the States but would contact them after we were reestablished in Europe. I hope that was okay."*

"Merde," Pierre said gruffly, *"I had a trap set for our American friends and put a virus on the tapes which would destroy their software when they ran it on their computer. I think what you took was put there by them or Clive. They'll probably try to track down the members of our hacker ring but it shouldn't matter. After I went back to the cabin from my vacation in the Berkeley Springs jail, I crashed the computer setup with the code that Julian gave me and installed a dummy network. As I was leaving, I saw a U.S. government car pull into the road. I assume that it carried some FBI computer specialists."* He smiled to himself.

"I hope they're having fun trying to find out who our hackers were and our passwords which I changed. Julian faxed me the real passwords for the group which I received before I left Paris. All the information should be in my trunk. I wish I could see the faces of the stupid Americans when they try to figure out the system." Pierre relished beating the FBI and CIA at their game. He continued.

"I think it's important for us to find a place to settle and establish our computer setup so we can replenish our bank accounts. The passwords of the NSC and the office of the Secretary of Defense which I retrieved

earlier that night should provide a tidy sum, especially from Syria's Assad, Usama bin Ladin, the Iranian military establishment, or all three. They can keep up to date on what the American military have in mind for them, n'est pas?" Pierre was very satisfied with his accomplishments.

"Perhaps I'll also try to sell them to the disgruntled Saudis in exile trying to unseat the Saudi monarchy. The only thing that is saving them is the American military. I know they'll pay well and, Miriam, ma cherie, we can then live in much more luxury."

"You don't think the Swiss police will hunt us down?" Miriam asked, as they strolled along the boulevard near their pension.

"No. The Swiss will be quite content to bank our money and keep quiet about its residents unless we create problems. I think we are safe for awhile," Pierre reassured her. "You don't have any regrets, do you?"

"Non, mon cher. But this cannot be the end of our activities. A short vacation, perhaps, but then we should start up our business again." Pierre agreed, already planning their next move.

ABOUT THE AUTHOR

An avid reader, writing fiction has always been one of Rose Bannigan's goals. The Purloined Encryption Caper is her third novel. Her two previous novels, The Snowstorm Murders and Riddle of the Five Buddhas, were also published by AuthorHouse.

Rose Bannigan worked for the Central Intelligence Agency in Washington, DC and Germany. Because of an evolving interest in Asia and international economic and social development, she joined The Asia Foundation and served in their San Francisco, New York and Afghanistan offices. Her assignment in the Foundation's office in Kabul led to travel in India, Pakistan and other parts of Asia. After leaving that Foundation, she joined the staff of the National Academy of Sciences which was becoming more involved in scientific collaborations with developing countries. Assigned to their international office, she concentrated on staffing and managing collaborative scientific programs whose activities involved travel to the Middle East, Africa and Asia as well as extensive report writing and editing of scientific studies and reports on many aspects of development. She was mainly responsible for developing and administering scientific and technical programs in Indonesia and Thailand for over ten years.

A native of Ohio, she currently lives in Arlington, Virginia with her husband, John, a lecturer and writer on Asian affairs. They still travel abroad and spend time at their vacation homes in Southern Shores, North Carolina and in Hampshire County, West Virginia.

Printed in the United States
53290LVS00001B/1-66